SUMMERTIM

BY CHUCK GOULD

Published by Starry Night Publishing.Com

Rochester, New York

To Cindy Shephard

Chuck Gould

Chuck Gould

Contents

Acknowledgments:

Some people to thank for support during this project include:

Jan Gould, my wife of 44 years. She knows be better than anyone else would care to, and has the miraculous capacity to love me anyway. Back atcha. Thanks for giving me space to write.

Various Seattle area novelists who read through early manuscripts and were kind enough to be very, very frank. Special shout outs in this regard to Michael and Lauren Barnhart, Larry Moller, Maeve Murphy, and Stanley A. Williams; all of whom put up with more than a fair share of Summertime.

Old friends Larry and Dorothy Dubia. Larry and Dorothy were among the beta readers, and Larry did the cover art for both books.

Paul Steinke, Dean of Students at the Seattle School of Philosophy and Theology, and a beta Reader. Sarah Steinke, a gifted poet, was also among the beta readers.

Other beta readers included Teri McGrew, a gaggle of critics from the Scribophile web site, and a list of people from the site affiliated with the British Arts Council, youwriteon.com

Proofreader Heather Strong. Nice job, Heather.

My friend and immensely patient bagpipe instructor, Tyrone Heade.

Wesley, Rebekah, Vanessa, all the members of Memphis Rail, as well as Ira Miller, Joseph Smith, Little Willy and the Bluesbirds, Red Scarf, The Cardinal, and the rest of the fictional characters in the book. It was a pleasure making their acquaintance, I am humbled that they allowed me to record their story, imperfect as the effort proved to be.

And finally, my readers. Thanks for your interest in the tale, your investment of a few dollars and many hours of time to allow me to share it with you.

Chuck Gould

Part One, Chapter One

Redd Wilmott owned a shopworn beachfront condo, in a pink stucco building in Fort Lauderdale. For Redd, it was a special place of rest and refuge. After Memphis Rail concluded their tour in Vancouver, Redd flew to Florida. The rainy Pacific Northwest dampened his soul, and it would take a week or more of steady sunshine to dry out. The concert schedule always wound up in December. After a few weeks off, Memphis Rail would get back together to tighten up the act and rehearse new material before hitting the road again in early spring. These winter weeks were precious. Redd lay on a lounge, behind the glass railing of his seaside deck. He watched the light begin to fade from the beach, as shadows stretched to bizarre, distorted, elongated shapes. The old bluesman fretted as he nursed a Vodka tonic.

During the last few years, it was becoming harder to book the best venues. Redd was sure that Ann, Mary, John, and Art were noticing, as he had, that the average age of their audience seemed to be going up by about eleven months every year. Sure, there were always a few new faces, but overall the number of fans under 40 was dwindling. The audience called out for tunes that had been big R&B hits for the Rail two, three, and sometimes four decades ago. Every member of the group except John Flood wrote new material for each tour. Some of it was clearly better than the selections on their "Greatest Hits" album, but not many of their fans seemed interested in anything except the old standards.

"It ain't the size of the crowds," thought Redd, "so much as it's the makeup. There's more white folks than ever. If we keep fetchin' in all these old busted down hipsters, we'll be soon be rotatin' between some tiny 'has been' room in Vegas and the Indian casinos. That ain't no way to end up. Hell, no it ain't."

Behind him, Redd heard the glass door sliding open.

"Hello, Baby" cooed a familiar female voice. "I knew you wouldn't mind if I used my key."

Redd rolled onto his right side to face his guest. "Wo-ho, Mama, if you ain't a sight for sore eyes!"

Gloria Gordon laughed. Her cobalt blue eyes glistened as she undid her hair. She shook the long blonde tresses out to their full length, down to her elbows. With one expert motion she undid her bikini top and let it fall to the ground. She grabbed two handfuls of hair to conceal the stiff nipples on her ample breasts. She tilted her head and wiggled her hips provocatively as she responded, "Redd, you old bullshitter. We both know it ain't exactly your eyes that's most excited to see me, don't we?"

"Ok, you got me there. You want a drink or somethin'?"

"No drink, but the Or Somethin' will be fine," giggled Gloria. "You been away a long time, Redd. I couldn't wait to come over, but we got to get down to business. My husband's at a meeting over at the country club."

Redd sat up on the edge of the lounge. Gloria let her hair fall away from her breasts and extended both hands to Redd. "He ain't supposed to be home for about an hour and a half. Sometimes though, he don't go into the meeting. He sits in the bar and gets plastered. The old fool never did know the difference between drunk and horny, so he comes home lookin' for somethin' he couldn't handle if he found it. There's always a chance he could come home early."

"So, then what?" said Redd, "You tellin' me we just got time for a quickie?"

Gloria pulled Redd's hands to help him rise up from the lounge. Backing through the doorway into the condo, with a less than reluctant Redd in tow, she dropped her bikini bottom. "Shit, Redd. A quickie with you can be about fifteen minutes. Let's start with that, and then see what we feel like doin' afterwards."

"And what if your husband comes home?"

"No problem. I got Julie MacPherson keepin' watch on the gate. If his car pulls into the complex, she's gonna ring your house phone. So the only rule, Baby, is that if that phone goes off you better be going off too; I'll need to be haulin' this ass down the hallway, pronto."

Red was unbuckling the canvas belt holding up his shorts. "Rule? Mama, you gotta know I ain't really into any sort of rules. Nobody rules this roost but the rooster."

"Maybe not, but your little hen is a gonna be flyin' if that phone lights up. Fair warnin'."

8

"Sure 'nough," said Redd. "Now, about that quickie..."

Gloria threw her arms around Redd's neck, and her legs around his waist. They disappeared into the bedroom.

A few minutes later, and long before either Gloria or Redd were the least bit satisfied with their encounter, the phone began to ring. Gloria panicked.

"Oh my god, he's getting home way early! Really, really fuckin' early! Goddam it, Redd, get off me. Get off me right away! Oh shit, oh dear, I gotta go!"

"Well, I'm a tryin' to get off," joked Redd.

"Fuck you, you know what I mean. I gotta, gotta, gotta go, right now!"

"Well, piss," said Redd, rolling over to the far side of the bed. "That sure turned out to be a tease, didn't it?"

Gloria scrambled to the living room, picking up her bikini top and bottom. The phone continued to ring, and with each ring the guilt and the urgency seemed to increase. "Oh god!" wailed Gloria, "If he catches me here again he'll kill me. He might even kill you."

"That fat old bastard can't kill nothin'; 'cept maybe a fifth," chuckled Redd. "Maybe one of these days you'll get smart and walk out on him. You can do better. That wheezin' old fart sure doesn't deserve a good woman like you."

The phone continued ringing, and Gloria raced for the door. She looked both ways, up and down the hallway, to confirm there were no witnesses in sight. She sprinted three units down the hall to the condo she shared with her husband, retired plumber Emerson Gordon. Gloria raced to the shower, certain that she was barely in time to avoid her husband's re-discovery of her serial infidelities with Redd. Gloria could not know she would be showered, dried, moderately drunk, and extremely perplexed when Emerson finally did return home, almost two hours later.

Redd became annoyed with the phone ringing endlessly in his living room. Julie MacPherson was taking standing guard a little too seriously. Redd picked up the receiver and barked, "All right, goddam it! I got the message!"

Redd was astonished to hear a familiar voice in the receiver. It certainly wasn't Julie MacPherson, it was Mary Towne.

"Whoa, Redd!" said Mary, "What the hell crazy kind of way is that to answer the phone?"

9

"Oh, shit," responded Redd, aware that his disappointment was evident in his tone.

Mary laughed, "OK, man, happy to talk to you too. I was about to give up ringing your phone, but I'm really glad you answered. I'm still up here in Seattle. There's somethin' going on that's pretty damned amazing."

"Wait a minute," interjected Redd. "Please don't tell me this has anything to do with the drunken white guy and his lucky accident with the saxophone. Shit, Mary, you've been stewin' on about that freak show for about a week now!"

"Hey, I'm not going to lie to you, Redd. He's part of this whole thing, along with those two sisters; Rebekah and Vanessa."

"Same Vanessa from that hotel in Seattle, right?" asked Redd, in a voice seasoned with a note of cautious optimism.

"Yeah. How many sisters named Vanessa do you think a guy like that would know?"

"OK, Mary. If it's got something to do with Vanessa, then fill me in. But this better be pretty damn good. You owe me. Your call sort of interrupted somethin', if you know what I mean."

"Redd, it don't take no serious amount of imagination to know what I probably interrupted. Sorry 'bout that. Pass my apologies along to the lady for me, will ya? But now, Redd, listen up. Somethin' is comin' down that I think could change a lot of stuff for the Rail. Don't know about you, but I'm pretty much lookin' forward to going home. At least home a lot more often. So, here's where it's at....."

Part One, Chapter Two

The Mini Cooper was stopped, motor running, next to an open drainage ditch in the Lake City district of North Seattle. The prospective landlord was already twenty minutes late. Wesley, Rebekah, and Wesley the Dog kept adequately warm as well as dry, breath steaming the windows of the tiny car.

"Do you think this guy is even gonna show up?" asked Rebekah. "If he isn't here in the next few minutes, I think we should forget about it. This is a strange neighborhood, anyway. No sidewalks, almost no street lights, it would sort of freak me out to walk the dog after dark."

"I see your point," agreed Wesley Perkins "It's just that this place looked like it would be perfect for us, in our situation that is, in the Craigslist ad. Two bedroom house with a separate "mother-in-law" apartment down in the basement. Furnished. We can live together without being 'together', if you know what I mean."

"You got that straight!" quickly affirmed Rebekah. "At this point, we're just barely friends. I don't personally see it getting to anything else, either."

"Yes, of course. We're roommates, nothing more. But it would be hard for you to afford a place on your own, I can't go back to Bainbridge, and Mary said we need to spend at least a couple of hours every day rehearsing."

"Yeah, so a house is better than an apartment, there's no neighbor on the other side of the wall. But I ain't gonna sit here all night waiting on this guy. Why don't we send him a text and make sure he's coming?"

"Go ahead," said Wesley. "I don't really ever text."

"God!" mocked Rebekah. She laughed as she put one hand on her side and contorting her posture as if any type of movement were difficult. "How do you old folks get along, anyway?"

Rebekah was beginning to type into her phone when a battered white cargo van crossed through their headlight beams and turned into the gravel driveway. A huge, unkempt man emerged. Something rather suspicious looking was smeared on his Levi jacket and tattered overalls.

He approached Wesley's car. "Hi, guys. Sorry about runnin' a little late. Had a toilet overflowin' in one of my places about a half mile from here. Woman was screamin' bloody murder into the phone. I thought I could fix it a little quicker than I did. Finally had to run a snake down the pipe. Turned out to be a bunch of toilet paper and some other stuff- backed up behind a tampon, of course. Name's Adam Turner, by the way."

Wesley got out first, while Rebekah gathered her handbag. Adam had extended his right hand toward Wesley. Wesley was debating whether to risk shaking a hand that had just been dealing with the contents of a clogged sewage pipe, but the hand was slowly withdrawn when Rebekah stepped out of the car.

"Oh, shit," thought Rebekah. She had seen that look almost every day of her life. She immediately understood that Adam Turner was not pleased to discover that one of his prospective tenants was black.

"Uh, none of my business, really," said Turner, "but is the house going to be for the both of you, together?"

"Yeah, if we like it, that is," said Wesley.

"Well, as you can probably figure we're getting a lot of emails on this place. I'll go ahead and show it to you. If you like it I'll have to, er, I mean I would be pleased to, let you fill out an application."

"Your ad did say that dogs were OK, right?" asked Rebekah.

"Yeah, but you need to put up another $200 deposit. It's non-refundable, so we can clean the carpets after you. Wait, I meant after your dog, of course."

Rebekah's tone was curt. "Of course, Mr. Turner. What else could you possibly mean?"

Adam Turner grabbed a square, battery powered lantern from behind the cargo door of the van and led Wesley and Rebekah up the driveway toward the front steps. Their footsteps crunched in the deep gravel. Even in the dark, Wesley could see that the lawn was overgrown. There were rough patches at the edge of the grass where the weeds were different than those in the larger expanses of turf. Wesley assumed there might be salvageable flowerbeds.

"Watch this top step," warned Adam Turner. "It's sort of loose. I need to get over here with a couple of nails or something. "

Adam fumbled with a huge ring of keys and finally located one that fit the door. He reached just inside, and flipped a switch for the porch light. Wesley was able to confirm that his assessment of the landscaping might have been too generous.

Turner stepped through the door to switch on more interior lights. Rebekah tugged at Wesley's sleeve to get his attention. When he looked in her direction, she was holding her nose. "Yeah, I agree," said Wesley.

"So this is the living room," said Adam. "Don't worry too much about the soot over the top of the fireplace, I had the chimney cleaned out in October and I understand it hasn't been smoking hardly at all since then."

"Smells like the last people had a dog," observed Vanessa. "When were you going to clean the carpet?"

"Actually, they had three dogs. One of 'em was a female, and she kept havin' litters of pups here. But we did clean the carpet! Can't you tell?"

Rebekah frowned. "No, not exactly."

Adam wasn't sure whether he wanted to change the subject and try to convince his prospective tenants to rent the house, or whether he should just allow the black woman's reservations to go unanswered. The easiest thing, really, would be if she just talked herself out of the place. He ultimately proved to be even more mercenary than he was racist.

"Be sure to check out the furniture!" said Turner. "The last folks got transferred overseas and couldn't take it with them. I paid them for it. Got the receipt somewhere, too. I'm sort of hoping to find somebody that wants to take it with the furniture, that way I don't have to rent storage or something."

Wesley and Rebekah wandered through the main level of the home. The kitchen was filthy. The bathroom looked positively contagious, with rusty streaks below dripping faucets on pitted ceramic fixtures. All of the furnishings had to be at least 20 years old, with a few pieces obvious relics from the 1960's and 70's. The last coat of paint was no fresher than the furniture.

The mother-in-law apartment, on the lower floor, was even dirtier. Mold was scaling an outside wall.

"Wes, this place is a real pig sty!" groused Rebekah. "I feel like I need to go back to Vanessa's and shower, just from stepping in here."

"Yeah. But the concept works for us pretty well. If I take on getting the place painted and cleaning up the bathrooms and kitchen, what would you think?"

"Wes, it's the damn smell as much as anything. I'm pretty sure that smell is down into the carpet so deep it will never come clean, I don't care how many times you try to clean it."

"OK, but cleaned up, with new carpet, what would you think?"

"Yeah, the only two things I can't stand is the stink and the filth," laughed Rebekah. "I mean, other than that, and the trashed yard outside, it's probably fine. But between you and me, I think old Adam there doesn't understand how things are between the two of us. I think he has some sort of problem with our living arrangement. He would never agree to clean this up for us, and I wouldn't trust him to do it right, even if he did."

"I think I know how to handle that," confirmed Wesley.

"Yeah? This I'll have to see."

They went back upstairs. Adam was wiping up a puddle in front of the refrigerator- the result of the last tenants unplugging the appliance without first defrosting the freezer.

"So, what do you guys think?" said Adam. "Do you want to fill out an application? Oh, did I tell you there's a $90 application fee- for each of you?"

"What's the rent here, again?" asked Wesley.

"Two thousand five hundred a month. First and last in advance, plus a thousand dollar deposit. Plus another couple of hundred deposit for the dog. It will cost you sixty-two hundred to move in, providing that we're able to approve your application."

Wesley reached into his pants pocket, and pulled out a large roll of cash. "There's a hundred $100 bills here. So here's the deal. I'll give you six thousand two hundred to move in. That leaves me with thirty-eight hundred. I'll use that to hire some guys to clean this place up, throw on some paint, and replace the carpet and pad. You don't jerk us around with some crap about applications, and you get to keep all the improvements after we move out."

"Oh," scoffed Rebekah, "so your solution is just to throw money at it?"

"Yeah. Money's just a tool."

"Oh, shit. I don't know," complained Adam Turner. "That seems pretty risky. What the hell do I know about you guys? For all I know, you could be plannin' to cook meth or something here. Then the cops come around and bulldoze the place. What would I do then?"

"Tell you what, Mr. Turner. Let's make this deal tonight. We're trying to share space with Rebekah's sister, and her little cottage is way too small."

Wesley sorted through his stack of bills, and extended a handful toward Adam. "You take the $6200. We won't move in before we have paid to clean the place up and replace the carpet."

"That's a fact," muttered Rebekah.

Wesley continued, "You can inspect it when the work is done. Then, when we do move in, I'll give you another ten thousand dollars; the next four months' rent in advance. Sixty-two hundred cash, right now, and a total of sixteen-thousand two-hundred in the next few days. Plus, we'll do the improvement. What do you say?"

Adam Turner stepped toward the door, as if ready to end the showing. With some hesitation he enquired, "Are you guys runnin' from the law, or somethin'?"

"Nothing that dramatic, not at all. Rebekah here, she just moved out from Boston. She's a nurse. Hasn't found work yet, but she will. We need somebody to take a chance on us. With enough cash in the pot, it's not much a chance though, is it?"

"So that's her story, and how about yours?"

"It looks like I'm going to be getting a divorce. Right now, the less paperwork and fewer credit checks, the better."

Adam Turner chuckled, and winked at Wesley. "Getting a divorce, eh?"

Rebekah scowled. Why did she dislike Adam Turner so much? She pulled on Wesley's arm until he took a step away from Adam. "Wes, are you sure you want to do this? We can probably find some place that doesn't need all this work? Besides there's no way I can come up with my share of the rent four months in advance."

"You're right. But we don't have a lot of time. You can pay me back for your share of the rent each month as the money comes in. I sure as hell don't want to live in a dump, and I can tell you don't either. We're not going to find a rental that's as clean as we expect unless we get involved with cleaning it. I got a few bucks severance pay when they fired me. Seems almost like justice, or something, to use it for this."

Turner raised his voice to reenter the conversation. "So you'll give me $6200 tonight, you'll pay to have the place cleaned, painted and re-carpeted, and you'll give me another four month's rent in advance when you move in?"

"Yup, that's the deal" said Wesley, "or, you can let us walk and you can go on trying to rent this place, stink and all, to somebody who probably can't afford it. The shape this place is in, the only people likely to be interested would be folks who can't bet approved anywhere else."

Turner sighed. "Almost sounds like you've been over here showin' this place. OK, deal. But don't be screwin' me over here. I'm going out on a limb, renting you this place without checking your credit and stuff. And I'm not sure what the neighbors will say."

Rebekah frowned, and turned her back on Adam.

Wesley concluded, "You don't live here, do you? These are going to be our neighbors, not yours. They're going to think it's neat that you found somebody to take care of the place again. You probably have some rental agreements out in that van of yours? Let's get this down on paper."

Part One, Chapter Three

Like a wary antelope in tall grass, Ann Foster looked nervously at her surroundings. She parked her Audi outside Ira Miller's office; two blocks off the main drag. Ann feared for her tires, as this street was virtually paved with smashed glass vials and broken bottles. Everyone said that Miller, manager of Memphis Rail and a dozen other acts, was worth hundreds of millions of dollars. Nobody visiting his dirty little office would ever suspect that. However, when invisible on the telephone he was as powerful a rainmaker in the entertainment industry as anyone working from a penthouse in Manhattan.

Across the street was the back side of an abandoned auto dealership, with stacks of old tires and discarded batteries towering over all but the tallest weeds. The plastic was smashed out of a sign frame shaped like a Chevrolet emblem, revealing peeling brown paint reading "Nash-Rambl," below. The "er" had fallen off the building when a corner began to crumble.

Next door, a cement block building once housed a four stall self-service car wash. Vandals stripped all the copper pipes and wires from the wash bays when it closed. The graffiti that covered the cracking walls claimed the site for the Satanic Apostles, one of the more ruthless street gangs ever to run drugs and hookers in Montgomery County. Copper colored sparks erupted as the sun reflected off several un-retrieved shell casings scattered across the heaved and failing asphalt lot.

Ann decided it was safe to leave the car. The only person she could see was the fry cook for Wilma's Chicken House, sucking down a cigarette just outside the kitchen door and perched on an overflowing trash can. Even so, she reached into her handbag for reassurance that her pistol was there and ready for action. Ann would never come to this neighborhood at night, packing or not. She visited rarely and reluctantly. Most business with Ira Miller could be conducted by phone or email. Ann knew that if she had to go to extraordinary lengths to persuade her manager, she had certain means to do so more effectively in person.

Ann walked quickly to the door and buzzed Miller's office on the intercom. Ira Miller recognized Ann in his security camera monitor and pressed a button to unlock the front door. Only a week into the New Year, the window mounted air conditioner in Miller's office was unplugged. "That's a blessing," thought Ann. "When that noisy damn swamp cooler is runnin' you almost have to shout to be heard in here."

"Ann! Good to see you! I trust you had a good Christmas? Good New Year's, too?"

"Darn straight I did. Flew back home after that show in Vancouver, and I been restin' up a spell. It's nice to sleep in the same bed several nights in a row, eat some home cookin', and see the family. Yeah, it's goin' pretty good right now."

"So what brings you by? I mean, I guess I probably know but just in case..."

"Oh hell, Ira. I need an advance again this year."

"I figured. How much this time?"

"Can I get thirty? I need to pay off a couple of credit cards and get by another two months until we start getting paid regular again. But there ought to be somethin' in royalties, right? Maybe I've got a big chunk of this covered already?"

"I wish. Royalties are way off." Ira clicked a mouse to refresh his computer screen and called up a spreadsheet. "If you remember, we settled up on your share of the royalties last September. You got $4300 comin' now."

"Three and half months and my share from records is $4300? Wo, damn Ira. I mean, I trust you and everything but Jesus, why ain't anything selling? Some of our new material is damn good."

"Yeah, a lot of the new stuff is great, but we have to mix in a bunch of the old standards to get anybody to buy Memphis Rail at all. I agree with you, your latest material is killer. Hell, that one that you wrote last year, Mean Cruel Mama, got a lot of airplay; but the album we formatted around it is standin' still. We're gettin' way too many 99-cent single downloads, and you know what those pay- it ain't shit."

"So can you cash me out on the 43-hundred and advance me another 25-thousand?"

"Well," began Ira.

"C'mon, man. Don't make me beg."

"I sort of like the way you go about begging," teased Ira. He changed his tone when he noticed that Ann looked annoyed. "OK, OK. Give me a minute."

Ira stared at his computer screen and clicked his mouse. "Alright, you've got $29,346.15 added to your checking account. Don't spend it all in one place."

"Wouldn't be your business if I did," insisted Ann.

"You're right of course. But I'd hate to think you're gonna use it to hurt yourself."

"I've been clean a long time now, Ira. A girl's got expenses, though."

Ira smiled. "Hey, by the way, what do you think about this new act that Mary is trying to develop?"

"Between you and me, I think she's nuts. She's staying up in Seattle, coachin' the hell out of a couple of nobodies from up that way. She's got some old white dude playin' the sax; and I got to say that I did hear him play one night and it was damn nearly unnatural, the sound he got out of that old horn. He was pretty drunk. Lucky drunk is what everybody thinks that was there. Ain't no way he actually plays like that when he's in his right mind. Can't be."

"You sure?" asked Ira.

Conversation was interrupted while a pair of cop cars, sirens wailing, roared down the street. When they passed, Ann said, "Pretty damn sure. I know a musician when I meet one. This guy ain't the real deal. Supposedly Mary's got some gal with a high pitched voice. At least she's a sister. Mary says she's really good. 'Course that makes me a little nervous, Ira. What if Mary isn't trying to develop these guys into a new act and starts thinkin' we should try to fold 'em into the Rail?"

"And, what if?"

"Hey. I'm the second female voice in Memphis Rail. Mary and I are damn good together. I sure as hell don't need some amateur gal from Seattle screwin' things up. What did Mary say that broad used to do? She was a stripper, or a pole dancer, or some kind of hooker or somethin?"

Ira laughed. "Pole dancer? Hooker? Really? I've talked to Mary a couple of times and she's told me this gal, Rebekah, used to be a nurse."

"Nurse, stripper, hooker, who cares? Mary better not be thinkin' of shakin' up the band. We got a good mix right now. We ain't really got enough money to go around now, at least not the way it used to. Maybe it would help if most of these older folks comin' out weren't too fat for a tee shirt and didn't already own all our CD's. Anyway, we can't change people in or out unless you give the OK."

"Gates and records, Ann. That's what it comes down to. Who knows how this thing Mary's working on is going to pan out, if at all. But don't worry about your spot in the Rail. You've got a lock on keyboards, and at least some vocals."

Ann planted a light kiss on Ira Miller's cheek as she stepped around him to leave his office. "I'm gonna hold you to that, Ira. I'm gonna count on it."

"Well, you can. But damn, now that I'm thinkin' of it, I probably should have made you beg."

"You old sum-bitch," teased Ann. "You ain't never gonna change!" She stepped briskly to the front door and waited for Ira to buzz it open. She blew him a kiss as she disappeared into the combat zone between the entrance way and her car at the curb.

Part One, Chapter Four

Wesley scrolled through a screen on his cell phone. He was sure he had the number he wanted. Two of the unidentified numbers were only vaguely familiar, and he wasn't certain which of the two would connect to the party he needed to find. He tried the one he felt was just slightly more likely, and was relieved when Phedra answered the phone.

"Hello, Phedra, this is Wesley. Mr. Perkins,"

"Oh, yes. Hello Mr. Perkins. Are you coming back home? That man, Walter, you know the one who has been staying with Mrs. Perkins and Miss Brianna the last couple of weeks? I hate to say it, but he's a real pendejo, if you know what I mean."

Wesley laughed. "My Spanish isn't all that great, but yeah- I know exactly what you mean."

"That man," complained Phedra, "he yells at me and Diego like we're dogs he's telling to 'fetch' or something. Mrs. Perkins doesn't like it much, we can tell, but she seems afraid to say anything about it. Are you and Mrs. Perkins getting back together, I hope?"

"No, Phedra. It doesn't look like we're going to be getting back together. I'm sorry if Brianna's father is hard to be around. I never cared much for him. But I always figured that was because he was Ruth's first husband. Anyway, that's not why I called. I need a little help, and I thought about seeing if I could hire Diego for a few days. Is he there?"

"Yes he is. I'll get him. Nice to talk to you, Mr. Perkins."

"Nice talking to you too, Phedra."

After several seconds of silence, Diego picked up the phone.

"Hello, Mr. Perkins. This is Diego. Phedra said you might have some work for me?"

"Yeah, I think I do. I'm cleaning up a place over here in Seattle so I can live in it. Yesterday I hired a crew of guys standing around outside Home Depot."

"Oh, oh" I think I know where this is going.

"Well, they came ready to work, tools and all. It seemed like a pretty good deal. Fifteen bucks per man per hour is a lot cheaper than paying a contractor, but I think I screwed up hiring them by the hour and not by the job."

Diego chuckled, "Let me guess. Once they are on the job, what little bit of English they once had seems to disappear right away, right?"

"Bingo, you got it."

"And," continued Diego, "they are working pretty cheaply by the hour so hanging out in a house, out of the wind and the rain, looks like a much better place to be than freezing their cajones off outside the hardware store. So if I guess correctly, progress is very, very slow. You know, at fifteen bucks, it takes a lot of hours to make a decent check."

"You must have been reading my mind," said Wesley.

"So, you want me to come to Seattle and translate or something?"

"Yeah, I think need somebody to talk to the crew in Spanish," agreed Wesley.

"I can do better than translate, Mr. Perkins. I know repair and remodeling pretty good. I spent one summer painting and laying carpet for an apartment guy down in Texas."

"Great!"

"But I thought you spoke some kind of Spanish, with that weird accent. I'll never forget how you stood up for me and my family at that fancy dinner. I still wish my boy hadn't told those bigots what you said. Phedra says that's part of the trouble between you and your wife. Mi Dios, I hope that is not true."

"Nothing going on between me and Mrs. Perkins is your fault, or your son's. None of it. As far as my Spanish, let's just say that it comes and goes. It's usually gone, and damned if I can find it when I need it. Yeah, I could use your help. I need to get this project wrapped up. What's a fair price?"

"If you're paying the Home Depot guys fifteen bucks an hour, I will work for twenty. That's probably too cheap for what I know and what I can do, but I owe you. The guys from Home Depot? They wouldn't respect me if they thought I was getting paid less than they are. Anyway, I will get their lazy asses in gear without some bullshit language barrier. In the end it will cost you a lot less."

"Ok, deal." said Wesley. "Why don't I pick you up at the ferry dock about eight tomorrow morning?"

"Ok, deal. I will look forward to seeing you again, Mr. Perkins."

Part One, Chapter Five

Diego's skill and supervision was a godsend. Within two twelve hour days, the walls were sealed and painted, the carpet and pad replaced. Everything in the Lake City rental was scrubbed clean.

One of the crew found a rusty lawn mower in the carport, under a pile of soaked cardboard and moldy maple leaves. After a difficult start, the engine smoked and clanked. The mechanism did a ragged job of chopping down most of the overgrowth. On the final pass, the blade hooked a loose wire concealed in the high grass and screeched to a halt. Efforts to restart the mower proved unsuccessful, so one edge of the yard remained unkempt.

Adam Turner dropped by to inspect.

"I have to say, this place hasn't looked this good in years. Heck, I don't think it looked this good when I bought it- but I can't remember, exactly. But I noticed you put some of the furniture in the carport? What's going on there?"

"That stuff stinks!" snapped Rebekah. "There ain't any way to get that smell out of the cloth furniture. So we're gonna keep the wooden stuff in the house. Maybe you got someplace else you can use the sofa, the easy chair, the mattresses, and the like?"

"Aw, shit," complained Turner. "I didn't want to have to deal with it."

"No problem," said Wesley. "Don't deal with it. We can leave it in the carport, where it will be out of the rain. Mostly. We'll even throw a plastic tarp over it, if you like. This place is going look like hell itself to anybody out the street, though. And who was concerned about what the neighbors are going to think? Haul if off, of leave it in the carport. We just can't take the smell of it in the house."

"OK, OK, I'll come over with a bigger truck and clear it away. You got the four months' rent in advance, like we talked about, right?"

"Yeah, here you go. Ten-thousand dollars. When that runs out, stop by and get some more."

Turner backed his grimy white cargo van out of the gravel drive just in time to make room for the arrival of Vanessa's Honda Accord. Mary Towne was riding along, and Wesley the Dog had his head sticking out of a back window.

"I brought over the dog, along with his food and blanket. My cat is too freaked out for him to stay at my place any more. I also brought you guys some pots and pans, and some plates and stuff."

"Good," said Rebekah. "Hope you brought some for my apartment in the basement too. I don't know how much we're gonna be eating or cooking together. When all this Judah Jones crap sifts out, we all feel a little safer and I've got some money, I'm gonna look for a place that's just my own. No offense, Wes."

"None taken."

"I brought a little house warmer, too," smiled Mary. She pulled a bottle of red wine from a sack, along with a fifth of rye whiskey. "Wes, fish three glasses out of that stack Vanessa brought and let's celebrate your new place. Plus, we got a few important things to go over and now's as good a time as there is gonna be."

"About the only place we have to sit right now is around the kitchen table, and none of these look like wine glasses, exactly." apologized Wes.

"That's no big deal," said Vanessa. "Mary and I have been talking through this thing and we all need to be on the same page on a couple of items."

The four gathered at the table. Wes poured the wine, along with a large shot of rye for himself. Wesley the Dog sniffed the new carpet, circled three times around a spot that must have seemed most suitable, and curled up in a shaggy yellow ball.

"Well, cheers y'all" said Mary Towne as she raised her wine to offer a toast.

"Cheers!" replied Wesley, Rebekah, and Vanessa. Four glasses clinked together.

"OK, then," continued Mary. "From what I can see, there's at least three things going on here. The first is what I can do for y'all. And that's something that not just anybody could do for you."

Wesley contemplated that statement, rubbing his chin.

"The second is what y'all can do for me. And just bein' honest here if you couldn't do somethin' for me I wouldn't be botherin' to do anything for you. The third thing is whatever is maybe going on in the background, and we need to make sure that doesn't screw up what I can do for y'all and what y'all are gonna do for me."

"We've really appreciated the coaching you've offered us so far," said Rebekah.

"Sounds a little complicated to me," remarked Wes. "I thought we were just trying to sort out this entire Judah Jones thing and hope to get life back into some kind of order. I mean, the rest of my life just fell apart and I'm screwin' around learning to play the saxophone?"

Mary nodded, and smiled. "Hear me out. Let's start with what I can do for y'all. That's the easiest. Wes and Rebekah, I have heard you guys enough times to be sure both y'all got some kind of talent on steroids. Nobody gets that kind of gift without some purpose to it. I suspect it might even be an important purpose."

"Gift? Sometimes it seems more like a burden," grumbled Wesley.

Mary continued, "There was a time I had that much talent, or thought I did. I spent a lot of years just trying to get the right people to listen to me so I could have somethin' of a career. Those years are precious time. I can get the right people to listen to you, almost right away, but I need to be sure you're completely committed, first. Before you run up and holler that you're committed, you deserve a warnin'. There's somethin' you need to know about the blues. Somethin' maybe a little dark."

"It's tough to imagine anything much darker than the crap I've gone through the last couple of weeks," Wesley remarked,

"Well, that's it. Or at least sort of," confirmed Mary. "You see, the blues ain't like no other kind of music. You can play a march without becomin' John frickin' Phillips Sousa. You can play a Brahms concerto without wearin' a powered wig and snortin' snuff. Christ, you can even play rock and roll without ever bein' Jerry Lee Lewis, Kurt Cobain, or Keith Richards. But it ain't that way with the blues. If you are ever gonna do more than just dabble in it, y'all are gonna wind up livin' it."

"So what's that like," asked Rebekah, "to live the blues?"

"It's a lot like bein' married to a curse. You're gonna love the blues more than the blues is ever gonna love you back. There are some bad times, in fact there are some terrible times. You hold out for the good times, hopin' they will make up for the rough ride you been havin'. Seems like the good times ain't really ever that good. Oh yeah, sometimes there will be money enough. Once in a while there's gonna be more money than you know what to do with. And there's a downside to that, too. Someday you wind up holdin' more money than you ever thought you were gonna see, and realize the same old problems and feelin's of bein' dissatisfied still dog you 'round. That's a hell of a shock for most people, findin' out that havin' money, or not havin' money, ain't really the root of all evil. Getting' well, stayin' happy? Ain't got nothin' to do with gettin' rich. Blues feeds off a hunger in your soul, so the blues is gonna make sure you stay plenty hungry."

Nobody spoke for moment. Vanessa stared intently into her wine glass. "Why would you stay with it, then?"

"After a while, you got no choice. Blues is a long, long road. It don't matter how far you go, or how many years you spend on that road, it seems like it takes you everywhere except some place you could really be at home. After a while, that's the only thing that seems like it would be really important, goin' home."

Wesley stroked the dog between his ears. "So, why don't you just hang it up and go wherever home is?"

Mary refreshed her red wine. "Maybe because the blues ain't gonna let you go. Maybe because you ain't sure where or what home really is, not after all those years on that twistin' and windin' road. Blues don't let you go until it's done with you, and it ain't never done with you until you find somebody to take your place. That brings us to the second part of our discussion, what y'all can do for me if you decide to let me do for you."

Part One, Chapter Six

Before Mary could continue, Wesley the Dog snarled and sprang to his feet. He streaked to the front door, growling and snarling menacingly. He crouched low to the ground in the entry, muscles as tense as cables. He stared up at the knob, slobbering and growling between angry barks.

"Lord!" exclaimed Mary, "what's gotten into your dog?"

"Don't know, really," said Vanessa. She pushed her chair back from the table, as did Wesley and Rebekah. "He can be really protective, especially around Rebekah. He must think something's goin' on outside, we better take a look." Wesley and the sisters moved to the living room window, and Mary followed closely behind. Wesley the Dog remained fixed in place; ancient sounds from deep within his throat threatening death to any intruder.

There was nothing to see, or so it first appeared. The uncertain and fading afternoon light of mid-January played a demon's tricks with shapes and shadows, progressively fuzzing the edges of objects farthest from individual gaze. There was nobody on the porch. The freshly mowed lawn seemed empty. There were no children playing in the street, and no cars driving by.

"Musta been a false alarm," suggested Mary.

Rebekah bent down to caress Wesley the Dog beside his jowls. "Hush, boy. That's a good boy now," she soothed and cooed. The dog responded to her touch, but reluctantly- as if unconvinced that the danger had passed.

Vanessa was the first to notice, and she gasped as she pointed to the left hand side of the yard. "Oh, shit! Look over there!"

In the tall grass remaining on the far edge of the lawn, at almost the exact point were the mower destroyed itself on the wire, a long red scarf lay in an abstract heap.

"I don't see nothin' but some nasty ass grass, and an old rag," said Mary.

"Maybe that's all there is to see," said Wesley. "You know, Mary, you were asking about whether we were committed. Let me tell you, we're not committed- we're compelled."

"How so?"

Vanessa continued to stare at the red scarf on the unmown lawn. "We don't really have a choice in this thing. We're pretty sure it's something that's happening to us, or through us. Rebekah, and me, and Wes, and Wesley the Dog; we're together for some kind of purpose."

Wesley took a large sip from his glass of rye His voice changed, to one that Vanessa and Rebekah heard first at the Elliott Plaza, and assumed was the sound of Judah Jones. "There ain't no way out of this thing by goin' backwards. Not no mo. Me, the sisters, and the dog? I think I's talkin' for all of us when I says we need to stick together 'til we get through this thing. Don't matter much where it takes us, we can't be goin' back to where we been. 'Cuz where we been? It don't be there no mo."

Mary was startled by the transition in Wesley's voice. "What the hell was that?"

Rebekah grimaced. "Sometimes that happens when Wes drinks rye. It blows your mind to hear it, I know, but Vanessa and I are pretty sure it's not something he can control."

Mary closed her eyes and sighed. What sort of madness she was wading into? Was she somehow compelled as well? Was there still time to bail out of this weird opera? Why did she think this old white guy and the untested female vocalist could possibly be a ticket home- for her or for anybody else?

Wesley the Dog shook his coat, and walked cautiously back to his place on the carpet. Vanessa and the three musicians returned to the table.

After a final moment of self-doubt and silence, Mary continued. "As I was sayin', y'all got to do somethin' for me in exchange for somethin' I can do for you. It ain't much, really. I'm gettin' to be an old woman. I'm just about ready to go home, but I need somebody to take my place. Unless I miss my bet, that's going to be Wes, or Rebekah, or maybe even Wes and Rebekah together. Nobody gets to just quit. When you're ready to go home someday, you won't get to quit either. You will havta find somebody to take your places. You need to pass it on."

Wesley and the sisters said nothing for a moment, each contemplating the gravity of Mary's "bargain." Vanessa was the first to speak, "But what about me? Rebekah's got a voice, Wes plays the sax, but I'm supposed to be part of this too. I'm pretty sure that whatever we do isn't going to work unless we stick really close together. That probably means the dog too."

Mary spanned her eyes with her left thumb and index finger, making a rubbing motion toward her nose. "Lord, 'Nessa! Anybody else? You people ain't an act, you're a whole damn tribe."

"Exactly!" emphasized Rebekah. "That's what we are, sort of a weird family."

Mary shook her head, and finally in a tone of resignation asked, "OK, Vanessa. You do anything at all with music? Do you sing? Play somethin'? What can you add to the deal? What the hell, we need some excuse to bring you in."

"I sort of thought I'd be handling whatever managing might be required."

Mary shook her head. "Nope, that ain't happenin'. Not unless you want to start all by yourselves, down at the bottom, and most likely never get nowhere. Let me tell you, one percent of the people in this game get ninety percent of the audience and ninety-nine percent of the money. The other ninety-nine percent of the people in this game? They get to divide up the ten percent of the audience and one percent of the money left over. I ain't gonna manage you either, not once we get you goin'. There's just a handful of the right people in a position to take what you got and turn it into somethin' that will be heard. Somethin' that will be remembered. Somethin' that will sell. I can get you next to the people who can do that for you, after we spend a little time gettin' you ready."

Wesley spoke up, again in the voice of Judah Jones. "We needs to be t'gether. Ain't you noticin' that I plays better when both Rebekah and Vanessa is around? 'Nessa don't know it yet, but I just gots a hunch, almost for a certain, that she's gonna prove a natural on the blues harp. She can whack a tambourine or bang a cowbell or somethin' times other than that. She's gotta be in, 'long with the dog, or it ain't gonna be happenin'. Least not the way it needs to."

Mary frowned. "Wes, I ain't got a lot of patience for talk about "naturals." I ain't never met one, 'cept you, maybe, and I'm not all that sure I've got the whole story on that. But, in this case we'll give Vanessa a try on the blues harp because it can't be any stranger than anything else goin' on around here."

Wesley sipped his rye, and replied "Gots to work, Mary. We gotta stick together here. We can't be goin' home, less'n we're goin' together."

Mary was resigned to Wesley's unnatural voice. "There ain't a lot of ladies playing harmonica, Wes. Guess maybe it ain't considered proper for us to be so nimble with our lips and tongues, or somethin'. Blues harp and sax are weird together, but we can try to figure that out too."

Wesley returned to his normal voice. "Weird together? Jesus, Mary, we're pretty much all weird together in this thing."

"Maybe so, Wes. But the dog? What the hell, guys? They don't just be lettin' a dog in to most of the places you need to go. They don't let no dogs in, unless..." Mary paused, laughed heartily, and reached for her purse. She pulled out a pair of dark sunglasses. "Unless the dog's one of them seein' eye dogs! Try these on, Vanessa. Far as anybody knows, you're blind as a bat and you need your dog to get around. But hey, the first time that animal takes a pee or shits on stage, it ain't gonna go well."

"I don't know," countered Vanessa. "It seems pretty bogus to me."

Mary persisted. "Bogus? Child you don't know from bogus. Your whole gig is as close to unreal as ever I seen. But there's a long tradition of blind blues musicians. If you can actually pick up the harp and fill in with some percussion, we can make a spot for you somehow. Frankly, though, I'm only doin' that to get Wes and Rebekah, no offense meant."

Vanessa laughed as she mugged an exaggerated pose in Mary's sunglasses. "None taken. As long as we three can be together, I don't care."

Part One, Chapter Seven

The four migrated back to the table. Wesley the Dog lay on guard with one eye open, and one ear tossed back along his shaggy neck. Mary resumed her lecture.

"Well, then, the final thing comes down to this bizarre crap goin' on behind the scenes. I know y'all think that Wes is somehow the livin' reincarnation of Judah Jones. I saw the album cover over at Vanessa's, and except for the twist in the neck? Yeah the sax on that cover looks a lot like Wesley's horn. I even agree that Wes sounds a lot like Judah Jones on that record. But, I ain't buyin' it as anything more than coincidence. That's all. Y'all gotta swear that you won't be talkin' 'bout no Judah Jones, no Caroline, and none of these crazy damn notions that Wes and Rebekah are someways or 'nother Judah and Caroline come back to life."

The room was silent for a moment. Wesley and Rebekah looked perhaps instinctively at Vanessa, waiting for her to speak.

"Mary, that's fine. But we aren't the only people who are going to remember Judah Jones. Somebody else is going to have a copy of that old album from the 1950's. We can't just pretend that Wesley popped up out of nowhere. And, what about the similar appearance of the sax?"

"We build a backstory for Wes. He's been a lifelong fan of Judah Jones. Years of practice later, he can play a lot like Jones did. After a long search, he even found a horn that looks a little bit like the one once owned by Judah Jones. Trust me, people are going to be amazed by a white guy playin' like Wes can play. It's unusual, like a rhinoceros shoootin' pool, or what not. Nobody will ask too many questions. Ain't no frame of reference to form questions from."

Wesley took another sip of rye. "Oughts to work. Oughts to work out fine."

Vanessa looked puzzled. "I guess we can do that. Mary, though, you need to know we've got something going on here that's sort of unfinished business."

"Listen, sister," counseled Mary, "whatever little private hell y'all are decidin' to wade through- there's a bunch of us you need to leave out of it. You see, I got plans for you. The blues has got plans for you. I'm gonna do for you, you're gonna do for me, and unless I miss my guess there's one hellacious number of folks gonna go home in the end. We're all just waitin' for somebody to take our place. That's gonna be Wesley, Rebekah, and if you want to ignore my earlier warnin' it's gonna be you too."

"OK, so what's next?" asked Rebekah in a practical tone.

"On my end, I need to get Ira Miller to appoint me A&R executive for you guys."

"Uh, what does A&R mean?" asked Vanessa.

"It stands for artist and repertoire. I help you guys get started, and normally I would hook you up with a producer and a label. I really got to be entirely honest with you, though. There ain't no way to make a record with a saxophone, a soprano voice, a dog, and somebody whacking a cowbell. We're gonna start off pickin' up local sidemen for your rhythm section. My plan is to before long have you openin' for Memphis Rail. After that, I got some ideas- but we'll need to see how things work out."

"Sounds like a win-win," said Rebekah.

"Damn straight. But get this and get this well; ain't gonna be nobody outside the four of us ever hear any talk about Judah Jones, Caroline, magic jewelry, or haunted frickin' saxophones. You OK with that? I'll drop this whole project like a hot rock the first minute I start lookin' like a nutcase. We stick to the back story. Agreed?"

There was a moment of silence around the table. Wesley extended his left hand to Vanessa and his right hand to Rebekah. Vanessa and Rebekah reached out in turn to grab Mary's hands. When the circle was complete, the three said, simply, "Agreed."

Part One, Chapter Eight

Blow, draw, blow, draw, blow, draw, draw blow. Vanessa practiced her harmonica scales with growing frustration. Mary didn't play harp, but still coached her as much as she was able. They discussed the theory of second position cross harp, as well as the circle of fifths. When Vanessa finally grasped the circle of fifths, she seemed confused whether she was supposed to use a harp one step clockwise, or counterclockwise, from the primary key.

"It's up a 4th, 'Nessa. Like you use an A harp when the rest of the band is playin' in E."

"I get that Mary, but it doesn't make all that much sense to say we're goin' up a 4th when we're goin' backwards on that circle diagram."

Blow, draw, blow, draw, blow, draw, draw, blow.

"Well, then do this," suggested Mary. "See where the key is stamped in at the edge of reed cover?"

"Of course."

"So, get yourself some tape, put it over the stamping, and mark the cross harp. Take your G harp and mark it D. Then when somebody calls the tune in D, you'll be squared away. Lord, 'Nessa, you got more than enough on your plate without strugglin' to remember which key to play. We been after this a couple of hours a night all week and you still ain't close to any kind of harp player a 'tall."

"Damn, Mary. I've been trying, really hard, and I got blisters on my lips to prove it!"

"Ok, let's try somethin'" said Mary. "I'll clap out a four-count rhythm, and you work up and down the scale. This is the blues, not some kind of freakin' parade. Be thinkin' to emphasize the second and fourth beats, not the first and third. Let's see what happens."

Mary clapped and Vanessa played. Blow, DRAW, blow, DRAW, blow, DRAW, draw, BLOW. Blow, DRAW, draw, BLOW, draw BLOW, draw BLOW.

"You're more or less gettin' the rhythm just fine, but I can't begin to guess why Wes thinks you're gonna be some sort of natural. We'll have to start you out maybe exclusively on the cowbell, tambourine, and what not. Ira sent me some computer files, mostly rhythm tracks from the last album. We're gonna use those to rehearse with tomorrow. You, me, Rebekah, and Wes. We'll have you try some harp, but I got to say that you ain't even close to ready."

Vanessa cried herself to sleep. She was desperate to be included. Somebody needed to keep a watchful eye over Wes and Rebekah. What if they were all twisted up somehow with Judah and Caroline? Things might go wrong. She knew she had the gifts of sensitivity and observation. Vanessa worried that perhaps she was all that stood between her sister, her friend, and the dark destructive snakes now slithering around the perimeters of their lives. During her agonies, she slipped into a dream.

Vanessa immediately recognized the cave. More than once, she and her mother visited this location during her childhood. The mouth of the cavern was almost insignificant, rising like an eyebrow arched above a grassy hillside. In summertime, the field before the opening filled with stalks that were dry, brittle, and rattled as anyone passed through. In her dream, it was spring. The grass was dazzled with dew. Buttercups and daisies raced the soft emerald spires toward the sun.

The cave was said to be miles deep. Rumors were that nobody had even been to the far end and emerged to recount the experience. Cold, winds scented with copper and sulfur whistled in the dark recesses, punctuated by a low whoosh of water rushing through an invisible crevice. There were faint odors of urine and beer just inside the mouth of the cave, with brown and green bottles kicked to one side of the entrance.

Vanessa remembered the cave, but never an experience like this. She was a plant, growing just inside the lip of the cave. Enough rainwater dripped or blew through the opening to sustain her growth. She had sprouted up at the innermost edge of the sunny spot, nothing but moss and lichen could grow only a few feet deeper.

She was self-aware, with a nervous system that allowed her to feel but not move. She reached tendrils down to tap the wisdom of the earth, affording her access to thought but not speech. She communicated across reasonable distances with sister plants, alerting one another to danger. She understood and accepted that she was more a manifestation of a life force permeating the soil than an individual, living a life rooted in place and flourishing in a natural sphere.

In her dream, Vanessa began vibrating. She produced a warm, bright, and well regulated tone. After a moment, she paused. A sister plant in the meadow vibrated in response. The sound was higher, and compared to Vanessa's vibration gave the impression of being more intense. Based on her current drills with cross harp and the circle of fifths, Vanessa recognized the tonal interval between the two vibrations as a fourth.

Pleased that she had been heard, Vanessa vibrated her original tone in response. From far across the meadow, at the edge of the stream, a new tone emerged. It seemed slightly more intense, and drew the ear a greater distance from Vanessa's original sound. "That's a fifth!"

The sister plant in the meadow resonated a fourth in response, and Vanessa finalized the exchange with a long, happy vibration of her original, fundamental tone.

Vanessa woke with a start. Short of breath. Ecstatic. She had cried herself to sleep, but now she wept for joy. Vanessa, the sensitive and the perceptive, knew she had received a priceless gift. Now she would absolutely be included. Vanessa had the blues.

Part One, Chapter Nine

Mary Towne was relaxing in a bubble bath, with a pink towel wrapped around her hair. Her cell phone was sitting on a nearby stool, and she reached out to pick it up when it rang.

"Hello?"

"Mary, this is Ira. What in the name of hell is going on up there in Seattle? I just played that file you emailed me. The one with that bunch of supposed rookies you took under your wing."

"Yeah?" responded Mary, "and what did you think?"

"Shit oh dear, Mary. Shit oh dear! Where did these people come from?"

Mary sat upright in the tub, dabbing her phone dry with a wash cloth. "What do you mean by 'shit oh dear'? Ira. Just come out and tell me plain whether or not you liked it."

"Like it? I think you're screwing with me. I don't know who you recorded in that rehearsal session, but they sure as hell aren't some bunch of wannabe nobodies like you've been telling me. Ha, ha, ha, the jokes on me. Why are you fucking around in Seattle instead of gone home to spend some time with your grandkids? Instead you're pulling my chain about some bunch of supposedly unknown amateurs you think are almost ready to roll with the Rail."

Mary reached her free hand through the bubbles, searching for the plug. "Shit, Ira. I got no time to be jerkin' you around. No energy, neither."

"Oh, year? Well let's start with that vocalist you've been telling me about; Rebekah, right? I can't place it, but I swear I've heard that voice before. But then again I think maybe I haven't heard it before, maybe I'm just remembering some idealized concept or something. Jesus, Mary, she's right up there with you as far as talent goes- and God knows I have nothin' but respect for you and what you can do."

The plug released, with a deep gulp. "Damn well you better."

"Yeah," continued Ira, "she's just an octave or so higher, and the edge isn't quite there, yet, and maybe that's because she's still young. But good lord, when she starts wailing it reminds me of church bells, and xylophone, and maybe even the whistle on a locomotive. With those pipes? It's a serious fucking waste if she's not in the trade. I say, no way. "

"Way, Ira. That's Rebekah, nobody else, and she's got one hell of a voice. We're starting to work up some harmonies, and she gets it almost the first time, every time. But, what else do you think?"

"Well let's talk about the sax player. Shit, Mary, nobody plays like that. Not consistently. We spend all afternoon in the studio doing 25 takes to get one horn player to sound like, (what did you say his name was? Wesley Perkins?)... for a 20 second solo and this guy is just cranking along, live, like it's normal. I've heard legends of guys who played like that, maybe 50 or 60 years ago, and there's even a few scratched up old records kicking around here and there, but almost nobody plays at that level today. Especially some middle aged white guy who just pops up out of nowhere."

Mary stepped out of the tub and reached for her bathrobe. "You're gonna hear this sooner or later," confided Mary. "Wes has been a huge fan of Judah Jones for his entire life, and he spent a long, long, time..."

"That's it!" agreed Ira. "That's where I heard about the same style before. Yeah, Judah Jones, that's it! Didn't he have like one fantastic album in the late 1950's? If I remember right, his Cadillac ran off the road down south someplace and his career was cut short."

"Maybe might not have been a car crash," responded Mary, "but from what I know, he never made it back to Harlem after a trip home to see some woman or another. Anyway, Wes has spent years and years learnin' to copy those chops." Mary wondered, nervously, if Ira could detect she knew a bit more than she was revealing about Wesley Perkins, Judah Jones, and a lynching in Indianola.

Ira was quiet for a moment. "Maybe there's some possible angle there? No, forget it, I'm just having crazy thoughts. There's no point thinking them out loud."

"What do you mean, exactly?"

"What I mean is, what if we dig up a copy of that old Judah Jones album and recut it, track for track, in a modern studio using this Wes Perkins guy to play the sax? Do you think he's got that much shit in the bag? Could he give us ten, and do it clean? Maybe that's just way too insane. Stuff like this doesn't happen in real life, we both know that, right?"

Mary stepped into her fuzzy slippers. "Who knows what we know, or think we all know. But we should give it a little while. The three of them get better and better, every time we rehearse. I ain't never seen anything exactly like it, but it sure it fun to be around while it's happening."

"That's right," said Ira. "There are three of them. I almost forgot that lady harp player. She's pretty good too, but just journeyman stuff. I don't hear a lot of featured solos there. I take it that's her on the percussion? It seems to shut off when the blues harp kicks in."

Mary looked into the mirror, applying moisturizer to her face. "Give her a little more time, Ira. This time last week, she couldn't play a note."

"What! Don't bullshit me, Mary. Nobody learns to play like that in a week. Now I think you're screwing with me again."

"That's Vanessa, Ira. And if I'm lyin', I'm dyin'. She brings a lot of energy to the set. She uses a dog to get around."

"A dog? What for? Is she blind or something?"

"Not exactly. But Wesley and Rebekah? They need her. They need the damn dog, too. I can't put it into words 'xactly, but Wesley plays pretty good by himself. He plays better when Rebekah is around, better yet when Vanessa's there, and all three of them take it up a notch whenever Wesley's in the room."

"What do you mean whenever Wesley's in the room? Wesley is there playing the sax, right?"

"Yeah, but the dog's name is Wesley, too."

"Oh my aching ass, Mary. It sounds like a fucking circus or something. I haven't had a drink all day, but I swear I'd have to be drunk to just buy into this shit."

Mary opened the bathroom door. "Buy or not, Ira. It is what it is. You know me. I ain't got the time to be screwin' around for no reason in Seattle. I wouldn't be here, if this wasn't something exceptional. Have I ever let you down? Have I? I mean in all the years, I ain't ever screwed with you and I ain't about to start now."

"Well then, let's put these guys to the test. I need a second opinion. You ever hear of the Gridiron Grill? It's across the street from the football stadium in Seattle."

"Hell, no, Ira. I don't get out to football much. But I'm sure I can find somethin' the size of a stadium."

"I've got Little Willie Maxwell and the Bluesbirds booked there next Sunday, playin' for a big bash right after the Super Bowl."

Mary chortled "Oh, yeah. Little Willie. You know, he always get pissed when I call him that?"

"Maybe it's the way you say it, or something" chuckled Ira Miller. "Try saying his name without pointing at his crotch. Anyway, the Grill likes to have live music during half time on TV. I guess it sells more liquor than the Super Bowl show. Get your guys to work up a tight 30 minute set to cover halftime. We'll put the Bluesbirds on right after the game ends, keep the crowd hanging around and buying drinks. But, I'll have them standing by in case your guys get up there and choke. You ready for that?"

"Ira, I ain't never been so ready. You be ready too, because things are gonna be changin'. I know what I know, and I know what I don't know, and I know what's happenin' up here is special. Really, really special."

"OK then, prove it on Super Bowl Sunday."

"Watch our smoke, Ira. Watch our smoke."

"Let's just hope that smoke ain't from goin' down in flames. See ya later, Mary."

"Yeah, Ira. See ya soon."

Mary flipped off the bathroom light and walked down the hallway. The water was gone, but bubbles remained in the tub.

Part One, Chapter Ten

The February rain ran down the jagged crimson clinker bricks, teasing the scent of musty lime from the mortar. Second story windows, unwashed for decades, were black within their wrought iron frames. There was a time when Puget Sound washed against the base of Beacon Hill, far to the east. That was before the proud citizens filled the bay with sawdust, garbage, and, (during a series of "regrades"), sluiced tons of dirt into the bay. The Moran Brothers shipyard once stood here. In the late 1800's the battleship "Nebraska" came down the ways. After the Moran brothers made their millions, the shipyard was displaced by ravaged hilltops and industrial wastes. In the late 1900's Seattle erected football and baseball stadia at the site of the old shipyard. Millionaires minted here were now athletes, not industrialists.

The red brick structure, 80 feet wide and a city block deep, stood at the edge of the original shoreline. The edifice originally served as a barn for 25 teams and wagons, employed to haul steel a few miles from the Bethlehem mill. Now, it was home to the Gridiron Grill- one of the busiest sports bars in Seattle. The fire marshal posted a sign, "Maximum Capacity 1250," but during every Seahawks game, at home or away, the fire marshal's edict was clearly flaunted. The original, rough-hewn plank floors undulated gently from wall to wall. Light fixtures with huge white-glass globular shades descended on skinny, black cables from the ceiling-like so many hovering spiders. Tabletops crafted from the ends of wire spools, 4-feet in diameter and smoothed by lathering on a half inch epoxy gloss, were loosely arranged throughout the old stable. No fewer than 60 enormous video screens ensured that every play, of every game, would be clearly visible to every patron, in every seat.

Amos Beckstein noted a crowd beginning to gather outside the door of his Grill. He began a slow stroll around the room, noting with satisfaction that everything seemed to be in place. Super Bowl Sunday was always enormous. Better than any home game, even during those years when the Seahawks managed to make the playoffs. Better than any away game.

Better than the more subdued crowds that wandered in for a beer or two during the Mariner baseball season. After trying it both ways, Amos concluded that no live entertainment during the pregame show, live music during halftime (with silent video on his 60 monitors), and a strong performance immediately after the game sold substantially more beer and booze than the TV game alone.

Ten minutes later, after a final warning to his extra servers, Amos gave his bouncer a nod that meant "unlock the door." The line reached the end of the block and disappeared around a corner. "This could be the best Super Bowl Sunday yet," thought Beckstein.

The storm filled every dip in the pavement with a puddle. An anonymous looking black tour bus splashed down the side street, air brakes hissing when it came to a stop immediately outside the Gridiron's stage door. Little Willie Maxwell and the Bluesbirds, the headline act of the day, had arrived. Moments later, while the Bluesbirds were still schlepping their gear into the building, a Honda Accord pulled up behind the bus.

"Hey, you guys can't park back here!" protested one of the Bluesbirds. "This part of the lane is just for the band."

Mary Towne opened a back door of the Honda and stepped out into an inch of water. "That you, Marvin?"

"Holy shit! Mary Towne! What are you doing here? Slummin? And riding around in some crapmobile too! You with the rest of the Rail, or up here in Rainattle by yourself?"

"Neither, I'm sort of with the half time show."

"The hell you say! Willie said Ira Miller called and said he was breakin' in a new act at halftime. Hell, he couldn't have meant you. So how's this shakin down?"

Just then Little Willie Maxwell stepped out to grab something else from the bus. "Hey, babe!" he teased. "Anybody ever tell you ya look a lot like Mary Towne?"

"Yeah, actually I get that a lot," laughed Mary in reply. "Anybody ever say y'all look like a little Willie?"

"God, but I hates it when you call me that!" joked Willie as he walked over to Mary and gave her a brotherly hug.

"She's here with the half time show!" said Marvin.

Willie broke the embrace and stepped back to an arm's length. "Oh really? You mean after all these years we've been openin' for Memphis Rail and now you're here with some local fakes that are supposed to open for us? That's gonna be pretty weird. This is a fair sized place. Seemed like a serious gig for guys right out of the box."

"Not really. They've got 30 minutes down really tight. It's set up so I can jump in durin' the last two numbers to pump things up if we start losin' the crowd, but mostly we're tryin' to see how these guys do when haulin' an actual load."

The rest of the occupants of the Accord emerged. Vanessa stepped out from behind the steering wheel and put on her dark glasses. She pretended to fumble in the air as she reached for the assist bar attached to a harness worn by Wesley the Dog. Everyone laughed hysterically at her antics. "'Splains the crazy damn drivers been all over the road up here!" snorted one of the Bluesbirds.

Mary handled the introductions. "This here is Vanessa. Plays the blues hard and percussion. That there is Rebekah, just wait until you hear her sing. This here is Wesley Perkins, on the sax. He's gonna surprise you, trust me."

Marvin looked with open skepticism at the single white face in the crowd. "Sax, you say? A bluesman? Yeah, OK, I'll be pretty damned surprised. He don't exactly look the part, if you know what I mean."

"And this here is Wesley the Dog. He's a part time seein' eye dog, so we can get him up on stage."

"I suppose the dog is a bluesman too?" joked Willie. "So how the hell you planning to pull this off, Mary? You got no rhythm, and I ain't just talkin' about your sax player."

Mary held up a tiny computer drive. "We've got 30 minutes of stuff to plug in from the last Memphis Rail album. Bass, drums, and guitar. No solos. We've been rehearsin' to this for hours every night. I think they sound pretty good."

"So, shit," groused Willie. "We're not just following a bunch of wanna-be's, we sort of have to follow the Rail. Thanks a lot, Mary. Hey, we're gonna sit out here in the bus and smoke a while, care to join us?"

"Nah, it ain't never really much been my thing. I think we'll just go inside and get a table off in the corner till there's maybe 5 minutes left in the second quarter. Might help to let everybody get a feel for the place, maybe."

"Ok, then Mary. You guys go ahead and blow 'em down at halftime, but leave some ham on the bone for us, if you know what I mean."

The four musicians and the dog entered through the stage door, and found access to main floor of the Gridiron Grill. A nervous server started to object to the presence of the dog, but backed off immediately when Vanessa said "Service animal."

They ordered a round of drinks. Red wine for Mary, martinis for Vanessa and Rebekah, and a shot of rye, straight up, for Wesley.

"You probably don't want to hear about any advertising crap, Wes," said Vanessa, "but you might want to know that Dyna Cola is going to use the skydiver stunt you thought of as part of the half time festivities at the game. The parachute commercial is going to play at the first commercial break in the 3rd quarter, sort of as a tie in. It pisses me off a little that Benniston is back at the Super Bowl, sitting in the Dyna Cola suite with his nose way up Magruder's butt."

"Don't worry," said Wesley, "I'm beyond caring."

"Well, I still think it sucks. You ought to get the credit for that spot, but instead you get shit-canned and Benniston gets the glory."

The waitress arrived with the drinks. "You guys with the band or something? Amos said to comp you tonight."

"Thanks," said Mary. "We're the halftime show"

"Sorry about all that, Wes" sympathized Vanessa. "But as long as you and me and Rebekah stick together, we're going to be able to protect each other. At least until stuff gets resolved with the guy in the red scarf. Maybe we even need to stick together until we find somebody to take our place, like Mary says."

As the Super Bowl began, every kick, every run, every pass, and every tackle was displayed on 60 different video monitors around the Gridiron Grill. The combined effect of the repeated and colorful motions imbued an almost psychedelic ambiance, reflecting off the upturned faces and balding heads of the patrons. The Seahawks were done for the season, so different portions of the crowd cheered for either the St. Louis Rams or the Baltimore Ravens.

The noise roared like an angry river, substantially louder in the second quarter than in the first.

"I wonder if we'll even be heard over this bullshit," said Mary. "Y'all are gonna need to be tight, start stronger than hell with "Dust My Broom," and get control of this crowd right away. I'll talk to the dude on the sound board and tell him to push it as far as the system can go. Makes me nervous we didn't do a sound check, but this guy runs the board here all the time and he swears he knows where everything needs to be set."

Rebekah stared over her cocktail glass. "You seem sorta nervous, Mary. Hell, we ought to be nervous more than you."

Mary fussed, "Vanessa, you and I better get up on stage with the dog- and line up your harps and stuff. Won't do a bit for you to be seen findin' anything except by feel, would it? Rebekah, you and Wesley come on up right after the two-minute warnin'- that will probably be about five minutes or more before it's actually half time."

Just then, Amos Beckstein wandered up to the table. "I assume you guys are about to get ready? I'll try to introduce you, if I can be heard over all this damn noise. What do you call yourselves, anyhow?"

"Call? What do you mean?" asked Wesley.

Beckstein looked slightly annoyed. "Call your group, man. What else? Hell I can't just say, 'Ladies and Gentlemen, here's a bunch of folks who came down to play the blues!' now, can I?"

A terrified silence ensued. In all the effort to prepare the set, it hadn't occurred to anybody, incredibly enough not even Mary, to suggest a name for the act. Rebekah boldly broke the silence. "Call us the Jones Family," she said.

"Jones Family?" confirmed Beckstein.

Vanessa rushed to correct her sister. "No, sorry, that's not quite right. We're the Family Jones!" The sisters and Mary burst in laughter, and Amos Beckstein nodded and grinned. The joke was lost on Wesley Perkins, and the dog did not possess a sense of humor.

The musicians assumed their places on stage, each at the appointed time. At the last second of the Second Quarter, the board man fired the spots, cut the audio to the TV monitors, and potted up the mics. The crowd noise subsided for a split second in response to the activity on stage, long enough for Amos Beckstein to say, with a sweeping motion of his arm, "Ladies and Gentlemen! For your half time entertainment, we proudly present The Family Jones!"

Beckstein handed the wireless mic to Rebekah. Wesley Perkins detected the golden retriever exuding a soft, subtle, yellow glow. Redd Wilmott's recorded bass line began thundering through the Grill and the world would never be the same again- at least not for the Family Jones.

Part Two, Chapter One

Ira Miller picked up his phone. There was a lot of noise on the caller's end, but he quickly recognized the voice of the owner of the Gridiron Grill.

"What the Sam hell is going on here, Ira!" demanded Beckstein.

"Oh, shit! What do you mean? It's still half time. God, don't tell me they didn't show up..."

"Fuck no, Ira. Showing up ain't the problem. The goddam place is in chaos. Chaos, I tell you! I've never seen a show have this kind of effect on people!"

"What are you saying, Amos? Did they bomb? Sorry about that. Hey, they're nobody man, just hustle them off."

"Are kidding me, Ira? I couldn't get within 20 or 30 feet of my own stage if I had a police escort! Nobody rushes the stage at a blues show, but that's what I got on my hands here. They've sucked the whole damn crowd into a giant wad of folks jumpin', clappin, swayin' and hollerin'. There ain't anybody at their right tables anymore, and no goddam way I can even try to keep tabs on who ordered what. People are just drinkin' anything they can reach. Everybody is too busy boogy'n down to order. Goddam it Ira, this bullshit is gonna cost me thousands of dollars in sales. What the fuck did you turn loose on me in here?"

"Hey, Amos, I'm really sorry about that. Mary told me these guys were pretty good, but she's always had a heart for orphan kids, stray dogs, and lost causes in general. We can fix it. There's a lot of half time left, and I've got the Bluesbirds standing by."

"The hell you do. After the second number using the karaoke bullshit from Memphis Rail, Little Willie and the Bluesbirds came charging in from the bus, hooked up, and there's some kind of goddam jam session going on up there that's like nothing else you've ever seen. Then Mary Towne stepped up to do vocals with this new gal, Rebekah? Right? Omigod, Ira, the two of them together, you ought to hear it. It ain't fucking natural, Ira. I swear, it ain't natural at all. It's like somebody, or something, grabbed everybody in the room by the balls and won't let go."

"I can hear a lot of noise over the phone," agreed Ira. "But I can't make out much about the music. There, listen to that, it's a whole lot of people just screaming at the top of their lungs! What's going on, Amos?"

"It's your goddam sax player, Ira! Where in hell did you find a guy like that?"

"I'm not really sure I've got the whole story on him."

"Yeah? For shit's sake, he looks like some sort of middle age nerd who couldn't probably spell s-o-u-l, let alone have any! He's getting sounds out of that fancy old horn of his that most guys would be pleased to make once in a lifetime, and he's makin' it look easy. He just finished a solo that put the whole place into a total frenzy. How the hell can he do that? It ain't natural, I tell you! It can't be! Omigod, Ira, you won't believe this- a couple of the sidemen with Little Willie are actually bowing to your sax man, right this minute."

"Sounds like the halftime show is a success," chuckled Ira.

"Success my ass!" argued Amos. "Success is pouring $2,000 in drinks every minute for 30 minutes during half time. Ain't happenin' today, not by one hell of a long shot. My goddam servers, or half of 'em anyway, are up there in that fucking crowd jammed around the stage! I'll be damned before I pay staff that ain't keepin' their noses into business. This shitting fiasco is your fault, Ira. I should never have let you talk me into this bullshit act, the Family Jones."

"The Family Jones?" asked Ira.

"Yeah, that's what they say they call themselves. But it seemed like they just made it up on the spot. Your lady harp player seemed to come up with it. And what the fuck is with her? She seems too spooky by half, and the whole blind blues woman shtick is just crap too. Somebody said they saw her drive up in an old Honda, before the game started."

"I'll have to talk to her about that," said Ira.

"What? About being too spooky by half? I fucking guess so!"

"Naw, about driving up to a gig and then bringin' out the seein' eye dog. Hey look, Amos, I'm really sorry if your till is down over this thing, but it sounds like this act has...." Ira's comment was interrupted as the volume in the Gridiron Grill reached a fever pitch. The audience was whooping, clapping, stomping, and shouting at a volume that almost matched that of the amplified performers.

"Oh, shit!" said Amos. "Maybe I better go. This is getting way, way, out of hand. I've got people dancing on table tops, and just now two fell off. Aw fuck! Looks like some fat broad just tried to stand on a couple of stools and one collapsed! Sure hope she doesn't sue."

"Calm down, Amos. Look at the bright side…:

"Bright side? Damn it Ira, I don't know where they came from, but there's a maybe couple of hundred people outside trying to jam their way in through the goddam door. I gotta keep them outta here. If the fire marshal came by with a stick up his butt I'd be out of business as it is. You fucking owe me, Ira. You pay the damn Bluesbirds for this gig. I'll be damned if I'm going to take this kind of loss at halftime and pay your guys to boot."

"Wait! Amos! What the hell am I hearing in the background? Your crowd is out of control, and I'm sorry about that, really, but I need to know what the hell they're playing that has everybody so stirred up!"

"That old Broadway tune from the 40's or 50's. I think it's called 'Summertime,' from Porgy and Bess. Your sax player, the white guy? He's either really good or really crazy. In either case, it's like he's put a whole new meaning to that tune. And this bogus blind gal on the blues harp? Awesome, Ira. Really, she's awesome too."

"Amos, I'll make this up to you when I can."

"You owe me big time, Ira. Really big time. Now I gotta go tell the sound man to shut off the spots and cut the mics when we get close to the end of half time. That's assuming he ain't up there in the middle of all those folks hootin', and hollerin' and wavin' their asses around in front of the stage. What a fucking mess, Ira. What a fucking mess!"

Chuck Gould

Part Two, Chapter Two

The Baltimore Ravens kicked off to start the second half. The St. Louis Rams returned the ball to their own 34 yard line before the runner disappeared beneath a tsunami of opposing uniforms. A nine-yard run on first down was followed by two incomplete passes, bringing up fourth and one on the St. Louis 43. The St. Louis punting squad stood at the sidelines, ready to take the field.

The TV producer had a hunch. "Keep camera three on the Rams' coach. They're behind 17 to 6, and I think he might decide to go for it here." The producer's instinct paid off. After a visual moment of indecision, captured eloquently by camera three, the Rams' coach signaled his quarterback to go for the final yard on 4th down. The crowd in the stadium went berserk when the decision was apparent. Half of the ticket holders hoped the bold move would benefit the Rams, while the other half rooted for the Ravens to take over on downs- and with excellent field position.

One of the Rams moved before the ball was snapped, resulting in a "false start" penalty. It was now fourth and six. Would the Rams decide to punt, with six yards now separating the extension of the current drive from handing the ball over to the Ravens? The Rams' coach shook his head, expressing disgust with the player who penalized the team. Everyone in the stadium cheered, for differing reasons, when the Rams coach left the normal offensive squad on the field and kept the punter on the bench.

The Rams quarterback took the ball from under the center, stepped back and faked a handoff to the halfback. The Ravens were not fooled, and the blitz was on. Baltimore sent almost everybody they could find through the line of scrimmage. The Rams' quarterback spotted a wide receiver, only one step ahead of a pursuer, running along the edge of the field and approaching 44 yard mark. The quarterback drilled the ball to the receiver, who caught it just before being shoved out of bounds by the Ravens' safety. Depending on the camera angle, it was not entirely clear whether the Rams' player managed to touch both feet to the field while still inbounds.

The officials called the play a first down for the Rams. It was questionable, a matter to be resolved by replay and experienced judgment. Few spectators were surprised when the Ravens' coach threw in the red flag, asking for an official review of the first down call.

"Time out," thought the producer. "So next up is the Dyna Cola commercial and the spot for Continental Airlines. Two minutes to take a piss. No problem, everything will be a no-brainer, and I'll be back before anything else happens." The producer left his headset on while he stepped through the door to the restroom adjoining the studio. He had his fly unzipped, when a panicked voice began screaming in his ear.

"Hit the fucking dump button, you moron! Dump! Oh Christ, this is going to ruin us! Get this shit off the air! Aw fuck, we're way past the seven seconds! This means your job, you dipshit! Your goddam job! Oh fuck oh dear! We're so goddam dead!"

The TV producer urinated on his pant leg as he raced back to the console. He arrived just in time to see a young blonde woman, on her knees, in front of the opened fly of a black man's trousers. She wiped her mouth with the back of her hand before saying, "It tastes so good, going down."

The voice in the producer's headphone screamed so loudly it was all but unintelligible with the static and distortion. "You ignorant fuck! That went out on the network feed! If the local affiliates didn't kill it, and you know goddam well a lot of them wouldn't be hovering' over the dump button during a Dyna Cola spot, millions of people just saw that. That might mean our corporate ass. It means your ass for sure. Dipshit!"

Benniston ran, as if for his very life, from the stunned silence and fermenting rage in the Dyna Cola suite. He was out the door and down the hall even before Magruder turned to say, "This tears it with us, you miserable puke! You told me this footage had been destroy..." Realizing Benniston had left the room, Magruder addressed one of his subordinates. "Pull that fucking account. Cancel any payable invoices. See if they've got anything worth suing for. We'll shut the bastards down. This is going to cost us millions, maybe billions in sales. This crap ain't gonna fly anywhere, and it sure don't fly down south."

The crowd at the Gridiron Grill was stunned. An ominous silence, antipathetic to the shouts and celebration only a few moments before, prevailed. "Oh shit!" whispered Vanessa. "How did that happen? We destroyed every trace of that file."

Wesley had his forehead in his palm, shaking in disbelief. His voice trembled. "Red Scarf. I think he said he can't create anything, but he can move stuff around as much as he wants," During a timeout at the beginning of the fourth quarter, the Super Bowl broadcast cut to a local news snippet. "This just in from the Georgia Dome, local Seattle advertising executive Alexander Benniston was discovered hanged by a heavy scarf in a VIP restroom following the broadcast of a controversial Super Bowl commercial. A police spokesperson, speaking on the condition of anonymity, says the death initially appears to be a suicide. Benniston apparently stepped off a hand sink. The Atlanta medical examiner's office will announce an official cause of death following examination of the body."

Vanessa wailed. "Oh, God no. Not Mr. Benniston!"

Rebekah replied. "That's really awful. You're probably out of a job, sis. But if the same thing we think might be after us just got to your boss, that's the least of our problems. We're doin' the right thing, stickin' together."

Part Two, Chapter Three

Ruth gripped the steering wheel of her Lincoln Navigator until her knuckles were white. She wept. She had just been shunned by everyone at the Bainbridge Golf and Country Club. Her oldest friends ignored her when she approached, or excused themselves, and moved away. Back in her car, humiliated, Ruth experienced a despair she had never known. She was ostracized- a pariah. Time might staunch the bleeding, but even her family's money would never erase the scar.

Alternate waves of red hot anger and icy blue shame raced through her body, like competing electrical shocks. She thought of a pop song from her childhood, something about "Tears of rage, tears of grief." She wondered how Wesley could have betrayed her so badly. Everyone on Bainbridge Island, at least everyone who mattered, knew that Wesley had been the account executive for Dyna Cola. He held one of the most prestigious jobs in the advertising industry, until he managed to get fired.

A day after the Super Bowl, there was more news coverage about the flagrantly indecent commercial that aired at the beginning of the third quarter than about the outcome of the game. Benniston's suicide was discussed in ghoulish detail. One of the tabloid sites was loudly speculating whether the commercial had been planted by a "disgruntled employee, recently discharged by Benniston's agency."

"That miserable son of a bitch!" fumed Ruth. "How could he do this to me? He's embarrassed me in front of everybody I know! I wouldn't be surprised if he actually did have something to do with that obscene commercial. What did I ever see in that bastard? At least with Walter, weasel that he is, I know exactly what I've got."

Just then, her cell phone rang. Ruth pulled over to the shoulder and answered.

"Hello, Ruth Perkins? This is Ken Farnbarger, a counselor here at the middle school. I'm calling about your daughter, Brianna."

"Is something wrong with Brianna?"

"Not really. I mean she hasn't been hurt or anything like that, but I think it might be best if you came by and took her home for a few days."

"Oh, no- what did she do?"

"She didn't do anything, but the kids are teasing her about her stepfather."

"He's almost the ex-stepfather," insisted Ruth.

"Well, whatever. Point being, it's really out of hand. They're chasing her down the hallways yelling about her 'pervert stepfather freak'. We've been confiscating cell phones all day. There's a pretty graphic video version of that soda pop commercial available on-line. People keep logging on and shoving their phones into her face."

"Oh God, no. That's ridiculous. And you can't do anything about it?"

"We would if we could. We're outnumbered."

"I'll be right over. Keep her away from the other kids. But I don't get why you're kicking her out over this and not the other kids."

"Don't get this wrong, Mrs. Perkins. We're not kicking Brianna out of school, we're suggesting she take a few days off until this thing dies down. We'll get her teachers to send her work home and she will get full credit for the days she misses."

Ruth tucked held her phone to her ear with her shoulder and pulled back into traffic. "So, where is she now, exactly?"

"She's in the nurse's office right now. Shaking and crying, but really she's one tough young lady, most kids would have cracked a lot earlier in the day."

"I'm on my way. I'll be there in a few minutes. But I have to say, this doesn't seem fair."

"Mrs. Perkins, I would agree that it probably isn't fair. Lots of times things turn out a little unfair. It's just easier to have Brianna stay home a couple of days than to send home the 40 or 50 kids who are giving her grief over the videos."

"That many? 40 or 50? Oh my god, poor Brianna. What do you mean by 'videos', is there more than one?"

"Well, yeah. There's the commercial from the game, and then there's something that turned up on one of the amateur video sites. Looks like a riot in a sports bar in Seattle, but I guess it's just the crowd going crazy over some blues band up on stage with a dog.

One of Brianna's so-called friends stumbled on that, and I think everybody in the school has seen it by now. There's a guy playing saxophone in this band on Super Bowl Sunday that everybody says looks exactly like Brianna's stepfather."

"Oh crap. I hate to say it, but it could be Wes Perkins."

"Yeah? He really seems out of place, he's, how would I say this, 'ethnically dissimilar' from everybody else on stage and he seems to be the star of the show."

"OK, look. I'm just a couple of blocks away now. I'll see you in a minute or two, Mr. Farnbarger." Ruth drove aggressively to rescue her daughter. She thought, "How could I be married to a guy for ten years and have no idea he could play the sax on a professional level? How could I have been such a fool? We'll never live this Super Bowl nonsense down. Not ever. Fuck you, Wes, and all of your dirty little secrets!"

Part Two, Chapter Four

Rebekah was spending more time on the main floor of the Lake City rental house, and less in her basement apartment. She realized her feelings toward Wesley were complex, but after an initial discomfort she no longer found her emotions as frightening. Could she really, when quiet and sober, be the Caroline, to Wesley's Judah Jones? Maybe; but if so the strengthening bond between them was now distinctly different than a romantic or sexual attraction. Caroline and Judah had been conjugally intimate, and Judah was proposing marriage on the night he was lynched. Rebekah couldn't imagine ever having sex with Wesley, but she was learning to trust him.

She confided in Vanessa. "Remember how, when we were little girls, we always wished we had an older brother? It's weird, really. I sort of think of Wes like an older brother. Like he's somebody who would stand up for me, and try to see that nothing bad happened to me."

"Anything going on between you two, Sis?"

"No. And maybe not all that likely to. I am starting to care about Wes, but not in the same way I usually care about a man. There's something different here. I guess I can't really explain it."

"I'll study on it a bit," said Vanessa. "Let's hope that makes it easier for us to stay together until all this weirdness shakes out. We don't know where any of this is going to take us, but we all agreed to stick together and that's what we need to do."

On Monday night following the Super Bowl, Wesley Perkins clipped the leash to Wesley the Dog's collar. "Hey, I'm taking the dog out for a walk!" called Wesley. "It's been a couple of hours, and he's probably about to burst. You can come too, if you want."

"Naw, that's OK" answered Rebekah. "It's cold and dark out there. But I'm going to make some tea. You want some tea? I can just as easy boil enough water for two cups."

"We got any Chamomile? With a little honey?"

"Yeah, I think so. Take the dog out to do his business. Should be ready when you get back."

Wesley Perkins and Wesley the Dog crunched down the gravel driveway, turning left on the unpaved shoulder of the asphalt street. The dog raised his leg next to a utility pole, one of a seemingly endless line of gargantuan tree trunks lining the road side. The once proud woodland giants were now stripped of branches, soaked in creosote, and employed to suspend electrical wires, TV cables, and street lamps. Insulated frames and arms, fastened to the top of each pole, kept the lines running straight and separate. Wesley once remarked that they reminded him of a row of crosses.

Wesley the Dog sniffed a likely looking pile of weeds, walked around it in a tight circle, then changed his mind and tugged at the leash to go farther down the street. As the almost invisible path along the open drainage ditch brought them near the outer fringes of the next oasis of halogen light, Wesley the Dog suddenly lost interest in sniffing the ground. He froze in place, drooling and snarling. Wesley tried to pull him along with the leash, but the dog grew increasingly hostile and would not be moved.

A transparency of the figure with the droopy overcoat, slouch hat, and long red scarf appeared in the light. At first, the image seemed two dimensional, but it rapidly evolved to become solid. Wesley the Dog placed his body across the knees of Wesley Perkins and growled menacingly at the unwelcome intruder.

"Looks like your dog doesn't like me much," said Red Scarf, followed with a sinister laugh. "But we're really old friends, Wes, your dog and me. I guess you could say we play on opposing teams. He hasn't always been a dog, you know. Hell, he's been a human being a handful of times. I guess he just shows up in whatever shape he thinks is going to be most effective."

"You bastard!" cried Wesley. "What the hell was with that Super Bowl stunt? I know damn well that had your hand in it. And you didn't have to kill Benniston."

"I didn't kill Benniston."

"Oh, bullshit! He was hanging in the restroom, from one of your red scarves. Hanging like Paul at the Pawn Palace."

"If you're making a list of hangings that affect your life, Wes, don't forget Judah Jones. But I didn't really, entirely, actually kill any of those guys. Couldn't if I wanted to. I can't."

Wesley the Dog attempted to lunge toward Red Scarf, but Wesley Perkins kept a tight rein on the leash.

"What the hell do you mean, you can't kill anybody? I saw you lurking around during the fire at the Pawn Palace, and we know damn well you were involved with the commercial that led to the death of Benniston."

Red Scarf sighed, and kicked at some gravel with his boot. "Oh hell, Wesley. I'll only explain myself to you because it amuses me to do so. Remember when I told you I wasn't allowed to create anything, but I get to move stuff around as much as I want? OK, that's exactly how that Dyna Cola spot got put together. It got assembled, not created. It had its desired effects."

"Yeah, you bastard. Everybody thinks I used Vanessa to sabotage the file and get even for being sacked. She got fired thirty seconds after getting to work on Monday. There's talk of a police investigation. It has embarrassed all my friends and family..."

"You mean your ex-family..."

"Well, shit, yes I guess I do. Whatever, I've never felt so isolated and trapped."

"As I said," chuckled Red Scarf, "it had its desired effects."

"So what do you mean you didn't kill Benniston, or Paul Feldman, or who knows how many other people. How do I know you aren't going to kill me, or Vanessa, or Rebekah?"

"Wes, just like I told you I don't get to create anything, I don't get to destroy anything either. What I get to do, though, is to give you some tools you can use to destroy yourself. There's actually an element of choice, but y'all come in for a taste of sugar- and wind up with diabetes."

The dog lunged again, but was restrained by Wesley Perkins. "You bastard! It sounds like you really enjoy your role."

"I might as well enjoy it, Wes, I don't have any choice. Think about that, why don't you? Oh, shit! Look at what you guys imagine to be time! I've got something important going on in Washington DC, and I need to be there about three days ago. If I leave now, I can still make it."

A spark burst from an overhead electrical wire the instant the figure in the red scarf disappeared. Although the apparition was out of sight, his voice remained. "Protect Rebekah, Wes! There are a hell of a lot of us trying to get home."

"Home!" thought Wesley. "Oh God! Rebekah's there by herself, and this bastard is hanging around." Wesley unsnapped the leash from the dog's collar, and the dog ran at full speed back to the rental house. Wesley followed behind, as well and quickly as he was able, but he stumbled over unexpected obstacles in the dark.

Part Two, Chapter Five

The email sent two days earlier read, "Expect a conference call at 11." A few minutes before 11, Ann Foster poured a final cup of coffee and trundled to her favorite easy chair. She wore a flowered shower cap. She propped her feet, in fuzzy pink bunny slippers, on a footstool. One knee jutted through the gap in her polka dot bathrobe. Whatever Ira had on his mind, she would be ready to discuss business.

The phone rang a minute or two after the appointed hour. "Hello, Ann? Ira here. Hey, hope you don't mind but I need to put you on hold while we get Art Abbott on the line. I guess he forgot. Some woman answered a few minutes ago. Sounded like we must have woke her up. She said Art was still sleeping, but that she would get him up right away."

"Yeah, sure. OK. But what's this call gonna be about? Has it got anything to do with that video of Mary and the Nobody's that's been circulatin' round? What the hell is she thinking? She needs to give some thought to her career, she needs to consider the rest...."

"Ann, hold on, please. Let me get Art on the line and then we'll patch everybody in together."

Ann waited, increasingly perturbed. Some cell phone video on the internet was logging about fifty thousand views per day. In the video was Mary Towne, on stage with one of Ira's second-tier acts, Little Willy and the Bluesbirds. Also on stage were two black women, a yellow dog, and the goofy looking white guy playing sax. The audio quality was awful. It was impossible to draw any musical conclusions over the noise of the crowd, but from what could be heard they seemed unusually tight. "'Specially since these Family Jones people couldn't ever have rehearsed with the Bluesbirds."

Each time Ann watched the video she paid particular attention to the young female vocalist. "She's got hot looks, I'll give her that," thought Ann. "But it takes more than a little ass shakin' to carry your weight in the blues. She's gotta be a lightweight- all legs and a skinny little voice. Still, she's got a lot of stage presence. More than you would guess."

Ann was startled, slopping coffee on her fingers when Ira's voice was returned to the phone. "OK, have we got everybody now?"

"Ya got me," said Redd Wilmott.

"And me," confirmed John Flood.

"Me too," agreed Ann.

"How in hell did it get to be eleven o' clock all of a sudden?" grumbled Art Abbott.

"Good!" concluded Ira.

"Uh, where's Mary?" asked John

"Mary's still up in Washington. I just got back from spending three days up there, going over a few things. There's some big stuff right around the corner for Memphis Rail. Unless I'm entirely screwed up on this, and that don't happen that often, there's some hot opportunities. It's no secret that the Rail has been flying level for a while now. Maybe even losing a little altitude every year."

John Flood interrupted. "You been readin' my mail."

Ann could no longer hold her coffee steady. She sat the cup on the side table. "Readin'? He's been sendin' the mail."

Ira continued. "We're ready to put the Rail back in overdrive, start selling a lot more recordings, and get the money back to where it used to be."

"Uh, Ira. That sounds like a lot of rah, rah, bullshit," said Redd. "We been down the road too many times to be impressed with cheer leadin'. I think most of us are half ass afraid this has something to do with Mary's little freak show up in Seattle. Tell it like it is, Ira. What's up?"

"OK. Here it is. Once in a long, long time there's some kind of lucky accident, or fate, or something else, that comes along and puts just the right people together. These folks that Mary has been coaching along, the Family Jones? They're one of those collections of the right people."

Ann stood and began pacing. "I'm getting a weird feelin' about where this talk is headed."

"Ira, that's gotta be bullshit" objected John. "There ain't really any first class acts that didn't pay their dues. Nobody that didn't earn every one of their chops. Yeah, almost anybody can poke around a little at the blues, but first you got to live the blues to really pass 'em on."

"John, I didn't buy it either," replied Ira. "Amos Beckstein let them do a set in his sports bar during the Super Bowl and..."

"I think we've all seen the video, Ira," interjected Ann. "The crowd was ridiculous, but you couldn't tell much about the music..."

"Exactly. That's why I flew up to Seattle. From what Amos told me, and then from what Mary and Little Willy both told me, I had to go see this thing for myself. I was sure it had to be a load of crap. Only, it isn't."

"Oh, God, Ira," said Redd, "speaking of accidents what the hell happened to the harp player, Vanessa? I met her when we were up in Seattle last December, and she sure as hell wasn't blind then."

"Don't know about that," gruffed Art. "I mean if you consider her taste in men..."

"She isn't really blind now, either," said Ira. "It's just a ploy to get the frickin' dog up on stage."

Ann snorted. "Figures, that broad is phony as hell."

Ira continued. "I thought at first they ought to scrap the dog. An animal is a lot of hassle. But they think they're a lot tighter with the dog around, and I'll be damned if I don't agree with them. It's kind of like he runs some sort of invisible board. This whole situation ain't like nothing I've ever heard before. I heard about a few things like this, but never saw it firsthand."

"So what's that got to do with us, really?" insisted Ann. "You're not thinkin' of expanding the Rail are you? God, Ira, we're not makin' half the money we used to as it is. Wouldn't be no way to bring in three more people. And a dog too?"

"Here's where it is," said Ira. "We're going to go into the studio in March and do an album. We'll schedule Rain Crow, in Seattle, the week before our make good at the Paramount. Wesley Perkins is gonna be the sax player. He'll work for scale, and we always hire a horn player anyway. Vanessa will play blues harp and some percussion, she's very damn good."

"How can she be any good at all?" countered Redd. "She didn't mention playin' any kind of instrument at all when I saw her in December."

"That's just it, Redd. I don't know how she can be any good, just that she is. We need to get some of this stuff recorded before the clock goes midnight and everything turns back into some kind of pumpkin or something. This is nothing less than a once in a lifetime opportunity. This will get us another ten or fifteen good years for Memphis Rail. Hell, it might even revitalize the blues!"

"Ten or fifteen more years?" grumped Art Abbott. "I ain't got that much more gas in the tank."

"So the crazy drunk Perkins guy will play sax and the bogus blind bitch bang the tambourine and such. And the skinny little broad with the ass and legs?" asked Ann.

"You have to mean Rebekah. Yeah, she's part of the whole project too. Her voice pairs with Mary's really well."

"Oh shit," said Redd.

Ann grabbed a vase of cut flowers and hurled it against the wall. "Damn it, Ira. I'm the second female voice in the Rail!"

"Don't worry, Ann. We'll feature you as much as we can fit in. Tell you what, I'll see that you get lead, such as it's going to be, on one or two tracks. But the whole album isn't going to be as much about vocals this time. Yeah, we'll have lyrics in each cut, but most of what we're going to be doing is instrumental. Lots of solos, especially saxophone."

"I wrote some damn good material recently," said Art, (his voice steadily improving as the conversation went on). "I can build in some more solos."

"Yeah, I got a few new tunes too," said Ann. "They really show off the keyboard, and if we use any of them I get lead vocal."

"Hold up!" said Ira. "We're not going to do any new stuff. We're going to rearrange and recut an album from the late 1950's. Track for track. We won't need anything original this time around. We're not going all the way back to the roots, but we're going pretty far down the trunk to get our stuff for this record."

"Sounds sort of weird," complained John. "What's up next? Sammy Davis, Dean Martin, and Frank Sinatra?"

Ira replied, "Weird or not, that's the plan. I have a nose for this sort of thing and one hell of a lucky sense of timing. This is exactly the right moment to reach back. When you guys all hear what I just heard in Seattle, you'd be excited about being part of the project."

"And then after we make this record," pouted Ann. "I suppose we'll be takin' this new broad and her friends on the road with us? What about the money?"

"I won't lie to you Ann, likely so. I'm not yet clear how Memphis Rail and the Family Jones will do some combined shows. As far as the money goes, imagine bringing in about four or five times what we grossed last year and cutting out three more shares. Do the math. And, if doesn't work out we forget the Family Jones and go on back to what we've been the last few years. That's if it doesn't work out. But I think, no, make that I'm certain, that it's going to."

"So what's this album from the late 50's Ira? Anybody ever heard of it before?"

"It's pretty obscure. Some of the wonkiest record collectors know it. It was a huge hit in its day, but the guy that did all the featured solos died just after it was released. Anybody familiar with 'Blues Breakout' by Judah Jones?"

"Yeah," said John. "I mean I've heard there was one hell of a sax player on that album, but nobody ever seems to be able to find a copy anyplace."

"Well, we've got a copy!" said Ira. "It's way worn out, but it won't be hard to pick up the sound. This sax player, Wesley Perkins? He's about a note-for-note dead ringer for Judah Jones."

"Oh, bullshit!" scoffed Redd.

"No bullshit," countered Ira. "You guys will see when we get together in studio. Watch your emails, I'm sending out an mp3 file we made with an old record player and a mic. What you hear is what we need to play, or at least a rough outline. Go ahead and work out your licks, and I'll let you know in a few days where we're going to be recording."

"So is Mary going home before we get back to work?" asked Ann.

"No, she's hanging around Seattle, keeping an eye on the flock so to speak. The Family Jones is playing some dates in the tribal casinos with Little Willy. They may have the talent, or the gift, or whatever but they will benefit a hell of a lot from a bit more experience. Mary said she would try to get us a better video. I think you're all going to be amazed."

"Oh, I'm amazed already," pouted Ann. She contemplated the water running down her living room wall.

Part Two, Chapter Six

Harp through a mic is like fire in a wire. The brass reeds marry their quivering hearts to the cardioid soul of the diaphragm. The sound is not only amplified, it's purified, in a way that no wooden reed or string can ever hope to duplicate. The energy, the joy, and the urgency fills the hall like shimmering silver raindrops. Vanessa puckered her cheeks to change the pressure on the draw notes, bending the tones around invisible anvils as she sucked them another half step flat. She marveled that this new skill felt so natural, as if she had been playing blues harp for hundreds of years. The crowd at the Copper Raven Casino was overwhelmed. It responded with electrified applause- so intense and immediate that few realized it was a desperate prayer for survival. Clap, clap, clap clap; as if to erase the challenge to their souls and erect a barricade of atonal sound.

The Bluesbirds rollicked along, hitting three triplets on the major, stretching to a 7th and then giving the 4th one beat on the road back home. Four bars from the I chord, two bars from the IV chord, two more from the I chord, one bar from the V chord, another bar from IV, and the last eight beats of the twelve bar progression back at the nominal key.

Mary Towne remained off stage, nodding a nervous approval of the performance.

Rebekah stepped to the mic, fingering her onyx necklace. "How y'all like the show so far?"

Thunderous applause, and the band played on.

"Well here's something brand spankin' new. Called Bucket Blues. Hope y'all like it"

Went out and got a bucket
Took it to the well
Strung a hundred feet of barb wire
And rode that bucket down
To hell-low Mama?
There's a new mare in my stall
But I told my friend the bucket,
Bucket, you know I don't care at all

Wesley Perkins stepped up for twelve bars of solo. Running on the fumes of rye whiskey and the soft glow of a yellow dog, he fired off lightning fast staccato explosions. He bent and twisted long, warm colorful notes in a way that would leave a vaudeville balloon clown seething with envy. Nobody understood how that much sound could be voiced by a single instrument. Nobody cared. The audience edged toward pandemonium, averted only as the twelve bar interlude came to an end and Rebekah began again.

Me and my friend the bucket
We wandered up the hill
If you won't fill my bucket
Then I know your brother will
Oh hell, oh Papa?
Bill collector's at my door
But I told my friend the bucket,
Bucket, you know I don't care no more

Vanessa switched to tambourine after Rebekah began to sing. Little Willie stood near her, on the left side of the stage, playing rhythm guitar. He stepped to the mic as Rebekah ended her second verse and said, "Ladies and gentlemen, that's Rebekah of the Family Jones!" The band ran through the last four bars of the progression to give the audience a chance to applaud, and then Marvin Cooper stepped to the front of the stage with his vintage Fender Telecaster.

Marvin's solo wrapped iron tentacles around the crowd, shooting darts of flaming sonic brimstone directly through the booze numbed skulls. Even Little Willie was impressed. "Marvin's always played the stink outa that guitar," he thought, "but damned if there ain't somethin' special about the way he's puttin' it down tonight. Somethin' about this Family Jones bunch. Don't know what it is, but they sure seem to wear off easy on just about everybody. The Bluesbirds is almost bein' upstaged, but damn my ass if it isn't sort of fun."

You know I got the bucket ramble
I got the bucket walk
I ought to take the gamble
But I knows y'all would talk
Hell-low sister?

Your man's been hanging round me double time.
I told that brother buckin' bucket,
Bucket, he's a nuisance, not a crime.

Vanessa blew four bars on the harp. Like a call and response, her phrasing was answered by Wesley with four bars on the sax. Before the twelve bars were finished the crowd began rushing the stage. A panicked security officer fingered his radio and shouted, "Mayday! I need three of four guys right away. Longhouse Lounge. The band's got these people out of their chairs and it don't look good."

The security guard's fears proved unfounded. The audience approached the stage, but stopped several feet away from the performers. There was a ragged gap along a universally understood "no man's land." The crowd reached out, but were reluctant to touch the energies of smoke, black lava, sweet cider, and incendiary plastics that emanated from the speakers on stage. It was as if their instinctive understanding of the danger trumped their inexplicable lust to be consumed by the flames.

The Family Jones and the Bluesbirds jammed with the progression for another three minutes. They shared the solos in turn, drawing ecstatic applause with every passing.

The 60 minute set extended to over 90, with the room demanding no fewer than three encores. Little Willy and the Bluesbirds, with special guest the Family Jones were being called back for a fourth when the house manager waylaid them back stage. "Hey, guys. You're fantastic. But starting about ten minutes ago you're stepping on our Hendrix tribute act, Purple Craze."

Little Willy laughed. "So, you s'pose we warmed 'em up enough?"

The house manager shrugged. "Nobody's gonna follow that act, but I gotta pay the Craze whether they go on or not. I'll be damned if I'm payin' them not to play. I told the house manager to comp you all at our Sweatlodge Bar. It's way over on the other side of the casino, in sort of a quiet corner. I'll take you around the back side of the house. I'll pretend I don't see that dog goin' through the kitchen."

The Sweatlodge Bar was as remote as the manager implied. There were less than a dozen drinkers, sprinkled among thirty tables and a visually impressive bar created from electric lights shining through a polished slab of translucent yellow crystal. Nobody paid any attention as eight musicians and a golden retriever entered through a service door and sought the most isolated seats available.

There was an empty seat the immediate left of Rebekah. Little Willy approached, pointed to the seat and said, "Do you mind?" Before Rebekah could answer, Willy assumed the seat.

"So, what was with that thing you did, The Bucket Blues? I been playin' this stuff a long time, and I ain't never heard of Bucket Blues. I thought the words were pretty clever, I'll give you that. Seemed to be one of the highlights of the show."

"Well, thanks, Willy," replied Rebekah. "I guess it did go over well."

"You blew 'em down, Sis." confirmed Vanessa.

"Not so much," demurred Rebekah. "Shit, I coulda recited the Declaration of frickin' Independence, propped up by the rhythm and instrumentals, and everybody would have been just as excited."

"Not so," argued Willy. "You were like unnatural, or somethin'. You just wrote that tune today, right?"

"Well no," said Rebekah. "I sort of lied and I'm sorry. I didn't really write it earlier today. I just made it up on the spot. I didn't have any idea what the second and third verses were gonna be while I was singin' the first. Glad it worked out, though."

"Oh, shit!" exclaimed Little Willy. "You just improvised those killer lyrics? Where does that come from?"

Mary Towne interrupted. "Damn, Willy. How many years you been doin' this? You know better, or should, than to ask where any of this stuff comes from."

Little Willy agreed. "Yeah, ain't none of it really ours. Not like we own it."

"Zactly. We got it from some folks who went before, and we gotta keep it until we find some folks comin' up behind. Christ sakes, Willy. The older I get the more I think we ain't but steppin' stones somebody else is usin' to get across the pond. We get our turn to be stepped on, and then we ain't much use no more."

Wesley got the attention of a server. "Rye whiskey, double shot, straight up."

Vanessa started to look at her watch, and then remembered her shtick. She wondered how many people noticed that even though she was supposedly blind, she wore a wrist watch. There was no need to keep up the pretense with the Bluesbirds or Family Jones, but she thought it might be advisable to remain in character.

"Hey," said Vanessa. "What time is it?"

"Twelve-forty-five." responded Rebekah.

"Wo. Let's not sit here drinkin' all night. It's about two hours back to Seattle, I'm tired, and I'm about ready to go home."

"Just you wait, girl," chuckled Mary Towne. "You ain't even begun to get tired. Not yet. I'll go get us three rooms so we don't have to drive back. Ira will step up for the bill. He don't know it yet, but he will."

"We could make room for y'all in the bus," offered Little Willy.

Mary waved him off with the back of her hand. "In your dreams, babe."

Part Two, Chapter Seven

Wesley fumbled with the key card. He became increasingly frustrated with every futile swipe. No matter how he ran the card through the slot, it failed to turn activate the green LED signal indicating that the door to his room at the Copper Raven Casino Hotel was unlocked. Mary Towne had experienced no trouble with her key in the room next door. Vanessa and Rebekah's room, immediately across the hall, opened on the first try as well. Just as Wesley was ready to give up, return to the reception desk and ask for another key, a uniformed security guard walked down the hallway.

"Say, there!" hailed Wesley. "Can you help me out here? I think there might be something wrong with this key."

"No, it's the lock. Everybody has trouble getting through this particular door. Management replaced the card reader two or three times this month, and that's just during my shift. Maybe it's been more. May I see your key a minute, please?"

"Sure, but I don't know what you can try that I haven't..."

Wesley watched as the security guard placed the card between his muscular black hands, pressed together as if in prayer. The guard began rapidly scraping his palms back and forth. "Sometimes, I think the solution has something to do with static electricity. Don't know why this works, but a lot of times it does. Here- if you'd care to try this again now. Let's see what happens."

Wesley took the card, noting that it been warmed by the friction created by the guard. The door unlocked on the first attempt.

"Thanks, very much!" said Wesley as he turned the handle and pushed open the door. "Saved me a trip to the front desk."

"Always glad to be of service. Have a nice rest, Mr. Perkins."

Wesley closed the door and was no more than a couple of steps toward the bed when it occurred to him that there was no way the guard should have been able to call him by name. Did the security staff routinely know the names of all the guests in every room? It seemed doubtful. Maybe the reception desk sent the guard to see whether Wesley was going to have trouble with the lock?

Curiosity motivated Wesley to open the hallway door so he could question the guard, who certainly could not have gone far in the very few seconds since Wesley entered the room.

Wesley began speaking before the door was entirely open. "By the way, I'm just wonder...." Wesley immediately realized that the hallway was empty. He could trace the carpet's red and black totem pattern for 50 feet in one direction and 70 feet in the other. The hall was a long, empty box filled with an artificial, silent, sacrificial light. "Must have been the front desk," concluded Wesley. "But where the hell did the security guy disappear to so quickly?"

Wesley sat the snakeskin saxophone case next to the bed, laid down, and kicked off his shoes. He was almost immediately asleep, and he began to dream.

***

Every window on the clapboard sided schoolhouse was open, but there wasn't enough breeze to dispel the sopping oppression or pungent humidity of the Mississippi morning air. The interior walls and ceiling were initially painted white, but the color had turned mouse grey. Chunks of the old paint would lose tenuous holds on the walls and ceiling, fluttering to the rough plank floor like escaped butterflies in final flight. A dark, foreboding image of George Washington and a US flag were both nailed to the wall above a cracked, slate chalkboard. Most of the wrought iron frames supporting the desks and chairs were fractured, or had sections broken away. There weren't enough desks for all the students. Many sat in wooden chairs without desktops. A few kids sat at the side of the room, with their backs against the wall.

To the left of the chalkboard was a Confederate battle standard, something the local white folks often referred to as the "Stars and Bars." The Confederate flag was smaller than the US flag, but managed to assume greater prominence in the room. Just below the battle standard, the ink was still bright on a calendar page just recently turned. "September, 1946"

Wesley looked around the room at his classmates. A few were eleven years old, most were twelve, and a few boys were thirteen or fourteen. Clarence Williams, sitting next to Wesley, said, "Hey there, Judah. First day of school and we's made it all the way to grade six! My pappy done told me, this heah will be my last year. I gots to get to work. Pappy says six years of school is a hell of a lot more than any negruh needs. Sides, there ain't no colored high school 'round heah no how. Did you get a good look at some of these girls? Damn if they didn't do some blossomin' out during the growin' season, if you knows what I mean."

"Sure enough I did," answered Wesley. "But look at them, they're all goin' out of their way to ignore them older boys - Eustis, LeRoy, and Horace. I'd say they probably ain't lookin' at the older guys because they're actually gettin' a shine for 'em. Look at them all, just a- fannin' themselves like they're in danger of meltin'. Makin' like actual ladies or somethin'. Shit, Clarence, ain't even two of 'em weren't buck naked with us down at the swimmin' hole- and some of 'em no more'n two years ago at that. A might too high and proud now, ain't they?"

Miss Barker, the sixth grade teacher, slapped a wooden pointer down on Wesley's desk. "Judah, if you've got all that excess energy that you can be talkin' to Clarence, you get up here and help me pass out the history books. There won't be enough to go around, so pass out a book to every other student. Everybody will have to pick a partner and share."

Miss Barker stepped back to the front of the room. "Class, class! May I have your attention, please? We've got a special treat to start the year. The kids over at Mayfair Private Academy and Preparatory School got new history books this year, and they were kind enough to let us have the old ones. Judah Jones is passing them around. There's just enough for every other student, so we will have to share, but it will be such a treat to actually have a book to study from."

An unidentifiable voice in the back of the room wise-cracked. "Just pass out the books to the kids who knows how to read. Oughts to be mo than enough." Miss Barker ignored the remark.

Even though the Mayfair Private Academy and Preparatory School only accepted students from the most privileged families, (and none of those so privileged were black), it was obvious that their cast off history text books had seen better days. Even lily-white fingers soiled the edges of the pages. Some of the covers were bent, and a few missing completely. Bored but wealthy students had scribbled on every imaginable surface of the books. A number of the books had sections of solid black ink. Miss Barker spent several nights looking through the old text books, blacking out the most racially offensive doodlings.

A female student among the first to get a book from Wesley raised her hand. "Miss Barker?"

"Yes, Effie May?"

"Is they gonna be another book too? I just looked at the last chapter in mine, and it's got a list of wars. It shows the War of Northern Aggression, back in the 1860's, and finally it winds up with the Spanish American War. It says heah' the Spanish American War was in 1898. Ain't there been some sort of history since 1898? I mean what about that war we just won against them Nips and Kikes?"

"Effie May," scolded Miss Barker. "Where ever did you hear people called disrespectful names like that?"

"At home, Miss Barker."

LeRoy Wilson spoke out of turn. "Lawd, Effie May! You don't need to know a thing about history no how. You're a girl! You'll be makin' babies 'fore very long. What use you got for history anyways?"

Miss Barker corrected LeRoy. "LeRoy, you aren't supposed to speak without raising your hand. Maybe it's time we all learned, and I mean all of us learned, that we can be a lot of things or do a lot of things that people might tell us we aren't able to do."

"What do you mean by that, Ma'am?"

"I mean the girls don't have to stay home, watch the babies, and keep house. And they don't have to settle for cleaning house and watching babies for somebody else, either. They have options. They can even be nurses or teachers. Who knows? Someday a colored nurse might even be able to work in a white hospital. Maybe get the same pay as a white nurse, too."

"Look at me, I'm teaching school and making my own way in the world. LeRoy, I won't be havin' you or anybody tell these girls that they don't have a future outside of makin' babies. No. No way."

Wesley raised his hand.

"Have you got something you would like to say, Judah?"

"Yes, Miss Barker. I think I knows why the history book ends up with the Spanish American War."

"Why would that be, Judah?"

"Because they's still some old guys around who fought in that war. Nothin' newer than that can really be history. I'll bet that it ain't really history until most everybody that was there is dead. Ain't that right, Miss Barker?"

The class found the theory hilarious. In his dream, Wesley stared through the eyes of Judah Jones to witness all of the students pointing at him with outstretched arms. They were laughing so hard that some were beginning to weep. Some of his classmates' faces became contorted, appearing to be middle-aged or older rather than in the throes of puberty. They mocked him in chorus, "Cain't be no history 'less most everybody who was there is dead!"

***

Wesley awoke with a start, and dreamed no more that night.

81

Chuck Gould

Part Two, Chapter Eight

The first night back in Seattle, Art Abbott and John Flood shared a table in a dark corner of the Quixote Steak House. A flickering candle in a cut crystal table lamp cast a soft, pepper-yellow radiance across their exquisitely prepared entrees. Movie posters from the 1940's and 50's were framed on the walls. The posters were apparently selected more for the liberal usage of red and brown ink than for the relative quality or popularity of the films. Some titles were extremely obscure, and other posters were printed in French or Italian.

At 10PM on a Wednesday night, there were few other diners. Art and John found their waitress almost too attentive. How are the steaks? (Fine, thanks). Did they want another round of drinks? (Sure, and how about some more bread, please). Here you go, two more drinks and a basket of hot bread. I'll be back to see if you need anything else.

"I'm sure she will," smirked Art. "I think we must be her only table. Poor kid, she'll be hoping for a decent tip."

"I don't mind a fair tip for proper service," said John. "It really pisses me off when you get treated like shit and they 'spect you to add 20% to the bill anyhow. She's doin' all right, if she'll just stay out of our face a bit."

"Oh, yeah. I agree really. She's expected to pay off everybody from the hostess down to the dishwasher and tip out to the kitchen too. Hell, John, you and I used to play for drinks and tips for how many years, 'fore we caught on with Memphis Rail?"

"Sometimes I miss those days, Art."

Art agreed reluctantly. "Well, yeah. Me too, I guess. God knows the money wasn't shit. We never knew where we were gonna sleep, and if and when we were gonna eat. Days we couldn't ride the goddam bus, let alone find cab fare. But, there was somethin' different about the music then. Somethin' special. I don't know for sure what it was."

"I been studyin' on it some," said John. "I have somethin' of an idea."

Art leaned back, cocked his head, and raised his eyebrows to indicate surprise. "Well, don't keep me waitin', brother. Tell me about this here theory of yours."

"OK, then. Here goes. When we really weren't playin' for money, why were we playin' at all?"

"Playin' in hopes that someday we would fall into makin' some money?"

"Naw, that ain't it, not really," insisted John. "We were playin' because we loved the music."

"Well, if you say so, John."

"Yeah, I do say so. And you know what was different then, when we played because we loved the music?"

"Sure. We couldn't make rent. Hey, pass that bread basket over hear, would ya?"

"God, Art. Anybody ever say y'all can be a bit negative sometimes? Yeah, we couldn't always make the rent- but the important thing that was different when we played because we loved the music is that the music sort of loved us back."

"What the hell do you mean by that?"

"It's like this," continued John. "You know how it is when you see some good lookin' woman, and the next thing you know she's bein' fairly obvious about lookin' at you in return?"

"Shit, yes! Holdin' out hope for moments like that is one of the main reasons for gettin' up in the mornin'!"

"OK, now hear me out. When it just happens, sort of natural, ain't that a hell of a lot better than havin' some gal pretendin' to be excited with your company 'cause she's gonna be stuffin' a few hundred bucks in her purse before the night comes to its final conclusion?"

"Conclusion?" chuckled Art. "Sure you don't mean climax?"

"Hell, you know what I mean. It's the same with the music. Doin' it because you love to do it is way different than doin' it because you're gettin' paid."

"Maybe not," countered Art. "What if I said I love to get paid? And hey, speakin' of gettin' paid, you heard about Little Willy's sales the last couple of weeks? Damnation! That crazy assed video of the Bluesbirds, along with the white guy and those two sisters, has been seen somethin' like a million times. What the fuck is with that? Everybody's jumpin' on line and downloadin' Bluesbirds' albums. That fuckin' act was never that good, but Ira says since that video went viral they're outsellin' Memphis Rail!"

"It ain't gonna last," observed John. "Everybody's lookin' for the sound on the video, and of course they ain't never actually recorded anything with that new group, The Family Jones. That's over, at least for now. We go into the studio tomorrow with that Jones bunch, and then we'll see what happens."

"Well, I'm tellin' you right now I ain't gonna have a lot of patience for amateur night," grumbled Art. "And what the hell is with that dog they drag around? Shit, I think I'm allergic to dogs. I know I'm allergic to somethin', anyway. When we were here in December, weren't anybody but the white guy- the one on the video blowin' that impossible soundin' stuff on the sax."

"Damn shame we were stuck in that other hotel. Redd, Ann and Mary are still talkin' about that night."

"So whatcha think of the material for the remake of that old album, Art?"

"Some of the most old-time, simple shit imaginable. I think St James Infirmary might have been about the second or third song I learned on the guitar. My daddy taught it to me, of'n an old Josh White record. Hound Dog has to be done just right, no faster than about 60 or 65, or it comes off too rock-a-billy. Big Mama Thornton's Ball and Chain is always a winner. Never cared much for Nobody Knows You When You're Down and Out, but Judah Jones did a hell of an instrumental on it in the '59 album. I guess what sticks with me the most is that tune Family Jones does on that video with Little Willy, Summertime.

"Yeah, I don't know what Ira's thinkin' with this goof ball project. Redoin' some old album. But, I do gotta say, if we can get the same kind of response to Summertime that Little Willy got from the video, we're sell a shitload of stuff."

Chuck Gould

The waitress silently approached- her footfalls muffled by a deep Persian carpet stretched over a thick foam pad. John Flood was almost certain, but wasn't entirely sure, that her blouse was less buttoned up than earlier in the evening.

"You gentlemen care for some desert?"

Part Two, Chapter Nine

The light changed, and Wesley Perkins throttled up his Mini-Cooper. He shifted through the first three gears, and began descending the lazy left hand curve on the ramp from Lake City Way to southbound I-5. He was pleased to see the mainline traffic moving at 55 or 60 miles an hour. If things didn't bottleneck under the convention center, he would make it to Georgetown and the Rain Crow Recording Studio with time to spare. Vanessa and Rebekah left earlier, planning to stop by Sea Tac airport and meet Mary Towne's flight from Alabama. During the last portion of the Family Jones mini-tour with the Bluesbirds, Mary finally found the confidence to fly to Birmingham and spend a few days with her new grandbaby.

In the center of the Ship Canal Bridge, Wesley's radio crackled to life. "Oh, shit!" he thought. "Here we go again! This is probably more of that Brother Benjamin crap."

Wesley looked into the mirror, inspecting the back seat for the presence of the figure in the red scarf. There was nothing except traffic in the mirror, but Wesley knew that didn't guarantee he was actually alone.

A familiar voice invaded the Mini-Cooper. Wesley knew from experience that it would be pointless to try to turn off the radio or lower the volume.

"Hallelujah, Brothers and Sisters! This here is the Hour of Holy Gospel Power, comin' to you from the shores of West Moccasin Springs down here in Iberia Parish, Lesiana. Hallelujah and Amen! The Holy Spirit is a walkin' among us now, right there on your radio dial and here on the shores of West Moccasin Springs. I'm Brother Benjamin..."

The speaker paused for an awkward interlude before a second voice began to speak, with decidedly less confidence and authority. "And this here's Brother Abner Culliford. Me and Brother Benjamin has partnered up here at West Moccasin Springs. We're bringin' the Kingdom of God to Lesiana."

A sarcastic cackle erupted from immediately behind Wesley's head. A glance in the mirror confirmed the presence of the figure with the red scarf.

"I should have known!" said Wesley. "I figured you wouldn't be far away when Brother Benjamin came on. I didn't see you just now, though."

"You aren't going to see me unless I want to be seen, Wes. You ought to know that. But hey, there's nobody else that can see me right now so if you have any thoughts about trying to use the carpool lane..."

"Is every goddam thing a joke to you?" complained Wesley.

"Funny choice of words in your question, Wes. But hey, I'm gonna shut up a minute and let you listen to my man, Brother Benjamin."

Brother Benjamin was in mid-sentence. ."..and out of our four-hundred seventy-five acres here, we have set aside twenty-five acres for the temple. If your Christian family is looking for a home, we have four-hundred 1-acre home sites available, with access to the fifty-acre common garden. If the Lord doesn't see fit to award you one of the home sites, we'll have space for you in the family dormitories. The Lord is a workin' miracles here on the shores of West Moccasin Springs. Put the material world behind you. The Lord has given us authority to help free you from the bondage of your homes, cars, and other material distractions that might keep you from entering the Kingdom of God."

"He's just trying to rip everybody off!" complained Wesley. "Why the hell do you keep playing this really sad, sad, crap on my radio?"

"Ain't your radio, Wes. It's our'n"

"Well, whatever the hell- obviously he got poor old Abner for his lottery winnings, and now he's out to get anybody else. I thought the golden ribbon scam was awful, but this is really over the top! There ought to be a special place in hell..."

"Trust me, Wes. There is. But for now, listen and learn, Wesley. Listen and learn. Brother Benjamin's into his hour of power. In fact, a lot further into it than he realizes. But take note, Wesley. He's reaching out to people trying to find a home. That's what you're about, helping people go home. You've got an hour of power coming soon. Sooner than you think. Protect Rebekah, Wesley."

"Shield her. Take the terrible, terrible beating. Because as we move this thing along it's going to be mostly about you. From the minute you were born you were destined for this time. These people need you far more than you need them. You'll be discovering that soon enough. You're going to be a bright and shinin' star, Wes. A beacon calling people home."

Part Two, Chapter Ten

There are homeless specters of grand ambition, unbridled consumption, and economic dislocation. They swirl among the dusty vortices of moldering litter and cigarette butts, wandering in frustration through dead end echoes and unclaimed spaces. They move small traces of grit from place to place in Seattle's Georgetown, in futile attempt to rediscover or re-create a prosperous time of abundant harvest- a time no longer remembered and seldom imagined.

More than a hundred years ago, they brewed beer in Georgetown. Smoke poured from a forest of stacks. Cargoes of hops and barley steamed into Seattle from the hot, dry, plateaus east of the Cascade Mountains. The switching tracks ran down the center of the street. Horses, carts, and passenger trolleys would pause throughout the day to make way for short sections of grain cars destined for the sprawling brew houses.

The brewery also manufactured ice. The delivery wagons were insulated by burlap bags filled with sawdust. Iron shod hooves sparked while wheels rumbled on the cobbles. Axles creaked as teams of horses pulled the loads up steep Seattle hillsides. Muscular young men with leather aprons and wrought iron tongs ran from both sides of the cart, supplying 30-pound blocks of ice to subscribers wealthy enough to afford the luxury of an icebox in the pantry.

The entire enterprise was long abandoned. Only some of the brick structures remained, and most were in disrepair. Throughout the district, scars of less weathered brick covered gashes on the sides of surviving structures to commemorate the point where a neighboring edifice once shared a common wall.

The location of Rain Crow Studios was marked by a remarkably bright sign, painted on the vintage masonry. Contrasting with the drab background, the image appeared to be as vivid as fresh acrylic artist colors, wet and shining, shimmering from the tube. A huge black crow, leaning on an ornate walking stick with one wing and ostentatiously tipping a stove pipe hat with the other, was depicted above orange letters silhouetted with black borders. "Rain Crow Studios, established 2008"

Wesley Perkins parked his Mini-Cooper. He was pleased to see Vanessa's Honda Accord already arrived. He was about to meet a lot of new people, and the greater the number of familiar faces in the crowd the better. He grabbed his snakeskin saxophone case and proceeded into the building.

The young woman at the reception desk was so covered with tattoos and piercings she reminded Wesley of a porcupine involved in the sabotage of a paint factory. She looked at a list. "OK, so you must be Wes Perkins, the sax guy. Come on back, everybody else is here, and I mean everybody. Most of the time, we only get a couple of people here at once. People lay down tracks and they get combined later on. This is so retro, man- I mean it's like the 70's or 80's or something!"

"Well, let's hope it's like 1959," said Wesley. "We're going to be doing a modern remake of an old album."

"1959? Damn, that was a long time ago! I think my grandparents were still kids back then."

They entered a large, space with unusual shapes and textures. There were five walls, so no two were parallel. One wall was covered in rough wood planks, one was made of concrete, one was hidden behind thick drapes, and two were covered with a multitude of cones fashioned from foam. Portable glass walls were apparently positioned for a purpose, and John Flood's drum kit was contained within a Plexiglas cube. Vanessa, Rebekah, Wesley the Dog, and Memphis Rail were seated in wooden chairs along the wooden wall. "Here's Wes now," said Mary Towne.

"Sorry if I'm late."

"No, man, you ain't late," said Redd Wilmott. "Just the last one to get here."

Mary Towne handled the introductions, then addressed everyone with, "OK, y'all ready for the warm up?"

Vanessa, Rebekah, and Wesley were unsure how to respond. Redd sensed they were perplexed.

"Hey, it's like this. We got this tradition in the Rail. We started it hell, maybe 40 years or so ago. When we first get together every day, before we rehearse or perform, or record anything, we do this group warm up. It ain't really the blues, it's more of a spiritual. An old, traditional thing, you know."

"Yeah," added Ann Foster. "We all do the chorus together. There ain't enough verses to go around, so we take turns starting off. If we use up all the lyrics before it gets to be your turn, you either ad lib some new lyrics or play an 8-bar solo. John don't neither sing nor write, so he just sets a slow, steady tempo."

"Redd, you start off today," suggested Mary. Then Ann, then me, then Vanessa, then Art, then Wes, then Rebekah. So, Rebekah, be ready to show us what you can do when it comes round to be your turn- you're going to have to create somethin' fresh. Then, of course, everybody together for the first verse to finish stuff up."

Wes unpacked his horn, anticipating an 8-bar solo during his turn.

John Flood began to clap out a 4/4 rhythm, as relentless as a mortgage and slightly slower than a heartbeat. After four beats, everyone clapped along in perfect unison.

Memphis Rail began to sing. Family Jones joined in on the second line.

Swing low, sweet chariot
Comin' for to carry me home
Swing low, oh, oh, sweet chariot
A Comin' for to carry me home

Ann Foster took the first verse, her light and bright voice in rested and polished form. The entire group clapped with an even precision, as though a complex instrument willed into conformity by John Flood.

I looked over Jordan
And what did I see
Comin' for to carry me home
A band of angels comin' after me
Comin for to carry me home

All joined in for the chorus, and then Mary Towne was next. The dusky resonance of her seasoned intonations created a sensation that each individual note was a living being, hovering in the air.

Some days I'm up
Some days I'm down
Comin' for to carry me home
But I know this road is heaven bound
Comin' for to carry me home

Vanessa, remembering the order, was ready to follow the chorus with a harp solo. She played three solid low notes, caught a high contrast, and then bent her way back down to the bottom of the scale. Art Abbott nodded approvingly. As Wesley clapped along and concentrated on the phrasing of Vanessa's harp, his mind raced to an imaginary dice game. Craps on a scrap of canvas. Nickels and dimes exchanged hands at the community pig roast, shielded from view by a tan colored Studebaker.

It was Art Abbot's turn. Art sang with spirit, if not precision.
If you get there
Before I do
Comin' for to carry me home
Tell all of my friends I'm a-comin' too
Comin' for to carry me home
Wesley was up. He caught a glimpse of yellow radiance from the dog, then closed his eyes and stepped into a process he had given up trying to understand. A high tone, long and round and clear as a glass rod, emerged from the old silver sax with the twisted neck. Wesley snaked down the scale to a low note, reached back to duplicate the original high sound, and then resolved to something closer to the middle of the range. Wesley's solo concluded with the last two lines of tracing the traditional melody note-for-note. Wesley opened his eyes in time to see Redd Wilmott give him a congratulatory wink.

It came around to Rebekah. She would need to invent a verse for the old standard. With astonishing tones, apparently enhanced by the unique environment of the studio, she added;
Ain't got no lamp
Or light to guide me
Comin' for to carry me home
Got friends and family here beside me
Comin' for to carry me home.

Ann Foster glared.
Memphis Rail and The Family Jones sang the final chorus together. As they were finishing up, a voice from the control booth was heard on a studio monitor.
"Hey, keep it up! That's gold. Let's get everybody plugged in and do it again with a full instrumental background!"

94

The producer remarked to the receptionist, standing to the side of the board. "That's not on the 1959 album, but unless I miss my guess we're about to hear somethin' pretty incredible. I'm going to get this on file. I've heard Memphis Rail for years, and they ain't ever been this dynamic. Keep your eyes and ears peeled, Alice. I've got a rare feelin'. You're gonna want to be able to say you were here when this went down!"

Chuck Gould

Part Two, Chapter Eleven

Like a cannibal clown at a penny arcade, Red Scarf prowled stealthily around the settlement at West Moccasin Springs, Louisiana. He chose to be unseen. The pilgrims returned to work after lunching at 50-foot tables in the mess tent. Dust flew as bags of concrete were poured into the gaping maws of gasoline powered cement mixers. Young and middle aged men in work boots and overalls framed up walls and rafters. Women in loose blue jeans and deerskin gloves shuttled small truckloads of materials between building sites, and brought water to the carpentry crews. Four shoeless teenage girls in ankle length dresses kept the young children occupied. They played a game of hide and seek through the shade and shadows of a pecan grove.

Even after thousands of years, (according to the imaginary concept his prey considered time) Red Scarf never tired of the hunt. Everyone had a weakness that could be exploited, and Brother Benjamin's colony was overflowing with possibilities. There was never much difficulty, or even a challenge, in wrecking the righteous. They were vulnerable because they believed their religious faith made them special. They assumed they were separate from their fellow humans, closer to and more beloved by God. There was always greater satisfaction in rupturing a soul from a stealthy, subtle perspective. Red Scarf surveyed the field.

The large, athletically built youth with the Nordic facial features? Oh, my! He thinks he is destined to be a great spiritual leader. Lots of possibilities there.

The dark haired woman with the red Coleman water jug? Why, of course! She secretly believes that she is wildly desired by nearly every man.

This one thinks he can sculpt. That one believes she's an amazing singer. The woman with the puffy face and broad ass? She's sure that if she could only lose 25 pounds she could be a professional ballerina. The twenty-five year old man with the home made haircut is convinced that he will eventually become a wildly successful businessman. The red haired girl, one of those watching the little children, dreams of marrying for love.

"What a jackpot!" muttered Red Scarf. Unable to resist, he moved a red scarf into a bush near the aspiring ballerina.

"Oh, look!" she exclaimed. "Here's a scarf! Anybody know who dropped this?"

After a moment of silence, she wrapped her find around her neck.

"Hey, that looks very nice on you," remarked the great spiritual leader. The sculptor, the temptress, and the singer all agreed.

"Thanks very much," she blushed. "If nobody recognizes it, I think I'll keep it."

Red Scarf considered the case of Brother Benjamin. "Brother Benjamin, indeed! He wasn't so religious when he needed help with that time-share condo scam in the 80's. I saved his ass a hundred times when he was in prison in the early 90's. Then those horrible X-rated movies he shot with little kids in Columbia. Even I was appalled, and that takes some doing. Back to prison again, and finally he emerges as Brother Registered Sex Offender Benjamin and the Hour of Holy Gospel Power. He's fairly well served his purpose. It's time. Time to stop shielding him from his own impulses. Time to put the businessman, maybe the ballerina, the great spiritual leader, and Abner Culliford in play here. "

Red Scarf resolved to allow Brother Benjamin to destroy himself. He almost immediately visualized a plan.

Bridget Bishop was tasked with watching the small children, and she grew bored. The others of her own age group remained apart from her, and were frequently whispering. Bridget wondered whether they suspected she had chosen to wear no bra or panties under her full length, floral print shift. Scandalous, to be sure; but at West Moccasin Springs there were few other ways for a rebellious young woman of fifteen to express her independence.

Bridget sat on a rock at the edge of the pecan grove, soaking her feet in an irrigation ditch. If there were an upside to her widowed father's relocation to Louisiana, it had to be that Cliff Martinez was now a two-day drive away. She would never forget the first of several midnight rendezvous in the hayloft. It wasn't long after she and Cliff initially crossed the line that she realized she didn't really love him, after all. She missed the sex, but she didn't miss Cliff.

If she had stayed, she would likely have become pregnant. A life as Mrs. Cliff Martinez would have been pure hell. Or, perhaps her parents would have discovered her secret and banished her from home.

Mrs. Pudeator approached. Bridget found her comical. The plump, middle-aged woman never failed to talk about how close she came to enjoying a career as a professional ballet dancer. Bridget remembered that years ago, before her family found Jesus and threw out their television, she used to watch a video tape of a Disney movie called "Fantasia." It was easy to imagine Mrs. Pudeator as one of the dancing hippos in a frilly pink tutu. Today, Mrs. Pudeator was wearing a red scarf. "That would really clash with a pink tutu," thought Bridget.

Mrs. Pudeator said, "You're Bridget Bishop, right? Brother Benjamin sent me to find you. He wants you to see you in the tabernacle, right away. He says he's got a special blessing for you."

"For me? Why would Brother Benjamin want to bless me?"

"I don't know child, I'm just the messenger. But, run along now. It isn't every day somebody gets a chance for a blessing from Brother Benjamin."

When Bridget knocked on the door, Brother Benjamin was sitting alone in his office. His pants were down around his knees, and there were pornographic images on his computer screen.

"Who is it?" called an angered and irritated Benjamin. "Can't you see the sign? I'm in prayer, here. That's why the sign says Do Not Disturb."

Benjamin heard a young female voice from beyond the door. "I'm sorry, Brother Benjamin. It's Bridget Bishop. Mrs. Pudeator said you wanted to see me right away, so I knocked. She said you had a special blessing for me."

Brother Benjamin had no idea why Mrs. Pudeator would have sent Bridget Bishop to his office, but he sensed a rare opportunity. He pulled up his pants, shifted to a different window on his computer, turned on the light, and opened the door. Bridget Bishop blinked up at him, with soft blue eyes framed by a perfectly proportioned face.

"Yes, child! Please do come in! I have a special blessing and a prayer for you. It's good that you came when you did, you're going to need healing prayer- and the laying on of hands."

Silas Bishop and Mark Wardwell were laying an ornate rock wall, bordering the entrance to West Moccasin Springs. They stopped and cleared their tools out of the drive so an overheating minivan, so heavily loaded that the tire tops scraped the fender wells at every moderate bump, could pull off the road. The driver stopped and rolled the window down.

"Is this here the Christian community?"

"It is!" said Mark Wardwell. "Welcome. Where y'all from?"

"Pennsylvania. Long drive down here. Are there some home sites left?"

"Should be. Folks have been showin' up all week. You're about the fourth or fifth car so far today. One batch from California, another from Illinois, and I forget the rest. Pull on up ahead there, next to the mess tent. Look for a table sitting under a canopy with a Welcome banner across the front. Brother Abner Culliford, one of our founders, will help you get checked in."

As the newcomers pulled into the compound, Silas Bishop said, "Mark, I need to take a break for a couple of minutes. I can't explain why, exactly, but all of a sudden I think there's some urgent reason I need to go see Brother Benjamin."

"What the heck for, Silas?"

"Don't know for sure, but I do know that I won't be able to concentrate on these doggone rocks until I go and see. It's a strange feeling, and I need to check it out."

"OK," said Mark Wardwell. "I'm ready for a lemonade break, anyway. See you back here in fifteen minutes?"

Silas Bishop was already stepping briskly toward the tabernacle building and Brother Benjamin's office. He called back over his shoulder, "Yeah, fifteen minutes should be fine!"

Silas Bishop reached Brother Benjamin's office to find the door closed, and a Do Not Disturb sign hanging askew. He was ready to return to work when he realized that he was hearing sounds of passion from within. Rhythmic grunting, and female calling "Oh, oh, oh, oh my god! Don't stop!"

Although he had never heard it in that context, Silas immediately recognized his daughter's voice. He kicked open the door, startling the naked couple sprawled out on Brother Benjamin's office couch. "You bastard!"

Bridget shrieked, "Daddy!"

Brother Benjamin jumped up, awkwardly, with his erect manhood waving like a preposterous flag. Brother Benjamin's last words, before enraged Silas Bishop's rock hammer shattered his temple, were "It ain't what it looks like, man, it ain't what it…."

Part Two, Chapter Twelve

Ira Miller was effectively barricaded in his office. He seldom slept, and often spent the night at his desk. Outside the building, he would routinely hear random shouts and curses. There would be gunshots nearly every night. Sometimes, the short explosions resolved into nothing more than silence. Once in a while, the gunfire would inspire one of the employees or a customer over at Wilma's Chicken Shack to call the cops. Those would be one-siren nights. Most of the gunplay was braggadocio, but there were times when somebody caught a bullet. Those were almost always two siren nights, one cop car and one ambulance. Typically, there would be gunfire but no sirens. Sometimes, somebody would find a body in the morning.

Ira never felt unsafe, even as the neighborhood changed. Few businesses remained, but Ira was a neighborhood deity. He had launched and managed the careers of several legendary acts. Many of his performers began as small time local talent; kids from the local neighborhood. Even the most violent youth still dreamed of the day that Ira Miller would recognize their obvious talents. Ira was the gatekeeper. He could open the door to a life of easy living and untold riches beyond the 'hood. Nobody messed with Ira, and word on the street was that nobody ever better.

When the phone rang at 11 PM, Ira answered.

"Miller Entertainment."

"Ira, hey it's Martin from Rain Crow. It's done."

"What's done? Christ, you just started this morning. How many tracks did you get?"

"That's what I'm trying to say, Ira. We got all of them."

"In one fucking day? That's impossible. These people have never even played together before. Redd, and especially Mary would not be cool with turning out some sloppy shit. What you've got can't possibly be any good. At your rates, I expect professional results-not some one-take bootleg crap."

"Bullshit, man. I been engineering recordings for more than 20 years. I know mediocre shit when I hear it. I also know when you've got a mother-fucking monster record. Maybe a dozen times in my career I've been this psyched about something I've had a hand in. And most of the stuff today, we did get in a single take."

"My aching ass, Martin. We're trying to recreate at least the spirit of the Blues Breakout album. The Rail doesn't even normally play most of that old shit from the 50's. We've got an amateur horn player, a brand new vocalist, and some gal that's been playin' blues harp for about two weeks mixed in here. I went up to Seattle and heard them play before I decided to go ahead with this recording, but they've never played with the Rail before. Hell, they didn't even rehearse! And now you're telling me some of this shit is in the can after one take?"

"Yeah, most of it. You don't want to change a goddam note. As far as your three newbies go, there's something pretty odd going on. They're like some kind of catalyst or something. A lot of people would say you've got the top blues act in the country, maybe even the world with Memphis Rail. With these three new faces, something has happened. Everybody is playing up to a higher level. It's nothing short of fucking amazing. They are so inspired, and incredibly tight. Sort of like the entire group is being controlled by some invisible musical genius."

"I'm having a hard time believin' this shit. It sounds like some Tin Pan Alley fairy tale, Martin. Email a couple of files, I need to hear this supposedly miracle bullshit for myself. You're right, the Rail is the best in the business, and the Family Jones act has a lot of promise, but it doesn't make sense that you mix these two different groups together and come up with some over-the-top fantasy band. I figured it would take a lot of time to get this together."

"I sent you the email just before I dialed the phone. You got "Hound Dog," and "Summertime." Hey, Ira, the video for "Hound Dog" is gonna go beyond viral. You know that yellow dog the blind harp player uses to get around with? I swear to God, Ira, I mean I swear to God that damn dog was keepin' perfect time with his tail! Never say anything like it. People who aren't even fans of the music will be checkin' out the dog. Everybody will argue over whether it's faked, of course, but between you and me, it ain't!"

"There may be more fake about that so-called 'guide dog' than anybody realizes," replied Ira. "Give me a half hour to listen to the files, and then I'll call you back."

"You got it. I'll wait for your call in about half an hour."

Ira opened his email and found the files sent from Rain Crow Studios. He opened "Hound Dog," and it began to play through an elaborate system built into his office walls.

Wesley Perkins opened with a two bar sax intro, eerily note-for-note identical to the opening notes played by Judah Jones more than 50 years earlier. Ira was astonished with the sound. Was it the tone, the technique, or both? Whatever, there was no doubt that the opening phrase was compelling.

Substantially down tempo and with a lot more "swing" than the ubiquitous Carl Perkins version, the rhythm section kicked in. Mary Towne began singing about her man being "nothing but a 'hound dog, just a hangin' 'round my door" Wesley's sax was mixed low in the background. John Flood drummed with slow, steady joy. Ann Foster's keyboard simulated the clonking, percussive sounds of a 50's era stage piano, with some notes convincingly almost a quarter tone out of tune. Redd used a special pick to recreate the "slap" of an upright bass, and Art Abbott dialed up the midrange and treble tones on his Fender. "Damn," thought Ira, "but that does sound a lot like the late 50's, early 60's! Only a whole lot cleaner."

Consistent with the "Blues Breakout" format, Wesley Perkins launched into a sax solo after the first verse. For two eight-bar segments, the old silver horn with the intricate etchings, purple velvet stops, and the twisted neck moaned, and laughed, and shouted, and whispered, and wept. There were runs where the notes were rapid fire as a pinball trapped between a bumper skirt and a rubber rail. The fast notes were offset with long, fluid, tones that seemed extricated from a magical chant. Ira realized that even people who didn't care much for the blues would likely be fascinated with the almost impossible performance of Wesley Perkins. "Where does that shit come from, anyway?"

Redd Wilmott picked up the lyrics at the second verse, singing back to Mary. "I ain't gonna be your hound dog, just a hangin' round your door" Vanessa wedged some quick bursts of blues harp in between his phrasing. When the second verse of lyrics concluded, Wesley soloed again.

He played the same note for eight beats, but kept the sound fascinating with an almost abstract syncopation. The frame of reference established, Wesley soared up and down the neck of his horn in a pattern that alternated rhythmic triplets with high stress squeals. "Well, I'll be damned!" exclaimed Ira. "That's better than anything I heard him play when I was in Seattle. How good is this guy, anyway?"

Mary Town picked up the lyrics again, her lead vocal energized by an electrifying higher harmony. "Rebekah! Omigod, she's got one of those voices that record even better than she sounds in person!"

The final instrumental highlighted the saxophone, well supported by the other musicians.

Ira clicked off his computer and picked up the phone.

"Hey, Martin. Ira here."

"Well that was fast. You couldn't have listened to both those files already."

"I don't need to listen to them both. You're right, Martin. If the rest of this thing is like 'Hound Dog', it could be the biggest damn record in the entire career of Memphis Rail!"

"Oh, you listened to 'Hound Dog'?"

"Yeah, of course. You sent it to me, what else did you think I'd do with it?"

"Well, yeah. I wanted you to listen to it. I guess if you were only going to listen to one of the files you probably should have done 'Summertime'," replied Martin.

"Why so, exactly."

"Because it's better than 'Hound Dog'. Maybe a lot better. Maybe even as good or better than anything I ever recorded- and I shit you not."

"What?! The hell you say! Stay on the line, Marty, while I get back on the computer and open the other file"

Part Two, Chapter Thirteen

Most of Memphis Rail taxied back to downtown Seattle. Wesley, Rebekah, and Wesley the Dog drove home to their Lake City rental. Vanessa and Redd Wilmott said they were "going out for a drink," and left in her Honda Accord. There was at first some awkward tension, ultimately fractured when Redd joked, "You know, you drive pretty good for a blind woman."

Vanessa laughed slightly, and replied, "For some reason, we play a lot better when the dog is nearby, and Mary figured that we could get a guide dog into places that wouldn't allow a regular dog."

"Ain't nothin' regular about that dog," grumbled Redd. "He keeps sendin' out spooky little signals, like he's tryin' to let us know he understands what we're sayin' and doin'. Did you see him tappin' his tail when we played 'Hound Dog'?"

"Yeah. That was a little unusual. I didn't think animals had a sense of rhythm."

Redd let a sea of ominous silence build for several seconds. When the pressure behind the dike became too great, he remarked slowly, and deliberately "You gotta tell me, 'Nessa, just what the hell is going on. I'm just an old blues man. I guess most people would say I'm a damn good blues man. But in all my years I can't say I ever saw or even heard of anything half as strange as this crazy situation."

Vanessa stalled for time. "What do mean, exactly?"

"I exactly mean that when we were up here last December, I saw a confused lookin' white guy stumble on stage with a twisted saxophone. He reeked of cheap whisky, could hardly stand up, and played the living shit out of that horn until he passed out. We spent a whole night together, and you never even mentioned playin' blues harp. You didn't utter a word about your sister havin' a voice."

"I don't know exactly what to say. I just took up the blues harp recently. Ask Mary, she coached me along in the basics. I guess I would have told you Rebekah could sing, if you ever asked me."

"I been around the barn a few times," countered Redd. "I gotta say I'm more than a little disturbed by your whole Family Jones deal. Look at Wes Perkins, for example. He was bombed out of his mind last December, and I just thought he played lucky drunk. Has he had anything to drink all day? Sure didn't seem much like it, and he played even better."

"Wes has been working on his confidence, I guess. Yeah, he used to drink a lot. It always made him talk funny, like some old country field hand. He's been tryin' it without the rye, and it doesn't seem like the liquor makes any difference any more. He's just that damn good on the horn, Redd. And, I think he keeps getting a little better all the time. There aren't many people playing at that level."

"There ain't anybody playin' at that level. That's my point. You'd have to practice about a hundred years to get where he's at, maybe more. It's beyond any kinda explanation. "

"So, Redd, why not just leave it there and not worry about an explanation? Just enjoy it for what it is, for however long it lasts."

""Cuz, dammit, Vanessa it ain't just your white freak with his antique sax. It ain't just your instant ability to play harp, and it ain't just your mysterious little dog either. You probably can't tell because you ain't been around us, but Memphis Rail is caught up in this whole thing somehow. We're not the same blues band when we play with your Family Jones."

"I think you guys are sounding great!"

"That ain't the point! Look at what just happened in the studio. No way in hell could we ever just walk in and damn nearly play straight through some old album. We'd be bickering over how this or that phrase should sound, whether to leave out a verse, where the solos should go and who should play them."

"So then, it went well." suggested Vanessa.

"Well-hell. That ain't the way it's done. Bands are a collection of egos that most of the time can't barely figure out how to put up with each other long enough to perform. Today, it was like we were all just instruments being played by some supermind someplace. Everybody knew what to do, when to do it, and it worked out better than almost anything we've ever done."

Vanessa pulled her Honda to the curb, but left the engine running. Silky waves of rainwater raced down the windshield, only to be wiped away by the relentless swiping of tireless rubber blades.

"Redd, I want you to listen to me, please. I'm going to say something pretty serious, and I don't want you to laugh. OK?"

"How do I know I'm not gonna laugh before you say it?"

"Take my advice, and don't laugh. Did you ever stop to think what people are?"

"What do you mean by that? That's a goofball question. Hell, everybody knows what people are."

"Well, maybe. You ever go to Sunday school, Redd?"

"Yeah, when I was a kid. Until I got old enough and big enough that Mama couldn't force me no more. You ain't gonna go all religious on me are you? Talkin' about Adam, Eve, gardens, and snakes and stuff?"

Vanessa sat in silence, apparently contemplating what to say- or whether to say anything at all.

Redd tried to ease the conversational load by interjecting a bit of humor. "I don't personally care much for snakes, you know. However, if you happen to have one of them apples handy..."

"Redd, if there's one true thing in the entire Bible it doesn't have to be the story about Eden. But before that, at the very beginning of the beginning of the very first story. You remember what happened, right?"

"Yeah, God created the universe."

"Ok, right. Now how did God do that?"

"Shit, I don't know. God didn't ever tell me how he created the universe. I gotta say, God and I don't talk much. Ain't especially lookin' forward to the day when I might meet him, neither."

"Seriously, Redd. Genesis says that God created the universe by creating energy first. God said 'Let there be light,' and there was light. It just happened. There was no other choice."

"Uh, 'Nessa, I'm sorry. But is there some reason I'm confused about why we're goin' out drinkin' if you're gonna turn into some kind of preacher here?"

"I'm not preachin', I'm trying to answer your question about Family Jones and Memphis Rail and exactly what the hell went on at Rain Crow today."

109

"OK, but see about comin' round to the point, please. This religious crap gives me the jeebies."

"Here's the point, straight at you. God doesn't create by hammering stuff together. God creates by what we would consider thought, and by will. So, what is man? Most likely, each one of us is a unique God-thought, and those individual thoughts are parts and pieces of a much more complex idea."

Redd squirmed, uncomfortably. "This is gettin' way to heavy, Vanessa. Shit, talk about a buzz kill. You say that you, and me, and everybody we know are all God-thoughts? Hate to break it to you, but I sort of think my Mama and her first husband had something to do with creatin' me."

"Yeah, but you're not just an animal, Redd. Animals can only make more animals. People are different because we're God-thoughts in an animal body. And consider this about thoughts. Some of those tunes we played today were written in the early 1900's. How old do you suppose the folks who wrote them are today?"

"Oh, hell, 'Nessa! All of them have to be dead by now."

Vanessa flipped on her left turn signal, checked for traffic, and pulled back into the traffic lane.

"Yeah, they're all dead. At least the animals are dead. Would you suppose it would be OK to say that since we're still playing their music that somehow their thoughts kept on going long after their bodies gave out?"

Redd rubbed the side of his palm across his chin for a moment of silence. He then responded, "Oh, Christ. I think I'm startin' to get what you're sayin'. I ain't never thought of it exactly like that. You think there's some big idea, maybe, that's just usin' all of us as little thoughts in the plan? An idea that goes way back before some of us, maybe even any of us were born?"

"Could be, Redd, I can't say for certain. But I suspect."

"You ain't mad at me, are you?" asked Redd with a hopeful tone. "We're still goin' out for drinks, right?"

"You got it," smiled Vanessa. "We might be unique little God-thoughts, but even if we are that isn't all there is to bein' human."

Part Two, Chapter Fourteen

About 4 AM, (still slightly drunk, and sexually satisfied), Vanessa fell asleep next to the muscular presence of Redd Wilmott. She dreamed.

Vanessa dreamed of cosmic dice tumbling high overhead, clacking thunderously together while rolling across the sky. Streaks of light and tongues of fire telegraphed the results of every roll, electrifying the cardboard universe below.

Vanessa, Rebekah, Wesley, and Wesley the Dog walked through a city with painted streets. In each block, there was a row of Christmas green plastic cubes with peaked tops- intended to resemble houses. There did not appear to be any actual doors of windows, only impressions on the cubes to suggest where such openings could have been. After every clap of thunder, their small party would advance another block.

In each new location, Rebekah walked up to one of the green cubes. In some inexplicable manner, she converted one of the plastic outlines to an actual door. A dark mist, comprised of swirling abstract shapes suggestive of human bodies formed spontaneously at every stop. A cacophony of sighs, wails, moans and weeping was audible before the cloud formed a horizontal helix and twisted through the door like water circling a drain.

Wesley Perkins shielded Rebekah from the animated fog. Enormous piles of absurdly colored money gathered everywhere. Vanessa kept occupied shoveling the currency out of the way, so that when the thunder tolled again the Family Jones could advance to the next set of houses. Wesley the Dog watched, approvingly.

At the last stop, Wesley Perkins disappeared under the money. Wesley the Dog burrowed frantically into the pile of paper. Vanessa and Rebekah dug as well, calling "Wes! Wes! Where are you?" Vanessa was not surprised to see Rebekah in tears.

Vanessa awoke.

Part Two, Chapter Fifteen

Ira Miller raced to the airport.

"When's the next flight out to Seattle?"

"There's a direct flight boarding in 30 minutes, sir. Let me check. We have three seats left in First Class, nothing in Business Class or Coach. There will be another flight in four hours, would you like me to check..."

"I'll take the First Class ticket. Here's my frequent flyer number. I'm in a hurry. How much?"

"That's a seventeen-hundred and sixty-five dollar fare, but based on your mileage we can sell it to you for eleven-hundred fifteen. That includes three free beverages and no charge for baggage. Do you have any baggage, sir?"

"Yeah, more than I care to think about sometimes," grumbled Ira. "But if you're asking about luggage, nope. Just this little case with my laptop. I'll carry that aboard. I assume there's Wi-Fi on the plane."

"Yes, and that's also complimentary in First Class."

"Put it on my American Express."

"Of course sir. Let me see your photo ID and I'll print up a boarding pass. What should I put for a return date?"

"Tomorrow. Late afternoon. I should be done by then."

The ticket agent's fingers rapid fired across the keyboard. A thin cardboard document emerged from the computer keyboard. "You're boarding at Gate D7. Thank you for flying Sky High Airways, Mr. Miller."

Ira waltzed through the First Class security line in moments, and proceeded toward his assigned gate.

Like many of the airports in the Deep South, where tobacco farming is an important portion of the economy, smoking was allowed in designated areas. There were large glass smoking rooms in the center of every concourse. Smokers could enter through double doors and light up in an atmosphere isolated from the non-smoking public.

Fresh air was piped into the room from a dedicated source. The "exhaust" from a room full of tobacco addicts was removed through a central hole in the ceiling and carried through a black plastic hose to a vent at the roof of the terminal. The glass was tinted an iris green, in a worthless effort to disguise the yellow-brown scum clinging to the inside of every pane.

Ira normally sped past the smoking rooms without giving them any particular consideration. This day was different. He thought, "Those people remind me of the hamsters Mrs. Krenshaw kept in that aquarium, back in second grade." His mild amusement was interrupted when, through some trick of airport lighting and an apparently weird angle of sight, his dark shadow on the glass cage became a multi-colored reflection.

"Well, piss on that!" scoffed Ira. "Somebody ought to figure out how to build that effect into a carnival fun house. I sure don't have time to worry about it now."

Ira arrived at the gate ten minutes before boarding was to begin. He found a plastic chair without any visible goo globs or grease, and sat where he could watch the clock behind the gate agent's podium. Ira's mind went into overdrive, while the digital hours and minutes appeared to slow to a glacial crawl.

This could be a disaster unfolding. If so, it would be mostly Mary's fault. Why the hell did she get tangled up with those three strange people in Seattle? And where did they come from? Nobody ever heard of this Wesley Perkins guy, and yet he could possibly prove to be the most elite sax player in the world. Rebekah has a voice that few singers could rival. She clearly puts Ann Foster to shame, and Ira was sure that even Mary Towne realized she was no better than close second to Rebekah in solos.

Damn, damn, damn. Why had he so foolishly consented to let the Family Jones get anywhere near Memphis Rail? He had to beg Ann not to quit before he could get to Seattle and sort things out. Redd was concerned, but apparently so enamored with Vanessa that he seemed willing to go with whatever might flow. Mary was defensive of Family Jones. Ira expected no less, Mary was ever the mother hen.

Art and John were simply confused and freaked out. Ira had listened to all the files from Rain Crow, and there was no doubt that it was the Rail's best work. Ever. Especially "Summertime." The journeymen drummer and guitar player seemed proud of the results, but couldn't be comfortable with the process. They insisted that nobody ever played brand new material that flawlessly, and so dynamically, without rehearsal and in a single take. They were right.

Maybe it's just chemistry. Put the wrong people together, no matter how talented they might be as individuals, and the results can be disappointing. Why should chemistry only work one way? Maybe the Family Jones and Memphis Rail, together, were some sort of bizarre chemistry that just happened to take the blues to an entirely new level.

Maybe, just maybe, this was going to turn into a triumph. If so, it would be because Ira followed his instinct and took an unusual chance. Maybe he could mollify the keyboard player with a solo album. Ann would probably go for that, especially if they found a flattering photo and printed her name large enough on the cover art. Mary would support whatever Ira did, as long as he showed her some respect. Redd would do whatever Mary and Vanessa told him to do. Art and John? He just needed to convince them to hang in there for a while longer, see how the album sold, and see how many extra shows and bigger venues they could sell for the upcoming tour season. Wes Perkins? It's likely there's no getting rid of Wes Perkins. Maybe, whether things are about to go fabulously well or the group was about to de-Rail, it was actually Wes Perkins at the core of the problem.

Ira was only half sure of what he would need to do to salvage Memphis Rail. Whatever it would prove to be in the end, he realized he would need to do it in Seattle.

"Ladies and gentlemen. Thanks for waiting. Sky High Airways is now ready to board Flight 66 to Seattle through Gate D7. Please have your boarding passes ready to show at the gate. We'd like to invite our First Class passengers, or anyone traveling with small children to board at this time."

Ira was halfway to the gate before he realized he forgot his laptop and its case. He spun around in time to see a ragged looking man, overdressed in winter clothing and a red woolen scarf, begin reaching for his case on the vacated seat. "Hey, you! Leave that alone! That's mine, goddam it!" The man in the red scarf left the case in place, and seemed to virtually dissolve into a crowd of travelers headed down the concourse toward Baggage Claim.

Part Two, Chapter Sixteen

During a stressful and contentious meeting in Seattle, Ira hammered out a consensus among his musicians. He reluctantly employed his most reliable and effective tool; cash.

In a private conversation with Ann Foster, Ira forgave her significant advance of a few weeks earlier and committed to producing a new Ann Foster CD. The compilation would consist of Foster's original work, backed up by studio musicians rather than Memphis Rail. Ira wasn't confident in the ultimate commercial success of Foster's solo flight. Her talent, and material, were fine- but the contemporary market was looking for something else. Ira sensed he may have stumbled upon that something by combining the Family Jones and Memphis Rail. "Cleaning up the old standards," mused Ira. "Who would have thought we'd wind up with this kind of sound, and so damn much energy in the music?"

Ira's remaining problem with Ann was her jealousy of Rebekah. That wasn't going to be solved by a sack full of money and a record deal. Mary Towne agreed to do what she could to monitor the situation, and intervene as peacemaker when possible. Mary was more often complaining that she was "tired, and ready to go home," but Ira had heard that from so many musicians, so many times, that he no longer worried much about it. Mary was wedded to the blues. She performed because she was compelled to do so. Maybe she was already "home," and simply didn't realize it.

John and Art were suspicious of the Family Jones. During the meeting, Art had no reservations about remarking, "I'm damn nearly 60 years old. Been playin' guitar for over 50, and playin' professionally for more than 40. Suddenly I run into a handful of people who ain't paid their dues, at all, and are blowin' me off the stage. What the hell is with that? Was there any goddam value, at all, to 50 years of sweat, blood, and bullshit if somebody just walks in off the street and beats you to death? I mean, what the fuck has my whole life been about?"

Ira strategically reserved an announcement until the right moment. Art's rant required a strong rebuttal. "OK, listen up. We were scheduled to make up that concert at the Moore a week from now. The one that got canceled in the power outage last December. I thought you would be recording right up until the concert. But, anyway, we're not playing the Moore."

"What!?" frowned John.

"Hear me out," said Ira. "I got the Seattle Theater Group to move the gig to the Paramount instead. They own both venues, so it's no skin off their nose either way. Twelve hundred seats is a sellout at the Moore. We can bring in about twice as many at the Paramount. We'll add a second show, if need be. We might sell five-thousand tickets at sixty dollars each. If we do a second show, we'll probably move five-hundred copies or more of "Blues Breakout.""

"That starts to sound like some serious money," acknowledged Redd.

"Hell yes it does. Art, John, Ann, Mary, Redd; most of you have spent your entire lives in the blues. Most of that time, for most of you, with Memphis Rail. We did what we were doin' for as long as we could. But you know what they say, if we keep on doing what we've lately done, we're going to keep on getting what we've already got. There can't be anybody all that satisfied with where the money's been these last few years, can there?"

Part Three, Chapter One

The wind blew a bitter breath across the cobbles. A light frost had settled the previous evening, removed by a couple of boot tracks and scored by the iron rims of a baker's wagon. Brother Joseph pulled his hooded cloak tightly to his body, although the more he tried to protect his chest the more he bared his calves and sandaled feet. The Cardinal's note conveyed such an ominous tone, "Come early, come alone, and tell no one." Brother Joseph hoped he remembered the count correctly. He slammed the wrought iron knocker against the unnumbered black door, seventh from the corner. Brother Joseph waited. Just as he was ready to conclude that there would be no response, the door opened to a slow groan of rusty hinges. Brother Joseph recognized Agnes Zsabronka, housekeeper for The Cardinal.

"I'm Brother Joseph, The Cardinal summoned me."

"Indeed he did, Brother Joseph. Indeed he did. Won't you come in please? Wait here. I'll make The Cardinal aware of your arrival."

Joseph stepped through the door into a coal black alcove. When Agnes closed the door, there was not a trace of light with which Joseph could visually follow her progress up the stairs. In the darkness, every footstep on every tread resonated like a drum beat. He heard, but could not see, Agnes step through a doorway at the top of the steps. Alone in the darkness and absolute silence, Brother Joseph was aware of a unique odor. Although Joseph didn't own a firearm, he recognized a smell that seemed similar to gunpowder.

After perhaps a minute, the door at the top of the stairway burst open. There, backlit in a blinding white light, was the silhouette of a figure in a long, thick robe- The Cardinal. Light cascaded down the steps, illuminating a clear path to the top.

"Brother Joseph! Praises be. I am so pleased you were able to come so quickly. Come up here, man. Sit by the fire. It's a nippy morn' for sure, is it not? I have already asked Agnes to bring some hot tea and sweet cake. Welcome, Joseph."

Brother Joseph hitched up his robe and scaled the stairs to The Cardinal's library and study. A vigorous blaze crackled on the hearth, creating a warm, dry atmosphere that contrasted well with the piercing chill of the morning. The Cardinal's pet raven flapped to a high perch when Brother Joseph entered. "Sit ye down, man," implored The Cardinal. Brother Joseph found a seat on a long bench near the fire, covered with a well-worn leather.

"So tell me, Joseph, how are things with the hives? You are still charged with keeping of the bees?"

"Yes, Your Eminence. The brothers have an insatiable demand for honey, most frequently for making mead. The chandlers ask for more wax than I can supply. But the hives are healthy, and expanding."

"I'm so pleased to hear that, Joseph. It's time to give you a small break from your duties. In fact, I'll be sending you across the sea and around a corner of the cosmos. There's something we must do, and opportunity is ripe."

Brother Joseph struggled to maintain silent composure. Several monks previously disappeared from the monastery without explanation. Whispered rumors persisted that each departed on an important mission for The Cardinal.

The Cardinal looked sympathetically at Joseph. He smiled and said, "I understand your reluctance. Yes, it's unlikely that once you turn a corner in the cosmos you ever will find your way back again. Worry not, Joseph. Worry not. Those who have gone on before have prepared a home for you there. You will have new memories, a new face. You won't even remember our little village, or keeping bees in the monastery. But, you will remember your mission. There is a critical task for you to perform. When you arrive, your assignment will begin but your memories will give you the same tools you would have had if you had been preparing since childhood."

The Cardinal extended an empty hand toward the fire. His raven battered the air with his wings, energizing the flames with a satisfactory crackle.

"Which childhood, Eminence? My own childhood, or the one around the corner?"

"I can promise you, Joseph, you already don't remember your actual childhood. It was not of this life. Whichever childhood you imagine is of little consequence, but you will imagine a childhood associated with your new home. You will speak the language, read the signs. You will recognize and use the tools. You will be tuned to that portion in space, and have no conscious memory of this one."

"I am yours to command, Eminence."

"Of course you are."

"What must I do?"

Agnes entered the library with a silver tray. Steam poured from the spout of a cream colored pot. Two porcelain mugs, several small pastries, and a sharp knife flanked the teapot. She pulled a small table to a spot near the fire, placing it between The Cardinal and Brother Joseph. After resting the tray on the table, she nodded to Brother Joseph, bowed deeply to The Cardinal, and backed out of the room.

The Cardinal motioned to Brother Joseph in a manner that communicated, "Help yourself." Brother Joseph poured two cups of tea, offering the first to The Cardinal and placing the second next to his own seat on the leather bench. As Brother Joseph reached for the pastries, The Cardinal continued, "What must ye do? More than anything else, you need to make a delivery."

"What shall I deliver?"

"Some time ago, Brother, I created a splendid musical instrument. A horn, with floral etchings that spelled out a blessing in a tongue even more ancient than our own. I entrusted this horn to a priest, and sent him around a corner in the cosmos. His instructions were to sacrifice the instrument at a sun festival, on the morning when what we know to be the three moons of Eklon align with a star that is invisible to us- yet anchors the center of the universe. The priest failed."

Brother Joseph stirred the emerald green tea with a gleaming silver spoon. "In what fashion did the priest fail, Eminence?"

"He discovered the power of the horn, and began using it for his own amusement and ambition. The sacrifice was never made, and darkness assumed nearly an equal measure with light."

"So, you need the horn back?"

"There's no bringing it back, Brother Joseph. The sacrifice cannot be removed by force. It must be voluntarily surrendered by whomever holds it. I can send forth, around the cosmic corner, but I cannot recall. Were it otherwise, this would have been resolved long, long ago. What I need, what we all need, is to keep the horn moving."

"Will the renegade try to reclaim it?"

"He cannot. He chose darkness, and now serves darkness. He can never again handle the horn. But he can influence anyone who holds it to use it for his benefit."

"Do you know exactly where it is?"

"Yes. It's currently in a very dangerous place, involved with people who may not realize it- but they have handled it in previous turn. Soon, with the benefit of such experience, they may become so adept that they will be priests as well. If our own renegade cleric can control three priests, he will become a Cardinal as well."

"So, what do I deliver, and where?"

"Your assignment will be waiting for you. You will know it. In fact, you will be compelled to fulfill your mission. You will have no other choice."

The raven squawked and danced before the hearth, flapping its wings, temporarily disrupting the flow of smoke up the chimney. A cloud of smoke entered the chamber.

"When will I depart?"

"Drink your tea, Brother Joseph. You have already departed. In fact, you are already there. The tea will put you into a short sleep. When you awake, you will clearly see exactly where, when, and what you are. You will have no conscious memory of this place or position in the cosmos."

"What shall I do if I run into the renegade priest, your Eminence? And how will I recognize him?"

"You will indeed encounter the renegade priest. You will have to outwit him. And that won't be easily done. He's a trickster. Always was and always will be. Typically, he wears a red scarf- even when the weather is far too hot for it."

"Outwit him? Can that be done?"

"Yes. I know his limitations better than anyone else. He's my brother."
*****

Joseph Smith jerked awake at his desk. "Oh Christ! How long have I been sleeping? I hope nobody saw me dozing off. Full partner with the firm for barely a week, and asleep at the desk. Damn! I hope I didn't snore." He twisted his wrist for a better view of his virtually new Patek Philippe. His desperate need to know the time was a good excuse to admire the watch again. Only three minutes had elapsed since he last consulted the chronometer. He could not have been sleeping long. Not at all.

With his partnership, Joseph had been assigned a prestigious client. An eccentric and reclusive nonagenarian who spent most of his life locked up in a hotel room. Joseph's firm, Cardinal, Chandler and Meade, defended him, usually in absentia, in a variety of civil litigations. The general public believed the urban hermit's fortune was approximately one-hundred-billion dollars. Joseph had reason to suspect those estimates were low.

It was a rare thing for the old man to venture out, but this morning his secretary had called the law firm to announce he would be making a short visit. In particular, he wanted to meet his new barrister, Joseph Smith.

Joseph's legal assistant, Max Schlossen, stood in the doorway of the office. "Security phoned up, Mr. Smith. The limo just pulled into the garage. We might want to consider moving to the conference room. They could be up the elevator in the next few minutes."

Joseph said, "Go ahead, Max. I'll be right behind you." Whenever possible, Joseph preferred to rise from a chair without anyone watching. A prosthesis replaced that portion of his left leg he sacrificed for his country in some shit-hole village in Iraq. The mechanical limb normally worked well, but no amount of adjustment ever resolved a moment of awkward balance when first standing. Some of Smith's jealous peers suspected that those small stumbles made him, and by extension his clients, more sympathetic to judges and juries. One legal adversary had once gone as far as motioning during a case "opposing counsel should be ordered to use a wheelchair, as his disability is apparently distracting the court." Motion denied.

Part Three, Chapter Two

Ira Miller worked his contact list. Publicity exploded like a molten, eruptive child, birthed by an overdue volcano.

"This is KPLU, Tacoma Seattle, coming to you from the campus of Pacific Lutheran University in Tacoma. There's something brand new from Memphis Rail, expanded by a new group from Seattle called The Family Jones. The new release, 'Blues Breakout Redux' is a modern remix of an album recorded in 1959 by Judah Jones. Jones might have been the best horn player of his day, and we're already hearing that the sax man from The Family Jones, Wes Perkins, has somehow captured his style, phrasing, and tone. Here are a couple of cuts from 'Blues Breakout Redux'. We're all excited about this at the station, we hope you enjoy it as well. By the way, tickets are on sale now for next week's appearance at the Paramount. The first show is already sold out."

"This is the Bad Axe Blues show, with Phillip Ryan, WLEW, 102.1FM, broadcasting the best blues in northern Michigan. Memphis Rail just released a remake of an old album, check this out!"

"You're listening to WDCB Chicago, 90.9 FM. You ain't heard the blues 'til you heard the latest from Memphis Rail, give it a listen."

"Blues 'Til Noon, with Jerry B, on 103.9 FM, Quincy. You ain't gonna believe the latest from Memphis Rail, helped along with a brand new group called The Family Jones!"

"Listen up, blues fans. There's something entirely new, but also very old from Memphis Rail. They teamed up with some fresh trio out of Seattle, The Family Jones. You're a gonna' wanna hear this. We'll be playing tracks throughout the day, here on KPFK 90.7 FM Los Angeles, 98.7 FM Santa Barbara."

They all bought in. WRBV in Macon, KGSR in Austin, WBAI in New York City, KPOO in San Francisco and thirty or forty more; every metropolis, town, and village where Ira Miller could call in a favor. After so many decades in the business, Ira owed, and was likewise entitled to, a lot of favors.

The Rain Crow video of "Hound Dog" went viral, as predicted. Even people who weren't ordinarily fans of the blues were fascinated with Wesley the Dog's uncanny ability to keep rhythm with his tail. Viewers were hitting the web site almost 500 times a minute, or three-quarters of a million views per day. Local news shows in several cities closed with a few seconds of the "Hound Dog" file, following the canned strategy of wrapping up the dismal news of the day with something more lighthearted.

Traditional fans of Memphis Rail began buying "Blues Breakout Redux." More significantly, legions of younger people were texting, tweeting, posting, and chatting about the "new blues group" they just discovered. The first of hundreds of four and five star reviews read, "I remember my parents listening to blues. I wish they were still around to hear this. I'm not only in love with this album, I've fallen in love with the blues as well! Easily worth owning. Oh, and the guy on the horn, Wes Perkins? He plays a really wicked sax!"

Part Three, Chapter Three

Ira booked Rain Crow for six days, so Memphis Rail and The Family Jones gathered for daily rehearsals. Virtually everything they played together was flawless. Rebekah's voice grew stronger and more compelling. Wesley Perkins usually played with his eyes closed, eerily suggesting that he was mailing in his performance from another spiritual plane. Vanessa played a competent blues harp, with Wesley the Dog pressed up against her thigh for most of her performances.

Redd Wilmott was jealous of the dog's customary post.

Art Abbott and John Flood slowly warmed to the newcomers, but kept skepticism at ready hand for easy expression when required. The daily sales reports helped- a lot. The last text from Ira read, "Downloads now running about 20-times what they were prior to 'Blues Breakout Redux'. Trending up. Second show at Paramount selling fast. Congrats, Rail and Jones."

Mary Towne was proud of the virtually instant success of her protégés, but wary as well. While others might have speculated, among Memphis Rail she was the only one who knew the whole story of Judah Jones, Caroline, and their daughter and granddaughters. She was walking a high wire home. If she made if before the stars realigned, there was surely somebody to take her place. If the insanity and improbable circumstances of The Family Jones became widely known before those last few treacherous steps, she would crash to her doom. Somehow, Mary realized she had long ago pawned the net.

Ann Foster became increasingly bitter. While her phenomenal keyboard skills were unquestioned, she was suddenly upstaged on vocals by some unknown professional stripper. Rebekah was younger, with a sexier build and a better voice. Ann long made peace with being the second female vocalist in Memphis Rail, but wouldn't cede that position to Rebekah without a fight. "Hell," she thought, "I can't figure out why Mary ain't just as concerned. Rebekah ain't only a strong second, she's givin' Mary a run for lead- even if Mary don't realize it yet."

During a rehearsal, Ann was sure she noticed a chink in Rebekah's armor. Maybe only a woman would notice. In fact, maybe even Wesley hadn't noticed. It seemed apparent to Ann that Rebekah was more than moderately interested in Wesley Perkins. Rebekah was the last to watch whenever Wesley left the room, and the first to notice when he returned. Everyone respected Wesley's performance on the sax, but only Rebekah seemed exceptionally excited with almost every Perkins solo. "That," thought Ann, "may be my opportunity to take her down a peg. Wesley's as clueless as any other man. He don't do a thing for me, but he'd be easy pickin's if that seems like my best odds to show the bitch her place in the pecking order. "

On the third day of rehearsals, Mary Towne was approaching the rest room as Vanessa walked out.

"Hey, 'Nessa. Things are going pretty well in there."

"Yeah, Mary. I think we're soundin' pretty good."

"Yes, we are. But hey, I want to pass a couple of quick things along. Sort of just between us girls. Nobody else is around. This is as good a time as there is going to be."

Vanessa instinctively became slightly defensive. "And, what would those things be, between us girls?"

"The first is, be a little careful with Redd. He gets fixated pretty easily. You're the brand new bright and shiny toy right now, but just the same as he seems to fall for you hook, line, and sinker there will be somebody else along, soon enough, to take your place. It ain't Redd's fault. Like most men, he makes decisions with the head of his dick, instead of the head on his shoulders."

"Oh come on, Mary. Really, I appreciate your concern, but it isn't like I don't have a lot of experience with men. Hell, I was married once, for a while at least. I'm a big girl. I can take care of myself. I'm smart enough not to expect more from Redd than he's willing to provide. But he's a lot of fun for now. So what else is on your mind?"

"You're gonna think I'm some kind of doomsayer, Vanessa. But there's something you're going to find out soon enough, living the blues. You should probably prep Rebekah and Wes for this too. They listen to you."

"And that would be?"

"Most folks, when they first get involved with show business? Most folks dream of a day where every place they go, everybody they meet will already know their name and who they are."

"Well. Yeah," agreed Vanessa. "Isn't that more or less what being famous is about?"

"Maybe," conceded Mary, "but it doesn't seem to take long at all before that dream changes. You know what y'all gonna dream instead? That you can just go about your regular business and nobody will recognize you, know you, or even give a damn who you are. The day will come when you'd give your soul to be an unrecognizable nobody, only you ain't got your soul to give no more. You already gave it to be somebody. There ain't no second chances. You tell Rebekah and Wes, OK? Ain't none of you gonna listen, for sure, but at least I get this off my conscience."

Part Three, Chapter Four

The folding chair standing next to the vending machine was missing one of its rubber feet. It assumed a crooked posture as Wesley Perkins, enjoying a fifteen minute break from rehearsal, leaned back against the break room wall at Rain Crow studios. He took a few sips of Dyna Cola, and then tossed the paper cup and remaining contents into the trash. There was no doubt, he had lost his taste for the beverage.

Ruth's offer awaited a decision. Her proposed property division was surprisingly favorable. By any reasonable reckoning, she offered Wesley everything he owned when the marriage began as well as a generous cash settlement. Wesley's attorney characterized the proposed dissolution one of the more unusual arrangements ever encountered. Ruth offered Wesley two-million dollars to dissolve the marriage, with another million dollars placed in escrow.

The million dollars in escrow would be released to Wesley on Brianna's 18th birthday, providing Wesley avoided any contact with Ruth, Brianna, or with Walter Graham during the intervening three years and seven months. It was easy money, but also a clear signal that Ruth wasn't simply through with the marriage, she was anxious to completely discard Wesley Perkins. "She's taking off, once again, in search of that perfect life," mused Wesley. "She'll be lucky to find it, and obviously I'm not going to be part of it. Why would I want to be part of her life, or Brianna's, when I'm not welcome? It really makes sense to go along with the escrow deal."

John Flood wandered into the break room.

John dropped six quarters into the coin slot and selected an orange soda. "Hey, Wes."

"Hey, John."

"You gotta minute, man? I keep hearin' all these ridiculous damn stories about you not even really bein' a musician. If that's the straight dope, how you goin' about gettin' that kind of sound and performance out of that sax? And don't bullshit me. Somethin' don't seem close to right, and I'm pretty damn sure it ain't my mind."

"OK, between you and me it's exactly like I've told everybody all along."

"That you been a lifelong fan of Judah Jones and finally learned how to duplicate his licks?"

"Hell, no. That's just the press bullshit. I'd never heard of Judah Jones till last December, right after I bought the saxophone in a pawn shop."

"Yeah, that's what Mary keeps sayin', along with Vanessa and Rebekah too. That's gotta be total crap. Sorry, but that just don't wash. What the hell are you up to, man?"

"Shit, John. You're asking me to explain something that I don't even understand myself. I pick up the horn, and I play. What you hear is what you get."

"You play? Or are you maybe just holdin' the horn while it plays? Don't take this wrong, man, but it ain't natural for you to play like that. It ain't in the DNA, if you get my drift."

Wesley sighed. "I get the drift. You ever play sax at all?"

"Some. Back in high school. It was somethin' I tried out for a while before switchin' to the drums."

"Were you any good at it?"

"Fair. That's why I ain't buyin' this bullshit that you just picked up the horn and all of a sudden you could play. That don't happen in real life. There's gotta be somethin' special about the horn."

Wesley stood up and folded the chair against the wall. "C'mon then. Let's get back in the studio and I'll let you try the horn. If there's something special about the horn and it can just be picked up and played by somebody without any talent, you'll know right away, won't you?"

"You're on, man. Somethin' ain't half right. Let's see what's really goin' on here."

The saxophonist and the drummer walked into the studio. The silver saxophone, with intricate etchings and bright purple felt stops, was sitting on a chrome and plastic pyramidal stand. Wesley handed the horn to John Flood. Wesley the Dog, prone on the ground near Rebekah, lifted his head and growled.

"It's OK, boy," soothed Wesley.

John Flood fingered a few keys to adjust his grip and confirm finger position. "You won't be pissed if I make this sound as good as you do?"

"Not at all. Go for it, John."

The drummer nodded, winked, and put his lips around the mouthpiece. A ragged, uneven, and distressed sound- difficult to characterize as musical, shocked everyone in Rain Crow studios.

"What the hell was that?" scoffed Redd. "Leave the sax playin' to Wes. You make that horn sound like somebody is stranglin' a goat!"

"Bullshit!" protested John Flood. "He did something to screw up the horn when he handed it to me. OK, Wes. Don't touch nothin' to do with the reed, or anything. Just pick this up, the way you handed it to me, and let me hear you play somethin'"

"You sure?"

"Damn right I'm sure. And no funny business, man. I'm gonna be watchin' real carefully."

The saxophone changed hands. Wesley the Dog rose, walked across the studio, and sat down next to Wesley Perkins. Wesley put the saxophone to his lips and closed his eyes. He envisioned a warm yellow glow. He blew a round, resonant, electrified E-flat that seemed to shimmer like a crystal chime.

John Flood was in shock. "What the hell?"

Wesley opened his eyes, then winked and nodded. He proceeded to play a dozen bars of a rollicking, 6/8 march.

Wesley opened his eyes, shrugged, and smiled. "Was that OK?"

"Sounded like circus music," said Mary. "You have any idea what you just played?"

"None, really. It was just the first thing that came to mind."

John Flood was obviously affected by the performance. He stepped to his drum kit, kicked over the snare, and then spun around to address Wesley. "No fucking idea? That was my high school fight song. Note for god damn note. No way you could know that. Where the hell did that come from?"

Nobody knew exactly how to react. Mary broke the silence. "Y'all know better than to ask where any of this stuff we do ever comes from. Let's just be grateful that for now, at least, it's here."

Chuck Gould

Part Three, Chapter Five

"Praise Jesus! Brothers and Sisters, this here is Brother Abner Culliford. I'm a broadcastin' to you today from the Christian Community at West Moccasin Springs Louisiana. This here is the Hour of Holy Gospel Power, where we mourn the passing of the late, great Brother Benjamin. His name is surely added to the golden ribbon. The ribbon with the names of the saints, and all the supporters of our mission, that we will wave in celebration when Jesus returns to establish the Kingdom of God on Earth."

"We're a gonna share with you the testimony of Bridget Bishop, one of the younger sisters in our community. Say hello, to the faithful listeners, Bridget."

"Hello, I'm Bridget Bishop. My family and I moved here, not long ago, to set up a new life at West Moccasin Springs."

"Hallelujah, and amen, brothers and sisters!" interjected Abner Culliford. "The holy spirit is a walkin' among us, right now and right here, on the Hour of Holy Gospel Power! Sister Bridget, what can you share with our listeners about your new life in our community?"

"Brother Abner, before we came to West Moccasin Springs, Satan was a workin' on my heart. Not to mention some other parts of my body as well. I was a lustin' after men. Young men, old men, good lookin' men, ugly men. It didn't matter much. I was on the verge of becomin' a slave to temptation and sexuality. Praise Jesus! Here at the Christian Community, He showed me the light! I learned I don't need any more lovin' than I can get from Jesus, and that there ain't no other lovin' worth havin', no how."

"There you have it, brothers and sisters! Sister Bridget is still a teenager, and already she is on God's path. What more could you hope to offer your own sons and daughters? They's still a few home sites left, here at West Moccasin Springs. If you feel the Holy Spirit a callin', leave your worldly cares behind and come an join us. We have even specialists on staff to spare you the nuisance of disposin' of your worldly properties. Come to West Moccasin Springs! Bring your family. Be really and truly free in Jesus. Hallelujah, and amen!"

Part Three, Chapter Six

Ruth Perkins took one of the pens from the holder on her attorney's desk. It was of substantial diameter and felt unusually heavy in her grasp. An antique mechanical wall clock clicked the seconds away, as a tarnished brass pendulum swung its arc in a dark mahogany case. Ruth drew a deep breath, and began applying her signature to lines indicated by yellow plastic arrows, temporarily stickered to the page.

Attorney Alex Swanson remarked, "This is one of the fastest dissolutions of marriage and property agreements I've ever been involved with. Mr. Perkins didn't challenge a thing."

"I didn't expect him to. He's walking away with everything he had when we married, plus interest, plus that other million for agreeing never to contact me or Brianna before she turns eighteen. By the way, what do I do if he doesn't honor that?"

"You let me know, and I'll start the process to have the funds released from escrow and returned to you. Do you have any reason to suspect he's going to be hanging around in violation of the agreement?"

"No. As far as I know, he hasn't even been back on the island since we broke up. No phone calls. Nothing. The only thing we've heard from Wes is what he's told his attorney, and the attorney has told you."

Alex Swanson absent mindedly thumbed his appointment calendar. "I will have to admit that he took one of the strangest turns I've ever seen. He had a great career, and now he's playing saxophone with that rag tag group of musicians? I even saw him on the news the other night, in some video of a dog that can keep time with its tail."

"You, and I think everybody else on the island saw it. Oh God, but he just needs to disappear, and the quicker the better. As you know, and somehow nearly all my friends have found out, he's living with one of the women in that band. I know he's at least spent the night with another one. If he was going to start running around on me, he didn't have to go so far down in class."

Ruth finished her signatures. She pushed her chair back from the desk, while gathering her purse.

"How soon will this be absolutely final?"

"It will take a couple of days for the formal processing at the courthouse, and then it will be filed and done."

"Excellent. Brianna's father, Walter, and I are going to remarry. Our daughter has a few years left before she goes away to college. She deserves to grow up in a perfect family, with her real parents."

"I wish you every happiness, Ruth."

"Thanks, Alex."

Part Three, Chapter Seven

Joseph Smith cursed the jet lag. Smith slept intermittently on the leg from New York to Zurich, but his circadian sensibilities were almost always disrupted when flying into the sun. Even the plush accommodations of the eccentric old client's private jet didn't prevent the grogginess and disorientation. The plane taxied to a halt and a black Mercedes limousine began approaching the runway. Joseph checked the document again. There was a coarse, waxy feel about it; not like modern paper at all. Was it parchment? The highly processed skin of some animal? Strangest of all was the message, intricately drawn with several different colors of ink. There were no consecutive symbols that seemed to create words or letters, only an abstract design.

Joseph recalled the meeting with the old man, and how his client responded to Joseph's obvious surprise at the nature of the document sandwiched in a cordovan leather portfolio.

Zaccheus had smiled. "You don't get it, do you? Let me explain. When something must be communicated very exactly, it's more useful to draw a picture than to rely on language. When we put letters on a piece of paper, those letters represent sounds in speech. The sounds form words, the words from sentences, and the sentences convey thoughts. That's inexact. There's too much left to the imagination. Images are the oldest language. This drawing represents the idea itself, not something that needs to be assembled and interpreted in order to be understood."

Joseph's response was, "Forgive me, Sir, but I can't visualize exactly what idea your message is trying to convey."

The old man laughed so hard he began to cough. "Of course you can't. Only those who share the required consciousness will recognize the idea. Know this; there is as much information in that diagram as in that set of legal textbooks lining the wall of this conference room. You're new. My associates don't know you. A portion of the image is actually your credentials. Just take it to Switzerland. Deliver it as instructed. You will be given something in return. Bring it back to me. Do not fail me, Joseph. When you return, I will let you know about your next task."

The jet stopped on the runway and steps were lowered. Two burly men emerged from the formal black automobile and looked warily in every direction. Finally convinced that there were no random strangers or unpredicted conditions to deal with, one of the men motioned Joseph down the gangway and toward the opened back door of the car.

"Welcome to Switzerland, Mr. Smith. I believe you will find everything is prepared for you. You have the courier's portfolio and the document? Excellent."

"Thanks. Shouldn't I be checking in with Customs, or something?"

"No. You're not officially in Switzerland. Outside of the people you will meet this afternoon, nobody will know you are here or ever were here. We have only a short drive to make. Please, take a seat and make yourself comfortable. For security purposes, we will be blacking out all the rear windows. You cannot know our route, or the appearance of our destination from the street."

"That's awfully damn secretive. Is it really necessary?"

"We apologize, Mr. Smith. We're all working for the same employer. We can only assume you are being well paid for your cooperation. We will try to make your short time with us as pleasant as possible, given the circumstances and situation."

After the doors closed, opaque black panels emerged from the doors to cover the side windows. A similar partition folded down from the headliner and created a tight seal against the front of the passenger compartment. Another rose from the trunk to block out the back window. The air in the back seat turned a butterscotch yellow, inadequately illuminated by courtesy lamps with thick plastic shades reminiscent of 1930's streamlined styling.

One of the burly men sat with Joseph in the back seat. He reached for a cigarette, but did not insist on lighting it after Smith cleared his throat to indicate his displeasure. Cooped up in the semi-darkness, Joseph was aware of the sound of the tires on a high speed throughway. After a momentary stop, the ride and the sound suggested a slow drive along a rough brick road. There was a stretch of gravel, two or three sharp turns, and another section of brick road.

The Mercedes stopped. Joseph could hear the clanking and banging of a motorized garage door as it rose to permit the vehicle an entrance. An ear-splitting metallic racket became painfully loud as the door opened and the limousine pulled in off the street. A few seconds of additional motion were followed by a stop. The garage door clattered shut, and the black panels were retracted from the windows.

The limousine was parked in the middle of a vast warehouse. Perhaps forty charcoal black fire pits were evenly spaced on the same floor, each with an anvil and a bellows. Huge, shirtless men with shaved heads, wielding hammers the size of 5 gallon kegs, beat sparks from smoldering steel. Bored apprentices worked the bellows. The air smelled of burning rust. Joseph's eyes watered from of the fouled steam rising from the obsidian water vats- where the glowing orange blades were drenched for temper.

It was impossible to speak, or to hear. One of Joseph's escorts motioned him toward an aluminum stairway. The escorts followed Joseph. They climbed through the fiery cacophony, to reach a private office accessible only by a catwalk thirty feet above the lower level.

One of the escorts opened the door to a brightly lit, modern office. The moment the trio stepped through the door, there was no suggestion of the smithing and chaos through which they had passed.

A woman with a radiant complexion was seated behind a desk. Although she otherwise appeared young, she had silver hair. She wore a luminous pearl white gown. Her hands were perfect. "So, you're Joseph, then? Have you the document from Zaccheus?"

"I do," said Joseph, handing the portfolio to the woman.

"Excellent." The woman glanced briefly at the drawing. "I had no idea things were becoming so complex. If there were such a thing as time, Joseph, there would be none to waste."

She stood up and turned her back. Joseph was entranced by the graceful flow of her garment as it cascaded down her back, crested over her buttocks, and barely caressed the floor. The woman opened a portion of the rear wall, withdrawing a titanium case from a compartment that had not been detectable when closed. Even with her back turned, she sensed Josephs' gaze at the suggestion of her thighs below her gown.

"Don't be ridiculous, Mr. Smith. And don't get distracted. Take this back to Zaccheus. I will warn you; it's worth your life if you open this case or if you lose it. It's worth your soul if you steal it. Zaccheus will instruct you further. You must excuse me now. Napoleon is about to march on Moscow. We're the neutral party. We have a lot of pikes and bayonets to forge."

Joseph slept soundly between Zurich and LaGuardia. Zaccheus dispatched a Lincoln Town Car to meet the plane upon arrival. Moments after deplaning, Smith's cell phone rang. He recognized the number of his firm, Cardinal, Chandler, and Meade.

"Mr. Smith, this is Mr. Cardinal's secretary. Please come directly back to the office. Our client is eagerly waiting for your return."

"I can do that, but I haven't changed clothes or showered in almost 24 hours. I'm hardly presentable..."

"Never mind the formalities. Our client is really eager to receive delivery of the package are you are bringing back. Mr. Cardinal instructed me to convey the urgency of your immediate return. The driver has already been instructed to bring you to the office."

"OK, if that's where the driver is going that's where I'm going to be, isn't it?"

"Yes, Mr. Smith. By the way, you do have the titanium case?"

"Of course"

"And you have not opened it, correct?"

"Yes, of course. I was told it would be worth my life to open it. I'm maybe dying of curiosity, but that doesn't mean I'm all that eager to actually die."

Part Three, Chapter Eight

It was early in the morning of the equinox. Darkness and light achieved their semi-annual balance. The concert at the Paramount would be the business of the day, but for now Wesley dreamed.

He followed a trail in a treeless and arid wasteland. There were mountains of purple sand, hills of dull brown dust, cliffs of crimson peril, and canyons of invisible despair. High upon one of the hills was Wesley's destination, Camp Haven. Rebekah and Vanessa were expecting him. Wesley was late. He hurried through the unfamiliar landscape with only his trust in the path itself to sustain him.

He crested the top of an intervening hill and began a shallow descent. The left hand side of the trail was cut into a bank. Wesley was startled to see a stream of transparent, star-studded water emerge from the bank and flow along the edge of the pathway. The water increased in volume and flow at every step. Soon, Wesley and the growing stream were in a footrace- barreling downslope, around curves, and through a patchwork chessboard of searing white sunlight and inky shadows. The sound of the water increased from a love breath, to a whisper, to a murmur, to a crystalline trickle, to a symphony of gurgles, to a joyful gale. The faster the water flowed, the faster Wesley ran alongside in wild abandon, and the more the volume of water increased.

As Wesley ran along the howling, moaning, clattering hiss of the expanding river, he became gradually aware of a deeper roar that grew steadily louder. He leaped over a boulder and followed the stream around a sharp left turn. The deep roar surpassed the sound of the river and became intense. The water disappeared into a cloud of silver mist. Wesley abandoned the race, edging slowly forward into the fog. There was an unusual smell, of wet dog and gunpowder.

Wesley stopped at the edge of a great bowl. The stream continued over the lip, disappearing from sight along a compound curve. Wesley realized that he stopped just in time. A few more steps, and he would have fallen into the abyss. A freak breeze separated the silver mist for a moment.

Wesley realized that the great bowl was miles in diameter, and noted hundreds of other streams, similar to that which he had followed, cascading over the brink and disappearing into some invisible depth.

"It's an eye!" exclaimed Wesley. "It's filling up with tears." Wesley realized the scene must have been created by a sculptor with perfect hands. "Oh, hell. I'm off the trail. I better backtrack so I can meet Vanessa and Rebekah."

Despite his long and joyful romp along the descending stream, only a few dozen steps brought Wesley back to the point where he recognized the trail. An unfamiliar voice from a ledge, above him and to the right, called out, "Hey, man! Are you nuts? Get up here right away! They can't get to us here, but you're dead if you keep standing where you are!"

Wesley found a path, less than a shoe width in size. He edged carefully along the extended crack and joined some strangers on the ledge. "Who would get me if I didn't come up here?"

A bony finger extended from a ragged sleeve. "Look!"

On the trail below, Wesley observed a great beast. It was the size of a bison, but stood on two legs. Its eyes blazed like charcoal before a bellows, and a smoke that smelled like burning rust puffed from its nostrils with every breath. The monster bellowed with frustrated rage. His most terrifying and dominant attribute, his size, prevented him from walking the tiny ledge along the cliff and destroying the pilgrims there.

"Whoa, shit!" exclaimed Wesley. "Where did that come from?"

"It's been there all along," said the traveler. "It will remain until its ready to leave. We can't will it away."

"I guess I got distracted and lost the trail," said Wesley. "I was trying to get to Camp Haven."

"That happens a lot," replied the traveler. "You celebrated with the stream on the left, and failed to see the bridge on the right."

The traveler pointed down the trail, just beyond where the monster stood only moments before. A sturdy bridge, with intricate black iron railings and a smooth slate walkway, extended across a chasm. "Camp Haven is across the bridge. You were off the trail the moment you started following the water, Wesley."

"How do you know my name?"
"How do you not know mine?"
Wesley awoke.

Chuck Gould

Part Four, Chapter One

A rollicking tussle tumbled through the illusions of time and space. Forces of darkness and forces of light cast competing shadows of essential perceptions and envisioned realities, all while trying to unweave the tapestries of rivals. From the surface of the earth, the chaos appeared like a sliver comet on a still-expanding concept of cosmos. A comet ultimately destined to become a black star- a vacuum where a brand new home could be described as having neither form nor void.

Ira Miller flew back to Seattle for the concert at the Paramount. He ordered 500 copies of "Blues Breakout Redux," 200 copies of older CD's by Memphis Rail, and 200 tee shirts. Ira feared that he might have ordered too many shirts and CD's, even for a two-show event.

Little Willy and the Bluesbirds opened for Memphis Rail and the Family Jones. Backstage, Mary Towne worried that the applause for the Bluesbirds was tepid. Sure, two shows were sold out, (barely), but Mary wondered how many ticket holders were paying to see Wesley the Dog, the star of tail-tapping viral video? It's one thing to be upstaged by some unknown white guy with a literally unbelievable talent on the sax, another thing entirely to be nothing more than the rhythm section for a dog. "We're making some damn good music," fretted Mary. "The question is really whether there's a genuine market for it."

The Bluesbirds turned out a barely adequate performance. "Too much of that funny smoke in the bus," chuckled Redd Wilmott. "Works fine, if the audience is just as stoned. Obviously ain't the case here today. Good to know. I always said one of the best reasons to trot out a warm up act is to take the temperature of the crowd. So far, these here Seattle folk seem a little cold and distant."

"Shit, Redd, it's always that way in Seattle," insisted John Flood. "This place has to be the biggest hick town in America. People running around thinking they're oh-so-cool and hip- but they don't really connect with the blues. Never have."

Chuck Gould

"Maybe I should have worn my red plaid shirt. Lumber jack boots, and suspenders," joked Wesley Perkins, "being from Seattle, and all."

Art Abbott was not amused. "What the hell would you know about it anyway, Wes? You better not choke out there. This ain't some sports bar or Indian casino. We've got a crowd that ain't mainly here to drink, and probably for the most part ain't already drunk. We're countin' on you, and the rest of Family Jones, to keep up your end of the deal."

"No need for that, guys," counseled Mary Towne. "Just play like we've been doin' out at the Rain Crow and it's gonna turn out OK."

The Bluesbirds opening set wound up, to slightly more enthusiastic applause. Mary wondered if the audience clapped because they appreciated the music, or because Little Willy and the Bluesbirds were finally stumbling offstage. Nevertheless, Mary said, "Hey, good job!" as Little Willy passed down the backstage hall.

"Thanks, Mary. I hope we left a little ham on the bone for you guys."

"I'm sure we'll be alright, Willy. I'm sure we'll be fine."

The curtain closed. A crew of stage hands scrambled to swap out keyboards, foot pedals, and drums. They connected guitars to the sound system and propped them up on stands, in places marked by tape on stage. They reconfigured the microphones. A DJ from KPLU stepped in front of the curtain and pattered to the crowd. "So, let's have another hand for Little Willy and the Bluesbirds!"

There was a smattering of polite applause.

"Up next is our main attraction. Among blues fans, Memphis Rail needs no introduction." A voice near the back of the hall screamed, "Yeah!"

"But here today, for the first time ever, they are appearing in concert with a freshly expanded format. In fact, the group they have incorporated into their act is right here from Seattle, The Family Jones." Another voice, from the balcony shouted, "Family who?"

"We've been playing their latest album, along with all their old standards of course, on the radio. Our listening audience is pretty excited about what they have heard so far." A few whistles, shouts and some applause erupted from scattered places in the hall.

148

A voice from behind the curtain whispered, "Give us another 30. We need another 30."

"By the way, folks, if you like what you hear today I understand there are some CD's and other stuff available in the lobby. Just like public radio, don't be afraid to step up and support entertainment that you really enjoy. Now, without further ado, we are proud to present," (the DJ consulted a crib sheet), "Mary Towne, Redd Wilmott, Ann Foster, John Flood, and Art Abbott of Memphis Rail, along with Vanessa Hayes, Rebekah Brown, Wesley Perkins and Wesley the Dog of Family Jones. Let's give them a warm Seattle welcome!"

The set was designed to get the audience involved as early as possible. The curtain opened as the first notes of the bass line for "Hound Dog" (Big Mama Thornton style) rumbled into the gilded and ornate atmosphere of the Paramount. Mary Towne began the lyrics, accusing some un-named man of being "nothing but a hound dog." John Flood made astonishing use of his floor tom and high hat, while Art and Ann entwined their efforts to round out the rhythm section; Art with his Telecaster and Ann with her keyboard programmed to simulate a 1960's stage piano.

Rebekah stood quietly behind the mic, waiting for her backup vocals in the second verse. Wesley rocked from the waist up, awaiting his turn in the arrangement as well.

Behind her dark glasses, "blind" Vanessa Hayes stared out at the crowd and beat time with a tambourine. After just a few notes, the golden retriever at her side began tailing a precise time. The portion of the audience with seats high enough in the hall to see the floor of the stage went nuts as Wesley the Dog began performing with the band.

"Shit!" thought Mary. "Maybe they really are here just to see the dog!"

A few patrons in the front row, strategically comped by Ira Miller, raised hands overhead and began to clap along with the band. In moments, most of the audience were sucked in to become part of the performance.

Ann Foster wrinkled her nose as the second verse began and Rebekah filled in behind Mary Towne with backup vocals. "That should be me," brooded Ann. "It's always been me. That bitch has a lot of nerve."

The second verse came to an end, and Wesley lifted the antique, silver saxophone to his lips. It was time for his first solo of the show. He closed his eyes, imagined a yellow universe, and blew.

The effect was astonishing. Nearly everyone in the seats swore they heard the sax playing all around them, as if the sound came from a circle of instruments instead of a soloist on stage. There were those, in fact there were many, who imagined the sound was originating within their own minds, and only incidentally detectable by ear. Wesley poured out a torrent of intricate staccatos, inspired legatos, and welded it all together with a tone that suggested two fires having intercourse in a house of mirrors.

"What the fuck?" thought Redd Wilmott. "I'll be dammed if the guy doesn't just get better and better every time he plays!"

The audience was passively and politely appreciative during the warm up act, but just over a minute into the performance of Memphis Rail and the Family Jones they were out of their seats, jumping up and down, clapping and screaming. As many as could jam into the aisles were dancing. Ushers appeared to try to shepherd the dancers back to their seats, but gave up when it was obvious the crowd was out of control. Two of the ushers joined the dancers.

"Well, looks like they ain't here just to see the damn dog," mused Mary Towne.

Wesley finished his solo, to thundering applause, and a few of the dancers returned to their seats. The appearance of a few off duty cops, in uniform, finally restored the audience to tenuous order.

The set progressed. "Hound Dog" was followed by "Little Schoolgirl," with Redd Wilmott on lead vocals. Ann Foster backed up Mary Towne for vocals on "House of the Rising Sun." Vanessa evoked a rapid series of notes from the blues harp that suggested an insect in flight when Mary Towne performed "Queen Bee," and Rebekah surprised the gate with an inspired rendition of her recently composed "Bucket Blues."

As credibly and capably as everyone else performed, nothing could compare to the moments when Wesley blew his horn. The audience, on the verge of bedlam during other portions of the show, went completely berserk during each and every saxophone solo. After 55-minutes of performance, the ticketholders as well as the performers were drenched in sweat. Hands were clapped raw, feet were danced sore, and voices hoarse from cheering.

The set was scheduled to conclude with "St. James Infirmary," followed by "Summertime." Both were heavy with sax solos, and featured tracks on "Blues Breakout Redux." They relied on the same A-minor, D-minor, E-seventh progressions. The performance was to morph directly from "St. James Infirmary" into "Summertime" and create an extended final number prior to any encores.

Chuck Gould

Part Four, Chapter Two

Memphis Rail and the Family Jones were through two verses of "St James Infirmary." Rebekah became increasingly annoyed with some middle aged white woman in the second row. Every time Wesley played a sax solo, she would begin waving her arms and screaming his name. "How pathetic," scoffed Rebekah. "We shouldn't have to put up with that!" Wesley ignored his ecstatic fan. Rebekah wondered whether that was because he was just totally clueless about an absurdly horny woman coming on to him, but finally wrote it off to the fact that he played most of the set with his eyes shut tight. "Ironic," thought Rebekah. "Vanessa, who sees on several planes at once gets up here and pretends she is blind. Wesley makes no pretense of being blind- he just closes his eyes in order to see."

Whatever portions of the crowd were not already standing leapt to their feet as Wesley began slicing the air and weaving the shreds with his saxophone solo. The purple felt stops hammered against the mysteriously etched silver horn faster than the eye could follow- or with the languid unbroken perfection of evenly spaced ripples crawling across a slice of mercury. Almost everyone stood, noted Rebekah, except Wesley's ecstatic fan. She seemed to take advantage of the momentary distraction to wiggle rather suspiciously in her seat. In a manner of moments, she was leaning back, with her knees raised under her long skirt. "Oh, God no," worried Rebekah, "tell me she's not about to do what I think she's about to do."

She did it. The woman in the second row reached under the edge of her skirt, slipped her panties off around her shoes, and threw them onto the stage at Wesley's feet. Ann Foster watched with a cunning eye as Rebekah reacted to this spontaneous offering to Wesley, the god of the sax. Rebekah swooped up the panties in a smooth, sexy motion that could have been honed during her career as a pole dancer.

Rebekah upstaged Wesley for a moment as she held the panties near her nose, and made a disgusted face. She fingered her jewelry and then said in flawless French, "Comment répugnant! Vous avez besoin à la douche plus fréquemment, la dame!" She tossed the panties back to the second row. Everyone who could speak French laughed at what she said. Everyone else laughed at how she said it. Wesley was unaware of the entire incident, immersed in a yellow universe where sound, light, reality, and illusion coalesced. Ann Foster was even more certain that Rebekah had some not-very-suppressed feelings for Wesley; and again resolved to use that to future advantage.

The band played on.

In the lobby, Ira Miller fretted over the trade in CD's and tee shirts. Initially certain he had ordered too much merchandise delivered to the Paramount, it was now apparent that everything would be sold out no later than the first part of the second show. "I'll won't make that same mistake in 'Frisco, LA, Dallas, or New Orleans," vowed Ira.

"St. James Infirmary" gave way to "Summertime," with an extended Wesley Perkins solo creating the bridge. Mary Towne stepped to the mic, and crooned the opening line, "Summa time, and the livin' is easy." The audience realized they were being drawn from one old standard into another, with seamless grace and precision. The new tune was like an unexpected gift. The audience apparently sensed the performance had reached its zenith. From moment to moment and from his audio perspective in the lobby, Ira wasn't certain whether his musicians were barely drowning out the noise of the enthralled gate. It could have been true that the super-energized fans were a few decibels louder than the sound system.

"They're missing some damn good music, making all that noise," chuckled Ira.

A man dressed more formally than anyone else in the hall approached Ira. He walked as if slightly unbalanced. "I understand you're Mr. Miller?"

"That would be true." Ira refrained from extending his hand, but instead squinted at the stranger through a single eye and cocked his head in evaluation. "So, you have the advantage on me. You know my name, and I don't know yours. What do you hope I can do for you?"

Joseph Smith handed Ira a business card. "I'm Joseph Smith, with Cardinal. Chandler, and Mead."

Ira stuffed the business card into his shirt pocket. "I retain an attorney for my legal affairs. Should I be referring you to her? I'm sort of busy right now."

"Actually, Mr. Miller, I'm here to make a proposal on behalf of one of my clients. He's an eccentric collector of musical instruments, and he owns an interest in a very exclusive producer of premium woodwinds."

"What's this proposal then? Like I said, I'm pretty busy."

"We're prepared to offer an endorsement fee for your sax player, (Perkins, I think it is, right?) to play one of our instruments. In the same transaction, my client would add Perkins' current horn to his private collection. We believe there's some remote possibility the Perkins sax might have historical significance."

The conversation was interrupted as a petite young blond woman approached the table and fingered a pile of tee shirts. "Got anything in a small size? Maybe something with the dog on it?"

Ira smiled. "Nothing with the dog today. We should have some next week if you want to check our web site. But why not pick up a Memphis Rail shirt? They're selling out fast."

The young woman picked down through the pile. "I don't see anything here smaller than a medium. That would hang on me like a sack. Guess I'll check the web site. The music's pretty cool, especially that guy on the sax, but I really came to see the dog."

She walked away.

Ira retrieved the business card from his shirt pocket. "Ok, then, Mr. Smith. It sounds interesting, on the surface," said Ira. "But there's a couple of things you apparently don't know. I own the rights to the names Memphis Rail and Family Jones. I have the groups under contract, produce the shows, and deal with publishers and labels, but I don't own the individual instruments. Those belong to the performers. Much as I'd like a slice of that endorsement fee, I'm going to have to refer you to Wes Perkins directly."

"I see. I'll have to talk to him then."

"Don't be screwing around with this stuff until after the second show," insisted Ira. "I can't afford to have anybody messing with his mind. He's damn nearly carrying the whole gig. Frankly, I'd be nervous to see him switch horns. I get the sense he seems unusually dependent the sax he's got."

Joseph Smith looked around for a moment, as if uncertain how to proceed. "Well, then. It sounds like it's going to require the influence of somebody Mr. Perkins knows and trusts to bring him to a timely decision. That's going to be tough for me to accomplish, starting off as a complete stranger. But let me show you something."

Joseph Smith sat a titanium case on the edge of the CD sales table, opened the lid, and extracted a spectacularly polished horn. Ira couldn't avoid making a comparison with a gem stone. Brand new items, freshly made, often carry unusual smells. This horn was no exception, it had a not entirely unpleasant odor that somehow suggested "burning rust" to Ira.

"This is the prototype of an entirely new technology. My client's firm has fused the dust of industrial diamonds with molten glass. R&D spent several hundred thousand dollars perfecting the ultimate alloy for a woodwind. I can assure you, as well as Mr. Perkins, that whatever sounds he can produce from that old antique horn he plays will pale in comparison to what a man with his talent will realize from our Roten Schal 101."

"Hell, I don't know," said Ira. "I'm sure, that given a little time, I could persuade Wes to play your horn instead of what he's got now. But there's a risk it might screw up the music somehow. That's a huge risk. Definitely a financial risk, and things are just starting to gel. What kind of money would be involved? High six figures, maybe?"

"That would be more than we typically negotiate. My client is extremely keen to acquire that old sax for his collection and also begin promoting the Roten Schal line. I'm sure that money would become an issue at some point, but it would be tough to put a specific dollar amount to it."

Ira sensed one of those rare opportunities where desire, obsession, and financial ability merge. "Really? Then how about seven figures? You're going to need my help on this thing. Perkins doesn't know you from dirt. There's got to be enough money in it to make it worthwhile. Could it be worth seven figures?"

Joseph Smith appeared nervous and embarrassed. "Based on what you have told me, maybe I should risk trying to earn Mr. Perkins' trust myself."

"Oh, shit! You're telling me seven figures isn't out of the question!"

"No, Mr. Miller, I didn't make any such inference."

"You didn't have to. Let me ask you this, if I figure out how to acquire that old sax from Wes Perkins- if I'm the legitimate legal owner- would your client make the deal with me?"

"Getting the old horn is only part of the equation, Mr. Miller. It's equally important to promote Roten Schal. We need a performer of Mr. Perkins' caliber to play our instrument."

"So then let me ask you this," said Ira. "If I can get Wesley to give up his old horn, turn it over to your client, and begin playing a, a, what did you call it?"

"Roten Schal," Mr. Miller.

"Yeah, one of those. If I can get you that old horn, and get Wesley to play your sax in concert, would it be worth three-millon?"

"I think it might be worth two."

"Two and a half?"

"When could you deliver?"

Ira was pleased with himself, but consciously maintained a cool demeanor. "Something like this needs to be done very carefully. And, I'll need your diamond and glass horn to make it work."

"I can tell my client you needed 30 days. We'll need a surety deposit equal to the value of the Roten Schal before I can leave it with you. Just give me the name of your attorney and we'll get the process underway."

Part Four, Chapter Three

Following a coroner's inquest into the death of Brother Benjamin, a grand jury in Iberia Parish declined to press an indictment against Silas Bishop. Nearly everyone agreed that Silas responded in a manner that was easily understood, given the unique circumstances. Bishop's attorney discovered Benjamin's status as a registered sex offender in Alabama. The presence of the radio preacher's DNA proved that he penetrated the innocent young Bridget and had his way with her. As one of the jury members quipped, "Hell, if'n it had been me, and if that abeen my daughter, I'd have cut off his balls and made him eat them. Then I woulda gone ahead and smashed his skull."

The Community established by Brother Benjamin and Abner Culliford accepted carloads of pilgrims every day. A Community Finance Committee worked around the clock, liquidating stocks, bonds, real estate, and other worldly assets surrendered by Christian families journeying to West Moccasin Springs. To increase the number of residents, the original one-acre home sites were subdivided. One third interest in half-acre home sites sold for one hundred thousand dollars; or as close to that figure as an individual family could raise. The community kept title to two-thirds interest. Homes were framed in less than a day, and finished in less than two, by enormous crews consisting of other residents. Each believer who benefitted from a "house raising" was committed to help build a home for twelve subsequent arrivals. The community supplied all of the lumber, wiring, plumbing, fixtures, and finishing materials; and the community owned the finished structures. There were mandatory worship services twice a day, with community meals on Wednesday evenings and Sunday afternoons.

After the death of Brother Benjamin, the community was governed by a Board of Elders. Abner Culliford was the acknowledged head, with Silas Bishop and a few other male believers elected to the Board by residents at large. Thrice weekly meetings were semi-formal, with the Elders uniformly dressed in starched white shirts and red neckties.

Residents with a complaint of any sort could request a hearing by the Board, and were promised prayerful consideration and resolution.

Abner Culliford assumed his seat at the center of the table, with Silas Bishop to his immediate left. Mason Nordvahl, Secretary, read the minutes from the previous meeting. Following a subtle prompt from Silas Bishop, Abner Culliford called for a vote to approve the minutes. Approval was unanimous.

"So is there any old business?" asked Abner.

Near the far end of the table, Giles Corey raised his hand. Abner nodded in his direction.

"I need to report that I'm still trying to track down the owner of that small parcel and old shack on the NE border. It hasn't been all that easy."

Silas cocked his head inquisitively. "How tough can it be? What do the parish records show?"

"That's just it. There's something special about that property. It's exempt from assessment. Supposedly goes back to the Second World War or somethin'. I can't seem to get anybody all that interested in figurin' out who holds the deed."

Silas inquired, "So, how about anybody livin' on the place? Have you checked to see if they own it, or know who does?"

"Well that's the heck of it. People say they see a guy comin' and going, at least off and on, but there ain't no name on the mailbox and nobody's ever been around the dozen or so times so far I've gone knockin'."

Abner scratched the stubble of a freshly started beard. "Picking up that thar piece will give us another access to the road, and more frontage on the pond. Maybe can cut out another half dozen home sites for the Kingdom. Keep on after it, Giles. The Lord's work depends on it."

Silas whispered in Abner's ear.

"If'n there ain't no more old business, let's move on to new business," said Abner.

Virgil Brinkman had an appointment with the Elders. A welder by trade, Virgil was a man with gnarled hands and a short muscular frame. He wore his clean overalls and slopped some polish on his "good shoes." Virgil did not want to appear inferior before the Board. He had a serious matter to discuss. His wife followed him into the small boardroom, and quietly selected a chair in the second row. Virgil stood before the row of Elders on the far side of the table.

"Welcome, Brother Virgil and Sister Sarah!" greeted Abner Culliford. "What y'all got on your mind today?"

Virgil shuffled his feet, seemingly nervous to begin speaking. After the first few words, however, his voice began to sound authoritative.

"Well, brothers, I guess it's kind of like this. We'll be a-wantin' to get our money back. This ain't what we expected to find. Not at all. We're gonna pack up and go back to Colorado. That's where we belong. It was a mistake to come here."

Silas Bishop responded, "That's disappointing, Brother Virgil. How has the community failed to meet your expectations?"

"Well, we been a-thinkin this through a bit. We had our own ten acre spread back home. Nice place, too. Evergreen forests on the edges, a meadow in the middle, and a creek runnin' through it. We woulda never left, except we heard about this place on the radio and it seemed like God was a-callin' us to come and join with fellow believers and establish this here community."

Silas responded with sudden enthusiasm "And so He was, Brother Virgil. He called us all."

"Maybe not. Since we been here, we noticed a few things. For one, we're all havin' to work a lot of hours every day for no pay. Buildin' all these houses, especially."

Silas held his hands forward, palms up. "Don't you also have a house that others helped build, Brother Virgil? Isn't it satisfactory?"

"Well, yeah, I guess so. Heck, I guess it's a fine house, but it bothers us that we don't own the building. We only own one-third of the ground it sits on. We're not used to workin' this hard and turnin' up with nothin' to show for it. This just ain't for us. We were good Christians before we came here, we been good Christians while we been here, but now it's time to go back to Colorado. We can be just as good a Christians there as here."

161

"So, after such a short time with us you are willing to give up helping to establish the Kingdom of God in Louisiana? Have you thought this through carefully, Brother? Where will you go if you return to Colorado?"

"Why, back to our little ten acre spread, of course. We've got a double wide we live in there. Look, when we got here we gave up our retirement savings, eighty-five-thousand dollars, for the home site. We turned over a car that had to be worth twelve-thousand and I ain't seen it since. We'll call it square as far as the car goes if we can get about five grand so we can buy something to get home in. Get us back our money, pay us part of the price of our car, and we'll keep y'all in our prayers back home in Colorado."

The Board of Elders stared at one another in apparent confusion. One of the Board said, "Let's suspend things for just a second while I pull Brother Brinkman's folder out of the file drawer." The Elder shoved back from the table, and disappeared behind a screen. Sarah Brinkman looked very concerned, but said nothing. Virgil put his hands in his overall pockets, and shuffled his ridiculously reflective shoes. One of the longest minutes in Brinkman's life finally passed, and the Elder returned.

"Step up to the table, please, Brother Brinkman. Let's go through your file."

The Elder opened the folder and spread several documents on the table, side by side.

"So, what am I lookin' at exactly?" asked Virgil.

"This document on the left is our copy of the deed creating a life estate for you and Sarah on your one-third interest in your home site here."

"What's a life estate?"

"It means that you own your interest in your home site, as long as either you or Sarah are alive. After that it reverts back to the community. It means we can't just give you back your $85,000. That's gone. This is what you got for it."

"So, we should be able to sell out to maybe the next family that shows up, right? I reckon it ought to be extra desirable, with a house on it already."

"No, Virgil. You can't sell your one-third unless the community agrees to it. You can't just force the community to change partners in your home site."

Virgil flushed red with anger. Sarah began drawing heavy breaths, as if trying not to cry.

"We'll see about that!" sneered Virgil. "I've got a durn good attorney back in Colorado. I'm gonna give him a call as soon as we're back home. You ain't heard the last of this, not by a long, long ways!"

Silas Bishop closed his eyes and shook his head. "Brother Virgil, when you came to us we made some commitments. We agreed to take you in to be one of us in this community. To care for you, support you, and help promote your spiritual welfare. You made some commitments, too."

"Yeah, Brother Silas. I appreciate all that, but we just want to go back to our place in Colorado. It ain't workin' out. Sorry."

"Virgil," sighed Silas, "You ain't got no place in Colorado!" Silas reached into the open folder and pulled out another document. "See this? This is a quit claim deed. You signed it, handing over your acreage to the community trust."

Sarah gasped, and began weeping openly.

"Well, I thought you might try to pull that!" shouted Virgil. "I called our down the road neighbor this morning. He says the "for sale" sign is still up on the fence next to our driveway. Our ten acres ain't sold to anybody yet. Ain't no reason you can't just tear up that deed and forget the whole thing. Ain't that what Jesus would do?"

Abner Culliford spoke. "The ten acres is sold- by you to us. I'd have to check with Community Finance to see if they're actually tryin' to sell it again. Frankly, Virgil, I ain't got no idea what Jesus would do. We can see if there's anythin' in the Bible about lettin' you out of the deal once it's made, but I can't for the life of me begin to know where to look."

Sarah stood up and screamed at the Elders. "You bastards! You're just swindling everybody here! How in the name of God can you justify takin' everything we got, givin' us nothin' back, and then tellin' us we ain't got nowhere to go if we decide to leave!"

The Elders scowled. One said, "Virgil, you need to silence your woman. That ain't no way for her to talk to this Board. You might need to teach her to show a little bit of respect 'round here."

"You fuckers!" raged Virgil. "You ain't worth the respect due a busted slop jar!"

"Shut your face, Brinkman," hissed one of the Elders. "It may take us some time to decide on your situation. Maybe a hell of a long, long, time. Meanwhile, you better not be speadin' shit in the community. We don't need any trouble out there. You want any hope of ever getting' somethin' back? Keep your head down, keep your mouth shut, and keep buildin' houses for the new arrivals."

Sarah shrieked. "Lord Jesus, save us, please, please, save us!"

Another Elder, head of Acquisitions and Dispositions, chimed in. "Remember, we own the building you live in. You start making waves, and you won't live there no more. Greyhound runs down the highway three of four times a day. Give us any more crap, and about all you'll get out of us will be a couple of bus tickets to the first big town across the state line. Don't screw with us on this, Brinkman. Don't."

Part Four, Chapter Four

The first show ended triumphantly. After three encores, the house lights finally went up. The audience stood to applaud and cheer for another full minute. Memphis Rail and The Family Jones headed for the ready room, Vanessa careful not to remove her dark glasses before the curtain closed. Little Willy and the Bluebirds lined the backstage corridor, high-fiving the featured act as they passed.

"What the hell was that, Mary?" asked Little Willy. "I been playin' the blues for about 40 years, and I ain't never heard it any better. That's better than anything we played at the casinos. Way better. I ain't never heard the blues done anywhere close. What the fuck is going on? It's like you guys have reinvented the damn music. Keep that up, and hell, the rest of us just might as well go home."

Mary said nothing, but shrugged her shoulders with a raised eyebrow and an expression of confusion and concern. "What is happening?" thought Mary. "I never signed up for any of this. What started off as some sort of oddball joke with accidental musicians in spreadin' to everybody else. Wes and the sisters? They're changin' us more than we're changin' them. I don't know how I feel about that."

Ira Miller appeared backstage and nodded toward Little Willy and the Bluesbirds. "Good opener, guys. Second shows kicks off in an hour and a half. Stay in shape, Willy. We'll all get together for one big giant ass party after the second show."

"You got it, Ira. I'll do a little to stay in the groove- but that's all. Gonna need my best stuff just to be in the same building with Rail and Jones."

"Hey, there's a lot of money changing hands up in the lobby. I'm heading back up there. But before I do, I had to come back and say 'Mary, Redd, Ann, Art, John, Vanessa, Rebekah, and Wesley, that was one hell of a show!' That's as good as it ever gets. You guys surprise me every time you play. I think it can't possibly get any better, and somehow it does!"

Everyone was standing around a table. A caterer had delivered bottled water, two cases of beer, and several bottles of expensive wine. There was a basket of rolls, and hot trays of mashed potatoes, chicken, salmon, and ribs. Rebekah reached into a large purse, and produced a fifth of rye whisky. "Say, Wes, you haven't been doing this much lately, but after that show you maybe want a little taste?"

"No, thanks, 'Bekah. I've been playing dry for a while now. There was a time the whisky was probably important. Hell, it might even have been critical, but somehow I've sort of, I don't know, maybe outgrown it or something. I never used to drink much before last December. But, hey, maybe I will have a beer."

Vanessa stepped from the ready room back into the sterile brick hallway. She had a concerned look on her face as she motioned to Wesley and Rebekah to follow.

"You guys, I'm starting to be afraid we were just part of something that's even bigger than we first thought. Wes, somehow you picked up where Judah Jones left off and you're taking the whole thing forward. Rebekah, you're blowing past anything Grandma Caroline ever hoped to do. I've got a strange feeling that there's something really powerful, or at least really significant, going down. I don't know what it is."

"Well, whatever it is, I'm beginning to like it!" beamed Wesley.

"That could be a problem," cautioned Vanessa. "We need to guard against getting big heads over any of this. You know what door the enemy uses more than any other?"

"No, what?" asked Rebekah.

"Ego. People in love sometimes do crazy things without thinking them through. It's even more likely when you've fallen in love with yourself."

"I think we have a right to be proud of what we're doing," protested Wesley. "I'm pretty new to this whole blues thing, but there's so much energy pouring off that stage it's damn nearly visible."

"Trust me, Wes. It's absolutely visible," said Vanessa.

"Well," continued Wesley, "the audience is really into what we're doing, and I'm really getting into it too. We've worked hard for this, we're earning the props."

"Worked hard?" challenged Vanessa. "Worked hard? Damn it, Wes! You could hardly play a note four months ago. You didn't earn your chops with years of practice, you bought Judah Jones' old saxophone in a pawn shop! You want to see hard work, take a look at Little Willy and the Bluesbirds. If hard work meant you deserved applause, they would have brought down the house."

"Hey, let's not fight," said Rebekah. "We got into this thing because we realized we needed to stick together. Vanessa, remember what you said about three energies? Two energies just make a line, but a third can make shapes? Let's stay on the same page here. I'm a little freaked out if Vanessa thinks this thing is even bigger than we suspected going in, but Wes is right too. We're doing one hell of a job right now. We're putting the blues on overdrive. Well, maybe 'under drive' is a better word."

"Oh, Christ," stewed Vanessa. "Not you too. Don't start thinking we're a bunch of stars or something, guys. We're an accidental family. The only thing we can do and hope to come out the other side of this thing is stick together. Remember, there's at least as much a chance that the music is making us as there is that we're really making any music."

"OK, I get it," said Wes. "Stay away from the big head. This whole thing could just disappear, and hell, I guess it might. And Rebekah's right, we shouldn't be fighting. We need to take care of each other. Hey, you need to excuse me for a minute- time to take a pee."

"OK, we're going back inside for a snack and stuff," responded Vanessa. "Those biscuits were lookin' pretty tempting, and I could use a glass of red wine."

Wesley walked toward the shadowy end of the hallway. A yellow safety bulb illuminated the rest room door. He pushed his way past the self-closing hinges, detecting that curious odor of wet cement, ceramic tile, ancient urine, and exhausted beer. Large, globular, white ceramic lamp shades descended on thin place shafts from the fifteen-foot ceiling. Wesley noted the aura was reminiscent of the Gridiron Grill, where the Family Jones played with Little Willy and the Bluesbirds on Super Bowl Sunday.

There was nobody else in the backstage Men's room. Wesley stood at a urinal, flanked on either side by a partition. He unzipped his fly, and began. Wesley was startled by the voice he associated with Judah Jones: so startled that he pee'd on his shoes.

"Damn fine job this afta noon, brother. That old horn of our'n, it never sounded no better. 'Leastwise, not when I played it. And, I played it damn good."

Wesley jerked his head toward the sound of the voice. Across the partition to his immediate right, he saw the shoulders of an old overcoat, a neck and face wrapped in a red scarf, and a disheveled hat with rumpled crown and soiled brim.

"What the hell?" exclaimed Wesley. "How did you get in here? I didn't see you come in."

The red scarf answered, in a voice that Wesley recognized as Paul the pawnbroker. "I've been here all along, Wesley. I was here before you came in. I'll be here after you go. Where you go next, I'll be there before you get there- but even so, I'll still be here."

"How do you do that?" demanded Wesley.

"Do what?" responded the figure at the adjoining urinal. Wesley was amazed that the voice now sounded like his recently deceased ex-boss, Benniston.

"How do you speak with so many voices? How the blazes can you be everywhere at once?"

The red scarf answered in a male voice that Wesley remembered hearing on the radio. "Hallelujah, brothers and sisters! I'm a walkin' among you, right here, right now!"

"Cut the crap!" demanded Wesley. "Why can't I just get rid of you, for Christ's sake? I sure as hell never asked for you to start showing up in my life. You aren't welcome. In fact you're a real pain in the ass. So, for real now. How can you speak with so many voices, and how can you be everywhere at once?"

"You won't like the answer, Wes."

"Fuck that. I don't care if I like it or not. You gonna dog my ass around like this, I deserve to know."

"OK, Wes. I'll tell you. Not because you really deserve to know. You don't, of course. I'll tell you because it amuses me to do so. I'm your lesser nature, Wes. I'm part of you, and in return you and everybody else are part of me. Wherever you go, there I am."

"So, what in hell do you want with me? I never saw you until last December, and now you're turning up all over the place. Look! I can't even take a piss in peace."

A female voice spoke from the scarf- a voice that Wesley slowly recognized as Debbie Kessler, office manager at Banes, McLeod, and Benniston. "I don't want anything from you, Wesley. You have that backward. Really, it is you who wants, or at least expects, something from me."

Wesley shook, and flushed.

"What I'd like from you is to be left alone."

The red scarf spoke in Wesley's own voice. "No, it isn't. That's what you might think you want, but it isn't what you need. You and everybody else? You live for the spiritual struggle. The "jihad," if you will. In fact, it's your only cosmic purpose after you fulfill your animal duty and reproduce. It's all that keeps you alive. Your internal war makes you stronger, or weaker. A lot of that is up to you. When you finally give up, when you can't fight any more, you get to go home- for at least a while, anyway."

"Suppose I tell you to just get the hell out of my life!" insisted Wesley. "Suppose I tell you I don't like you screwing around with people I care about? Suppose I tell you I won't do whatever it is you or my goddam lesser nature compels me to do? What then?"

Red Scarf disappeared from sight, but the voice Wesley assumed was Judah Jones remained. "Makes no dif'rence, either way. They say you ain't gonna get rid of no demon if you don't know its name. And when you does learn the name, you gonna realize that just 'cuz of that name you can't get rid of it, not no how. You gonna do some things. Things you ain't gonna be proud of. Things you gonna wish someday you could take back. Ain't no takin' back. They's only the struggle. You got no hope to 'scape. Best you can count on? Maybe you got a kinda outside chance to someday be forgiven."

"What the hell does that mean?" demanded Wesley.

The invisible voice grew softer, as if the speaker were walking away. It was Benniston, again. "All in good time, Wesley. All in good time. Keep up the struggle. You're going to take a terrible, terrible beatin'. By the way, now's the time to protect Rebekah. Shield your spiritual sister, Wesley. Stay the course. The hour is almost at hand."

Chuck Gould

Part Four, Chapter Five

Wesley walked back down the brick hallway, past the ready room. There was a dirty window in the outside wall. The heavy iron bars beyond the window were a sharp edged rusted reality, separating the distorted glass from the hazy shapes and dripping greys of springtime in Seattle. He became absorbed in the monochrome kaleidoscope of boots, buses, and beards beyond. "How could I spend my whole life here, and now seem to be seeing it, really, really seeing it for the first time?" wondered Wesley.

Wesley lost track of minutes and moments. He was only subconsciously aware of Little Willy and the Bluesbirds taking the stage to open the second show. He was immobilized by, yet simultaneously absorbed into, the traffic and pedestrians passing through his life beyond the window. Ultimately, a voice called down the hallway, "Hey, Wes. There you are! Get in here man, we're setting up for the second show. Wesley returned down the hallway, and opened the door to the ready room.

He heard rhythm and music. The rest of the group was engaged in one of the ritual warm-ups. Everyone clapped along in a steady, measured time. Redd Wilmott sang a Blind Lemon Jefferson number, first recorded in the 1920's. He was supported by Vanessa, providing a blues harp fill.

"I'm broke and hungry, raggedy and dirty too..."

Vanessa huffed two conservative but rhythmic bars through the harp, deliberately restricting her range to the lower pitched reeds. She bent the draw notes cautiously, and artfully. Everyone else continued to clap time.

Redd continued, "I says that I'm broke and hungry, raggedy and dirty too..."

Vanessa closely simulated her previous two bar fill.

"If I cleans up, pretty mama..."

Vanessa started at a high note, and skidded toward the bottom of the harp for a single measure.

"Would you takes me home with you?"

Redd joined the rhythmic clap as the blues harp wailed the bronze edged tones of a weeping angel.

Art Abbott took a turn at the lyrics, "I believe my good gal musta found my black cat bone." The clapping and harp breaks continued through his verse.

The rotation passed to Rebekah. A startling realization caused Ann Foster to jerk her head and neck as she watched Rebekah finger the necklace a second before beginning to sing. "Of course!" concluded Ann. "I don't have to make a play for that goddam Wes Perkins, I can take this bitch down without picking up any baggage I ain't got no use for! I ain't never seen her sing without that jewelry! It's got to be her lucky mojo charm! Oh, shit! Why didn't I see this before?"

Rebekah sang, "I'm a motherless, fatherless, sisterless, brotherless too. I'm a motherless, fatherless, sisterless, brotherless, too. You know that's gotta be the reason that I'm a takin' this heah trip with you."

Ann Foster was up next. She didn't sing a verse, but hummed with her eyes closed above a curiously satisfied smile. Ann looked as if she had drifted far away, but her humming was vibrant and intense.

Vanessa continued filling with the harp.

John Flood never sang, but took his turn pounding out an intricate percussion solo on the tabletop.

Mary Towne was up next. "Babe if you don't want me, get go on you gotta tell me so. Babe if you don't want me, get go on you gotta tell me so. Gonna get up in the mornin', and find me someplace else to go."

Wesley retrieved his silver sax from its snakeskin case while Mary Towne finished her turn on vocals. When the rotation came around to him, he was ready. His first four bars of instrumental filled the room like electrified water, or an energized gas. It was everywhere, omnipresent, vibrating through every person's body like a bolt of lightning or a sexually climatic shiver. Vanessa's contribution transcended the physical parameters of the harp. The old blues veterans clapped along, each in awe of the sounds that erupted from the blues harp and the sax. It was beyond the limitations of music. It flirted with the definition of a soul.

Wesley and Vanessa did an extra twelve bars of instrumental, joined by John Flood's enhanced expression of percussion.

Redd Wilmott wound up the cycle in the same mode with which it began. "I'm broke and hungry, raggedy and dirty too. Oh, ho, ho, I'm broke and hungry, raggedy and dirty too." He smiled directly at Vanessa as he sang the final line, "If I cleans up, pretty mama, would you take me home with you?"

Silence prevailed for a moment, following the final measures. Art Abbott, never one to be overly gracious or optimistic finally spoke. "Shit. You know what this is like? It's like being part of a goddam plant. A plant that's getting into full bloom. Just when you thought that the fucking blossom was really fantastic, a whole 'nother leaf opens up. We just stood here and warmed up better than we been playin' for the last five or ten years."

John Flood added, "Yeah, if you had told me a couple of months ago that we could add three general newbies and a damn dog to the band and be better than anybody ever imagined, I would have said you were nuts. We thought we were good? Yeah, but we weren't shit. We just been waitin' for this, without knowin' it. Don't know where the hell this is going to take us. I guess I'm excited for the sound, but nervous about the situation."

None of the Memphis Rail or Family Jones were aware of the scene outside the Paramount. People from the first show had tweeted and texted their friends, and a number of ticketholders who had seen the first performance were determined to relive the experience in the second. Scalpers demanded eighty dollars, then one hundred, then one-hundred fifty, and finally two-hundred dollars for the sixty-dollar tickets to the second show. It was later rumored that the last person to buy two tickets to the second show paid sixteen-hundred for the pair. Extra off-duty cops were called in to help confine foot traffic to the sidewalks. White news vans, with antennas on retractable cranes, pulled into every available parking spot and loading zone. Little Willy and the Bluesbirds wailed on, as rows of cameras and spotlights staked out territory in the aisles along both sides of the stage.

After a workmanlike performance, Little Willy and the Bluesbirds left the stage. The curtain closed, and a platoon of black-clad stagehands set up for Memphis Rail and the Family Jones. The applause never really stopped during the intermission. A chant, suppressed but audible, began sweeping through the crowd. "Perkins, Perkins, Perkins, Perkins." It was the audience expressing a demand for the music of Judah Jones, and music now evolved beyond. Somewhere beyond the very last row, a disheveled figure in a red scarf (invisible to most) nodded its head and grinned an arcane and secret smile.

"Lots of folks comin' to church, and then goin' home for sure," cackled Red Scarf. "And soon."

Part Four, Chapter Six

The morning following the concert at the Paramount, Wesley Perkins and Rebekah took Wesley the Dog for a walk. The vehicle parked across the blacktop road was new to the neighborhood. Beyond a uniform coat of gritty road dust, a crushed front corner, and a missing hubcap, nothing exceptionally distinguished the oxidized white handyman's van. Wesley and Rebekah didn't pay any special attention to the truck. They could not have known that a woman and two men, concealed behind front seats, watched them exit the driveway and stroll toward the end of the block.

"Oh!" sneered Ann Foster, from an uncomfortable perch on a wheel well. "They're holding hands! That will open a few eyeballs in this neighborhood. It's not exactly the 'hood hereabouts, if you get my drift."

One of two men hiding with Ann replied. "Nobody gives a rat's ass about that anymore. But, hey, lucky for you. We've only been out here about two hours, so you're only out $400 for hanging around and waiting. One time, we sat on a place for three days before it opened up. We didn't charge for the times we split to get a sandwich and crap like that, but our client was still out almost $7,000 before we even got in the house."

The second man confirmed, "Yeah, you got off light. Sometimes we make more hanging around waiting than we do bringing stuff out for people. OK, they're around the corner. Remind us one last time what is it that you want us to bring out for you?"

"A white gold necklace, with a black ornament on it. There shouldn't be more than one. There's a ridiculously large stone in the ornament. It looks like a diamond, but trust me- it's a cheap chunk of glass. There should be two matching earrings, each with a fake diamond as well."

"So," mused the second man, "You say these big stones are fake, so why are you going to all this trouble to have us bring them out for you? What if you're lying? $4,000 seems like way too much to pay us for picking up some worthless garbage. Maybe we might just toss your ass out, and keep the stones. If you're willing to pay $4,000, they must be worth a lot more."

"Bull-shit! Cousin Theo said you guys were professional. We agreed on a price. I've kept up my end, I've got your money right here!" Ann reached into her purse. Her companions became wide-eyed when she withdrew a pistol instead of a wad of cash. "Oh, silly me! I grabbed the wrong item. So, if you guys want to get cute, here's a change of plans. Jeremy, you're going in by yourself. I'll keep your friend here, Morgan, company while you're gone. When you bring out the goods, I really do have your money in the bag."

"Fuck that!" cried Morgan. "So he can grab the loot, split, and I'll get wasted? No fucking way."

"Way!" insisted Ann. "But I'm going to be paying you more than the stuff is worth. I don't go around ripping people off. It isn't about the phony jewelry, I've got a personal score to settle with this bitch. We don't have time for stories now. Jeremy, get your ass in there and find the jewelry. Let's hope the fucking dog is constipated this morning."

"You want me to mess up the place while I'm in there? Should I grab anything else while I'm at it?"

"No, I don't want it to look like a random rip off. It needs to look like somebody was targeting that costume jewelry. Somebody is. That will mess with her mind in a major way. If you're not out by the time they get back with that dog, we're driving off and you're on your own from there."

Jeremy opened the backdoor far enough to conclude that nobody seemed to be watching the van. He stepped down to the street, closed the door slowly and deliberately, and walked confidently up the drive to Wesley and Rebekah's house. He took special pains to act as though he had legitimate business there, or was perhaps calling on an old friend.

Jeremy eyed the keyway in the front door lock. "Kwikset, those are easy," he thought. He selected a bump key from an assortment on a ring, inserted the key into the cylinder and wacked the head of the key with the end of a screwdriver. On the third attempt, the tumblers bounced into place. The knob turned, and Jeremy disappeared into the house.

On the far side of the block, Wesley and Rebekah paused while Wesley the Dog lifted his leg against a phone pole.

Wesley confided to Rebekah, "I feel sort of weird about something Ira said to me after the show last night. Now that we're coming down off the high of playing the way we did, it's starting to bother me a little more."

Rebekah turned sideways to look at Wesley. "So? What did he say?"

"He says there's somebody making saxophones that wants me to play one of their horns."

"Oh, Christ, Wesley. That's out of the question, isn't it? All this stuff is going down because you started playin' Granddaddy's old sax. None of this is really about getting rich or being famous, although I have to admit that wouldn't be so bad. There just isn't any real meaning to it, at all, if you're not playin' Judah's sax."

"Well, that's pretty much what I thought."

"So you told him 'no', right?"

"I should have. I told him 'maybe'. But there's a little more to it."

"What do you mean by that?"

"There's a little money in it. $25,000 according to Ira."

"So, what- you just have to play the sax one time and have your picture taken or something?

"No, worse than that. I'd have to agree to play their horn from here on out. They want me to give up the one I play now, sort of as a guarantee."

"God, no, Wes! Don't do that. Who knows if you can even play some other sax? We can talk to Vanessa about this and find out what she thinks she can see, but there would just be somethin' way wrong about selling Judah's horn for $25,000."

"Yeah, I'm sure I agree with you. That's probably why I feel weird about Ira even saying anything. He doesn't understand that we got into this thing for a reason. He's never run into Red Scarf. He doesn't know about us probably being in danger if we don't stick together. He thinks it's just about money. Next time I talk to him, I'll tell him 'no'."

Chuck Gould

Jeremy was a professional. Although he worked quickly and deliberately, he was unable to find the jewelry on Rebekah's dressing table, or in any of the half dozen other likely places where experience taught him women commonly hide heirlooms and baubles. "Oh, shit!" brooded Jeremy, "what if she wore them to walk her damn dog? Maybe I have to go through her underwear. No time for that. It would be a lot easier if I just trashed the place, but who knows what that goof ball bitch cousin of Theo's would do if I did? No way she should have brought a gun. We're gonna ream Theo's ass about that, for sure."

Jeremy was almost ready to give up, when he spotted a saxophone case leaned up against an end table in the living room. The case looked very old, and was of an unusual material. Could it be snakeskin? On a hunch, Jeremy opened the case and found an ornate silver saxophone, with stops of deep purple felt. Behind a hinged partition, he found a mouthpiece with a twisted neck as well as the jewelry that Ann Foster described. Jeremy started for the door with the case in hand, but then remembered Ann's irrational behavior. She was still holding Morgan at gunpoint. It might be best not to toss any variables into the mix. Besides, the old horn might be just some piece of junk. Jeremy opened the lid, scooped out the jewelry, and sat the case down again exactly where he thought it was when found it. He opened the front door a crack. The van was still parked across the street, and at least from the vantage point of the front door the dog walkers were nowhere to be seen.

Jeremy walked calmly down the driveway, as confidently and openly as if he had just conducted legitimate business or visited a friend.

He opened the driver's door to the van and climbed in.

"Did you get it? Did you get it?"

"Hell yes I got it." Jeremy held the jewelry out for Ann's inspection. "So, here's where we trade $4,000 for bringing out the stuff and $400 you owe us for waiting for what you see in my hand. But, none of that happens until you take the gun down off my bro."

"Not so fast," said Ann. "The gun stays out until we're back downtown and you drop me off at the hotel. But, Morgan, reach into my handbag there. You'll find fifty hundred-dollar bills. Put six back in." Morgan did as instructed. "OK, now, put the money in one hand, and reach up to Jeremy with the other. Really slowly. Jeremy, you put the jewelry in Morgan's hand, and take the money out of the other. That's right. Now, Jeremy, you put the jewelry into my purse and let's get out of here."

Jeremy turned the key to start the van. "You know where that crazy gal keeps her jewelry? In some old saxophone case!"

Ann immediately realized she had lost an opportunity. She thought "The saxophone! Oh, hell yes!"

"Wait a minute! How long would it take you to get back in there and bring out the sax, too?"

"What, for the same fee? No fuckin' way."

"What if I add another $2,000? I can get the money when we get back to the hotel."

Jeremy was inexplicably fascinated by the sax in the snakeskin case. He could get back in and out in a matter of a minute or two. Once they got back downtown with Theo's crazy cousin, he could decide whether to let her take the sax for another $2,000 or maybe just keep it for himself.

"Ok, I'll go!" said Jeremy.

"Horseshit!" protested Morgan. "Tell you what, I'll run in and bring out the sax, you sit here with the fuckin' gun pointed at ya for a turn!"

"I know right where it is," argued Jeremy.

"So, tell me."

"Screw that, I'm going in!" said Jeremy.

"No, screw the whole thing," said Ann. "Look yonder, they're coming around the corner. We're too damn late for the horn. Maybe next time. Let's get out of here."

Wesley, Rebekah, and Wesley the Dog were about one-hundred feet from their driveway when the van parked across the street started its motor and drove slowly past. There wasn't anybody in the passenger seat, and the driver acknowledged the dog walkers with a friendly nod.

Wesley the Dog lunged toward the van, leaping frantically into the air at the end of his leash. He snarled, and barked, and growled. Wesley Perkins reached for the dog's collar to achieve a tighter grip on the animal.

Surprised and concerned, Rebekah asked "What do you s'pose that's all about?"

"I don't know, but I don't like it. He never acts like that unless Red Scarf is lurking around someplace."

Rebekah, Wesley, and Wesley the Dog crunched up the gravel driveway to their house. The dog darted back and forth on his leash, sniffing the ground and snarling. When they reached the bottom of the steps Wesley suggested, "You wait here a minute. I'll leave the dog with you for protection. I'll take a quick look inside and make sure everything seems to be OK. If you hear me start to yell, send the dog in, run down the street a ways and then call 911"

"Well, alright I guess," said Rebekah. "But I'm not gonna sit out here by myself very long. Take your look and come right back." She grabbed Wesley's shirt collar, pulled his face close to hers and kissed him on the cheek. "There. You left the dog out here to protect me, so that's a little something to protect you, too."

"Got it. If there's somebody messing around in there, I'll clobber them with that kiss."

"Don't make fun of it, Wesley. There ain't anything much stronger than the reason I kissed you."

"Stay, boy!" commanded Wesley, as he handed the dog leash to Vanessa.

Wesley climbed the steps and checked the door. It was unlocked.

"Didn't we remember to lock the door when we left?" he asked.

"Hell yes we did! At least I sure thought we did. I don't know, maybe we didn't. Be really careful, Wes. Maybe we should just call the cops. This doesn't seem right, not at all."

"I'd feel like an idiot calling the cops if we just forgot to lock the door. I'm going to take a look, and I'll be careful."

Wesley stepped into the living room. Everything appeared normal. He even opened the door to the coat closet- and found nothing but coats. The kitchen and bath were as expected. Wesley checked the bedrooms, including the large bedroom he now shared with Rebekah. The door to the mother-in-law apartment downstairs was bolted from the upstairs side- nobody could have entered that area without leaving the bolt unsecured.

Wesley returned to the front door, and found Rebekah and Wesley the Dog climbing the steps. "It was too weird standing out there," complained Rebekah. "I was getting worried about you. The dog is still all tensed up. I had to come in and see what was happening. You might have needed some help or something. I guess I don't mind so good."

"I think we must have forgot to lock the door, that's all," reassured Wesley. "I don't know what set the dog off, but there's no sign of anything wrong here. There's no red scarf laying around. None of the usual signs that he's been up to any mischief."

Vanessa stepped into the entry way and began to remark, "Well, that's good. Sometimes I think our cup of freakiness just runneth over, if you..." Rebekah froze in mid speech. Every muscle of her body tensed. She forced her arm to raise and her hand to point as she screamed, "Wesley, goddam it! Look! Somebody moved the sax case!"

"Huh?"

"It was leanin' against the other end of the sofa when we left. I absolutely know it was! Somebody was in here, fucking around with things! Quick, take a look! Make sure everything is still OK."

Wesley tossed the snakeskin case on the couch, flipped the latches, and raised the top to view the contents. There was Judah's saxophone, nestled into its felt cradle. "Looks like the horn's here," said Wesley, as he opened the hinged compartment in the case. "Oh, no!" cried Wesley. "Oh, fuck! Oh, dear! Rebekah, they got the jewelry!"

Rebekah rushed over to confirm Wesley's report. There was nothing except the mouthpiece in the internal compartment of the case. She fell prostate on the living room carpet and began to wail. Wesley lay down beside her, and gathered her into his arms. She turned to bury her face in his chest, and for a full two minutes sobbed without restraint.

"'Bekah, please, don't cry. This is terrible, but let's get busy and call the cops. Must have been somebody in that same white van that upset the dog. Maybe the guy's got a record. Maybe they can find some fingerprints or something."

Rebekah wailed for another several seconds and then inhaled a few wet sounding lungsful of breath. She pushed herself gently from Wesley's embrace. "Yeah, call the cops. And call Vanessa. We need to tell her what happened. Maybe she needs to know right away. Things are fucked up now, for sure."

"Maybe not," conjectured Wesley. "Let's get the cops and Vanessa on the phone. Maybe we can just carry on, without the jewelry."

"It ain't just jewelry, Wes. It was Grandma Caroline's jewelry, come my way by some once-in-a-lifetime coincidence- just like you wound up with Granddaddy's old horn. Hell, if it was just jewelry, it would be something to buy and sell. It's a lot more than that to me. It's a lot more than that to you and me. It's more than that to you, and me, and Vanessa, and the Family Jones. Honestly, Wes, I feel like I've been raped or something. Sort of like somebody just ripped a hole in my soul and tossed it into a ditch to bleed."

Wesley was dialing the phone. He paused to remark, "I love you Rebekah. Nothing bad is going to happen to you. Not if I can help it. Nothing bad can happen to you unless something even worse happens to me first. I won't let it."

"I love you too, Wes. But I don't know if either of us have the power to stop a damn thing anymore. What if this wrecks you and me, just as we're getting started? What if it screws up the act? We're scheduled to fly to 'Frisco tomorrow with Memphis Rail. Better get Vanessa over here right away. She'll maybe have a good idea what to do now."

"That's who I just dialed, the cops can wait for a minute."

Part Four, Chapter Seven

Bridget Bishop toyed with the fraying fringes of a dream as sat on at rock, at the edge of a deep, black pool. She was almost certain she was awake, or almost awake for certain, when the encounter began. A muscular young man, naked above the waist except for a crimson neckerchief, approached. In his hands he held two red gemstones, each the size of a small melon. The stones were joined at a single point. The man snapped the conjoined stones apart, in a motion that seemed inexplicably effortless.

"Here, Bridget Bishop," said the man as he extended one of the stones in his left hand. "This one is yours."

Bridget collected the stone, and was surprised to find it virtually weightless. She was enthralled. "I've never seen anything as beautiful!"

The young man's voice changed. "Look ye, Bridget, deep into the bowels of the stone. Tell me what thou see'st there."

Bridget's gaze penetrated the transparent gem. An image began to form.

"I see my reflection!"

The young man's voice changed again, adopting a coarse female quality. "No shit. Of course you do. You all do."

"Do I get to keep this?" demanded Bridget. "It's the most perfect thing imaginable."

The young man's voice assumed the tone of a field hand. "You gots to keep it. You cain't give it back. It's yor'n. But don't mess it up none. Right now, that's jest about as good as it's ever gonna get. See that there spot where the two stones come apart?"

Bridget turned the gem to concentrate on the point where her stone had been connected to the other. "Yeah, I see it. It's the only point on the surface that isn't perfect and smooth."

A voice reminiscent of a scolding school teacher warned. "Don't even consider trying to polish it! You can't make the stone any smoother than it is. The more you try to polish, the rougher the surface will become. Before long, the gem will become cloudy and fogged. Eventually, you will no longer see yourself in the stone. Most people can't resist, and they wreck it trying to perfect it."

"I do sort of wish it was completely perfect," sighed Bridget.

The young man's original voice returned. "Of course you do, child."

"So, why were there two? I'm very happy with my gift, but why is it one of a pair?"

"Look carefully at your image in the stone, Bridget. What do you see? Do you not see two eyes, two ears, two nostrils? Do you not have two arms, two hands, two breasts, two ovaries, two legs, and two feet? Every holy thing created has an identical twin."

"I'm not sure I believe that," countered Bridget. "It doesn't say that in the Bible."

"Noah gathered the animals two-by-two."

"Yeah, but Jesus had twelve disciples. God made the universe in seven days."

"But what if God made two universes?"

"Are you trying to trick me or something?" protested Bridget. "It would be the nature of an actual universe that everything would have to be included. You know, sort of universally."

"You are very wise for one so young, but in spite of that there may remain some hope for your redemption. So, Bridget- have you ever wondered whether Jesus could have had a twin?"

Bridget involuntarily jerked with alarm, but did not wake up from her dream. "You bastard! You could go straight to hell just for saying something like that!"

The figure in the neckerchief twirled the second ball on the tip of his index finger. "I know a wee bit about hell. There are plenty of ways to get in, and only one way to get out. But wondering whether Jesus could have had a twin won't get you in. Out neither."

"You're never going to convince me that's true. Never!"

A soft, motherly voice replied, "Then there's no harm done. Remember, I'm not saying that Jesus had a twin. In fact, I would actually recommend that you disbelieve the entire notion. Take it from me, it's probably not true. Not at all. Just try to forget I ever brought it up."

Bridget sputtered, "But just even considering the question makes me feel dirty. Are you trying to wreck my faith?"

"No, precious Bridget. Not at all. Your faith should not be structured on a list of things you deem true or untrue. Nor can you precisely determine the nature of good and evil. Making those lists and assumptions? That's belief, not faith. Faith is what transcends the details. Faith defies the details. Faith is what constitutes your stone. Don't scuff it up too much by trying to polish out the rough spots."

Bridget squinted and nodded. "I guess maybe I see, maybe."

"Excellent, child. I must go now."

"Wait! Can you tell me for sure that Jesus didn't have a twin?"

The young man spoke as the field hand. "Lord's mercy, gal. You ever listen a tall? I jest now got done tellin' you not to believe it. Put it outta your mind, child."

"When will I see you again? And what happens to the other half of the stone?"

The young man began fading from view, disappearing from sight without moving away. "You will see me everywhere and nowhere. All the time, and never again. As for the other half of the stone, it will be waiting for you at home."

Bridget sat up in her bed. The sheets were wet with sweat. She must have been dreaming, after all.

***

In opposite corners of the living room, Virgil and Sarah Brinkman sat stoically and silently. Although it was well after dark, neither of them bothered to turn on the lights. The pain was easier to bear in the darkness, and easier yet when separated by silence. A lifetime of hopes, ambitions, and accomplishments was bleeding away. The retired couple were held like prisoners, fates decided in an unconsidered exuberance of faith. The earthly version of the Kingdom of God in Louisiana was less than anticipated, or promised.

The Brinkman's had few friends in the community, so they were surprised by a knock on the front door. Virgil bellowed out, "Who's there?!" in a voice that dramatically ruptured the stillness.

"It's me, Brother Virgil, Abner Culliford."

Virgil sprang from his chair and started toward the front door. Sarah interceded, putting a hand on his forearm. "Now, Virgil, be civil," she warned.

Even with Sarah's wise caution, Virgil opened the door with a violent jerk.

"So, Abner, what's up? You come to tell us you're throwing us out entirely?"

"I don't blame you none for feelin' that way," replied Abner Culliford. "Don't blame you none at all. Would it be OK if I came in to talk with you a minute?"

Virgil retorted." Come in? You may own the walls and floors of this house, but it's still our home and I'll be..."

Sarah interrupted. "Of course, Brother Abner. Please, come in."

"Thanks very much," said Abner as he stepped through the door. "I really want this to be just between us. I've been in prayer about your situation. There's only one right thing to do, and I'm here to do it."

Virgil began to respond, "Somehow, I seriously doubt that you would..."

Sarah interrupted. "Shh, Virgil. Listen to what Brother Abner has to say. What can it hurt?"

"Thank you, Sarah," said Abner. "I do appreciate your hospitality. Would it be OK if we turn on some lights? I've got some stuff I need to show you."

Virgil flipped the wall switch. Maybe it was the quick transition for darkness to artificial light, but something about Abner Culliford's appearance was different. There was a healthy glow to his countenance. For a second, Virgil wondered if Abner had been drinking.

"OK, I'll be brief," said Abner. "I got to thinking about what you said at the meeting. Wondering what Jesus would do. I gave you some smart answer about looking in the Bible to see, but in my heart I already knew what the answer was."

Virgil's voice conveyed a shade of hopeful optimism. "So, has something changed?"

Abner opened a manila envelope and withdrew a folded document. "Yeah. To start with, here's a reconveyance of your property in Colorado. You guys are free to go home, and what's more you've still got a home to go to."

"Praise Jesus!" shrieked Sarah.

"Well thanks for that, Abner. But you said 'to start off with'. Are there some sort of strings attached here? What are we expected to be givin' up to get our acreage back?"

"Well, your car of course is sold," said Abner. "We sent it to auction right after you arrived. So that's gone, but here's the keys to my Cadillac, and I've signed off the title. Just consider it yours."

"That's a better car than we brought," said Virgil. "What about our cash? I gotta suppose that's gone?"

"Nope. The Elders may run the community, but they don't run me. I can override them when I choose to. So, I choose to. There's a check for everything you paid."

"Glory be!" cried Sarah.

Virgil looked skeptically at the check. "Abner, this looks like it's drawn on your personal account. No offense, but we turned our money over to the community. If we're really gonna get paid back, shouldn't the money be comin' from them?"

"Don't worry, Virgil, that check is good for every last dime you see written on it."

Virgil replied, "We'll be leavin' in the morning, Abner. I gotta say, you really surprised me. I didn't expect this, not at all."

"Fantastic, Brother Brinkman. I was about to mention that it would be best if you cleared out in the morning. We've got a new family arriving tomorrow. She's just about ready to give birth. Twins, even, and they can't wait for a house. Since you want to go in the morning, anyway, that works out all the way around. See how the Lord works, Brother and Sister Brinkman? When you were ready to go home, the Lord sent us somebody to take your place."

Part Four, Chapter Eight

Joseph Smith sat on the broken back seat, trying to avoid snagging his clothes on any of the springs sticking through the torn upholstery. The seat belt was missing. The scraps of carpet covering portions of the floor smelled like urine, and alcohol, and vomit. He stared warily through a smudged and greasy window. Block by block, the neighborhood progressed from questionable, to battered, to obviously dangerous.

The first two drivers he hailed near the hotel refused to drive to Ira Miller's office. The second one said, "Sorry, buddy, but we don't service that neighborhood. You take a cab in there, and you're lucky to come back with all your windows unbusted. You don't dare stop for a light. Some jackass will blow out a window with a tire iron, stick a gun in your face and demand all the cash. Cops won't even go in there unless somebody gets shot, and sometimes only if somebody gets killed. I wouldn't go in there if I was you. Frankly, you ain't exactly gonna blend in with the neighborhood, if you get my drift."

"It can't be that bad," countered Joseph. "I have a business appointment with a music industry executive who keeps his office at this address."

"Trust me, if he's doin' business on that street it's because he's got some kind of truce goin' with the locals. No way am I gonna go in there. I wouldn't take that fare for a $300 tip. But maybe Achmed will. I just saw his car a block or two away. For ten bucks, I'll give him a call and see if he'll come by for you. But remember, it might turn out to be your ass if you go in there. Don't say I didn't try to warn you."

Joseph produced at ten dollar bill, and the cabbie dialed his cell phone. There was an immediate answer, and the cabbie greeted the party on the other end of the line. There followed a thirty second conversation, in a language that Joseph almost instinctively identified as Farsi. Before the cabbie finished the call, the shambling wreck of a Chrysler mini-van rounded the corner and stopped immediately in front of the cab.

The back door was held shut with duct tape. At least one wheel cover was missing. There was barely enough of the original structure left undented for an observer to guess what shape an automotive designer must have had in mind when the vehicle was new. Sections of the body were repainted, and a blue side door scabbed onto a body that must been crimson when it rolled out the factory door.

"That's Achmed. He'll get you in for fifty bucks. You pay that when he gets you there. He'll wait for you for another fifty, and you pay that when he's done waitin'. He'll get you back out again for another seventy-five. He goes in there all the time and nobody hassles him. He blends in. That old wreck of his ain't a big yellow target sayin' "rob my ass.""

"I appreciate that, but isn't a hundred-seventy-five bucks a lot for a cab ride across town?"

"Where you're goin' ain't across town, it's the goddam wild, Wild West. I can tell you I wouldn't do it for that. Or for twice that. As far as Achmed goes, I don't think he speaks any English. At least none he admits to. But be nice to him. If he thinks you're going to screw him out of his money, he's just as likely to steal whatever you've got and dump you on the toughest block he can find. Not sayin' he's goin' to, and he probably won't, but don't get cute with him and just pay the fare without bitchin'. A twenty-five buck tip, to round it up to an even $200, wouldn't be unreasonable, either."

When the minivan pulled up to a stop, behind the abandoned auto dealership and next door to the fenced-off car wash, Achmed's command of English proved better than his cabbie friend suggested.

"OK, here is address you told me. Looks like nobody on street, so right now is OK to go to front door. I'll watch door for when you come out. Don't walk out to car until I give you thumbs up sign, OK? Now I need first hundred dollars."

"A hundred? Your friend said fifty to bring me in and fifty to wait. I thought I was going to pay the second fifty after you got done waiting?"

"You think maybe my father raised some sort of fool? Maybe I wait while you go in there, maybe your drug deal go bad, and maybe you don't come out again."

"This isn't a drug deal!" protested Joseph.

"Don't matter. If you're doin' business around this neighborhood people get killed over stuff less than nothing. Fifty bucks for waitin', it is in advance. And you only get 30-minutes. You think you gonna need more, you pay for more and you pay now. Otherwise, thirty-one minutes from now, I'm out of here and you can find your own way back. Sir."

Joseph handed Achmed two fifty-dollar bills. "Thirty minutes should be fine. I just have to drop off a package and collect a final signature. If I need more time, I'll come pay for more before I run out of the thirty minutes."

Achmed collected the money with a grin, and shoved it into his shirt pocket.

As he walked briskly to Ira Miller's office door, Joseph Smith wondered, "Why do I think I just should have got the title to that entire junk heap for a hundred bucks? What would Zaccheus think if he knew I was riding in that piece of shit to close a multi-million dollar deal?"

Chuck Gould

Part Four, Chapter Nine

Vanessa put down the phone, collected her car keys, and dashed out the door. Wesley had said, "You better come out here right away. It looks like somebody broke in and stole Rebekah's jewelry while we were out walking the dog. I'm about to call the cops, but we better get our heads together on this thing as soon as we can. There's no telling what this might do to the Family Jones."

"Oh, God no! How's 'Bekah dealin' with this? Can I talk to her?"

"She's a wreck. She's in the bedroom now. I got her to stop cryin' for a minute, but she's started up again. Can you come out, please? If I can get her to stop sobbing so she can talk, I'll get her on the phone to you."

"OK, Wes. I'm on my way. If I can get her on the phone, I might swing through downtown and pick up Mary at the hotel. She pretty much knows what's going on with the sax, the jewelry, and all that stuff. She coached us along this far. Maybe she can help us figure out what to do."

"Whatever you think best, Vanessa. Let's get the three of us together. You know, two points make a line but three points make..."

"Yeah, yeah. Wes, I'll be there as soon as I can. See what the cops can do. They will probably be useless. I don't give a damn about the jewelry, except that I care what losin' it might do to Rebekah."

Chuck Gould

Part Four, Chapter Ten

It was well before dawn. Virgil and Sarah Brinkman were mindful not to wake the neighbors. They whispered softly as they loaded their few remaining personal possessions and four suitcases into the Cadillac gifted them by Abner Culliford.

"Sort of feels like we're stealin' somethin', don't it?" suggested Virgil

"I wouldn't know how it feels to steal, dear. I never stole anything, ever."

"You know I cain't say the same, Sarah."

"Yeah, but that was long ago. Before you came to Jesus. Praise the Lord, you got to start over with a clean slate."

Virgil closed the trunk as gently, and quietly as possible. "You're right. But I'm just glad to get this chance to be startin' over again back home in Colorado. You got everything in the car that's goin' in the back seat?"

"Yeah, and I walked through the house to double check. Funny, ain't it? We're pretty well cleared out, but it doesn't seem vacant. Why would that be?"

"Don't know, don't care. I guess it always seemed vacant to me."

"I guess."

Virgil squeezed Sarah's hand. "I got that deed in my pocket, the check in my wallet, and the title in the glove box. Time to go."

The Brinkman's took their places in the front seat, closing the doors deliberately but without any resounding slam. Virgil felt a twinge of concern as he started the engine. "Sure hope we don't wake anybody up, it's pretty early still."

"Look around, Virgil, there ain't another soul stirrin' about right now."

"You're right."

The Cadillac headlights traced the pavement through the community, heading toward the freedom of the highway. As they approached the main gate, the Brinkman's were surprised to see the silhouette of a woman in a long skirt, standing in the middle of the lane. They slowed, and soon recognized the woman as Bridget Bishop. Virgil brought the Cadillac to a stop and rolled down his window.

"Is that you, Bridget?"

"Of course, Mr. Brinkman. I found out you were leavin' this morning, and I couldn't let you go without a goodbye. In fact, I was pretty much up all night bakin' for you. I'm glad I got out here early enough to catch you before you got away."

Bridget extended a wicker basket, with a looped handle. She pulled back a red cloth to reveal two loaves of bread within- fresh, steaming, and smelling of sweet yeast. "You're surely going to be hungry, somewhere along the road. When you do, have some bread. Don't be forgettin' about us here. I promise not to forget about you two, and I will keep you in my prayers."

Virgil hesitated, "I dunno, Bridget. I mean you really shouldn't have gone to all the..."

"Of course we'll take the bread! Thank you Bridget, that's so very kind of you. I got a sack right here we can put it in."

"Oh, no need to bother Mrs. Brinkman. Go ahead and keep the basket, along with the scarf to help keep the loaves warm."

"That's more than generous, Bridget" said Sarah as Virgil reached out to accept the basket.

"Not at all, Mrs. Brinkman. Not at all. Travel safely now, you hear?"

The Brinkman's drove out of through the gate, and turned west on the highway. At last, they were going home.

"Sarah, don't it strike you just slightly weird that young girl was waitin' for us in the driveway, with a hot basked of fresh bread, at ten minutes after 5 in the mornin'?"

"No more weird than anything else that went on in that place. We're lucky to be escapin'."

"Yeah, I reckon you're right. Hey, if you'll spell me a few hours so I can nap this afternoon, we can jest drive straight on through. Won't need to stop for anything except gas, piss stops, and maybe a quick dinner."

"I wish you wouldn't use that word!"

"What word? 'Dinner'?"

Part Four, Chapter Eleven

Vanessa collected Mary Towne from her downtown hotel and merged back into the slow crawl on I-5 North. Neither woman spoke for several minutes. The mood of concern for Rebekah threatened to morph into a feeling of despair for the future of Family Jones, and, to a lesser degree, Memphis Rail. Near the zenith of the Ship Canal Bridge, Mary broke the silence.

"You gotta know, Vanessa, that it ain't the damn jewelry. Not really. Not at all. If it was the jewelry, you could hand that stuff off to anybody and they could put it on and sing. 'Bekah's doin' it on her own. She's gotta be."

"But she never sang before," countered Vanessa. "At least she never had a voice for it. I've known her for her whole life. Until all this stuff starting coming down, and until she wore that jewelry, she had no range at all- and no sense of tune or timing."

"Well, consider that maybe she just didn't know she had the talent. Christ, Vanessa, it's all about confidence in show business. If you think you can do it, you're gonna try. If you try, you got a chance to succeed. Sometimes the only thing that separates somebody at the top of the game from a million unknown amateurs is the courage to step out and try."

"What if she's lost that, Mary? What if she's lost her courage?"

"Damn, girl. I ain't really got an answer for you. I mean, normally I understand the business. I can mostly tell who's gonna make it big, who's gonna almost get by, and who's better off just sittin' down, shuttin' up, and lettin' somebody else come forward. This whole freaked out situation with Wes Perkins blowing the shine right off that horn of his, Rebekah singin' like nobody's business, and you just almost instantly pickin' up the mean-ass harp is beyond me. I wouldn't believe any of it if I hadn't been coachin' you through it in the beginnin'. I keep thinkin' I should have let the whole thing be from the get-go; but I'm way ready to go home and I get this feelin' you guys are a key."

The Honda Accord picked up speed after gaining the Lake City exit. Mary and Vanessa fell back into a silence interrupted only by the wipers swishing a fresh rain torrent from the windshield.

Inside Wesley and Rebekah's house, Wesley the Dog stood up on alert at the sound of Vanessa's car on the gravel driveway. Wesley Perkins opened the front door as soon as Mary and Vanessa reached the porch, so there was no need to knock. Rebekah was on the couch, huddled in a blanket, with her feet tucked back under her legs. She looked exhausted, and her eyes were red from weeping. As soon as Vanessa was through the doorway, Rebekah jumped up and ran to embrace her sister.

"Oh, God, 'Nessa. What am I going to do? Grandma's jewelry is gone. Some bastard broke in and stole it! Nothin' else is gone, not even Judah's saxophone. I'm probably screwed without that, aren't I? How can we carry on?"

Vanessa was amazed at her own response. Her voice was authoritative, yet compassionate, and exuded a surprising air of confidence. "Listen, 'Bekah, we're all gonna be alright."

"How do you know that?"

"Well, I don't exactly, but I do know what to do. What would Mama do when things got all mixed up and crazy? Remember?"

"Hell yes, of course I remember, she'd take a minute and listen for an answer. But, Mama ain't here, so what are we gonna do?"

"We're gonna do what Mama would have done. We can even do it just like Mama used to do it. Wes, pull all the curtains shut, tight as you can. Grab that candle there on the bookcase and bring it over to the breakfast table. Light the candle, turn out the lights, and everybody pull up a chair."

When the room was dark, the candle lit, and chairs occupied around the table, Vanessa said. "OK, everybody hold hands. There's four of us, and sometimes that's better than three."

"What do you mean there's four of us?" asked Mary, cautiously refusing to extend her hands. "I'm mostly just along for the ride here."

"Two points can only make a line," sniffed Rebekah.

"Yeah, and three points can make a shape," added Wesley. "But, Vanessa, what happens when we add a fourth point? I mean, we've sort of had the dog, but I don't know if he really counts."

"The fourth dimension is the illusion of time," said Vanessa.

"What do you mean, callin' time an illusion?" asked Mary.

"I mean just that. At the farthest off edge of the expanding universe, it's still the first micro-second of Creation. So what time is it, really? Maybe it depends on where you are? Sort of like a time zone; Pacific Time instead of Central Time, maybe."

"How is any of this gonna help me?" sobbed Rebekah. "I'm so screwed here!"

Wesley the Dog put his forepaws in Vanessa's lap. "Down, boy. There's a good dog." Wesley the Dog assumed a position prone on the floor, with both paws over his snout.

"Everybody, now. Close your eyes. You will know when to open them."

The circle of four went silent. Small sounds, like the tapping of raindrops on the window and a soft tick of the kitchen clock with each stroke of the pendulum, marked the illusory passage of time. After a silent minute, Wesley was sure he felt a tingle of energy enter his left hand, which was locked in a grip with Mary Towne's. He was equally sure he felt the energy pass through his body, and exit from his right hand into Vanessa. A split second later, the flow of energy reversed and was stronger. Within moments, current was flowing rapidly around the circle. It seemed to reach a crescendo, and Wesley opened his eyes. The three women were blinking, as if they were seeing the world anew. The candle seemed brighter than when it was originally lighted.

Rebekah looked slightly hopeful. "I felt somethin'" she said. "It was sort of nice, but a little weird too."

Her sister, nodded, smiled, and confirmed, "I think we all felt it. Anyway, I heard the answer we were listenin' for."

"This is too strange by half," protested Mary Towne.

Vanessa shook her head. "No, not. Here's what we need to do. Remember the warm-up thing we did before the second show at the Paramount? Not the first show, the second?"

"Of course, it's one of the exercises we been usin' for years." agreed Mary.

"Good, I'll clap out the rhythm to get us started. Mary, you go first. Then I'll do a verse. Wes, we're gonna need you to come in on the chorus the second time around."

"Hell, Vanessa, you know I don't sing. Let me get the horn."

"No, there ain't no time for that. We only get a very short window here. Trust me, try to sing. You don't have to be very good at it- you just need to use your own voice. After that, Rebekah, you wait till I give you the nod and then you come in. Not before, OK?"

"Yeah, but I probably won't sound much better than Wes..."

"Hush!" admonished Vanessa, extending her raised palm toward Rebekah. "Just hush. Let's get started. Oh, but first, Wes- give Rebekah a kiss."

"What, just like that? I mean..."

"I said, kiss her, damn it!"

Wesley and Rebekah kissed. Vanessa clapped out eight slow, precise beats and then Mary Towne began to sing, "Wade in the water. Wade in the water, children. Wade in the water, God's been a workin' in the water."

Mary joined Vanessa in clapping out the rhythm, and Vanessa, with a voice no better than average and seldom heard in song, picked up the lyrics. "See those folks all dressed in white,"

Mary Towne filled in "Wade in the water,"

"Must be the chilin' of the Israelite,"

Mary concluded the line, "God's been a workin' in the water."

Vanessa nodded at Wesley, and he tacked a ragged, monotonic harmony onto Mary and Vanessa's duet, "Wade in the water. Wade in the water, children. Wade in the water, God's been a working in the water!"

Vanessa nodded at Rebekah to indicate her turn. Her voice was astonishingly changed. Wesley the Dog bolted up onto his forelegs, with his ears erect. Rebekah's voice was not only everything it had been before, it now seemed mysteriously perfected. Every surface in the humble house she shared with Wesley resonated like a perfectly tuned, electrified sounding board. The tones were rich, and pure. Wesley felt the energetic tingle he had experienced in the circle of four, even though nobody was holding hands.

Rebekah sang, "See the group all dressed in red,"

Everyone responded with increased volume "Wade in the water."

Rebekah resumed with a rapid fire two beat arpeggio that spanned almost two octaves, ("Holy shit!" thought Mary) then syncopated her lyrics to catch the measure, "They must be the chilin' that ol' Moses led."

"God's been a working in the water!"

All four vigorously clapped tempo and sang together, "Wade in the water. Water in the water, children. Wade in the water. God's been a working in the water!" Wesley the Dog thumped his tail.

Mary Towne and the Family Jones continued the old spiritual for several minutes. Mary and Rebekah alternated the verses, with Vanessa and Wesley chiming in on the chorus. Each time Rebekah did a verse, Mary would make a grand, theatrical gesture toward her. Both vocalists were nodding and grinning; eyes alight with joy.

They finished the warm-up, and all fell laughing and weeping into the arms of the others.

"Don't know what just happened," said Mary Towne. "I seen a lot in my time, but I sure ain't seen it all- and I ain't never, ever, in all my days seen or heard anything like that!"

"But Vanessa," insisted Rebekah, "how did you know that would work? That I could still sing, even without Grandma Caroline's jewelry?"

"I guess I didn't know, for sure. But while we were listenin' for the answer, I was sure I heard Mama singin' that very same old song, and maybe somebody singin' with her. Somebody better. Somebody that sounded like Grandma, at least to me."

"So I'm not gonna need the jewelry anymore?"

"No, you're not. It's like this. Judah gave that jewelry to Caroline the night he asked her to marry him. The night he got lynched. Well, Judah's love for her was wrapped up in the necklace and stuff. That's how you found your voice to start with. You were expressin' the love between Judah and Caroline. But since then, that love has sort of leaked out of the jewelry. It doesn't really live there anymore. It's alive, right here, right now."

Wesley blushed.

Vanessa continued, "And you and Wesley both know damn well what I mean. You got your own love, now, Rebekah, and you got a better voice because it is your love. It's the same kind of love that Judah had for Caroline, but now it's alive again and it's growin. You guys, take care of that thing you found. It's really special."

203

'Hey, if it's all the same to everybody else," sighed Mary, "we've got a plane to catch to 'Frisco in the mornin'. I still got some packin' up to do."

"Yeah, sure," said Rebekah in a voice that exuded confidence. "I know it's going to be OK. I can't thank you guys enough for coming out here. Vanessa, Mary, and Wes, you too, you're all the greatest."

Vanessa and Mary climbed into the Honda Accord. Mary noted that Vanessa looked extremely tired. As they reversed down the driveway, Vanessa said, "I don't know for sure how that happened, but I'm glad it did. Really wore me out, though."

Mary reached out and touched Vanessa's wrist, and when Vanessa looked her way Mary smiled a broad, and peaceful smile. Mary began to sing in a very whispery voice. She chose another spiritual. "My home's across the river. The great an tumblin' ri-i-ver. My home's yonder 'cross the river, and when the horn blows I'll be gone."

Part Five, Chapter One

A buzzer sounded in Ira Miller's office. He glanced at a security monitor and noticed Joseph Smith fidgeting nervously at the outer door.

"Hello, Mr. Smith! Wait for the click."

Ira shut down the alarm system. He watched with the monitor with amusement, as Joseph Smith yanked the door open the first split second permitted by the electronic lock. Ira stepped to the outer office to greet his visitor and usher him into his private chambers.

"Did you have a good trip?" asked Ira.

"Well the flight was fine, and hotel was great, but I have to say the ride over here was a real eye-opener. How can you do business in this part of town, anyway?"

Ira was aware that many of his visitors experienced substantial cultural shock when entering the neighborhood, but he always enjoyed toying with their discomfort.

Ira motioned Joseph Smith to a chair in front of his desk. "What's so wrong with this part of town, Mr. Smith?"

"Really? On the way over here we drove for at least a mile and a half down a main street where nearly every business was boarded up. The plywood over every window was covered with graffiti. Every little corner grocery and discount liquor store has an armed guard posted on the sidewalk. Judging by the piles of trash bags at the curb, it must have been weeks since they sent a garbage truck around here. People were trying to keep warm next to a pile of burning tires in the middle of the damn street! We had to back up and go around the block. I couldn't even get a regular cabbie to drive me in here!"

"No cabbie?" interjected Ira. "Let me guess, you stayed at the Four Seasons and tried to hail a cab out front, right?"

"Yeah, how did you know?"

"And," continued Ira, "One or two drivers told you they won't bring their cars into this neighborhood because it was too unsafe?"

"Exactly! I wound up taking some trashed out gypsy rig..."

Ira interrupted, "With a guy named Achmed, who's charging you about triple fare, and who drove all around Robin Hood's Barn to show off some of the scariest possible sights in the district!" Ira couldn't suppress his urge to laugh, and he began chuckling so hard that his sides were shaking.

Exasperated, Joseph asked "So how do you know about my ride?"

"It's a very old scam. Trust me, you're not the first. I'm very sorry you fell for that. I suppose I should have warned you. The driver who put you in touch with Achmed is splitting the take at the same time he's running other fares. People can drive pretty decent cars around here without any problems, at least in the daylight. There are a few cabs that won't service this neighborhood, but most will."

Joseph threw up his hands. "I feel like an idiot..."

"No need. How would you know? Is Achmed still using that banged up old minivan with the trashed interior? Shame on him if he is. He's got a late model Acura at home in his garage. His real name is Jack Wilson. When he's not scamming tourists, he teaches at the community college. English Lit, if I recall correctly."

"Oh, shit. He really suckered me."

"Hey, when we finish up here, you tell Jack, er Achmed, that as a favor to Ira Miller he needs to drive you back by the most direct route, knock off the no-speaka-the-English routine, and skip the part where he asks you for even more money before he agrees to start his shit box and haul you out of here. If he takes off without you, I can have a limo here in about five minutes."

"Ah, Christ."

"In fact, I'll call you the limo anyway. No point having you put up with any more crap from the cabbie cabal." Ira Miller casually pressed a button on the corner of his desk.

"Shall we let Achmed know not to wait?"

"No, let him figure it out when the Town Car pulls up behind him. There are a lot of ways to make money off these streets, Mr. Smith. The cab scam is one of them. I make money here too, but I go about it differently. I've been doing it for at least 45 or 50 years."

"That's hard to believe, Mr. Miller. You don't look that old."

"You really, really don't want to know how old I am," joked Ira. "I do fine here, because I give something back. I've taken kids with reasonable talent and big dreams, singing and hand jivin' under street lamps, and turned them into mega-millionaires. Sons and daughters of janitors and assembly line workers, kids with no real prospects. Kids that might otherwise wind up in prison, or bleeding out in a gutter."

"Yeah, but surely those success stories have to be an exception."

Ira opened a camphor wood box on his desk. A pungent aroma permeated the air. "Cigar? They're Cuban. Don't ask."

"Sure" responded Joseph. "Thanks. But like I was saying, aren't the success stories the exception?"

Ira trimmed the ends of two cigars. "Of course. I can't do anything for most of these kids, but I can do something for a few. That keeps the dream alive for every generation. That dream's what keeps me safe around here anymore. Nobody messes with me. Not because I'm an old white guy with a couple of dollars in his pocket, but because for at least a few of these folks I'm still one of their best chances for a better life. I'm the guy who gave Marissa Richards, Oscar Mason, Hannibal Kidd, and the Maxwell Sisters their tickets out of here. I'm the guy who books and manages Memphis Rail."

"Speaking of Memphis Rail, Mr. Miller," shall we proceed with the business at hand?

"Certainly. My attorney has confirmed that your firm put $2.5 million into escrow, and I assume you're here because my million dollar surety bond is in order."

"Exactly, Mr. Miller. Once I leave here, with the Roten Schal in your possession, our 30-day agreement begins. Should you fail to perform, that is to convince Wesley Perkins to surrender his saxophone for my client's collection and begin playing and endorsing the Roten Schal prototype instead, the $2.5 million is removed from escrow."

"I guess I am still unclear about one thing. What if I can't get Wesley Perkins to give up his horn but I return your Roten Schal?"

"In that case, Mr. Miller, you forfeit the surety bond. My client would suffer substantial opportunity cost. It was all spelled out in the agreement."

"Yeah, it was. For some reason I'm a little uneasy about that. So, in the unlikely event I can't pull this off and forfeit the bond, what incentive would I have to return your fancy saxophone?"

"If you can't pull off the exchange, and you decide to keep the horn, it would cost you much, much, more than a mere million dollars. You said I really don't want to know how old you are? Mr. Miller, you can be sure that you in turn don't want to know what it would cost you to keep the Roten Schal."

Ira smiled and chuckled again. "It's a pleasure doing business with you, Mr. Smith. I suspect we might have encountered one another before, somewhere."

"If we have, I certainly don't remember it," replied Joseph Smith.

"Most likely you wouldn't remember. I'm not sure I do either. It could have been a very long time ago."

"Do you have any doubt you can persuade Perkins to give up his horn?" asked Joseph. "It absolutely must be done voluntarily. If it were a simple matter of stealing it, or removing it from his corpse, there are options available that wouldn't cost $2.5 million."

"I wouldn't have bet a million bucks against your two and a half if I wasn't sure I could do this. It isn't every day a guy gets a chance to play a horn cast from diamond dust. Trust me, his ego is about to blow off the charts. I've seen it too many times not to know the signs, and I know how to manipulate it. Either that, or a clumsy wad of naked cash will do the trick- and easily within 30 days."

Part Five, Chapter Two

Little Willy and the Bluesbirds rolled out of Seattle immediately after the second show at the Paramount. The smoke filled tour bus weaved erratically down I-5 to Portland, for a date at the Crystal Ballroom on old Burnside Street. Ira booked the third story, with its legendary "floating dance floor" in a standing room only configuration. The fire Marshall would allow two thousand ticket holders in the former Cotillion Hall, as long as there were no chairs to impede exit.

The Bluesbirds set up on the corner stage, opposite the ornate, cast and chiseled plaster face of the sweepingly curved balcony. Rows of white light globes traced the arches of the floor to ceiling windows to the right. The lighted arch theme was repeated atop oval shaped classic style murals framed by wainscoted walls on the left. Elaborate crystal chandeliers dangled below octagonal skylights. As they were setting up the gear, Little Willy remarked, "I always like to play this place. I was here the night Marvin Gaye brought the house down. It never seems to change all that much."

"Yeah, so how long ago was that?"

"Early 60's."

"Willy, you ain't old enough to have been playin' with Marvin Gaye in the 60's."

"No, but my daddy was. Played bass guitar. From as long as I can remember, I used to spend school vacations on the road with him."

"Think we'll sell 2,000 tickets? That's a pretty big show when we're not openin' for The Rail."

When the doors opened, it would have been difficult to tell how many in the sold out hall were genuine fans of Little Willy and the Bluesbirds. The crowd repeatedly requested tunes normally performed by Memphis Rail. It was obvious that Little Willy's association with the meteoric explosion of popularity for the better known band was paying dividends for the customary warm up act.

The gig at the Crystal Ballroom was a staggering success; (at the end of the last set, a gaggle of drunken women staggered out to the tour bus). Satisfied that the ladies on the bus were all of legal age, the Portland cops chose to turn a blind eye to the festivities. Little Willy and the Bluesbirds left Portland a few hours later, well satisfied with the crowd, the gate, the fans, and their performance. Next stop for the Bluesbirds, a concert date with Memphis Rail in San Francisco.

****

Ira normally bought a first class ticket for Mary Towne and Redd Wilmott, but flew the rest of the group in business class or coach. Ira was suddenly more generous. The success of the Paramount concert and chart busting music downloads made it easier to justify first class tickets for all. Three shows were almost entirely sold out at the Bill Graham Civic Auditorium in San Francisco; twenty-one thousand tickets, and the cheapest selling for eighty dollars. The premium seats not comped in exchange for local promotion were bringing four hundred apiece. Ira was looking forward to a gate of nearly three-million dollars. He could afford to fly Memphis Rail first class, and he would travel out to meet them at the Civic for sound check.

Vanessa wore her dark glasses. She made a good show of grasping Redd's elbow with one hand as she gripped the guide bar worn by Wesley the Dog. Rebekah and Wesley Perkins followed behind, hand in hand, carrying only the saxophone in its snakeskin case. The two couples ignored a nearly steady stream of "Hey, wait, aren't you guys...." from fifteen or twenty strangers encountered before finally hooking up with their concierge from Alaska Airlines.

"Welcome, everybody. Sorry I'm a minute or two late. The rest of your party is already in one of our VIP lounges. I'll take you through special access security and then show you where they're at and you will be together."

"Sounds fine, thanks" said Redd.

"You have the front rows of the First Class section, and your company even booked a seat for the service dog. We will board you last, just before departure, so you won't be bothered by strangers trying to strike up a conversation or asking you for photos."

Wesley the Dog's service harness and vest went through the TSA X-ray machine without incident. When the saxophone case rolled along the conveyor belt and under the X-ray sensor, the security agent scowled. "I need a supervisor, please!"

Wesley, Redd, and Rebekah all looked toward the agent with expressions of mild concern. Vanessa remembered not to look. "This blind routine is a real pain in the ass," she thought. "How long until I screw it up out in public and somebody figures me out?"

The security agent rolled the saxophone case slowly back and forth beneath the sensor, staring intently at the screen. A supervisor approached.

"What you got?"

"I don't know. This is supposed to be some sort of musical instrument case, but I can't figure out why anybody would carry it aboard empty. And look at the weight. It's too heavy for this size case to be empty, but there isn't anything showing up on the screen,"

The supervisor activated the conveyor belt to shift the case back and forth a few inches, merely repeating the exercise just concluded by the agent. The supervisor shook his head and frowned. He questioned Wesley, "Is this your case, sir?"

"Yes, it is."

The supervisor moved the case beyond the scanning machine, to a stainless steel shelf at the far end of the security area. "Step over here, please, sir. I'm going to need to ask you to open this case."

"Yes, of course, no problem. I can't figure out why you can't see my sax on your camera. That's all that's in there you know, just my horn."

"We'll have to see about that." The supervisor shifted his weight to his rear foot and unconsciously leaned away from the case as he said, "OK now, open it up."

Wesley flipped the latches and raised the lid to reveal an obviously antique silver saxophone, covered with etchings that seemed as mysterious as they were meticulous. "See? Just my sax, nothing else."

"What's under the inner flap?"

"Just some spare reeds, and a piece of old cloth." Wesley lifted the door to the inner compartment.

"So we've got a problem, Sir. You're carrying a case that must have some sort of high tech shielding system to keep us from seeing what's inside. What's that about? There's a good chance this could be a dry run, just trying to see if this thing works. Christ Jesus, you could put who knows what in there and try to pass this off as an empty case!"

"That's bullshit, man!" protested Redd.

"I need security over here, right away!" shouted the supervisor. He glared at Redd and added, "And none of you are going anywhere until we sort this out!"

"This is crazy," said Wesley. "There's nothing high tech about that old case. Hell, there's just something wrong with your machine."

The guard arrived quickly. "Is there a problem?"

"I think so, this gentleman has a case that doesn't allow us to X-ray the contents. Must be lead lined or something. When I questioned him about it, his cohort over there got all smart assed. Something isn't right."

Vanessa spoke up. "Maybe it is your machine. Before we start getting all arrested and everything, try putting something else in the case and running it through again."

The supervisor hesitated a moment and said, "I suppose that wouldn't be too much to ask. We'll know if the case is some sort of shield." A short line of rather important looking, increasingly impatient, and progressively annoyed travelers was forming at the limited access security checkpoint. The supervisor handed Wesley the horn, carried the sax case to the other end of the inspection table, tossed his wallet into the case, and put it on the conveyor belt.

The sax case rolled under the X-ray sensor, with the wallet clearly visible.

"Well, if it isn't the case it has to be the horn. What the hell is that made of, Sir?"

"Silver, I suspect. Maybe silver over bronze. I never really bothered to analyze it."

"May I see the horn, please?"

Wesley handed the horn to the supervisor. "Be careful with that, it's pretty old."

The supervisor put the horn on the conveyor belt. Judah Jones' old saxophone did not show up on the monitor when the horn passed under the sensor.

"I don't think I can let you take this on the plane. I don't even know if I can let any of you get on the plane."

The Alaska Airlines concierge interceded. "Of course you can. Any passenger has the right to request that you inspect their luggage by hand, rather than by using the X-Ray. Haven't you just done that? Aren't you satisfied that this is just a regular instrument case and an ordinary saxophone?"

The supervisor looked momentarily bewildered, but then noted the security officer was standing with both palms upturned, shrugging, and nodding in apparent agreement with the concierge.

The supervisor slowly laid the saxophone back into its snakeskin case, snapped the lid shut, and slid it across the stainless surface to Wesley. "All right, I guess she's right. But, I'll be damned if I ever agree that there's anything ordinary about that saxophone."

The concierge whisked the four musicians and the dog down a back corridor. "I really apologize for all of that. Some of these security guys get a god complex sometimes. You really shouldn't have to put up with that. They just don't have their machine set up right today. It wasn't your fault. Sorry."

They arrived at an unmarked door. The concierge opened it with a key. Art Abbott, John Flood and Ann Foster were seated on a pair of contemporary style couches, elevated from the floor on stubby mahogany legs. The walls were an exotic hardwood, but finished with such deep gloss they appeared almost plastic. Some bottles were open atop a self-service beverage bar.

Ann Foster forced a smile as the new arrivals entered. She was careful to conceal her extreme surprise at the sight of Rebekah. Unaware of the previous night's events at Wesley and Rebekah's house, Ann thought, "That bitch might as well stay home. She ain't gonna be able to sing a note, not with her lucky jewelry locked up in that safe deposit box back downtown Seattle. She has to know it's gone, what's she even doing here?"

Art Abbott questioned Redd. "So what the hell took you guys so long? You were supposed to be right behind us. You love birds all stop off for a quickie, or something?"

"Nope. Nothin' that interesting. We had some trouble getting' Wesley's horn through the checkpoint. Some nonsense about the X-ray thing not bein' set up right. Shit, they started thinkin' we was about to blow up an airplane or somethin,"

Wesley laid the saxophone case on top of the bar. "You know, I better check to see whether that idiot at security put the horn back in here the right way."

Wesley flipped the latches, opened the lid, and cried out, "What in the Sam hell?"

With all conversation stopped, everyone looked as Wesley lifted Rebekah's missing jewelry from the case. The same jewelry that was not there minutes earlier at the security checkpoint. The same jewelry that Ann Foster and her hired confederates had stolen the previous afternoon. The same jewelry that Ann locked into a rented safety deposit box in the downtown Seattle branch of Wells Fargo bank.

"Oh my God!" screamed a terrorized Rebekah, "How did that get in there?"

Unaware that there had been any incident involving the jewelry, Art and John simply looked confused. Mary had a hand stretched across her scalp, slowly shaking her head in concern. Vanessa drew a deep breath, and was uncharacteristically speechless.

Ann Foster entered a new realm of hysterical fright. She shrieked in alarm, and pointed at Wesley and the jewelry, but was unable to find any breath for further expression. She began to choke, and put one hand to her throat while flailing violently around with the other. Redd ran down the hall in search of medical assistance.

Although nobody knew at the moment they wheeled her out on a stretcher, Ann Foster's last appearance with Memphis Rail would prove to be the triumphal show at the Paramount in Seattle. The official medical diagnosis was "severe stroke, and cerebral hemorrhage." While she eventually recovered most of her muscular functions, she would never again be an accomplished keyboard player. Her voice was stripped away. During her remaining years, she avoided any contact with the band.

Part Five, Chapter Three

Bridget Bishop and Billy Proctor sweated, gasped, and groaned as the two teens humped naked on her pink and white flowered bedspread. "Shit," thought Bridget, "I hope we don't leave a stain!" However, it was by then too far into the moment to take additional precautions. Philosophers have commented that each ensuing generation assumes it discovered or invented sex. The intercourse between Bridget and Billy was spiced by the comparative novelty, as well as by the remote danger of being discovered by Bridget's father. Bridget hadn't reached the ultimate moment of sexual ecstasy before Billy finished with a few particularly energized thrusts. He collapsed, and she pushed his dead weight to a spot beside her on the bed. He kissed her on the breast, immediately next to her thumping heart.

Billy rolled onto his back, staring at the ceiling. After a minute or two of silence, he spoke. "Bridget, I can probably tell you anything, right?"

"Uh, I would think so. For Christ's sake, Billy, look at us. It's not like we're holding back or keeping secrets."

"OK. Well, in the last few days I've been questioning something about our faith."

Bridget was surprised, and slightly disappointed by Billy's distraction from the moment, but decided to indulge him. "So, it's natural and healthy to question. Just as long as we stick to the Bible when we look for answers. That's what my daddy, and all the Elders say."

"Well, it's all that stuff about the resurrection and everything. What if Jesus actually died on the cross?"

"Oh my God, Billy. Of course Jesus died on the cross. He was dead and buried, and on the third day he arose and..."

"Yeah, yeah, of course. But somebody I know asked me something and I can't get it out of my head."

"And the question was?"

"What if Jesus had a twin?"

Bridget jumped up in alarm, stood next to the bed, and lifted the stained spread to conceal a nakedness of which she was suddenly ashamed. She began to tremble. "Billy, oh my God! He's been talking to you too, hasn't he?"

"You mean the old guy wearing the red scarf? The one who rows around on the lake fishing almost every day? Seems to hang around that old shack a lot? Yeah. He's the one who asked me if I ever thought Jesus might have had a twin. It really creeped me out. What did he say to you?

"Pretty much the same thing. He didn't say for sure that Jesus had a twin. In fact, he said I shouldn't believe it was true. He just said that all perfect things are made in pairs and..."

"Shit, Bridget, that's exactly what he said to me. What's he up to, anyway? Is he some sort of demon or something? Is he trying to sow doubt? Trying to ruin our faith?"

"So what are we going to do?"

"Right now, let's get down on our knees and pray. I don't know what's going on. But let's listen for an answer." Bridget and Billy knelt on the floor, facing across the mattress, eyes closed, arms reaching toward the center of the sheets and the fingers of each entwined with the other. Billy began praying aloud, "Our Father, who dwells in Heaven, may your name be sanctified above all. May your kingdom come, and may your will be done on Earth just as it is done in Heaven. Give us every day our earthly sustenance sufficient for that day."

Bridget joined in, and together they recited the remainder of the prayer. "Forgive us our sins in the same way we forgive those who do wrong to us. Be our advocate in the time of trial. Deliver us from wickedness. Amen."

A full minute of silence passed as though it were a glacial age.

"So what did you hear?" asked Billy.

"No, it was pretty weird. You go first."

"Something about you and me. We're a spiritual brother and sister?"

Billy took a deep breath and frowned. "Yeah, I got the brother and sister thing too."

Bridget became tense and anxious. "Does that mean it's wrong to do what we've been doing?"

"I don't think so. Even if we are spirit siblings, we're not twins. The guy with the red scarf, he's trying to confuse us with some question about twins. I'm two years older than you, so we can't really be twins, anyway."

"So, Billy…"

"Yeah?"

"I heard another question. What if there's only really one physical body in the universe, and we all share little portions of it?"

"Sorry, but I sure didn't get any of that. Let's try praying again, and listening for more answers."

"Oh shit!" cried Bridget. "Can you hear that?"

"Uh, we haven't started praying yet."

"No, you idiot! That's my daddy's diesel pickup! I can hear it when he's still about a block away! Fuck, fuck, fuck, we are so incredibly fucked! Get dressed right away. Just throw your shirt and pants on. Take your shoes and socks and put them on in the bathroom, and whether you have to pee or not, be sure to flush the toilet before you come out! Go, go, go! We've got maybe a minute or less!"

Billy shoved his legs frantically into his pants, and ran down the hallway to the bathroom. He carried his shoes in one hand, and struggled to button his shirt with the other. Bridget didn't bother with underwear. She tossed a sundress over her head, wiped her brow with a tissue, and passed a brush through her hair. She pulled shut a door to conceal the disarray of her bedding, and ran to take a seat on the living room couch. She was sitting with her feet tucked under her thighs, schoolbook in hand, when her father entered the house.

Silas Bishop greeted his daughter. "Hello, Dear. What have you been up to this afternoon?"

"Nothing, Daddy. Just doing some homework. Billy stopped by to lend me a hand."

Silas frowned. The toilet flushed. Billy Proctor emerged from the bathroom and joined father and daughter in the living room.

"You know the rule, here in the community, about calling on a young lady when she's home alone? Right?" scolded Silas.

"Yes, sir. I'm sorry, Mr. Bishop. I didn't really mean to do anything wrong."

"You know, Billy, the Elders and I have been impressed with the sermons you have been delivering to the youth on Sundays. We all think you've got a unique gift. You can really go somewhere and be somebody here in the community."

"Thanks, Mr. Bishop. That's encouraging."

"But you've got to follow the rules, same as everybody else. You can rise through the ranks and be a spiritual leader here, maybe a lot faster than you think. Don't screw that up."

As Silas finished his statement, he seemed to physically react to his own speech; especially the word "screw." His demeanor changed from that of a concerned parent, to something more akin to a suspicious accuser.

"Wait? Did you hear that?" asked Silas.

"What, Daddy?"

"There's a noise in your room, Maybe a raccoon came in through the window, or something. You kids sit here. I'm going to go check it out.'

"Daddy, there isn't any noise, and there isn't any raccoon! I was just in there and..."

"You were just in there? Odd, I thought you were sitting in the living room, reading school books with Billy."

"Daddy, please!"

Silas adopted an almost menacing expression. Bridget's mind electrified with memories of her father murdering Brother Benjamin as the wretched old con man devoured her relative sexual innocence. She panicked for her young paramour's safety.

"Don't either of you move a goddam muscle, understand? I'm going to check out that bedroom. We'll see what happens, after we see what I happen to find."

Bridget jumped up from the couch and ran to grab her father's arm. He shoved her aside. She tripped to the floor, and grabbed his leg. She knew that with one look at the torn up bedding, and the tell-tale stain, her father could easily become uncontrollably enraged.

Silas Bishop limped down the hall, dragging his wailing daughter with a death drip on his ankle. "No, Daddy, no! Please don't go in there!"

Billy Proctor realized that this might be his last opportunity to flee. Perhaps it was affection for Bridget, but he decided to stand his ground and deal with Silas Bishop man to man. His lover might need his protection. The time of boyhood was not only past, it was irretrievably lost.

Silas Bishop twisted the knob and shoved the door open with a violent sweeping motion. Before getting a clear look into the room, he began to snarl, "So Billy was just lending you ..." but he stopped in mid-sentence and his voice became calm and contrite.

"What the hell, daughter? Whenever did you clean up your room this nicely? Normally you've got clothes and stuff laying around in here. You put everything away, lined up all your makeup on the dressing table, and good grief, look at the bed? I didn't realize you could make such perfect hospital corners. There's not even a wrinkle in the covers. I'm really surprised."

Bridget gaped in disbelief. She knew, but her father did not, that the red scarf folded neatly at the foot of her bed was not part of her wardrobe. She seized the moment, and lied. "That's what I didn't want you to see, Daddy. I'm going to go through our whole house, room by room, and clean it up just like that. Just like Mama used to do when she was with us."

"Bless you, girl. For a moment there I was suspicious about something that I had no reason to worry about. Forgive me for being a cranky old man."

As father and daughter walked back to the living room, Bridget kissed Silas on the cheek. "You're the best Daddy anybody could ever want."

Billy Proctor tried his best not to look overly relieved as Silas and Bridget returned to the front room.

"So, what were you studying, Billy? What are they teaching you kids in Bible school these days?"

"Uh, well, I guess you could say we're doing a little research on the earthly family of Jesus. The natural children of Mary and Joseph."

"Oh, and what are you learning?"

"There's not all that much to go on in the Bible. The brothers and sisters are mentioned, but a lot of names are the same. Maybe one of the Mary's is a sister of Jesus, maybe not. We can be sure that James was one of the brothers, as Paul refers to him as 'the brother of our Lord in Jerusalem.' Beyond that, there's some pretty crazy theories."

Silas frowned. "They shouldn't be exposing you kids to crazy theories, not at your young age at least. The truth should be enough for you, and really all you need."

Bridget interrupted. "You're right, Daddy. There's no reason to go outside the Bible. Did you know that some people even believe that Jesus had a twin brother? How ridiculously weird is that!"

Silas gasped in surprise, with a gaze fixed on an empty corner of the room. Neither teen dared interrupt the pregnant and omnipresent silence, it was clearly owned by Silas Bishop. When the father spoke, it was in single words, spaced well apart rather than chained together in a phrase.

"What son of a bitch told you?!"

"Told me what, Daddy?"

"That Jesus had a twin brother."

Billy spoke up, "I'm sorry Mr. Bishop, blame it on me. I heard it somewhere and I mentioned it to Bridget. I apologize; I wasn't trying to put sinful notions into her head or anything. But it's my fault."

"Shut up, Billy." insisted Silas. "Just shut the hell up." He paced back and forth for a second, then took a seat in his easy chair. "Nobody is supposed to know about the twin. Do you have any idea how our enemies would misuse that? There would be stories that sightings of the resurrected Christ were just the twin brother."

"Daddy, that's crazy talk! Let's pray for your forgiveness."

"No, it ain't crazy talk, Bridget. It's a revelation that was given to brother Abner when he and that rapist bastard Benjamin first founded our community. Once somebody shares the thought with you, it's only a short time before you become certain that it's true. It's like a seed. Maybe even a wicked seed. That's how it spreads."

"So how many people believe this, Mr. Bishop?"

"All the Elders. We don't believe it, we know it. Everything perfect is always made in pairs and Jesus was perfect. Your parents will skin me for this, Billy, but you kids might as well know the truth. Billy, you can walk out of here right now, but if you stay and hear what I am about to say you need to know that you're committed to the community."

"What do you know, sir?"

"What do I know? That Jesus was the Son of God. The Roman soldiers who crucified him dressed him up like a King, in the tradition of a pagan sacrifice for fertile soil and abundant crops. He physically arose from the dead, demonstrating that the spirit owns the body and the body does not contain or imprison the spirit."

Billy knelt down next to the chair. "I guess I meant about the brother."

"Yes, he did have a twin brother, well known to both the Syrian Christians and the Essenes as Didymos Judas Thomas. Didymos means twin in Greek, and Thomas means twin in Aramaic."

"So, Daddy, are you saying that the twin brother is the one seen after the crucifixion?"

"No. That was Jesus. The twin brother, from the beginning, was a test of faith. The dark half of the day. When they learn about the twin, many will not believe. They will surrender to their doubt. They won't find a safe way home. Those who know about the twin and continue to believe? They will be the sons and daughters of Light, children of the Most High."

Billy stood up, backed up a few paces, and rubbed his chin. "I get the feeling you know something else, Mr. Bishop. Something you're not sharing."

"Brother Abner's revelation included the fact that Jesus will be coming again. Very soon. Jesus will be born as twins once again. Even more astonishing, according to Brother Abner, those twins are going to be born here- at our very own community in Iberia Parish."

Chuck Gould

Part Five, Chapter Four

Ira Miller's cell phone rang. He answered a call from Mary Towne and learned of Ann's collapse at the airport.

"God, that's really awful," agreed Ira. "Me? I thought maybe she was under a lot of stress lately, with the new adjustments to the act and all."

"She didn't look good at all, Ira. Maybe we should cancel the show?"

"Cancel? Mary we've got two sellouts at the Civic Auditorium. Fourteen thousand seats averaging about sixty-five bucks a pop. That's nearly a million dollar gate. Cancel, my ass. Anyway, hey, hang on a minute…"

Ira held the phone away from his ear to address a stage hand. "Those cheap ass mics aren't what I ordered."

"Sorry, dude, it's what they sent over…"

"Then send them the hell back and get the right shit, OK?"

Ira turned away from the commotion on stage and returned to the call.

"As I was saying, Mary, we can get Little Willy's keyboard player to sit in for her. Rebekah can cover the vocals. If she's up to joining us in LA or Dallas, that'd be super."

"She's probably my oldest friend, Ira. I'm really worried 'bout her."

Ira used a free hand to direct the placement of a vocal monitor and continued speaking into the phone. "Yeah, I totally get that. She's an important part of Memphis Rail. Let's hope she's back really soon, but meantime the show must go on. Hell, last time we played here we sold 5,000 seats at about $30. We need to think about what's best for the Rail. It's what Ann would want us to do."

"Still, somethin' doesn't feel right about leavin' Ann behind in Seattle." .

Ira heard a ping in the background, followed by an announcement. "Ladies and Gentlemen, thank you for choosing Alaska Airlines, Flight 306, to San Francisco. At this time, please turn off all cell phones and electronics."

"I gotta go, Ira. Still don't think this is entirely right."

"We'll make it right. See you for sound check, 10 AM tomorrow. You guys are gonna blow the doors off the Civic, Mary. Wait and see."

Part Five, Chapter Five

The drive from Bisbee to West Moccasin Springs was proving more difficult than imagined. Jose Cueva Reyes worried that his last $20 bill, stuffed into his Levi jacket, might not buy enough gas. There were still almost a hundred miles to go. The clutch was slipping, badly. The temperature gauge read much higher than normal. They were down to half a cold sandwich and one bottle of water. Worst of all, Maria was shifting uncomfortably in her seat. She could go into labor at any moment. Jose worried. He had delivered calves and colts. Could human babies really be all that different?

"There's a sign for a rest stop," said Maria. "We need to pull over so I can pee."

"Again?"

"Don't be such an asshole. Tell you what. I'll drive the damn truck a while and you try sitting here with babies on your bladder. See how it feels, maybe?"

"Hey, I'm pulling over. It's just that every time I shift gears the clutch seems to burn a little worse. Once we're up to speed and holding, it ain't so bad, really."

The exhausted brakes squealed in protest as Jose left the highway and slowed to find a parking spot.

"I'll see if I can find something really close to the Women's door, so you don't have far to walk."

Jose found a spot and got out of the truck. He needed to slam the door twice to get the latch to catch. He stepped quickly around the front of the hood, opened Maria's door, and helped her step down to the pavement.

"You want to lean on my arm?"

"Yeah, thanks. Maybe after this stop we can make it the rest of the way."

"Maybe."

Jose escorted Mary to the rest room door. "You better wait here," she said. "There's several cars here. Somebody else is probably in there too."

"OK. I'll be waiting here to help you back."

Jose waited outside the rest room, nursing his private doubts. He knew one thing for certain, he only gave the protestant pastor the time of day because Father McNeil made the introduction. Why, suddenly, in Maria's thirty-sixth week was it suddenly so urgent for them to travel to Louisiana? He was always against it. The truck was proving as unreliable as he feared. Maria's doctor was alarmed that she would even consider a cross-country trip.

He could still see Maria's face on the afternoon they made the decision. She glowed with a radiance and confidence that reminded Jose of their wedding day. "Just think, dear. A job for you, and a home of our own, and all we need to do is to be in Louisiana in four days? This is a once in a lifetime chance. We have to go."

He remained suspicious. "Why the rush? Why can't they wait until after the babies are born? You probably shouldn't travel. It can't be a good idea. Besides, the offer seems too good to be true."

"I've known Father McNeil for my entire life. He wouldn't steer us wrong, or deliver us to somebody else who would."

Jose trusted Father McNeil, but wasn't sure about the protestant preacher wearing a black suit, old time dress hat, and a red stole draped around his clerical collar. A job? A house? Sometimes God, and maybe even Protestants, work in mysterious ways.

Maria emerged from the rest room, appearing very concerned "How far is it to West Moccasin Springs?"

"About 90 minutes, but I can't push the truck too hard and we're gonna need to stop for gas. Better figure two hours. You OK?"

"Yeah. Help me back up into the truck, and let's get there quick as we can. I'm starting into labor, but I'm sure I can hold out for two more hours. Give them a call, and tell them to have a midwife standing by when we get there."

Part Five, Chapter Six

Ira lodged Memphis Rail and the Family Jones in the Fairmont Hotel on Nob Hill. Mary Towne retired to her room upon arrival. Vanessa and Redd Wilmott shared a room, as did Wesley Perkins and Rebekah.

Art Abbott and John Flood sought out the Tonga Room and Hurricane Bar. Back in the 1940's, the Fairmont converted the hotel's indoor swimming pool to a Tiki bar. The pool became a rectangular lagoon, with a floating stage. A ship's mast, topical huts, Polynesian sculptures, and the façade of an Asian house illuminated by paper lanterns instilled a dimly lit atmosphere. Faux thatched roofs hovered above tables around the perimeter of the pond.

A waitress approached their table.

"Tonga Mai Tai, please" requested John.

Art chuckled. "You really want one of those candy ass drinks served in a phony coconut shell?"

"Shit, ya."

"Make mine a Seagram's and Seven, please Miss," said Art.

John rested his elbow on the table and his head on his fist. "Gonna be a big day tomorrow. Two shows, sold out. Who woulda thought? Even six months ago, we'd be lucky to sell four or five thousand seats."

Art shook his head with a shiver. "Yeah, but are you really OK with this? I'm thinkin' about that incident back at Rain Crow. And a shitload of other stuff to boot. I heard you play the sax, once, a long time ago. You couldn't get a goddam note out of that Wesley Perkins horn. What's up with that?"

"Hell, I don't exactly know. Seems spooky as shit, if you ask me. For now, I've just decided to ride along 'cause the money's gonna be really good."

"Money? Holy crap man, is all of this reduced to bein' about money?"

"Well, no. But money's a bunch of it," said John. "Was a time it was mostly about love. Hell, I'da paid to drum for the Rail when we first started out. Now days, I'm mostly old, tired, worn out, and ready to give it up and go home."

Art was ready to change the subject. "Check out that floatin' stage."

"Yeah, so, what about it, other than it's pretty small?"

"Ever think that there's this invisible line?"

John shifted to the opposite elbow. "Huh? I don't follow you, really."

"Like there's this invisible line between where we are, and where everybody else is. It's sort of the edge of the stage, if you know what I mean."

"Oh, hell yeah. Most of the folks buyin' tickets think there's some magical divide. Like we never have to take a piss halfway through a set. Like we ain't put in 50 hours of rehearsal and made a hundred mistakes for every sixty seconds we have our shit together during a concert. Hell, yeah. I get that."

"So, that floatin' stage just makes the point more directly. Sort of like there's this middle ages moat or somethin'."

The waitress returned with the drinks. "Are you gentlemen staying here at the hotel? If so, we'd be pleased to start a tab and bill it to your room."

Art handed the waitress a twenty dollar bill. "Our company's payin' for everything. Go ahead and put the drinks against my room. It's, wait a minute," Art fished out his key, "Four Oh Seven. Come around once in a while, make sure we're not dried out, OK?"

"Absolutely."

A young woman passed their table. She stopped abruptly, and looked deliberately at the two musicians. She flashed a slow smile of recognition, coupled with a slow nod, before she waved very slightly and continued on her way. Art and John watched her hips shift back and forth under a short, tight skirt.

Art sipped his drink. "You see the posters?"

"Yeah. What's with that? 'Memphis Rail and the Family Jones' is bad enough. Seein' that line, 'Featuring Wesley Perkins and Wesley the Dog' doesn't sit so well. All these years, all that sweat, and the two things that yank us back to the big leagues is a goddam dog with a sense of rhythm and some insane white guy who 'parrently rules the fuckin' sax?"

"I sort of see it the same way," confirmed Art. "Still, though, I ain't sure what to do about it."

"Me neither. It seems to me more and more lately like we're caught up in some bullshit that's way beyond anythin' we can understand."

The lights went out in the Tonga Room. Thunder boomed, lightning strobed, and a torrential rain storm pelted the surface of the pool.

John looked around in shock. "What the hell?"

Art leaned back in his chair and laughed. "It ain't nothin. Just special effects. Goes off about every fifteen minutes, all night long."

Chuck Gould

Part Five, Chapter Seven

Rebekah offered Wesley the first shower. He finished, and Rebekah began her turn. Wesley wore the white Fairmont Hotel bathrobe as he sat at the desk and perused the Room Service menu. There was a knock at the door.

Wesley assumed the visitor must be Vanessa, or perhaps one of the other musicians. He gathered his robe, cinched the belt, and answered the door. He was astonished to see Sarah Cloyne, the best friend of his recently divorced wife, standing in the hallway.

Wesley struggled to be gracious. ""Uh, why, hello, Sarah. It's quite a surprise to see you here."

Sarah appraised Wesley's attire. "Oh, looks like I came at a bad time. Sorry about that."

"So, what brings you to San Francisco, and what can I do for you? I'd invite you in, but as you can see I'm not really dressed for company."

Sarah reddened with embarrassment. "I was just in town on business. I heard your band had a concert tomorrow, so I thought I'd drop by and visit. Maybe we could step out for a drink or something?"

Wesley was suspicious. Like his ex-wife, Ruth, Sarah lived on a family fortune established generations ago. She engaged in no form of business that would bring her to San Francisco. How did she find the right hotel? How did she find this room? Ira booked everything under one of his corporate shells. She must have bribed a housekeeper. Something didn't seem right.

"I don't know, Sarah. We've got two big shows tomorrow so most everybody is taking it pretty easy tonight. Are you going to the Civic Auditorium? Let me know where you're staying, and I can get our promoter to send you a pass. You can come back and meet the band after the second show."

"Actually, I haven't really found a room yet. I was hoping for something maybe here at the Fairmont. If I come back in fifteen or twenty minutes, would that give you time to get dressed? We really should at least do one drink, shouldn't we? For old times' sake? Ruth wouldn't care."

"Ruth has no reason to care," confirmed Wesley. "But…"

He was interrupted when Vanessa stepped into the room, wrapped in a Fairmont bathrobe identical to Wesley's. "Who's at the door, Wes?"

Sarah failed to control her short gasp. She flushed scarlet. "Oh. I'm so sorry. Really, I had no idea. I should never have come over. My apologies for disturbing you. I mean, disturbing you both."

Wesley was relieved that Sarah was attempting a gracious exit. "Not that big a deal, really. You wouldn't have any way to know that Rebekah and I are together now." He turned toward Rebekah, behind him in the room. ""Bekah, this is Sarah. She's an old friend from Bainbridge."

Rebekah's response was a unique mixture of polite remark and hostile gaze. "Oh. Well, nice to make your acquaintance, very old friend Sarah, from Bainbridge."

Sarah stepped back from the door. "Looks like my timing is even worse than I thought. I'll just go on about my day. Nice to see you, Wes. And nice to meet you too, Rebekah."

"No problem. Like I said I can get you a back stage pass for tomorrow."

"Don't bother. I just now decided to fly back to Seattle tonight."

Wesley closed the door. "What do you suppose that was all about?"

"What do you think? The woman is a damn stalker, Wes. How do you s'pose she found us, anyway?"

Wesley shrugged. "Can't say, really. Who knows? Looked like she had something pretty personal in mind. Not that it means anything, since we're together and everything, but a guy could find all this female attention sort of flattering."

"Yeah? Well I suggest you don't. Women like that don't necessarily think you look all that good- they just hope that being with you would make themselves look better."

"You're probably right."

"I'm damn right, Wes. Remember Vanessa warned us about letting any of this get into our heads. Something about the enemy coming in through the ego."

"Yeah. I think she said that people do strange things when they fall in love, and really strange things when they fall in love with themselves."

"So then pay some attention, Wes."

Part Five, Chapter Eight

Jose Cuerva Reyes pushed the battered old Chevy half ton as hard as he dared. Maria was slouched against the passenger door, biting her lower lip and inhaling with long, sporadic slurping noises. Darkness fell. It began to rain. The pungent air wafting across the cracked open windows in the cab was saturated with moisture. The wipers smeared across the windshield, and beyond them Jose called out the mile posts as they were detected by the headlights.

At sixty miles, "Hang in there, we're gonna make it for sure. Maybe just an hour to go."

Maria groaned. "I'm holdin' on, trust me. But I think things are developin' pretty quickly. Pray to God we make it. Like I said, we better call. You're drivin' so give me the phone and I'll punch in the number." Maria entered the number and handed the phone to Jose. "Here you go, let's hope somebody answers."

Jose held the phone to his ear. A voice answered, "Silas Bishop speaking."

"Mr. Bishop, this is Jose Cuerva Reyes."

"Yes, Mr. Reyes, we have been expecting you. Everything OK?"

"Yes, but Maria is going into labor."

"Oh shit! Where are you? Are you going to be able to make it?"

"We're maybe about an hour out. I'm going to have to stop for a little gas, but that shouldn't take long. I'm pretty concerned about Maria. She says she thinks she can hold out, but that it would best if there's a midwife standing by when we get there."

"No problem. Mrs. Pudeator delivers the babies here. She can be over to your new house in about 5 minutes."

Jose pulled around a dump truck full of gravel blocking the right lane. "So, Mr. Bishop, what do we do when we get there? Where do we go?"

"Let me know when you're about ten miles out. We'll put a car at the gate to meet you. Follow that car. You'll go straight ahead for three blocks, and then about two streets to the right. You will probably see a lot of people gathered around outside your new house. The mailbox says 'Brinkman, but don't worry about that. Maria's going to make it, right? There are some reasons it will be important that the twins are born in the community."

Slowed somewhat by the rain and a stop for gas, 75 minutes passed before Jose's overheating pickup truck made a right turn from the dark two-lane into the community. A white Mercedes sedan, with four way flashers blinking, pulled in front of the Chevy half ton and tooted twice on the horn. Jose flashed his headlights in response and fell in behind the car. Jose was grateful for the assistance. It was nearly impossible to see the small residential intersections in the darkness and the driving rain.

Maria moaned, and whispered hoarsely, "Hurry, please, please, hurry."

As they turned the final corner, Jose was surprised to see perhaps a few hundred people surrounding a small house. The crowd parted quickly to allow the Mercedes and the Chevy pickup access to the driveway. Jose noticed that everyone assembled was wearing a transparent plastic rain slicker and a wide brimmed hat. Each person held a lighted candle, and used a free hand to protect the flame from wind and rain.

Two women with a wheelchair stood on the passenger side of the driveway. Jose stopped the Chevy and the women immediately opened the door and assisted Maria into the wheelchair. As they pushed her into the house, Silas Bishop extended his hand to Jose Cueva Reyes.

"Welcome, Brother Jose. We're so glad you had a safe journey and made it here to join us."

"Yeah, I think maybe we made it just in the nick of time, sir."

"You can call me Elder Bishop, or even Brother Silas. We're not so much on formalities here."

As if the house inhaled them all, the assembled multitude pressed tightly against the exterior walls of the old Brinkman home.

"You know, Brother Silas, I never have quite understood all the urgency for us to get here so quickly. Father McNeil stressed how critical it was for us to make it before the twins are born. We risked a lot, crossing the country with Maria in her condition."

Silas Bishop rested a hand on Jose's shoulder. "We'll be able to tell you more very soon, I'm sure. For now, you have done your part. You and Maria are here. The babies still unborn."

"And we get a house of our own, and I get steady work, right?"

"Absolutely, Jose. This is going to be your house, right here. And we have lots and lots of work for skilled carpenters. Trust me, your needs will all be met by the community."

"Brother Silas?"

"Yes?"

"Look at the candles and everything. Does everybody always make this much fuss whenever a baby is born around here?"

"No, not really. Twins though? That's pretty special."

Part Six, Chapter One

Little Willy and the Bluesbirds were on stage, rocking the crowd to open the first of two shows at Bill Graham Civic Auditorium. As the opening act progressed, Memphis Rail and the Family Jones gathered backstage in the green room. Vanessa, Rebekah, Wesley Perkins and Wesley the Dog arrived to find the other musicians already gathered. Conversation ceased abruptly when they walked in.

Vanessa sensed an awkward discomfort in the room. "Hey, sorry, I guess we might be late or something? We really didn't mean to be. Everything's OK, right?"

John scratched behind his ear with a drumstick. "Sure. Of course. We've just been sittin' 'round doin' some talkin' 'bout the ways things are changin' all of a sudden. No big deal. Things change all the time, most especially in this business."

Art said, "Yeah, this is gonna be our first show without Ann on keyboards. We're still tryin' to figure out why she suddenly freaked out so bad yesterday. I mean, she was pointin' at Rebekah's jewelry and then just lost it."

Vanessa shot Redd Wilmott a look of concern, punctuated with an arched eyebrow. Redd realized that this would be a moment to exert some leadership. With a performance about to start, cohesive enthusiasm would be crucial.

Redd addressed everyone in the room. "Hey, we're all worried about Ann. But whatever happened to her is got nothin' to do with Vanessa, Rebekah or Wes. It's just some kind of medical thing, nothin' more. Let's get our heads straight here. We're going to have one of the biggest nights ever. We need to put out the same stuff we had at sound check this mornin'."

Mary Towne quickly reinforced Redd's assurances. "Redd's right. And hear that? The Bluesbirds are all the way up to 'Little Schoolgirl'. Second to last number in their set. We better start wadin' in the water."

Everyone looked at John Flood. John's concerned scowl morphed into a hesitant smile. He began tapping a slow and steady beat on the table top.

Mary began, "See that guy on the mountain top?"

All responded, "Wade in the water"

"He's gonna rock this world and never stop."

"Wade in the water, chilin', wade in the wa-ha-ha-ter, wade in the water, God's been a workin' in the water…"

Ira Miller made a final check of the merchandise in the lobby. There were more important tasks that could have commanded his attention, but Ira was always slightly distrustful of local strangers hired to peddle tee shirts and compact discs. He had developed a knack for keeping tabs on an employee while appearing to be looking in another direction. "So far, so good," he concluded. "But it's going to be crazy busy between shows."

Joseph Smith approached Ira, with his cell phone in hand. "That was my client. He's asking for a progress update on the deal with your sax player."

"I told you I needed 30 days, Mr. Smith. We've still got most of those days left. Assure your client I know what I'm doing. These things take some time. A little finesse, if you know what I mean."

Joseph put his phone into his pants pocket and fingered a CD. "Sure thing, but my client is extremely anxious to recover that old saxophone."

"Recover? What do you mean by that? Did he own that horn at one time? Something going on that I don't know about, here?"

"I'm sorry, Ira. Just a careless choice of words. Nothing to worry about. I should have said acquire, not recover."

"Well, tell him everything's going to be alright."

"He seems pretty confident that it will be, but he's eager for results. He wants to know if a little more cash might advance the issue."

"How much more?"

"What would you say if we raised the ante by a million dollars, in exchange for results in the next ten days?"

"So, we're up to three and a half? Tell your client that to bring about results as quickly as he's expecting, I'll need four. And I'll need to finesse the situation with a sledge hammer. Tell him I'll need one-million actual cash up front, in a big briefcase, in hundred dollar bills."

"I don't know what he would say. Your surety bond obviously doesn't cover another million in cash. "

"No problem, I can do it without the cash- but I'll need the rest of the original thirty days."

Joseph Smith grimaced. "I'll need to call my client again. I think first I'll need a drink."

"OK, I'll be here all night. Let me know if we're still on the original deal or if you want to raise the stakes."

Little Willy and the Bluesbirds concluded their final number, "Sittin' on Top of the World." The audience rewarded the spirited effort and accomplished performance with an energized and enthused applause. The curtain swept quickly across the stage. The stage crew began swapping out equipment, resetting mic stands, and preparing for the arrival of Memphis Rail.

Little Willy and the Bluesbirds met Memphis Rail and the Family Jones immediately outside the green room.

With a fist bump, Mary Towne said, "Hey, good show, Little Willy!"

Sustaining tradition, Willy replied, "I hates it when you call me that!"

Redd Wilmott cautioned: "Don't be disappearin' into a cloud of smoke out there in that bus of yours. You guys are back on in three hours for the second show."

Andrew Carrier, keyboard player for the Bluesbirds, groused "Yeah, everybody but me. I'll be on stage for all four sets. Sure hope Ann gets back up and around again."

"So, whatcha bitchin' for?" replied Little Willy. "You're gonna be makin' money while the rest of us are just kickin' back."

"Yeah, that's somethin'. Big night a paycheck, if nothing more."

Mary Towne asked, "So, Andrew, I asked you this ten times already but you're OK with all the keyboard parts?"

"How many years have we opened for the Rail, Mary?"

"Yeah, but a lot of our stuff is new."

"No, it ain't, really. It's from the 1950's. Relax, I got it. Let's just play the blues, and you guys can step up to cover if I come up slacking."

The audience, impatient with even the slightest delay, began a rhythmic chanting and clapping. "Rail, rail, rail, rail, rail, rail..." John and Art nodded and smiled, but then a second chant began burbling up beneath the first and soon became the dominant call. "Jones, Jones, Jones, Jones, Jones." As Vanessa, guided by Wesley the Dog and one of the stage hands, assumed her place behind the mic on the otherwise empty stage, the chant shifted to "Sax, sax, sax, sax," and then "dog, dog, dog, dog."

With the rest of the musicians poised for a quick entrance, the curtain opened on the San Francisco show.

Part Six, Chapter Two

Vanessa stood on the darkened stage, illuminated by a single white follow light. Wesley the Dog sat attentively at her side. She nestled her Blues Harp next to the mic and remembered the progression, now practiced perhaps two hundred times.

Blow the hole number four, draw number five, blow number five, blow number four, count to four, start again. Opening with the harp alone called for extra attention to rhythm and tempo, unaided by the drummer of bass player. Vanessa was always nervous that she might set the number up improperly, but the worry proved unjustified.

The blues savvy audience recognized the opening number immediately, "Hoochie Coochie Man," written by Willy Dixon and made famous by Muddy Waters.

Vanessa's harp continued to crow, as John Flood assumed his seat behind the drum kit. He began with tapping out basic time on a cymbal. After four bars, Redd Wilmott thumped in with bass guitar. The trio was soon joined by Andrew Carrier, chunking out the root chord with a tone-bar piano setting on his keyboard.

The audience was swept up before the rest of the band took the stage. Nearly everyone was standing, swaying back and forth in time and clapping hands above their heads.

"Jesus," thought Redd. "The Bluesbirds warmed 'em up more than we thought. We'll have to bust ass to build on this, that's for sure."

Redd stepped to the mic for lead vocal on the opening number, "Gypsy woman told my mother," (blow, draw, blow, blow) "Moanin' I was born" (blow, draw, blow, blow) "You got a boy child comin'" (blow, draw, blow, blow)

Mary Towne added a harmony for the fourth line of the first verse, "He's gonna be a son of a gun"

Vanessa continued to lay down rhythm with the harp. Mary and Redd, in a variety of combinations, sang about making pretty women "jump and shout" until the world would know just what it was "all about."

John Flood kicked the bass drum into gear. Art Abbott hit nineteen quick beats on the guitar. Rebekah shook a tambourine, and joined Redd and Mary as they sang through the portion of the lyrics affirming that "I'm here," finally resolving with Redd singing, "I'm the Hoochie Coochie Man," (and everybody knew that he was there).

During the eight bar interlude between the first and second verses, the animated crowd erupted with applause. "Guess they liked that," thought Redd. A disappointed moment later, it was apparent that the burst of enthusiasm from the audience coincided with Wesley Perkins appearing on stage. A follow spot illuminated the sax player, reflecting tiny silver sparks off the horn back into the audience.

Redd sang about having a black cat bone. Wesley Perkins took over Vanessa's duties, maintaining rhythm between vocal lines with his saxophone. He swayed back and forth, playing with his eyes closed, immersed in a private yellow fantasy. Even the simple, four note phrasing was so rhythmically perfect and tonally astonishing that the audience responded with shouts, whistles, and applause.

"Jesus," thought Art, "they're applaudin' the damn rhythm line 'stead of the lead vocal!"

Vanessa reached for her cowbell and drumstick, adding a punctuated "clunk" to the final beat of Wesley's regular rhythm lines.

Security guards Bill Lewis and Jim Taylor stood five rows deep in the auditorium, stage left.

"Pretty good show, don't you think?" asked Bill.

"Damn right. I worked this show a couple of years ago, but that was just Memphis Rail. They're like a whole new band with these extra people. A hell of a lot better, if you ask me. Listen to that guy on the sax. It's almost unreal. Wow."

The audience suddenly exploded with excitement. Cameras flashed from all corners of the hall.

Jim raised his voice to be heard. "Aw, shit. What part of 'No Photography' was too hard for these people to understand?"

Bill snorted, "We better just let it be. Looked like maybe a couple hundred folks takin' pictures. I wonder why all of a sudden, oh sure, look! The damned dog is getting' into the act!"

Indeed, Wesley the Dog was tapping absolutely perfect time with his tail.

"I never knew a dog could do that," marveled Jim. "I saw this in an on-line video a while ago and thought maybe it was faked."

"No fake, man. No fake at all. Hell, there it is."

Andrew Carrier performed an admirable piano solo after the second verse. "Not quite Ann Foster, but he'll do to get us by for a while," thought Mary.

Redd and Mary passed the lyrics of the third verse back and forth. Redd sang about the "seventh hour," Mary about the "seventh day." Following the line in which listeners were cautioned not to mess with a man who had "seven hun'red dollah" Art Abbott shadowed the vocals with subtle runs on his guitar.

Wesley Perkins never missed a beat. Every note was stunning. Wesley the Dog fascinated the crowd with his uncanny ability to keep rhythm. After the third chorus, Wesley began a saxophone solo.

The low notes growled, the high notes soared. Technique morphed seamlessly from moments where long, lazy tones seemed impossibly overlapped to runs where lightning would have struggled to keep up with Wesley's flying fingers. Mary Towne motioned toward the sax player with the sweep of her arm. Applause rolled in like a marble bowling ball down a cast iron alley. "What the hell," brooded John Flood. "It's pretty tough to take. This nerdy white guy and a damn dog, upstagin' us so badly."

The seats could no longer contain the audience. Suddenly fans were dancing in the aisles, standing on the cushions, and in some cases climbing atop the shoulders of others to get a better view. The first row stood and pressed up against that stage.

"Aw, shit," fussed Bill Taylor. "They just got started and here we go already."

"Yup. Time to get busy. Seattle said we can expect all hell to break out when they wind up with 'Summertime'."

Chuck Gould

Part Six, Chapter Three

Night rain fell on Iberia Parish. Hundreds of worshipers, wearing dark clothes beneath uniform transparent rain gear and wide brimmed plastic hats, knelt around the perimeter of the old Brinkman house. Each sheltered a single candle from the elements, accepting a relight from an adjacent congregant should the storm manage to steal the flame from the wick. All prayed in silence.

Maria Cueva Reyes lay on a birthing bed, head and shoulders elevated with pillows. Her moans and labored groans were omnipresent against the silence and patience of hope and expectation. Jose shifted uncomfortably in a wooden chair, one room away. He could not understand why the midwives were keeping him away from Maria in her hour of stress and fear, but he was willing to accept there was much he had not understood since Father McNeil sent them on this cross country quest.

Most of the Elders knelt before the front steps of the home. Silas Bishop would take a knee to pray, then stand up and look restlessly around. Each time he stood, Abner Culliford tugged on Bishop's rain jacket and encouraged him to resume the posture of prayer.

Billy Proctor and Bridget Bishop deliberately knelt at the outer edge of the circle. They left a gap of several feet between their position and the rest of the worshipers. Their candles both blew out, but neither bothered with a relight. They were more alone, at least for the moment, than Silas Bishop would have approved. In the darkness, and with some space, they whispered secrets of the soul.

"We could sneak off into that brush over there, that is if you wanted to," suggested Billy.

"Is that all you ever think about? Christ, Billy. We might be about to witness the Second Coming."

Billy frowned skeptically. "You really think?"

"Maybe. And if it is, we're like the shepherds or something, right?"

"I think we need be careful we don't turn out to be the sheep. Hey, I suddenly need to pee really badly. You stay here, I'll duck over to the brush by myself for a minute, then I'll be right back."

"Yeah, but hurry. What if something happens while you're gone?"

"Nothing's going to happen while I take a pee, trust me."

Billy Proctor stepped carefully through the darkness. Any trace moonlight was absorbed by the solid expanse of quilted black rain clouds. He reached the edge of the thicket, without stumbling, and opened his fly. As he began to urinate, he heard a familiar voice.

"Hello, Billy. Big night, dontcha think?"

Billy looked over his left shoulder. There stood Red Scarf, tonight wearing a transparent plastic rain jacket over his customary overcoat, and with his face wrapped behind a red stole.

"Oh, shit. You again? Every time you show up, all sorts of trouble seems to follow."

"Don't feel that way, Billy. The trouble's here all long before I get here. Maybe I just make it a little easier to find. But even that depends on what you call trouble."

Billy completed the puddle and zipped up his pants. "So, let me ask you. What's really going on here tonight? Is this just so much bullshit, or do Silas and the others really have this dialed in."

Red Scarf tipped his head back and roared with laughter.

Billy was alarmed. He looked quickly over his shoulder to see if Red Scarf had disturbed anyone else in the community. "God's sake, dude. Be quiet!"

"Nobody can hear me right now except you. Wouldn't matter how loud I yelled. Wouldn't matter at all."

"Ok, but what's so damn funny?"

"Well, let's start with the fact that we've got Mary and Joseph in the old Brinkman house. Joseph is a carpenter. They traveled a long distance with Mary about to give birth. Any of this sound familiar?"

"Of course."

"So then," started Red Scarf. "But wait a second, I've got an idea. Do you smoke?"

"Huh? No, not really. I mean I've tried weed a couple of times, and bummed a couple of cigarettes with beer once in a while."

"Time to start!" Red Scarf extended his wrists, palm down. When he rotated his hands outward, each held a thick, dark cigar tipped with a glowing ash. "Pick one, Billy."

"What the hell did you just do? It looked like you created a couple of cigars out of thin air!"

Red Scarf shook his head. "No, I didn't. In fact, I'm not allowed to create anything Creation is a special privilege."

"Then how do you explain…"

"But I'm allowed to move stuff around as much as I want. Makes for some real surprises, that does. Somewhere right now, there's a couple of guys wondering what the hell happened to their cigars." Red Scarf laughed heartily. "The hell indeed!"

Billy reached for a cigar, and examined it skeptically. "So, what's in this, anyway?"

"Tobacco, mostly. And beyond that? Nothing I wouldn't smoke myself." Red Scarf took a long drag on the remaining stogie.

Billy puffed lightly on the cigar, and was astonished by how much he enjoyed the taste. "Hey, this isn't half bad!"

"No it isn't. Not half at all. Now, about the events that will unfold here momentarily. They aren't going to turn out as most expect."

"I sort of thought that might be the case."

"It's been a great prank. Lots of fun. But some of the Elders have assumed too much. They think they are gifted with prophecy, but they cannot know the hour. Father McNeil owed me a favor. Something to do with an altar boy, a few years back. He helped me set up everything you see going down here tonight."

"Is there even any truth to the bullshit that Jesus had a twin?"

"Billy, you disappoint me. Didn't I recommend that you not believe it?"

"Yeah, but I don't trust you. You might tell me not to believe it because it's really true."

"I might. Or, I might not. That's where faith has to help you decide." Red Scarf laughed with such enthusiasm that he shook in place. Billy was glad that only he could hear the diabolical cackle. "But, I can tell you that just as Silas and the Elders have predicted, there will be twins born here. Tonight. On that you have my word."

Billy took a deeper draught of his cigar. "So why come to me with this, anyway?"

"There are plans in place that will need a man of your special talents. There will be an opportunity to lead this community, sooner than anyone can know. Sooner than anyone might imagine. I'd like you to be that leader."

"Me? I'm almost still a kid."

"You've got the gift of spiritual leadership, Billy. The people will trust you. I'll fill your mouth with phrases, sentences, speeches, and poetry that will build our flock, er, I mean your flock, of course, into a major church."

Billy shook his head in refusal and tossed his cigar onto the ground. "I can't go along with that, especially if you're involved."

"Don't be so hasty, man. There's plenty for both of us, and a very special gift for you."

Billy frowned with suspicion. "Yeah, what kind of gift?"

"Her name's Bridget. I think you know her. In fact I think you know her extremely well," chortled Red Scarf. "She will love you, and you alone, with unbridled passion from now until your dying day. Look forward to a love-filled life. Just allow me to help you build a church. It will be OK, and sometime years from now we'll settle, shall we say, miscellaneous accounts?"

Billy turned his back on Red Scarf to look toward Bridget. She craned her head to see if her boyfriend was returning from his trip to the thicket. Billy was sure he had never desired her more than in that moment. In fact, he was sure that no man had ever so desired a woman.

"Well, I'll be damned," said Billy, "but I'm goin' to say yes."

"Your wish is my command."

Red Scarf flicked his left hand, and another cigar appeared. "Here you go. Have another cigar. Bridget will actually like the smell. She's going to like it a lot. I'll keep you supplied with these, as many as you'll ever need, for as long as you're going to need them."

There was a shrill scream in the Brinkman house, and then another. A baby's cry was heard, and then a second.

"Better get back to Bridget, things are starting to come together." Red Scarf began fading into a mist. "Watch for me. We'll talk again soon."

Bridget, along with the rest of the worshipers, was standing and cheering. She motioned to Billy, "C'mon! The twins are born!"

Billy exhaled an aromatic cloud. "Yeah, so they are. But they're fraternal, not identical. These cannot be the twins we're waiting for."

Bridget was stunned. "How the hell would you know whether they were fraternal or identical? And what's that smell, have you been smoking?"

"I suppose I'm just guessing about the fraternal thing. And yeah, I had a cigar."

Bridget inhaled deeply. "I don't usually care for cigar smell, but there's something pretty special about that one. I like it."

The cheering and clapping subsided as Silas Bishop emerged from the Brinkman house. He looked troubled and pained. "Brothers and sisters, we have a new set of healthy twins here in the community. They're fraternal twins. One boy, one girl. We know that Jesus could not return as a woman, so these are not the twins we're expecting."

A sigh of disappointment swept through the crowd. Some voices farthest from Silas grumbled with discontent.

"But God hasn't said, 'no', He's merely said 'not yet'. Keep the faith, and the prophecy will be fulfilled."

Silas extended his hand through the doorway of the house, and motioned someone to step out. "Brothers and Sisters, allow me to introduce a new brother, Jose Cueva Reyes. The new mother is his wife, Maria. They will remain among us. Jose is a carpenter. May God be praised."

"May God be praised," echoed the congregation. Silas detected only a half-hearted enthusiasm among many of those assembled.

Bridget stared accusingly at Billy. "How the hell did you know? How in the hell?"

Billy shrugged. "Don't know, really. It just sort of occurred to me while I was smokin' the cigar."

Part Six, Chapter Four

Similar to Seattle, the audience was ecstatic and frenzied as "St James Infirmary" morphed into "Summertime" and the first show at San Francisco's Bill Graham Civic Auditorium climaxed. When the ruckus was finally contained, security guard Taylor phoned the dispatch office. "We're feeling a little unsafe here. Barely kept things from getting out of hand. Send us another 20 or 25 guys, at least. The second show starts in 90 minutes. Yeah, I agree. It's a pretty animated crowd for the blues."

Memphis Rail and the Family Jones retired the green room. Tables were set up along the perimeter walls. A catering company had laid out light beverages and snacks. Redd Wilmott, first through the door, high-fived the other musicians as they entered. "Damn good show!"

"We rocked 'em, and hard," agreed Rebekah.

"We killed em! And you never sounded better, Redd" said Mary.

"Thanks Mary, you too."

"That might be the most fun I ever had," confirmed Vanessa. "Time to come out of these glasses for a while."

"Is this just getting a lot easier, or am I getting that much better?" asked Wesley.

Everyone frowned. Vanessa and Rebekah exchanged a private glance of concern.

Art Abbott and John Flood slapped Redd's hand, but without any semblance of joy or accomplishment. Neither the guitar player nor the drummer said anything at all.

Redd congratulated Andrew Carrier as he entered. "Hey, nice work on keyboards. You're fittin' in like we've been playin' together for a hundred years, or somethin'."

"Thanks, Redd. You guys make me sound better than I am. Not sure why, but it's true. You guys blew down the house. Can't remember when I've heard anybody as good. Maybe never heard anybody better. It's damn nearly like magic, or somethin'."

"Or somethin'" grumbled John Foster. "Hey, y'all, me and Art are gonna slip out the back door and get some air. Be back in plenty of time for the next show. Hell, we'll be back before the Bluesbirds are up again."

Wesley the Dog whined. "Maybe we better take him out for a walk," said Rebekah. "Me and Vanessa. Wes, you come along too. Give the three of us a chance to talk."

Mary whirled around from a snack table, face creased with amazement and alarm. "You crazy, gal? No way can you go out this building right now with that dog. Especially the three of you together. Y'all won't make it fifteen seconds before there gonna be people just climbin' all over."

Vanessa was embarrassed. "Of course. But I think the dog has to go."

"Usually, we'd get somebody from the crew to take him out to do his business," replied Mary, "but the dog's as recognizable as any of the rest of us. Wes, why don't you take the dog down to the Men's and see if you can get him to piss on the floor or somethin'. If he sees you doin' it, he might get the idea."

"I'm not going to piss the floor."

"You don't have to. Just let the dog see you piss into the john. If you have any luck, we'll get somebody to go in after and wipe it up. We can't afford any accidents on stage."

"C'mon boy," called Wesley. The dog responded immediately and they disappeared into the hallway.

Mary grabbed a sparkling water, and motioned for Vanessa and Rebekah to join her. Redd and Andrew were swapping jokes at one end of the room. Mary Towne and the sisters gathered in a circle at the other.

"Somethin' up with Wes?" asked Mary. "Looks like he's startin' to think more of this is about him than actually is."

"I think we all noticed," agreed Vanessa.

"True," said Rebekah, "but give him a little break here. He's playin' the bejesus out of that sax. I mean, if you really listen he's surpassed what Judah Jones used to do. Yeah, he could be and should be a little more humble, but…"

"But," interrupted Mary, "he still ain't chopped enough wood to be struttin' the star. Egos have tore up more acts over the years than anything else. We always had a balance. If Wes goes down the road with some big ego, we're probably screwed."

Vanessa listened, with eyes closed and the bridge of her nose pinched between her thumb and forefinger. She nodded, opened her eyes, and responded, "Yeah. We'll talk to him. As soon as he comes back with the dog. Rebekah and me and Wes? We got into this because we were freaked out by some things goin' on and thought we'd be safer if we stuck together."

"I still feel like that!" insisted Rebekah.

"Yeah, me too. But what happens if old reliable Wesley starts getting some big head? Starts believing that he's so special nothing can possibly happen to him, or to any of us. Hell, it's not like he's here to protect us."

"Sometimes I feel like he is, though" countered Rebekah.

Mary Towne rolled her eyes, and reached out to put a hand on Rebekah's knee. "You obviously got more influence on him than the rest of us. Hell, it usually ain't that hard to bring your man to heel and you know damn well what I mean. See if you can't settle him down."

"OK."

"What's more, I get the feelin' that Art and John are pretty pissed off. Wes's remark about how he's just getting so much better didn't help a thing, trust me. Get him to reach out to those guys a bit."

Chuck Gould

Part Six, Chapter Five

Ira Miller made a final pass through the merchandise tables. He paused long enough to look over the shoulders of most contract vendors and offer some instruction.

"No, keep a variety in sight but don't fill the CD racks too full. Put "Blues Breakout Redux" in a separate row. Give the impression stuff is selling fast. Hell, shouldn't be too hard, because it is!"

As the crowd from the first show filtered out, Ira retired to the small office behind the door marked, "Agents and Promoters Only." He booted up his notebook computer, logged onto a secure web site, and reviewed sales numbers. Both shows were sold out. The 500 tickets personally acquired by Ira were all resold at huge markups from face value. Even in the original glory days of Memphis Rail, the money had never been this good.

Someone knocked insistently on the door. Thump, thump, thump! "Ira, you in there man? Hey, open up, we need to talk to you!" Ira recognized the voice; John Flood.

"OK, sure. Hang on a second!" Ira logged off the page detailing financial information about the concert.

Ira opened the door. Art Abbott and John Flood stood outside the office, animated with concern. "Yeah, come on in, guys. Great first show. Really. We'll own San Francisco by the end of the night."

Art Abbott was grim and direct. He extended his cell phone toward Ira. "Yeah, good show, but what's with this shit, Ira? What's up?"

"Sorry, but I don't have any idea what shit you're talking about."

Art shook the phone. "Right here. One of my old runnin' buddies down in LA sent me a text. Somethin' about 'how's it feel to be working for a white guy and his dog?'"

Ira stalled for time. "What do you suppose he meant by that?"

John Flood replied. "Don't bullshit us, Ira. How many years have we been doin' this? It's too late to start bullshittin' us now. We ran a search on the advance publicity for LA. What the hell, Ira? After all these fuckin' years?"

Ira tried to suppress a blush. "How could you have a problem with the publicity? Jesus, guys. Seattle? Two shows sold out. San Francisco? Two shows, sold out. We're damn nearly sold two shows at the LA Forum; so that's another 35,000 seats. We're three dates into the year, and there's more money here than any of us have seen since, well hell, maybe since forever."

"It ain't the money," countered Art. "It's the goddam insult."

Ira sighed and collapsed back into his chair. "Sit down guys. Obviously there's something crawling up your butts, so let's hash it out."

"Thanks, but I'll stand" said John.

"Me too," agreed Art. "Take a look at the poster on my phone. What the hell did you do? From what we can tell, every fuckin' poster hangin' in LA looks just like this one."

Ira took the phone from Art and made a pretense of examining the poster. There was no actual need to do so. The poster on Art's phone was exactly what Ira ordered. In the upper left hand corner was an artist's rendition of Wesley Perkins playing the saxophone. In the upper right corner, a drawing of Wesley the Dog, tapping tail in time to the blues. Large, bright text in the center read, "Blues Breakout Redux Tour! One Night Only! Wesley Perkins and Wesley the Dog!" In slightly smaller font, the text continued, "Appearing with Memphis Rail and the Family Jones" A group image of the original Memphis Rail was centered just below the middle of the artwork. Rebekah and Vanessa appeared in the lower left hand corner, in smaller scale than Wesley and the dog. The remaining text detailed the location, date, and the web address for tickets.

Ira smiled weakly. "Yeah, that's pretty much what we ordered," he admitted. "Looks like it's working, doesn't it?"

John balled up his fists. "Workin'? Workin' at what? You lose your damn mind, Ira? This Wesley guy is getting such a big head there ain't hardly room for the rest of us on stage. You gotta see that. But, hell, it's like you're tryin' to encourage it or somethin'"

"I'm working at selling seats, John. You know how long the videos of that dog have been viral on line?"

Art slapped the palm of his hand on Ira's desk. "But that's just it. A lot of these people are comin' to see the damn dog. We're playin' maybe the best we've ever done. I can't say why, but we ain't never been this good."

"Yeah," agreed Ira. "You ought to be pleased."

John said, "But the place only goes nuts when the dog starts waggin' his tail and our freak show sax player blows some sort of unholy, gotta be technically impossible, shit outa that old horn!"

Ira motioned emphatically with both hands. "What the hell do you guys care what they come to see? I'll hang my rosy red Jewish ass out for everybody to see if it will build the gate."

John snorted. "Yeah Ira, I believe you would. Me and Art, we've talked this out. We'd rather be playin' for seven hundred bucks a night in a roadhouse than whored out for forty thousand playin' side man to some wanna-be blues man and a goddam dog. It wasn't so bad when he was all humble and confused about how he could be playin' what he's playin', but now that he's got the big head, we're done."

Ira jerked to attention. "Done? What the hell do you mean you're done?"

Art laughed. "Well that got your attention, didn't it? What we mean, is that we ain't gonna just quit on you between shows. Hell, we'll even play LA. But, Ira, you best be auditionin' some drums and a guitar player. Shouldn't be too hard to find. Just look for a couple of guys willin' to sell their integrity for huge money. That just ain't gonna be us no more."

"Oh, shit, guys. Think about the act. All the years together. Don't just walk off like this. Give me a chance to straighten shit out. It can be like old times again."

Art and John began leaving the office. With his hand on the doorknob, John turned to say, "No, Ira. No matter what happens from here on out, it ain't never gonna be like old times. Not never again."

"Wait!" shouted Ira. "Have you told Mary and Redd?"

"Not yet. No need to mess with their heads before the second show. But they're soon enough gonna know you're lookin' for a drummer and an axeman. They deserve to hear it from us. You got us through LA, Ira. Then, contract or no, you're gonna cash us out. You owe us that after all these years."

Ira softened his intense demeanor. "OK, guys. Let's agree that you're committed to stay through LA. Beyond that, can I ask you to keep an open mind for at least a couple of days? See how things work out? Maybe you owe me something too, after all these years."

Chuck Gould

Part Six, Chapter Six

Abner Culliford, age eighty-one, beloved patriarch of the Christian community at West Moccasin Springs, died quietly in his sleep. Beyond the expected grief and despair, dangerously dark undercurrents of disappointment and anger swirled through the community.

The Elders met in executive session. The birth of the Cueva Reyes twins, fraternal rather than identical, fostered doubts among the faithful. Why had the prophecy, to which leadership was so committed, been corrupted? Had the pilgrims foolishly committed their faith, as well as most of their worldly goods, to an imperfect cause? There were whispered conversations about a class action lawsuit for recovery of assets. The Elders overheard, and realized the crisis called for a dramatic response.

Silas Bishop assumed his place at the head of the table, but immediately sensed a change among his spiritual brothers. All eyes were focused in his direction. The glare was almost as uniform as the starched white shirts and bright red neckties on both flanks.

Silas hesitated for a moment, and then resolved to look as confident as possible. "Welcome brothers. Let's open with a prayer. Brother Wilthaus, would you pray for us please?"

Brother Wilthaus did not respond.

Silas looked over the entire assembly. "Apparently Brother Wilthaus is not so inspired. Anybody else?"

None of the Elders responded.

Silas endeavored to disguise his disappointment. "Alright, then. I'll lead the prayer. Father God, author of light and darkness, we ask for your merciful guidance…:

Brother Aptford interrupted, "Enough! We been prayin' on this already, Silas. This whole community is on the verge of splittin' up. We got no choice but to do something about it. We risked everything to come here, and now we could lose it all."

Silas put his index finger behind his neck tie. He tugged at the knot to create a looser fit. "Yes, the death of Brother Abner was a shock. At least he went quietly. Without pain. It's the sort of death a lot of people hope for."

"It's not just Abner's death," insisted Aptford. "We could deal with that, and get past it. We disappointed everybody with the twins. Maybe we shouldn't have let that carpenter and his wife stay. Every time somebody sees those twins they're gonna know we blew the prophecy."

Another Elder spoke. "We don't know that the prophecy is blown. We don't know that Jesus won't be born again right here in our community. Maybe there will be more twins? Maybe these twins just weren't the right ones. Sort of like John the Baptist twins, or something."

Silas responded with a scriptural affirmation. "Good works in mysterious ways, and no man knows the hour."

Aptford slapped the table top with his palm. "Cut the crap, Silas. Maybe no man knows the hour, but we damn nearly promised these people the birth of miraculous twins. If we're gonna stand up and claim to know the hour, we sure as hell better know where the hands are sittin' on the clock. If not, shit is gonna blow back. Exactly like it's startin' to do."

A chair screeched when pushed away from the far end of the table. Brother Abaddon, undoubtedly the most superannuated resident of the community and among the earliest settlers, rose. Abaddon almost never spoke at community meetings. When he did, everyone paid careful heed.

Abaddon cleared his throat, and spoke in a weak, raspy voice. "When the crops fail, it's because the king is infertile. You have to sacrifice the king. It's time to replace the king with somebody younger. Somebody more virile so prosperity can return. We're nearly all agreed, Silas. It's time for a new king and time for you to go."

Silas surveyed the assembly. All but two heads were nodding in grim agreement with Abaddon.

"So you think this is my fault? How in hell is it my fault?"

Abaddon resumed his seat and Brother Aptford replied. "It doesn't matter about fault, Silas. We need a change to restore hope among the people. You're gonna be that change. We got somebody available to replace you, so it's time for you to go back home."

"My home is here," insisted Silas. "I got a house here. My daughter's here."

262

"It would be best for the community if you were simply gone," said Brother Wilthaus. "You need somewhere to go, so I already spoke to my brother up in Hibbing. Cold as a cast iron toilet seat up there in the winter, but he's got steady work available at decent pay. Job's yours if you want it, but you need to be up there by the end of the week."

"You think I'm just going to go quietly?"

"We voted you in, we can vote you out. Quiet or not, you're gone."

Silas struggled to maintain his temper. His voice sounded like steel and fire. He stood. "So, which of you thinks you're capable to stepping into these shoes? I don't see any obvious replacement. Not by a long, long ways. You need to pray over this again. There's still time to reconsider."

Aptford replied, "None of us. The people won't accept any of us, not after the twins."

"Then, who?"

"A younger man. One who just expressed his unconditional commitment to the community. One who has been inspirational as a preacher. He's the peoples' choice. He's our choice. Billy Proctor."

"That kid! Are you guys out of your minds? He's still a teenager."

In his distinctive, high pitched voice Brother Abaddon asserted, "Nevertheless. That's our decision. We believe it's divinely inspired. We will be installing Brother Proctor tomorrow afternoon, and it would be less awkward if you departed for Minnesota beforehand."

Silas began to speak, "You can't just..." but was physically unable to speak when Brother Abaddon rose again from his chair and extended a hand toward Silas.

"I believe that will be all, Brother Silas. We thank you for your service, but your responsibilities here are concluded."

In a single file procession led by Brother Abaddon, the Elders filed out of the meeting room and left Silas, alone, weeping in his chair.

Part Six, Chapter Seven

The second show exceeded all expectations. After every performance, audiences agreed that no act at any time ever played the blues as well as the nearly miraculous and energized audio experience just then witnessed on stage. Even so, each show was slightly better than the former. Redd, Mary, John, Art, keyboardist Andrew Carrier, Vaness, Rebekah and Wesley Perkins were all justifiably pleased with the performance.

Most of the trouble began when a few reporters from Bay area publications and radio stations leveraged their back stage passes into an impromptu press conference. The reporters assembled in a way that separated Wesley Perkins from the other musicians. Cameras flashed. Microphones were stuffed under his nose. Wesley Perkins was clearly the Man of the Hour.

Wesley knew this special attention could foster trouble. Rebekah and Vanessa warned him during intermission, "Don't get the big head, Wes. You're starting to piss a few people off. This isn't about you. It's not about any of us, individually. It's about the three of us sticking together until things get back to normal."

Wesley looked beyond the gaggle of reporters to his fellow performers assembled behind. None of them looked pleased with the situation. Art and John seemed especially disgusted, Mary Towne looked worried, Redd seemed confused. Vanessa put her hand over her mouth, as if to motion "be quiet." Rebekah looked on with a pained grimace and a furrowed brow.

The interview began. "Wesley, you sure kicked out the jambs again tonight. Some people are saying you might be the best blues saxophone player in history. Why is it that nobody ever really heard of you before now? Where have you been?"

Wesley blushed. He noticed John Flood, tapping with impatient annoyance on a table top. "Well, to begin with, it would be pretty tough to say that I'm the best sax player that ever was. I'm pretty sure I'm not. But I did start playing the sax back in high school and college. I made a different career choice. You might say I was sort keeping my light under a bushel. Playing professionally is brand new."

Another reporter pressed forward. "How long did it take the Family Jones to train that dog? Memphis Rail never had a dog. How do you get him to keep time like that?"

Art and John looked especially displeased, glancing sideways and frowning at one another. Wesley was aware that his first answer hadn't done anything to relieve internal tensions among the performers.

"Actually, we didn't have to train the dog at all. He's got some uncanny ability to keep time. Simple time, compound time, and virtually any tempo. I don't know if all dogs have a sense of rhythm and just don't bother showing it, or if there's something special about Wesley."

"That's another thing. Isn't it strange that you and the dog have the same name?"

"Yeah, but that's a long and not very interesting story." Wesley fought to get ahead of the interview curve. "Hey, I know you're supposed to be asking questions and I'm supposed to answer, but what did you think of the rest of the group tonight? Weren't they fantastic? Why don't you get their takes on tonight's show? I'm sure they can tell you a lot more than I can about what went down."

None of the reporters moved. Each seemed deaf to Wesley's suggestion that they interview anyone else in the room.

"Wesley, what can you tell us about your horn? It looks pretty old. Who made it? Is there a brand name?"

"No, not really. I don't actually know how old it is, or who made it. Honestly, I picked it up in a pawn shop and I don't think the pawnbroker knew everything there was to know about it, either. Say, I'm a little worn out. Why don't you folks grab some snacks and drinks and talk to the rest of the band? Mary was great tonight. Art drew flames out of that guitar of his. John drummed like nobody's business. See what they have to say."

The press seemed reluctant to back away. A reported asked, "One last question, please. How do explain the fantastic tone you get out of the saxophone? I mean, you play it really well but a lot of people think it's the quality of the sound that's even more exceptional."

Wesley held up both index fingers, as if stretching an invisible rubber band. He pointed them at the press like a pair of pistols. The other musicians looked increasingly annoyed with the adulation of Wesley Perkins. He needed to think quickly, to come up with a statement that would smooth things over with Memphis Rail.

"You said one last question, so here's one last answer. A lot of the arrangements in this show feature the saxophone, but let's not get carried away thinking that it's just about the saxophone, or about me, or about the dog. It isn't. Right here in this room are some of the finest musicians on the planet. If I sound any good at all, it's only because I've got people of this caliber to back me up."

Mary Towne gasped.

Unconcerned about being overheard by the press, Art Abbott sneered, "Oh, you've 'got people', Wes? Is that about it?"

John Flood threw up his hands in disgust. "Yeah, dude. Thank God we're standin' 'round ready to back your sorry ass up every time you wanna put on a show. I wondered what the fuck we were good for."

Wesley now ignored the press. "Hey, come on guys. That's not what I meant at all. Maybe it didn't come out right."

Redd Wilmott threw out his arms, as if to hug the assembled reporters, and ushered them toward the door. "Uh, I think we're all pretty tired after doin' two shows. We'll count on you guys to forget about the little tension you just saw. It ain't nuthin', not really. Kind of comes with stress of bein' on the road."

The press surrendered easily, yielding to Redd's authoritative confidence. As soon as the door closed, Art said, "I'm outta here for tonight. I'll be in LA in time for sound check, but I need some time to get my head together before we play another show."

"Me too," insisted John. "See you in LA."

Art and John walked out together.

"That could have gone better. A hell of a lot better," sighed Mary Towne.

"I'm really sorry. Crap, I didn't mean for it to come out like that. That's not what I meant. It isn't what I think. It's not what I feel. Jesus, I'm really sorry but I didn't do anything on purpose."

Andrew Carrier tossed a partially eaten sandwich into the trash. "Maybe somebody needs to spell it out for you, man. Take a look. You see any difference between you and everybody else here? Somethin' maybe just a bit obvious?"

"Oh, shit," complained Wesley. "You're not gonna go there, are you?"

Andrew softened his tone. "What you don't get, Wes, is that for us it ain't a matter of goin' anywhere. We live there. Stuff you can say to or about white people don't always come across the same when it's a white guy talkin' about black folks."

Wesley began, "I didn't really mean…"

"No, you probably didn't mean anything. You just didn't stop to think. There's a bunch of history involved. Stuff we can't any of us change. Just gotta try to go forward."

Mary Towne came to Wesley's rescue. "Speakin' of movin' forward, y'all, let's have the driver bring the car around and go back to the hotel. My butt's draggin'. Gettin' too old to do two of these in a night. One of these days I'm gonna just go home."

Vanessa stood up and removed her sunglasses. "Mary, did you ever stop to think that bein' home might have as much to do with who you are as it does wherever you're at?"

Mary sighed. "Not tonight, 'Nessa. I'm too tired get my head around all that voodoo bullshit. No offense."

Rebekah reached for Wesley's hand, and put it around her waist. "Yeah, it's time to go back to hotel. Vanessa, you stop by our room after we get there. The three of us need to talk a couple of things through here. Let's make sure we're stayin' on course."

Part Six, Chapter Eight

The Cardinal sat and brooded. He pulled the wolf skin cloak more tightly around his shoulders, and leaned closer to the central fire. His raven paced anxiously across the hearthstones, as if sensitive to his master's concerns. The Cardinal opened his left hand, and blew a steaming breath into the palm. The breath coalesced into a transparent stone pipe. The Cardinal held his right hand over the bowl, spontaneously lighting the contents. He leaned back into the chair and drew softly on the pipe stem. The cloud of smoke he exhaled was filled with images from around the corner of the cosmos.

The same trio of humans remained in possession of the sacrifice. The dog, dispatched to create a psychic channel to the humans, was serving well. Zaccheus appeared concerned about a lack of progress by Joseph Smith. Even so, Smith was the best currently available asset to recover the sacrifice. Perkins must surrender the sacrifice voluntarily. Smith was enlisting the help of Ira Miller.

The Ira Miller factor was predictable. Miller was motivated by money, entirely unaware that merely increasing the quantity of cash would never instill any permanent or genuine value in the common trash of currency. Miller would be easy.

Wesley Perkins held the key. Of course he would eventually succumb to the primary weakness of all human beings; self-awareness becoming self-importance. If Perkins surrenders the sacrifice to Miller, or Smith, the mission will be nearly complete. Red Scarf, brother to the Cardinal, remained a random variable. If Red Scarf regained possession of the sacrifice, nothing would be lost but everything would remain unfulfilled.

"In the end, my brother will fail," thought the Cardinal. "The sacrifice will never serve his personal amusement. He will never gain the power to create a priesthood. There is no question about the ultimate outcome, only the route we will be forced to follow in the process. If there were such a thing as time, it would be on our side."

The stone pipe and the cloud of smoke disappeared. The Cardinal bowed his head in prayer, and his raven responded by tucking his head under a wing. "Father, if it be your will to resolve the difficulty with the sacrifice, I am your humble servant. If it be your will to extend the conflict, grant me the patience and wisdom to persevere; once again as your humble servant."

Part Six, Chapter Nine

The shouting was heard well beyond the walls of the Silas Bishop residence in West Moccasin Springs.

Silas turned away from a half packed suitcase on the kitchen table and slammed his fist against the wall. "Goddam it child! For the last time, I said to get your stuff together. There's nothing more to discuss. We're clearing out for Minnesota."

"Daddy, I told you I'm not going!"

"The hell with that. You're not so old that I can't make you come with me."

Bridget Bishop pounded her fists into her father's chest. "And I'm not so young you could ever keep me from coming back. I love Billy Proctor. We're going to get married."

Silas threw the suitcase across the room. "Do you have any idea? Any clue? You want to hurt a man's pride, then you got a good plan. The crazy-assed Elders are replacing me with a damn teenager, and you want to go jump in bed with the kid?"

"It's not about that, Daddy. Hell, I've already been to bed with Billy."

Silas made a fierce and intense face. "Why am I not surprised? You're every bit as much the slut as your mother ever was."

Bridget collapsed, sobbing. "Oh, God, Daddy. Please don't say that. I'm no slut, Mama wasn't either. Why would you say something so hateful? Think about my feelings. I love you, Daddy. That was just plain cruel."

Silas fell onto the couch, also on the verge of tears. He extended his arms toward Bridget. "Come here, daughter. I'm really sorry. I shouldn't have said that. I didn't mean it."

Father and daughter embraced silently for a full minute. Silas caressed the back of his daughter's head, while she slowly regained her composure. The tender moment was interrupted by a tentative knocking at the door.

"Come in!" yelled Silas.

Billy Proctor stepped through the door. Silas stood up in rapid response, but Bridget grabbed his forearm and warned, "Now, Daddy…"

"Sorry to bust in right now," said Billy, "but I needed to talk to you about me and Bridget."

"Yeah? So what about you and my daughter?"

"To the point? I love her. She loves me. I want to ask your permission to marry her."

"Jesus, Billy. Looks like you haven't asked my permission about anything else so far."

"Daddy!"

Silas glared at Billy as he returned to his seat on the couch. He spoke with measured energy. "Well, I'll hand you this. You're enough of a man to face me, circumstances being as they are, and all. Probably don't make you enough of a man to marry my daughter, but it helps. You sure about this? Billy? Seems pretty sudden to me."

"Of course we're sure!" exclaimed Bridget.

"Hush, now. I'm talkin' to Billy. Why don't you go out for a five minute walk and let Billy and me have a little man-to-man talk? You guys are sort of ganging up on me here."

Bridget smiled and kissed her father on the forehead. She ran out the door, then disappeared around the side of the house where she could hear any conversation through the open kitchen window. Silas suspected she was still within earshot, but was mollified by her feigned compliance.

Silas stood up and walked to his liquor cabinet. He removed a bottle of single malt Scotch and two glasses. "Man enough to think about marriage, then you're man enough for a shot of whisky. I'll pour you one."

"Thanks, Brother Bishop." After a moment's delay, and obviously as an afterthought, Billy reached into his jacket pocket. "You brought the whisky, so let me offer you a cigar!"

Silas smiled. "I don't smoke much. Didn't know you did either. But sometimes I do like a cigar." He held the stogie under his nose and sniffed. "Smells really good!"

With glasses charged and cigars alight, Silas and Billy sat a few feet apart. They eyed one another suspiciously, but with a suggestion of admiration.

Silas broke the silence. "Well, I guess normally a father asks how a young man intends to support his daughter, but I guess we know the answer to that one, don't we?"

"I had nothing to do with how things turned out, Brother Bishop. The Elders came looking for me. They shouldn't blame you for the twins, and I told them so. They say God is calling me. I think they're right, and I want to marry Bridget. Getting you pissed off at me doesn't help that, though, does it?"

Silas took a long draw on his cigar, and then exhaled. "You guys are both so young. Kids, the both of you. You're old enough to marry in this state without parental consent, but she's more than just a little bit short. Why would I say yes? She's not a grown woman yet. She's gonna change some more over the years. You'll change too."

"Maybe so."

Silas sipped his whisky. "This place will change you. Count on it. Maybe not for the better. Getting excommunicated, or whatever the fuck you'd call it, puts a different light on it for me."

Billy searched for a confident and optimistic tone of voice. "Maybe you're right. Maybe neither of us is who we'll finally turn out to be and we will do some changin'. But think about it this way, as long as we love each other and stick together, won't we also be changin' together? You know, two married people are supposed to become one soul."

Outside the kitchen window, Bridget smiled excitedly. Her Billy was definitely holding his own.

Thirty seconds of silence elapsed. Billy debated whether to speak again, and try to restart the conversation, or to let Silas continue sorting out his thoughts. Silas took another deep drag on the cigar. "So, against my better judgment, young man, here's where it's at. You see that she gets at least her GED. You ever treat her like anything but a princess, you ever let her go hungry or be without a roof overhead, I don't care how far I might be from Louisiana, I'll be comin' back down here to kick your ass."

Bridget could not suppress a whoop of joy. Silas looked toward the kitchen window and smiled. "Short walk, daughter!"

Billy stood up and extended his hand to Silas, "Thanks so much, Brother Bishop."

"Yeah. But maybe you can practice callin' me 'Dad'."

Chuck Gould

Part Seven, Chapter One

Vanessa joined Wesley and Rebekah in their room at the Fairmont. They shared a bottle of red wine. The discussion was amiable, and predictable, until Wesley mentioned Ira's amended offer.

"One other thing. Ira's becoming fixated on this sax thing. He says the company that made this fancy new horn is anxious to tap into the publicity we're getting on the concert tour."

Vanessa scowled. "I don't always entirely trust Ira. There wouldn't be a problem with you holding that new horn for a photo, or something. We don't have any business giving up Judah's old saxophone as part of the deal."

Rebekah scratched herself on the shoulder and replied. "Twenty-five thousand dollars sounds like a lot of money, though, just to start playing a different horn."

Wesley said, "I'm confused. In some ways I'm not sure Judah's horn is ours to do whatever we want with. On the other hand, we saw how 'Bekah got along just fine without Caroline's jewelry. At least for a little while, until she got it back."

Vanessa closed her eyes and sipped her wine. "This whole thing, for the three of us, has always been about sticking together for protection and supporting each other. We don't know what the bastard in the red scarf is going to try next. Should Wes hang onto the horn? Maybe giving it up is how we'd finally get out of this trap. Maybe, if we don't have the saxophone we'll be out of danger."

"I get that," said Wesley. "But then what would the purpose be for everything we've gone through? It seems more and more to me like we're supposed to finish what Judah Jones started. Can we say we've done that, yet?"

"Tell you what concerns me," said Rebekah. "Look what happened to Judah Jones. What if there's something unlucky about that old saxophone? I don't want anything like that to happen to Wes."

"OK, Sis," warned Vanessa, "but before Wes makes, or we make, some decision to give up Judah's horn stop and think about something. What's happened, so far, not just to Judah Jones but all people that have been on the edges of this mess and sort and wore out their welcome? You know, like the pawn broker who sold Wes the horn and the jewelry. Like your old boss?"

Vanessa's point proved poignant. While Wesley and Rebekah contemplated her advice, the only sound was the clinking of a wine bottle against glass rims.

"Shit," groused Wesley, "Red Scarf once told me I'd serve his purpose either way. Maybe we're even more screwed if we try to get out than if we decide to stay."

Someone knocked. Wesley stood up and opened the door. There stood Ira Miller.

"Well," chuckled Wesley. "Speak of the devil."

Ira was puzzled. "What do you mean by that, exactly?"

"Nothing, really. We were just now discussing your offer to trade out my old sax for that new one. Hey, come on in and have some wine."

"Thanks, I will." Ira entered the room, carrying a titanium case sufficiently large and appropriately shaped to contain a saxophone.

Wesley the Dog lay quietly under a table, keeping a watchful eye on Ira Miller.

Miller nodded to the sisters. "Hello, Vanessa, Rebekah. Two exceptional shows tonight. I get tired of saying it after every performance, but Memphis Rail and you guys never sounded better. You're outdoing Seattle. The second show tonight blew away the first."

Vanessa pulled out a desk chair and offered it to Ira. "Thanks."

Rebekah poured a glass of wine for Ira. The promoter took a sip. "Wes, I want to congratulate you on being such a shrewd negotiator. Holding out, and not accepting the first offer for this new horn is paying some huge dividends. I managed to get the company up from twenty-five thousand dollars, all the way to fifty. That's one hell of a lot of money, just to trade your old saxophone for something brand new, and state of the art."

Ira sat the titanium case on his lap and opened the hasps to reveal a saxophone of such exceptional beauty it was as if the instrument radiated, rather than reflected light.

"Reminds me of the first time I saw…oh, never mind" said Wesley.

"So, what do you say?" asked Ira. "I've got some cash down in the hotel safe. Let's just swap horns and you'll be fifty thousand richer. Tax free. We can set up some publicity photos when we get to LA."

Vanessa responded quickly. "It's not that easy, Ira. Wesley, 'Bekah, and me? We're a team. We don't call ourselves Family Jones for nothing. Wesley wouldn't make this decision without us talking it all over first."

Ira became annoyed. "What are you saying? You each want a third of the fifty-thousand? Don't tell me you want fifty thousand apiece."

"It's not all about money," countered Rebekah.

"Well, not entirely," confirmed Wesley.

"And maybe not at all," said Vanessa.

"Well, then I guess you need another day or so to think it over," said Ira. "But what could you possibly lose? Look at this instrument. It's a prototype. There's nothing else like it in the world. Cast from diamond dust and molten glass, all fused together to be unbreakable."

"It's a great looking horn for sure," said Wesley. "Why don't I at least give it a try and see how it sounds. Who did you say makes this, again?"

"The guy from the factory calls it a Roten Schal. I don't know if that's the company name or the name of the designer, or what. The name can't be all that important."

Wesley began reaching for the horn. Vanessa lunged forward and grabbed his wrist. "No, Wes, don't. For God's sake, don't!"

Wesley was irritated that Vanessa interrupted his inspection of the horn. "Why not?"

"It's been a hell of a long time since my high school German class, but I just heard Ira say that horn's a Roten Schal. Means 'red scarf', in German."

"OK, so I'm confused," said Ira. "I don't understand how whatever the name means in German, even if it is 'red scarf', has to do with anything. Christ sake, Wesley. We'll get them to rename it. We can call it a Perkins-Jones, or whatever you want."

"Well," began Wesley.

Vanessa interrupted. "Where did you get that horn? Who brought it around?"

"Some guy named Joseph Smith. He represents the company that makes these saxophones, and I guess the owner of the firm wants to add Wesley's current horn to his collection. That's all I know about it, really."

Rebekah became more assertive than usual. She stood and walked to the door of the suite. Facing Ira, with a hand on the knob, she said, "Nothing's going to happen tonight. Maybe nothing's going to happen at all. Vanessa, Wes, and me? We need to talk this thing over some more. You wouldn't know how or why, but the fact they call this thing a Roten Schal is a sort of warning, as far as we're concerned."

Ira ignored the invitation to leave. "Look, I'm sort of hearing that time is an important factor in this deal. I don't know if I can do it, but what if instead of fifty thousand for Wesley I got you guys fifty thousand apiece? That sounds pretty tough to do, I know, but at least let me go back to Mr. Smith with some kind of counter offer. How about it?"

Wesley glanced back and forth between Rebekah and Ira. Vanessa noted his uncertainty with no small alarm. After an extended delay, Wesley said, "Let's just table this for tonight. Don't even ask about fifty thousand for each of us, because I'm not sure that would make the deal."

"For God's sake, Wes, give me something."

"Just tell the guy we're thinking about it," replied Wesley.

Ira Miller stood up to leave. "Careful. Sometimes if you think long you think wrong. You're not the only sax player who could introduce this instrument to the market."

"Thanks for dropping by," said Vanessa. "We'll talk this over among the three of us and get back to you. Maybe even as soon as tomorrow."

When he reached the door, Ira turned back and asked, "What if I could get them up to seventy-five thousand?"

"Good night, Ira," said Vanessa.

Ira shrugged hopefully, "Each?"

The three friends responded in unison. "Good night, Ira."

After Ira departed, Wesley Perkins sat on the couch. Vanessa sat on one side, and Rebekah on the other. Each of the women took one of Wesley's hands, as well as the free hand of her sister. The circle was silent for a moment.

Vanessa finally spoke. "Whatever is going on with Ira Miller, I don't think Red Scarf has anything to do with it. At least not directly."

Rebekah was surprised. "How so?"

"Well, what do we know about Red Scarf?"

Wesley spoke. "A couple of things, really. He claims he can't create anything, but he's allowed to move stuff around as much as he likes."

"Bingo," said Vanessa. "If Red Scarf wanted Judah's saxophone, he could just move it away from Wes to someplace else. Ira, and whoever is putting up the money, obviously can't just take it away from us- or they would."

"So maybe," added Rebekah, "what Red Scarf really wants is for Wes to have the sax? If that's so, maybe getting rid of the horn would get Red Scarf out of our lives. We could still go on being Family Jones, and playing with the Rail, right?"

"Don't forget what seems to happen to people when Red Scarf is done with them," cautioned Vanessa.

Wesley suddenly appeared worried. "Yeah, but there's something else we know about Red Scarf. He says he isn't allowed to destroy anybody, but nothing stops him from putting people together with stuff they can use to destroy themselves."

Vanessa broke the circle and rose from the couch. "Redd's waiting for me. I'm going up to our room. But let's just agree that there's more to consider here. Maybe we're damned if we do and damned if we don't."

Chuck Gould

280

Part Seven, Chapter Two

Rebekah opened the entry closet in the Fairmont Hotel suite she shared with Wesley Perkins. She pulled out a leash. Wesley the Dog frisked around energetically in response. "Probably time to walk the dog, Wes."

"Yeah, I'll take him outside to do his business. Care to come?"

Vanessa kissed Wesley on the cheek. "If it's all the same to you, I think I'll shower and get ready for bed. I'm just emotionally drained. Been a crazy day. Oh, and don't forget to put him in that Service Animal jacket."

The two Wesleys took the elevator to the hotel lobby. They passed through carefully arranged elegant furnishings, potted plants, and guests sufficiently sophisticated that the sight of a dog in the lobby was not especially disconcerting. A formally attired doorman assisted their egress, "Good evening, Sir."

"And to you as well, thanks."

Wesley the Dog sniffed inquisitively at a garden gnome positioned under a precisely manicured hedge of Japanese laurel. Wesley Perkins looked away, absent mindedly removing himself from the dog's impending moment of relief. Suddenly, the dog began to growl, then snarl, and finally tug violently on the leash. The garden gnome had disappeared. Red Scarf, appearing only fifteen inches tall, stood in its place.

"Damn it, Wesley. Don't let that animal bite me, or piss on me."

"Oh, shit! Why am I not surprised to see you just about now?"

"'Oh shit'? That's no way to greet an old friend."

The dog lunged at Red Scarf. Wesley pulled back on the leash, resulting in the dog being up on his hind legs. The dog jerked his head from side to side, as if fighting to be free of the leash.

"Old friend my ass," argued Wesley. "Can't think of a good reason not to just turn him loose on you."

"Get him under control," said Red Scarf. "I don't have any power to settle him down, but all you have to do is ask."

Wesley pulled steadily on the dog's service collar. "Easy boy. Easy now. Sit. It's OK."

Wesley the Dog sat next to Wesley Perkins, still tense and with teeth exposed, but mindful of the human's command."

"So what's with the little bitty size, tonight?" asked Wesley.

Red Scarf answered in the field hand voice Wesley always associated with Judah Jones. "Ain't but this much lefta me. Most the rest is already gone home. Caroline? She's all the way homes already. Won't nobody be seein' her no more. Rebekah, she stepped up an' took her place. Took it damn well, too. You protected our grandbaby."

"It didn't have a damn thing to do with you. I love Rebekah. I won't let anything happen to her."

Red Scarf vanished. The garden gnome reappeared. Wesley heard the voice of recently departed pawn broker Paul Feldman immediately behind him. He turned to behold a six foot version of Red Scarf.

"Nevertheless, a part of the plan is fulfilled."

Wesley the Dog growled viciously, but remained seated on his haunches.

"It gets pretty damn confusing," complained Wesley Perkins. "I would think if I needed to protect Rebekah, I'd be protecting her from you!"

Red Scarf's voice morphed into that of Debbie Kesslar, office manager at Wesley's former employer. "You would think. That's your great weakness, Wes. You think."

Wesley replied sarcastically, "Oh, really? Should I just thoughtlessly obey?"

Red Scarf roared a deep, dark belly laugh and continued in a strong, male voice. "Remember Seattle, Wes? When I offered you the Mark of the Beast and you turned me down?"

"Hell yes I do."

"You probably don't remember, but I told you then that made you the Chosen One. When you asked chosen for what, I told you chosen to promote my purposes anyway. Any of that ringing a bell?"

The sidewalk near the Fairmont Hotel was busy with pedestrians. Their universal lack of reaction assured Wesley that, as usual, his conversation with Red Scarf was entirely private.

"Cut to the point, man," complained Wesley. "Whatever it is you want me to do, let me know- so I can be sure to do the opposite. I've got no interest at all in promoting your purposes. I've seen you at work, you bastard. Shit, even the dog hates you."

"The dog has never liked me," agreed Red Scarf. "But that goes back a very, very, long time. Hear me out, Wesley. I'm mostly here tonight to give you some advice."

"And that would be?"

"Ira is not going to give up easily. He's become an agent for some forces who want to get that saxophone. Hang onto it. Don't give it up. We need it a while longer. You, Wesley, and the people you care most about in life right now, need it."

The wind freshened. Rain began to fall through the darkness. "Why would I listen to your advice? Hell, it sounds like if I do sell the saxophone to Ira I'd finally be rid of you."

Red Scarf threw up his hands and shrugged. "See there? That's what happens, every time. I try to give people useful advice and they resist. Gets old after just a few thousand planetary orbits. You have no idea."

"Well, of course we fucking resist. Any advice you give anybody is going to wreck their life."

"Or," countered Red Scarf, "maybe not. Maybe I count on you assuming the advice is destructive and then deliberately choosing to do the opposite thing. What you don't know, and can't know, is that there actually isn't any completely opposite thing. Maybe it's whatever you choose, regardless of what it is, and not my advice, that will undo you in the end."

The rain intensified.

"I got no time for riddles and games. If I thought I could get you out of my life, and Rebekah's life, and Vanessa's life by selling the horn to Ira, I'd give it to him. Hell, I might even pay him to take it!"

"Yes, and you might still."

Wesley pulled his jacket zipper to the top. He raised his voice to be heard above the intensifying wind. "How do I get Vanessa and Rebekah out of this thing without being destroyed? Heck, how can I be sure you won't destroy me, or even the dog, if you think we've served our purpose?"

"You should get in out of the weather, Wesley. Here's something else you can accept or not. You didn't take the Mark of the Beast. Had you done so, you would have had only one purpose-the purpose for which I traded the Mark. Yes, you are serving my purpose now, and you will continue to serve it no matter what happens to the horn."

Wesley the Dog rose. Red Scarf ignored the animal urinating on his faded overcoat. "You make it sound mighty damn hopeless," complained Wesley. "What about salvation, and all that religious stuff?"

"There's salvation available. It just ain't my department. Take my advice, Wesley. Hang onto the horn."

An especially cold gust of wind blew up from the bay, and Red Scarf disappeared.

Part Seven, Chapter Three

Regulations required every resident of the community at West Moccasin Springs to attend formal worship twice per day. The rule was not stringently enforced. The Elders overlooked the rare individual absences because nearly every member of the community was present for nearly every service. There were no empty seats, and no absentees, when Billy Proctor married Bridget Bishop.

A small choir, robed in white with crimson vestments, assembled to the immediate left of the altar. Smoke from votive candles in a hundred jars escaped through church windows and into the cool, damp, air of a Louisiana morning. Flowers festooned the church, with the scent of fresh cut blossoms accentuating that of molten wax. Although an acoustic guitar and piano provided music for most services, for this event the quilted cover was removed from the Hammond C3 organ and the rotating Leslie speaker.

Brother Abaddon wore a hooded black robe and stood before the altar with popular young preacher Billy Proctor. As if the wedding of two young people, known to be very much in love, were insufficiently inspiring to generate full attendance, Billy Proctor's recent elevation to spiritual leader of the community ensured that no resident of the community would miss the event.

Few in the church at West Moccasin Springs were aware that the marriage had not been licensed by the State of Louisiana. Brother Abaddon insisted that there would be sufficient time to worry about meeting state standards after the couple were united in the eyes of God.

The choir delivered an inspired performance of "Just a Closer Walk With Thee."

Silence prevailed among the crowd. Three rosy-cheeked toddlers proceeded down the center aisle with self-conscious uncertainty, throwing handfuls of red and yellow rose petals into the center aisle, (as well as a generous overflow onto any parishioners seated at the extreme ends of the pews).

The organist sounded a long, thunderous, chord; spun into intensity as the whirling speaker gathered momentum. Bridget Bishop appeared between the entry doors, radiant in a white silk gown, lacey veil, and a trailing cape trimmed with white fox fur. She held a bouquet of red and yellow lilies, laid against soft green ferns.

Everyone stood. The organist played "The Wedding March," while Bridget strolled slowly and majestically down the aisle. It was clearly evident that she was enjoying every step bridging the gap between her childhood and new life as Mrs. Billy Proctor. If only her father could have been present, the occasion would have been perfect. She timed her approach flawlessly, reaching the altar during the very last measure of her processional.

Brother Abaddon extended a hand to assist Bridget's ascension up two short steps to the altar platform. He smiled. "Brothers and Sisters. It is our solemn pleasure and holy responsibility to join these two young souls in holy matrimony. They come before us to publicly declare their promises and intentions to live together as husband and wife. It is a time of renewal and rejoicing. A time when the cycle begins again. Let us remember that as Jesus took the church to be his bride, so will Brother Billy be taking Sister Bridget."

As Brother Abaddon read some appropriate scriptures, two officers of the Louisiana State Police appeared in the church doorway. In deference to the occasion, the patrolmen stepped outside and stood near their patrol car.

Billy Proctor wondered if the cops knew they were proceeding without a license, but quickly decided they must be coincidentally stopping by while on some other business.

The ceremony continued. Vows and rings were exchanged. Brother Abaddon bestowed a blessing on the couple, and pronounced them "man and wife." Billy kissed Bridget tenderly but enthusiastically, eliciting wild applause from the congregation. Everyone stood as Mr. and Mrs. Billy Proctor walked down the aisle, arm in arm.

Well-wishers gathered outside the church, forming a tight knot around the Proctors. Brother Abaddon broke away from the group and approached the Louisiana State Policemen. "Welcome, officers. Is there something we can do for you today?"

"Yeah. We're investigating a possible auto theft. Is there an Abner Culliford living around here?"

"Sorry to have to tell you, but Brother Culliford is very recently deceased. I can't believe he would have anything to do with a stolen car."

"Where did he die? Here in your commune?"

Abaddon was annoyed. "It's not a commune, it's a community. Big difference. And yes, he died peacefully in his own home. Went to sleep and never work up again. And he would never steal a car, or anything else."

"We didn't think he stole the car. We thought either somebody stole his car or he might have been kidnapped. They found a Cadillac, registered in his name, just about a mile beyond the state line in Colorado. Nothing in the car but personal stuff. Two sets of clothes, wrist watches, wedding rings, some false teeth and a wig. The wallet and purse had ID for some people named Brinkman, and it's like they completely disappeared. Culliford ever go by the name Brinkman?"

"Sorry, I can't help you. Brother Abner never used the name Brinkman. He owned a number of cars. I don't recall him mentioning one gone missing. Whoever the unfortunate people were in whatever car you found, may God have mercy on their souls."

Part Seven, Chapter Four

The 11 AM sound check at the LA Forum was difficult for everyone involved. Art Abbott and John Flood didn't join the other musicians on the flight from San Francisco, but kept their promise to Ira Miller and appeared at sound check ready to play.

Redd Wilmott and Mary Towne were both conflicted. Redd's affection for Vanessa made him sympathetic to the Family Jones. Redd understood that Vanessa, Rebekah, and Wesley Perkins were bound together by some sort of superstition. Redd thought, "I care more about Vanessa than any woman I can remember, for a very long time. God, but she can be a pain in the ass though, all that psychic mumbo jumbo shit and all. Still, she's worth it."

Mary knew almost as much about the mysterious history of Rebekah's jewelry and Wesley's saxophone as did any of the Family Jones. She had chosen to disregard it. The music was spectacular. The results were clearly worth some minor risk. Mary remembered hoping that it would soon be her turn to hand off to somebody else and go home. Now, with the announcement that Art and John would be leaving the group as soon as Ira found suitable replacements, Mary began doubting the wisdom of her decision to include the unlikely sax player and the sisters in the act. And the dog? Mary regretted conceiving the "blind musician" ruse that put Wesley the Dog on stage with Vanessa.

Ira paced back and forth in the production booth. He grumbled at the technician running the board. "Too much bass. Can you take some of the top end out of the guitar? Sounds way too shrill. Back up vocal mic is too hot, and it looks like we need one for the floor tom. Christ, man, you ever mix a blues band before? You're making us sound like shit."

Despite chastising the technician, Ira was troubled. The sound had definitely changed. The magic of Seattle and San Francisco was missing. Memphis Rail and the Family Jones were playing like a group of strangers. It was if the musicians were distrustful of one another. None of the performers smiled. Ira could hear the difference. He hoped that by show time the problem would be resolved, or perhaps the audience wouldn't be too discriminating.

Memphis Rail and the Family Jones played through the first forty five minutes of their act before Ira indicated he was satisfied with the sound.

"Art and me will be back an hour before the show," said John Flood. The drummer and guitar player disappeared down the stairs behind the stage.

Ira ran down to the front of the house, eager to catch Wesley, Vanessa, and Rebekah while the three of them were together.

Ira felt like an insincere cheerleader. "Looks like we're set up for another huge night!"

"Think so?" replied Mary Towne. "To me, we sounded off a bit, 'specially at first."

"Nothing to worry about. We got things sorted out, and that's most important, right? Hey, Wes, Rebekah, and Vanessa, have you guys got a minute? There's something we need to go over." Without waiting for an answer, Ira strolled toward the stage manager's office. The door was unlocked, and the office almost entirely empty. It would do. The Family Jones, and Wesley the Dog, pressed in behind him. Wesley Perkins carried the snakeskin saxophone case.

"Gather 'round, everybody," invited Ira. "I've got some amazing news and it involves all of you." He put two objects on the desktop. One was the familiar titanium container for the diamond dust and fused glass saxophone, the Roten Schal. The other, a thick briefcase with an elaborate lock. "Where are you guys at on the proposal?"

Vanessa answered. "I think we're still not convinced. It seems wrong to basically sell off Judah's horn. There's more than money to consider."

"But," added Rebekah, "maybe there's something bigger than we can get our brains around, when it comes to that sax. We've been wonderin' if we wouldn't be just as well off, or better off, if it was out of our lives."

Everyone looked at Wesley, expecting a response. He said nothing for a long moment. "I've been thinking a lot about this. We thought Rebekah's jewelry inspired her to sing, but when she lost it for a short while we found out she could sing anyway. Lots of people think she's better."

Vanessa looked doubtful. "I'm not so sure that's the same issue, Wes."

"Yeah? Well maybe it's time to see if I can sound as good playing this other horn. I'm getting to be mighty damn good, if I do say so myself. Part of this whole thing has been a gift."

"A gift?" asked Rebekah.

"Yeah. I discovered this talent I never realized I had. We got together. If we take out the freaky stuff, some good things have already happened. If I can play just as well with another horn, and if the money's right, changing to a different instrument right now might solve a lot of problems for us."

Ira turned two keys and rolled some numbered cylinders on the face of the large briefcase. He sat the case on the stage manager's desk and opened the top. The air immediately smelled like currency; a bone dry dusting of paper, ink, and desire.

Rebekah gasped. "Jesus, Ira. That looks like a lot of money!"

"It is," agreed Ira. "There are four thousand hundred dollar bills in this case. Four hundred grand!" The Family Jones had no means of knowing Ira Miller skimmed six-hundred thousand of the additional million dollars cash Zaccheus funneled to him through Joseph Smith. They did not know that Ira would personally realize over three million dollars when the transaction was complete.

Wesley looked back and forth from Vanessa to Rebekah. "If we do this, let's make it a three way split. That's about a hundred and thirty three thousand each."

Vanessa thumbed idly through the top bundles of currency, then slowly withdrew her hand. "Nope. I won't stop you from doing this if you want to, Wes, but I don't want any of the money. You and Rebekah divvy it up between you. Me? I want to get past this thing clean, without any leftover energy hanging around."

Rebekah looked at Wesley. "It's really your horn, so it's your decision. Let's get it done or not, though. We're all living the dream, really. We're part of the best sound the blues has ever had. Let's concentrate on enjoying our fame and growing fortune instead of worrying about this old sax, and everything that comes with it."

Wesley reached slowly into the titanium case and withdrew the Roten Schal. He cradled it like a baby in his forearm. Ira suppressed a smile, the moment was close at hand. Wesley carefully examined the Roten Schal, then said, "Some things, Ira. We need to change the name. Red Scarf doesn't sound like a lucky name, even in German. I want my name on the company, and my name on the horn. Wesley Perkins Concert Series, by Wesley Perkins Woodwinds. Can you do that?"

Ira waved his hand to signify the request was incidental. "Done. I told the company that you were nervous about the name. They already gave me permission to let you change it."

"And I want five percent of wholesale, every time somebody buys a horn. They're going to be peddling these things based on my name and reputation, so I deserve a cut."

"That shouldn't be a problem. There's no pricing set up yet. They can easily pencil in another five percent."

"And finally, I need to be satisfied that I can make this new horn sound every bit as good as the old one. I can play it for just a few minutes, right now, and we'll know for sure."

"Go for it!" encouraged Ira.

Vanessa was more subdued and skeptical. "Yeah, Wes. Go for it. Let's see you make this horn sound like the one you've been playing. I'll be all ears."

Wesley Perkins lifted the sax to his lips, as carefully as a well-considered prayer. He reached down to scratch Wesley the Dog, who had shifted his position to sit immediately next to the musician's right leg.

The first four notes, were weak, ragged, and unimpressive. Wesley was not concerned. He relaxed, concentrated, drew a deep breath and closed his eyes. His consciousness was filled with a warm yellow light, radiating from the golden retriever at his side. The fifth note erupted from the bell, almost impossibly vibrant and bright. The sound had dominance over space and time. It carried a physical presence.

"Holy shit!" exclaimed Ira.

"Maybe nothing holy about it," mumbled Vanessa.

Wesley opened his eyes long enough to smile, wink, and then close them both again. He felt weightless. He escaped into a syncopated universe of rich, rolling, long, slow notes punctuated by rhythmic rhumbas up and down the blue scale. Flat thirds, fifths, and sevenths danced with ninths, elevenths, and thirteens. Tones were augmented, diminished, and turned loose to enjoy the freedom of flight. The new saxophone vibrated as if excited while Wesley Perkins coaxed, stroked, and tickled the stops.

The sound carried beyond the stage manager's office. Everyone in the LA Forum ran to hear, to see, and share the magic. After a two minute improvised solo, Wesley opened his eyes and set down the horn. Wild cheering and applause exploded outside the door.

Ira beamed, "Holy shit, Wes. Ho-ly shit. Whatever you just did, whatever you just played, let me tell you, nobody has ever gone there on the saxophone. Ever. You got whatever future you want to name in this business." Ira reconsidered his rave. "Um, of course I mean all three of you, Family Jones and all."

Vanessa arched her eyebrows and shrugged. "I'm damn surprised, Wes. I always thought it was just the horn."

Rebekah baptized herself in happy tears. Wesley the Dog thumped his tail enthusiastically.

Wesley grinned broadly, obviously impressed with his own performance. "I guess that settles it, then. Four hundred thousand now, my name on the horn and the company, five percent royalties every time somebody buys a sax. Done deal, Ira."

Wesley placed a long, slow kiss on the snakeskin case before extending it toward Ira Miller. Ira closed the lid on the briefcase, and shoved it across the desk to Wesley Perkins. The saxophones changed hands.

Chuck Gould

Part Seven, Chapter Five

Back in his hotel suite, Ira Miller answered the phone. The call was from Joseph Smith.

"I got your text, Ira. When you say 'it's done', you mean you're in possession of the saxophone, right?"

"Absolutely. I told you it wasn't going to be that hard, but you needed somebody that Perkins could trust."

"Ask the hotel to lock it up in their vault. I assume my client will want to fly to Los Angeles this afternoon and take personal delivery."

"Got it. In fact, it's there already."

"How much of that last million is left?"

"None. I said it wasn't going to be too hard, but I never said it would be cheap. The sight of all that cash had its desired effect. You guys got your horn. Oh, I had to promise you'd name the company and the instruments after Wesley Perkins, and he gets a five percent wholesale royalty."

Joseph Smith burst out laughing. "No problem, Ira. You could have promised him a hundred percent. Wouldn't have made a bit of difference. We'll wire the rest of the funds to your account, and release your surety bond, just as soon as we have physical possession of the horn."

Part Seven, Chapter Six

Little Willy and the Bluesbirds rocked the LA Forum. The packed house applauded enthusiastically after every number. The audience enjoying the Bluesbirds bristled with anticipation of the main act. Memphis Rail and the Family Jones were making history with every performance.

It was as though a cavern of infinite width had opened between the raucous energy in the main auditorium and the somber depression in the green room. None of the musicians spoke, exchanging glares and frowns rather than encouragement.

Mary Towne attempted to wrest control of the situation. "Hey, y'all. Take a look at us, will you? Sittin' here mopin' like somebody died or somethin'? We gotta take the stage before long, performin' for the biggest gate we've ever seen. Let's get this together and do one of our warm ups."

Mary clapped her hands four times and began, "Wade in the water…." The Family Jones joined in. Redd Wilmott, feeling some pressure from both Vanessa and Mary, picked up the warm up as well. The five musicians harmonized, "Wade in the water, children…"

An arrangement of flowers sat on a small table. John Flood smashed the vase to the floor, shattering the fragile optimism as surely as the porcelain. "Fuck that!" he screamed.

The clapping and singing stopped in mid measure.

"We're all goddam professionals here, or at least most of us are," hissed John. "If we haven't figured out how to keep fucking time by now, we ain't got no hope of doin' so. Soon as we're up, let's go out and do our thing. This show, and the next? It's the end of the line for me."

"No point bein' so bitter about it," groused Redd.

Art Abbott remarked, "Redd's right. Let's just call some kind of truce here. We'll go out and back up the goddam dog and the sax player, collect our money, and call it good. Most of us still like each other. Maybe we can act like it for a few more hours, anyway."

Wesley the Dog could sense the tension. He whined, and nuzzled Rebekah's leg. "It's OK, boy, it's going to be OK."

The Bluesbirds completed their set. A handful of people in the audience stood, but while everyone expressed appreciation for the Little Willy's performance it was evident the crowd was eager for the main event to begin.

The stage manager knocked on the green room door. "Ten minutes to curtain!"

Wesley picked up his instrument and started for the door. John Flood noticed the fancy titanium case. "What's that? You finally upgrade that rat's ass of an old sax case you been luggin' around?"

Wesley smiled. "Better than that, it's a brand new horn. Made out of diamond dust and molten glass. It's a prototype. The only one in the world so far. The company is going to name the line after me."

Art Abbott failed to conceal his sarcasm. "Oh, how special."

"Just wait until you hear it, Art. You'll see how special it really is. I sound a lot better with this than I did with the old one."

Vanessa motioned for Wesley to be quiet, but his newly emerging ego had already exacted a toll.

John Flood shook his head with disgust. "How long, exactly, until the end of the second show?"

Part Seven, Chapter Seven

Just as in San Francisco, the show began with a white follow light illuminating only Vanessa and Wesley the Dog on stage. Vanessa blew the first four notes of "Hoochie Coochie Man" and the audience was instantly involved in the performance. John Flood added rhythm from a single cymbal. Redd Wilmott built the bottom with his bass, and Andrew Carrier clattered out electric crystal notes suggesting muffled chimes on the keyboard.

Ira Miller's day had been sufficiently profitable. While he would customarily keep a hawk's eye on the merchandise vendors, he was ready to accept some losses through careless shop keeping or table help with sticky fingers. Tonight, he listened carefully to the performance. The group sounded a little more cohesive than during sound check, but Ira realized that might be the effect of overly optimistic ear drums.

Redd began singing the first verse, pausing for Vanessa to fill in with a measure of blues harp between lines. Their performance sounded especially fluid, yet cohesive. "They're an item these days," thought Ira. "Seems to be showing up in the act. They're really good together."

Wesley waited just offstage. The first verse and chorus concluded. He stepped confidently to the center of the stage during the eight bar interlude. The crowd was excited by his arrival, cheering and applauding as he readied to play. Wesley acknowledged the applause with a wave and a slight bow.

Redd began singing the next verse. Wesley substituted the sax for Vanessa's blues harp riff. Wesley was alarmed. Something didn't feel exactly right. His timing was almost perfect, the notes were clear and precise. Nobody but Wesley himself would be aware that something was missing. Maybe something important. Wesley kept animated time with his upper body. He smiled at Wesley the Dog, closed his eyes, and searched for the warm yellow light that normally inspired his performances. The butterscotch essence was thinner, and ragged around the edges.

"What the hell am I worried about?" thought Wesley. "I'm damn good at this. I've got the most unique horn in the world. When my solo comes up, I'll own this whole fucking building."

Two thirds of the way back in the crowd and seated on the aisle was a figure in a faded overcoat, a long red woolen scarf, and a 1950's style fedora. At the moment when Wesley the Dog customarily joined the performance to keep rhythm with his tail, Red Scarf stepped from his seat and stood in the aisle. He took the end of his signature garment, and spun it in circles over his head. Wesley the Dog growled, barked, and leapt from the stage into a group of VIP's comped in the second row. Pandemonium ensued. The golden retriever, in a bright orange "service animal" vest, leaped and lashed though the rows in a frantic effort to reach Red Scarf. People screamed, and some headed for the exits. Security guards, formerly invisible among the audience, suddenly appeared to be everywhere. Within a matter of only several seconds, Red Scarf fled the building, with an enraged golden retriever in close pursuit.

The band played on. Mary Towne signaled for a long segment of nothing by bass, piano, and drums. She stepped up to the mic.

"Hey, y'all. Sorry about the thing with the dog. He's never done that before. No tellin' what got into him. But, I can tell you what's got into us. Baby we got the blues, and we got 'em bad. We'll sort of restart the show from here. What do you say? Let's forget about that old hound dog and get down and dirty here in the LA Forum. Can I get an Amen?"

Mary's gambit settled the crowd. A weak round of applause blossomed into an ovation.

Mary projected a confident enthusiasm. The rhythm line continued. "Now, that's more like it! Let me introduce the band here tonight, and then we'll pick up where we left off. Y'all know Redd, on the bass. We got Andrew Carrier tonight on keyboards. Vanessa here, she plays blues harp and some rhythm. Art Abbott on guitar, and John Flood on bass. Rebekah does a lot of the vocals, and me, I'm Mary Towne. And oh yeah, we got Wesley Perkins on saxophone."

The audience applauded steadily as each musician was introduced. When Mary Towne mentioned Wesley's name, the applause went ballistic.

John Flood sighed as he kicked and hammered on his traps. "Gonna be a hell of a long final evenin'."

Mary waited for the right beat in the rhythm line and usurped Redd's usual line. "On the seventh hour," Redd instinctively picked up the lyrics normally handled by Mary and responded about the "seventh day." Wesley Perkins played his four note riff between the vocal phrases, now concerned that in the absence of the dog he no longer saw any yellow energy behind closed eyelids.

The lyrics wound through the third chorus. It was time for the saxophone solo. The sax stops felt foreign under Wesley's sweating fingers. His mouth was dry. His body trembled. There was no golden retriever exuding buttercup tinted light. "Hell," he thought. "What I wouldn't give for just a shot of rye whiskey just about now."

The progression matured to the beat where Wesley needed to pick up and solo. The saxophonist stood frozen in place, the horn was silent. Mary Towne made a circling gesture with her finger, and Memphis Rail repeated the four measures leading up to Wesley's solo. Silence again. The audience began to boo.

Mary Towne signaled for another four bars of rhythm. Everyone on stage, as well as in the audience, stared in disbelief at the Wesley Perkins, silent in the middle of the stage.

Two beats before his solo, Wesley sucked in a lungful of air and made his best possible effort to play. The saxophone did not sing. It did not resonate. There was no light, no energy, no magic, and no musicality to the tone. "Jesus," thought Andrew Carrier, "that sounds like somebody strangling a goat."

Wesley struggled for eight bars, and with every failed not the audience jeered and booed more viciously. Art Abbott stepped up with his guitar and signaled the booth. The technician cut Wesley's mike and slightly potted up Art's guitar for a substitute solo.

It was too late. The crowd in the LA Forum was lost, and angry as well.

"This is bullshit!" screamed a loud voice. "No dog? No saxophone? I want a fucking reeee-fund!"

The sentiment infected the crowd. Soon a dozen, then a score, and ultimately nearly everyone in attendance was screaming "refund, refund, refund, refund." Off duty cops and security guards made a failed attempt to restore order and get people back into their seats.

Memphis Rail and the Family Jones were confused and dismayed. Redd kept playing his bass, Mary attempted to sing, and Andrew Carrier played raggedly and entirely distracted on the keyboard. Art and John, walked off stage. The curtain closed.

Wesley Perkins sat on the floor, and cried.

Ira Miller rushed backstage, where he encountered an irate house manager.

"Show's over, Miller. We'll be lucky to get everybody out of here without some sort of goddam riot. Shit, people could get hurt, or killed. And forget the second show."

"You can't do that!" screamed Ira. "Hey, maybe we blew this one but we can get our shit together before the next crowd files in."

The manager grabbed a long handle and shoved it into a pair of contacts. The house lights came up, punctuated with a sharp crack. "Nope. Ain't happenin'. This is my house, and it's my ass if somebody gets trampled out there. We're done here. You figure out how to handle thirty five thousand refunds. This is all your fuck up, and none of mine."

Rebekah and Vanessa lifted Wesley from the floor. "Get up," snapped Vanessa. "We've got a few apologies to make. Looks like it was the horn after all, doesn't it?"

The three friends, joined Redd, Mary, and Andrew Carrier in the green room. Before anybody had a chance to speak, Ira walked in and announced the LA shows were both canceled. "I don't know if we should even try to do the rest of the tour. Word of this mess will be all over the country in about fifteen minutes. We've lost Art and John for sure."

Vanessa sounded hopeful but contrite. "Maybe we can still salvage something out of this?"

Ira did not mince words. "No 'we' about it anymore, Vanessa. You Family Jones people just about ruined one of the best acts in the history of the blues. The three of you are fired, as of right now. Goddam mistake from the get go, you were. I don't suppose there's any chance to get my four hundred thousand back, is there?"

"Not unless we trade horns again," sniffed Wesley. "Maybe if I had the old horn back…"

"No, it's too late for that. The guy who bought it will be at the hotel in about forty-five minutes to pick it up. Take the money and get the hell out of my sight. You're costing me millions of dollars here. We may never be able to live this down. You turned out to be a real jackass, Perkins."

Rebekah responded to Ira's insult. "Screw you, man. Yeah, this isn't Wes's finest hour, and yeah maybe a lot of this is his fault. I stood right there and let him make that decision without sayin' a damn word. There's no need to start calling names here."

Vanessa put a hand on Rebekah's forearm, a silent suggestion that she curb her tongue. "Ok, Ira," said Vanessa, "but before we go, do you know if anybody found our dog?"

"Shit no, I don't know." snarled Ira. "If he doesn't get killed out in traffic maybe you can pick him up down at the animal shelter. I could care less. Bogus blind woman, your phony ass seeing eye dog screwed up the show tonight before Perkins even got started."

"Sorry, I was just asking."

"Look, I need to run back to the hotel. Mary and Redd, give me a call later tonight. Andrew, you're still playing with Little Willy. The rest of you? I never want to see any of your sorry asses or even hear your names again? Clear?"

Ira slammed the door as he left. Silence hung like a rain soaked sleeping bag. Finally Wesley Perkins spoke. "Hey everybody," he said. He looked deliberately at Vanessa, and then Rebekah, "I can't even begin to apologize for how things turned out. I really messed it up for everybody. It feels so helpless, having nothing but 'sorry' to say after I fucked up this badly."

After a moment, Mary replied. "Thanks. I guess it means something that you're sorry. Still, knowing what I know about the things I know about, it's hard to say that you did any of this deliberately."

Redd concurred. "Yeah. Anybody could clearly see, that first night in Seattle, that you weren't in any sort of control. It's like somethin' got into you. We should all of been smarter. Some people are born to the blues. Others? They just ain't. Might be sorta our fault too."

Wesley Perkins sat with his elbows on his knees and his forehead buried in his hands. "I let everybody down."

"Hey, maybe there's a bright side," suggested Mary. "I've been wantin' to go home for some time now. Looks like the Rail is at least temporarily de-railed. I'll get to play with my grandbabies, and go all weekend without ever gettin' dressed- if that's what I get a mind to do."

"Besides, Wes," added Redd Wilmott. "If it wasn't for you, I might not never have met Vanessa. I guess I'll head back down to Florida and just hang out a while. Why don't you come too, 'Nessa?"

"Give me a day to think on that, Redd. Rebekah and I need to talk. We need to figure out a few things. Probably still including Wes, too. And what about the dog? That's sort of a sudden offer. I don't know if I want to say 'yes', but I can tell you I'm probably less inclined to say 'no'."

Part Seven, Chapter Eight

Zaccheus flew to Los Angeles. His assistant arranged for a limousine to meet his private jet on the runway. The car was there, as expected. Zaccheus disappeared behind the jet black bulletproof glass, and his assistant texted Joseph Smith. "On grnd. In car. ETA 20 min +/-, dep. traff"

Joseph Smith and Ira Miller sat in the hotel bar. A big screen television displayed the local news. An aerial shot depicted crowds pouring out of the LA Forum. The newscast cut to a ground level close-up, showing squads of LAPD personnel in riot gear attempting to keep the civilians moving along. The sound was turned off in the bar, but a banner across the bottom of the screen read, "Memphis Rail? Memphis Fail. Angry fans out of control."

Ira yelled at the barkeeper. "Change the channel? Please?"

Joseph Smith commiserated with Ira. "Damn shame the way that worked out. What the hell happened? I hear the dog ran off. Perkins laid an egg with the horn? Good thing there was never any serious plan to make more saxophones, the debut couldn't have flopped any worse."

"Christ, Smith. I'm going to need everything I stand to make out of this saxophone swap just to pay off my losses here in Los Angeles. My bread-and-butter act looks like it's out of commission. You can't possibly know what it's like to be starting over- at least not over and over again. More and more lately, I'd be happy just to hand this whole gig off to somebody else, go home, and put my feet up."

A very large man wearing a dark suit approached. He had a shaved head, and a patch over his left eye. Ira said, "Joseph Smith, allow me to introduce you to Giles Corey. Mr. Corey is head of the hotel security team."

"A pleasure, Mr. Smith. I spotted you gentlemen in here on the monitors, so I wanted to drop by and let you know that all three persons required to re-open the vault are now on the premises. Let us know when you're ready to reclaim your property, and we'll pleased to accommodate you."

Joseph Smith looked at his watch. "I believe my client is en route from the airport right now. He may be here in the next few minutes. Maybe we should all assemble at the vault? The gentleman accepting delivery of the item in the vault treasures his privacy. We should be prepared. He will definitely want to be back in the car as soon as possible."

"Certainly, Mr. Smith. Gentlemen, if you will follow me, please?" Ira and Joseph rose to join Giles Corey. Corey called to the bartender, "Whatever these guests enjoyed, it's on the house."

"Yes, Mr. Corey, Sir."

The three men entered an elevator. Giles Corey pulled a wireless control from his pocket. The controller incorporated a laser, and Corey aimed the tiny red dot at an ordinary looking screw on the elevator controls. A portion of the elevator wall slid sideways to reveal a second set of floor selection buttons. Giles used the buttons to punch in a sequential code, rather than select a floor. The car began to descend.

"Wow, that seems pretty elaborate," said Joseph Smith.

"Yeah, that's what I thought when I brought the horn over earlier today," agreed Ira. "Wait until you see their locking system."

Giles Corey explained, "We cater to some of the wealthiest travelers on the planet. Obviously I am not at liberty to mention the types of items we routinely secure for our guests, but our vault is more secure than the vast majority of commercial banks. By far."

The security manager touched a small plastic device inserted in his right ear. "Thanks."

"The rest of your party has arrived. Apparently they rated a police escort from the airport. They're on their way down with some more of my team."

The elevator reached the bottom of the shaft. Beyond the door were two armed guards flanking a black vault door with a silver combination lock. One of the guards nodded to acknowledge the presence of Giles Corey, then addressed Ira Miller. "Receipt, please."

"Sure. Here you go. One antique musical instrument and case."

"Very good. Please allow us a moment to check your face against the image on our computer."

"What? You don't remember me? I was just here this morning."

"Policy, sir." The guard referred to a computer monitor, and then remarked to his companion, "Receipt's good. It's him. Go ahead and access the first door."

The second guard pulled a retractable slide across the vault door, stood behind it, and began dialing the combination. A second elevator opened. Zaccheus, two security guards, and his personal assistant entered the secured area.

The first guard finished working the combination. He opened the vault door to reveal another immediately beyond it. "OK, your turn now." The second guard fingered the lock on the second door. Beyond the second door was a bank of safety deposit vault, each fitted with a unique combination lock. Only Giles Corey could open the individual lockers.

While the security manager was fingering the final lock, Joseph Smith made introductions. "Ira Miller, this is my employer, Zaccheus."

"Pleased to meet you, Mr. Miller. You've done us a great service."

Giles Corey opened the safety deposit door and yelled, "Good God! What in the name of seven hells is this! I put that goddam thing in here myself!" The security manager turned to face the rest of the group, holding a ragged red scarf in his hand. "It's gone! This is in there instead!"

"It can't be!" exclaimed one of the vault guards. "There hasn't been a single person in this room, let alone the vault, all day! Check the video! Nobody! There's absolutely no way that's not in there! Sir, is there any possible chance you opened the wrong locker?"

Ira Miller gulped and choked, fighting back the urge to vomit. There were millions of dollars at stake. "Who knows how well connected people like this Zaccheus might be?" thought Ira. "This could literally mean my ass."

Giles Cory began opening the vault immediately to the left. Before he could finish, Zaccheus said, "Don't bother. You've got the right locker. That red scarf is proof enough. The bastard just loves to taunt us. We get so damn close, time after time."

Ira began to apologize. "I'm really sorry. I can't explain what happened here, but…"

"You're right," interrupted Zaccheus. "You can't explain it. It has something to do with an ability to move things around. Your bond is forfeit, Miller. And expect us to bring an action to recover that last million dollars cash. And as for you, Mr. Smith, consider yourself terminated."

"It's not fair to fire me over this!" objected Joseph Smith.

"Oh, did I say 'fired'? I meant to say 'terminated'. I'll take that scarf, and we're going back to the airport. Very damn disappointing, all of you. Damn disappointing indeed."

Part Seven, Chapter Nine

Ernesto Montoya looked up and down the street before ducking into the abandoned Laundromat in South Central Los Angeles. At this time of night, there were no cars nearby. Ernesto was not surprised. Few people ventured into the district in the daytime, and virtually none after dark. Even the cops gave the area a wide berth, and were reluctant to respond to reports of the most minor crime without backup. Blood stained the concrete here, almost daily during the turf wars among rival gangs dealing crack cocaine. The murder rate was now less than it had been, partially because the worst actors were dead or pulling life without possibility of parole.

Plywood covered the windows of the Laundromat, although Ernesto and the friends he met here most nights were never sure whether the panes were broken before or after the glazing was boarded up. They were not the first generation to claim territory in this forlorn ruin. Perhaps they would not be the last.

The lock broke years ago. Ernesto shouldered the warped door open far enough to squeeze through, then backed his buttocks against it to force it closed. There was no light on the main floor, but Ernesto knew his way in the dark. Five feet from the west corner, a blanket hung in front of a stairwell. Somebody wired around a disconnected meter, so there was light beyond the blanket.

The sweet aroma of marijuana wafted up the stairs. "Marcus and Emilio must be here, already," thought Ernesto. His hunch was correct. Marcus and Emilio were arguing. "Arguing pretty bitterly, considering their condition," thought Ernesto.

"It's just an old piece of crap, man. You won't be able to pawn that for shit."

"Bullshit. You don't know quality when you see it. Look at all this engraving. Nobody would waste time doing that if this wasn't a good horn."

Ernesto interrupted, "Hey, guys. What you got there?"

"Emilio showed up here tonight with this screwed up looking saxophone. Top part of it seems like it's bent or something. There's some dark looking stain down in the bell. Look at the damn box, man. Smells really weird if you ask me, and looks like it's covered with scales or somethin'."

Emilio retorted, "You don't know shit. About saxophones or anything else. I think this is a score. You're just pissed off an' jealous."

Marcus laughed. "Don't know shit? Well I know that horn of yours don't play. Sax ain't my main instrument, but I can fart around enough to get by." Marcus snatched the horn from Emilio, "Check this out Ernesto. There's something entirely fucked up about this horn."

Marcus mouthed the reed and blew. The tone was weak and ragged, like a dying animal in distress. Marcus attempted a variety of notes, all with the same result. He looked insistently at Emilio, "You ain't gonna be able to sell this for two ass hairs, dipshit."

"Were did you get that?" asked Ernesto.

"Some bizarre lookin' drunk hombre. Freaky strange, if you ask me. Passed out between two dumpsters, and this was just layin' there beside him. Anybody could happen along and pick it up. I figured I would help myself before somebody beat me to it or the guy woke up."

"Why would you say he was freaky strange?" asked Ernesto.

"His clothes were way out of style. Wearin' some sort of overcoat, and a hat like they wore back when Kennedy or maybe even Eisenhower was president."

"White guy?"

"Hard to say for sure. Skin was on the dark side, but coulda been white. Most of his face was wrapped up behind a red scarf. Who the hell wears a heavy scarf around here this time of year? Don't matter, when he wakes up he'll be one hangover to the good and short one bitchin' saxophone."

Ernesto reached for the horn. "Let me see that thing. I took lessons up through middle school. Been a long time since I played the sax. I think I'll give it a try."

"What the hell for?" asked Marcus. "I just proved the damn thing doesn't play. Emilio will be lucky to get forty bucks for this old piece of junk on pawn."

Ernesto fingered the horn and mouthed the reed. He blew a rich, round, authoritative note that astonished all three friends.

Emilio taunted Marcus. "Doesn't play? Doesn't play? Maybe it's just that you don't play. It sounds mighty damn good."

Marcus took the horn from Ernesto. "Let me see that again."

A second attempt by Marcus produced no better results than his initial disastrous effort. He passed the instrument back to Ernesto. "Do something else."

Ernesto began again. Staccato, legato, low notes, high notes, long notes, and arpeggios flowed gloriously from the instrument in both syncopated and simple time. Each tone, each phrase seemed is if it were the voice of a living being. For two minutes he played, so immersed in the music he was only vaguely aware of his own performance.

"Jesus Compound Christ!" said Marcus. "That's almost better than I ever heard anybody on the sax. Bitchin' good, dude. What's the name of that tune, anyway?"

Ernesto shrugged. "Don't know, really. Surprised the hell out of me, just like it did you. Guess I just played the first thing that came to mind, whatever it was."

"I can tell you exactly what it was," insisted Emilio. "It's from some old Broadway show or something. Name of the song? It's 'Summertime'."

Part Seven, Chapter Ten

Wesley searched the neighborhood around the LA Forum for the golden retriever. There was no sign of Wesley the Dog, and no evidence of Red Scarf. Back at the hotel, the sisters took advantage of the privacy available pending Wesley's return.

"So what about you and Redd?" asked Rebekah. "You really think you'll try living with him in Florida?"

"Yeah. As long as he's asking and he's willing to have me, I'd like to give it a try. I don't suppose he's thinking marriage or anything, but I've already been there and done that. It's not everything it's cracked up to be. If Redd doesn't work out, I can always go back to Seattle."

"What would you do for work?" pressed Rebekah.

"Right now? I don't much care. I want to see about dialing into Mama's gift a little more, at least if I can. May not be much money in it, but there did always seem to be a bucket of peas or a dozen eggs on the front porch."

"Really? I just thought you might be done with all that mumbo-jumbo, especially after what we just went through."

Vanessa nodded reluctantly. "I guess that would make sense. Maybe I'm drawn more into it now because of what we went through. Speakin' of, what about you and Wes?"

Rebekah smiled. "It's going to take a lot more than today's disaster to bust us up. I haven't had a chance to talk to Wes yet, but I'll basically guarantee we work this out. Wes is the real deal, as far as I'm concerned."

Vanessa laughed softly, "Remember how you didn't even like him when you first met him? So, do you think you guys will go back up to Seattle?"

"No, I'm pretty sure we're going to make a fresh start. Remember that old sharecrop shack that's been in the family since just after the Second World War?"

"Yeah, I don't think we've been there since we were really little. What about it?"

"Well, I got an email this morning from some religious group. They finally figured out how to track us down from parish records, or something. They've been buying up all the property down around West Moccasin Springs. They'd like to make us an offer on it."

"What kind of offer?"

Rebekah shrugged. "They didn't say. Of course we'd need to agree before we sold it or anything. But I sort of thought that for now, at least, me and Wes could get back there and see what things are really worth. We're going to need someplace to call home, for a while, anyway."

Vanessa laughed. "For a while? I'd say, oh, for roughly another seven months, sister."

Rebekah blushed. "How did you know? Sometimes I run late, so I wasn't all that worried. I just did the test this morning. I haven't even told Wes yet. I don't know how he's going to take it."

"How did I know? Let's just say you can leave a bucket of peas on the porch. And Wes, he's going to be delighted. I've seen it, clear as day. Nothing less than delighted. Congratulations, Mama."

"Well, if you're in Florida and we're in Louisiana, we won't be as far apart as we used to be, Auntie 'Nessa."

Vanessa extended her arms to Rebekah. The sisters clutched in tight embrace. Vanessa kissed Rebekah on the forehead and said, "Oh, and by the way you're going to owe me another bucket of peas."

"Why so, Sis?"

"Twins, 'Bekah. You and Wes are going to have twins."

The End

<u>Starry Night Publishing</u>

Everyone has a story...

Don't spend your life trying to get published! Don't tolerate rejection! Don't do all the work and allow the publishing companies reap the rewards!

Millions of independent authors like you, are making money, publishing their stories now. Our technological know-how will take the headaches out of getting published. Let "Starry Night Publishing dot Com" take care of the hard parts, so you can focus on writing. You simply send us your Word document and we do the rest. It really is that simple!

The big companies want to publish only "celebrity authors," not the average book-writer. It's almost impossible for first-time authors to get published today. This has led many authors to go the self-publishing route. Until recently, this was considered "vanity-publishing." You spent large sums of your money, to get twenty copies of your book, to give to relatives at Christmas, just so you could see your name on the cover. Now, however, the self-publishing industry allows authors to get published in a timely fashion, retain the rights to your work, keeping up to seventy-percent of your royalties, instead of the traditional ten-percent.

We've opened up the gates, allowing you inside the world of publishing. While others charge you as much as ten-thousand dollars for a publishing package, we charge less than three-hundred dollars to cover proofreading, copyright, ISBN, and distribution costs. Do you really want to spend all your time formatting, converting, designing a cover, and then promoting your book, because no one else will?

Our editors are professionals, able to create a top-notch book that you will be proud of. Becoming a published author is supposed to be fun, not a hassle.

At Starry Night Publishing, you submit your work, we proofread it, create a professional-looking cover, a table of contents, compile your text and images into the appropriate format, convert your files for eReaders, take care of copyright information, assign an ISBN, allow you to keep one-hundred-percent of your rights, distribute your story worldwide on Amazon, Barnes & Noble and many other retailers, and write you a check for your royalties. There are no other hidden fees involved! You don't pay extra for a cover, or proofreading. You will never pay to keep your book in print. We promise! Everything is included! You even get a free copy of your book and unlimited discount copies.

In twelve short months, we've published more than three-hundred books, compared to the major publishing houses which only add an average of six new titles per year. We will publish your fiction, or non-fiction books about anything, and look forward to reading your stories and sharing them with the world.

We sincerely hope that you will join the growing Starry Night Publishing family, become a published author and gain the world-wide exposure that you deserve. You deserve to succeed. Success comes to those who make opportunities happen, not those who wait for opportunities to happen. You just have to try. Thanks for joining us on our journey.

www.starrynightpublishing.com

www.facebook.com/starrynightpublishing/

20082862R00178

Made in the USA
San Bernardino, CA
26 March 2015